Empire in Pine

Book One

The Green Veil

Empire Pine

Book One

The Green Veil

By

Naomi Dawn Musch

Empire in Pine

Book One: The Green Veil
Book Two: The Red Fury
Book Three: The Black Rose

Desert Breeze Publishing, Inc.
27305 W. Live Oak Rd #424
Castaic, CA 91384

http://www.DesertBreezePublishing.com

Copyright © 2011 by Naomi Dawn Musch
ISBN 10: 1-61252-968-2
ISBN 13: 978-1-61252-968-4

Published in the United States of America
eBook Publish Date: January 1, 2011
Print Publish Date: January 2013

Editor-In-Chief: Gail R. Delaney
Editor: Melanie Noto
Marketing Director: Jenifer Ranieri
Cover Artist: Jenifer Ranieri

Dedication

To the glory of God my Father and Jesus my Lord -- with wonder.

Acknowledgments

I couldn't be a wife, homeschooling mom, grandma, have a day job, and still be able to follow my passion to write if it weren't for the support of Jeff, my husband and lover of more than 30 years. He makes it possible for me to follow my dreams with tremendous freedom. Next to him are our five terrific young adults who've loved me and supported me, even though I sometimes get into "the zone" and don't hear what's going on around me. You guys are just the best.

I also want to note some special appreciation and lots of love to my mom and dad who are the best promoters any writer -- or daughter -- could want.

I've been waiting years for this one: a nod to my long-time friend Kim Maynard, who first sparked the idea for this story in a conversation we had way back in the day. All those improvisational mystery dinners, yuckin' it up with you at Fairlawn Mansion, fed my mental imagery for this series.

And thanks to several of my church friends who read the manuscript at various stages and always made me believe this was a dream worth pursuing. I am blessed with dear friends, a loving family, and a wonderful life!

Prologue

1848

Pain seared Colette's temples, neck, and shoulders. Behind her eyelids, everything blazed like a powder keg of dynamite going off inside her. Explosions roared and blasts glared -- red, and now and then a streak of hot white. She stirred on the bed, and her satin dress rustled.

"Wear the dress, Lettie."

She picked it up and held it before her in front of the oval mirror, noticing how the crimson sleeves would drop off her shoulders, and the bodice would all but reveal every inch of her form. The rest of the dress was cut to accentuate her womanliness, and the rustle of the fabric caressed her skin when it stirred.

"They all admire you. Tonight, I don't want them to be able to take their eyes off you."

"You would put me on such a display?"

A condescending laugh rippled out of him, and she pinched her eyes shut.

"A display? You want to help me succeed, don't you?"

"It's so degrading."

"Degrading." He didn't shout the word, yet it seemed so. "You never want to please me."

"I do."

"No. If you wanted to please me, you would do these simple things I ask of you."

"But--"

He stepped up behind her and slid his fingers over her shoulders.

"Vashti," he whispered. He tipped his lips to her neck and nuzzled her skin. "My Vashti. Wear the dress." His use of that name sliced into her. He caught her gaze in the mirror and entwined one multi-faceted ringlet around his finger, stroking it against the curve of her jaw. "And leave some of your hair down. Just enough to tickle you here... and here..."

His words echoed in time with the blood pulsing through the bruise on her cheek.

They all looked at her. There was no mistaking the hungry thoughts barely veiled in the eyes of the men as they regarded her. The women whispered behind fans and gloved hands, and she felt their rebuff.

Shame. Flooding her. Turning her cheeks crimson, which only seemed to attract more of their attention.

"Dance with the gentlemen, Lettie. It pleases me. That's all I'm asking. Only dance."

So she'd danced. But somehow, even that hadn't pleased him. Somehow, she'd done something wrong.

Tears crept out from under her swollen eyelids, and her shoulders rocked with quiet sobs. How had she come to this place? What had happened to all the dreams she used to harbor?

God, how could I have been so wrong?

Images from another life, a life she'd lived a long, long time ago, hurtled through the blare of her thoughts -- images of a small town with a street covered in pine dust, of a white house on a hill and a trip across the great lake into the shroud of forest where she'd first met her destiny.

A key turned in the lock of the door. Colette wished she could reclaim that other time from the foggy past. But now it was too late. She could never go there again.

Her body convulsed in a shudder as she willed her tears to cease. The door brushed open across the carpeted floor, and her husband treaded softly across the room.

"The heart is deceitful above all things, and desperately wicked. Who can know it?"

Jeremiah 17:9

Chapter One

1841

What could Papa and that man be talking about? Fourteen-year-old Colette Palmer sat still as granite on the Kades' front porch swing, and though she did not so much as sway even a little in the dry summer heat, her senses reeled. Oblivious to the sighs and gossip of her best friend Annie Kade, who sat beside her, Colette waited, watching for some movement from the little house down the road where she lived. Time shifted beneath her, rumbling like the earth and sky during a thunderstorm, making her whole body tremble with the suspicion her childhood might be dropping away beneath her feet.

She straightened again and smiled at Annie, pretending to listen to her friend as she surveyed the sawdust-covered road bending down the hill toward town. Towering trees hugged the perimeter of the town like sentinels. In the distance, out of sight but not out of hearing, came the faint, high-pitched whine of the big saw that cut the logs at the mill, the town's life-blood. From her perch, Colette could glimpse both churches, the company store, two of the four saloons, and a scattering of houses, including her own. Hers was white clapboard, not large like the Kades', but square and tidy with a neat little yard and vegetable garden in front, and a small barn housing her family's few animals in the back.

"Well, here comes Jean. Finally." Annie's voice penetrated Colette's thoughts. Annie stood and wrapped her arm around a porch column. "Wonder where they've been."

Colette inched forward as Jean and Manason Kade rounded the street corner below them. Manason gave Jean's shoulder a playful shove over some comment between them, and Jean smiled. Both of them had the Kade good looks, but Jean's creamy complexion contrasted with her brother's rugged tan.

"Manason's coming, too," Colette answered.

Annie slid her a sidelong glance. "The way you say it, one would think you were in love with him."

"I'm not."

Annie ignored her and called to her two siblings as they pushed open the iron gate at the end of the walk. "What've you two been up to while I've been sitting here being neglected?"

"You've been neglected, Annie? Since when would you allow it?" Manason said. He turned mischievous eyes on Colette. "Ah, it is the east, and Juliet is the sun. Don't let her corrupt you, Juliet."

Annie snorted. "Some Romeo you are. I saw you with Margaret Baker the other day."

"Spying is hardly a lady-like trait."

"Since when are you the judge of what is lady-like? I bet her daddy would like to know the things she's been up to with you. He'd probably pull out his shotgun and make you take her up to the church."

"You have a waspish tongue, little sister. Do you expect to catch a husband with it?"

Annie fisted her hands into her hips, her brown eyes snapping. Before she could reply, however, Jean remarked, "Careful what you say, Annie. You know he'll get you back."

Annie dropped back against the porch column, masking her countenance in a study of aloofness. "Really, Jean, anyone would think you've forgotten what it's like to be nearly sixteen. Can it be that you're twenty years old, and already you've no memory of what it's like to be almost in one's prime? I shouldn't be left behind on your secret outings anymore. That's all. You should both be treating me like an adult."

Jean laughed and tossed her head. Wisps of dark hair floated loose at her temples. "I don't think I'm yet in my prime, though you may think I'm ancient. I can assure you I haven't forgotten what it was like to be sixteen -- or fourteen either, for that matter," she added with a smile at Colette.

"Well, then," Manason said, challenging Annie with a lift of his chin, "If you want to be treated like an adult, perhaps you'd like know that we came to invite you to walk back down to the mill with us."

"I hate the mill."

"Then you don't care about our little surprise."

Annie stepped down the stairs toward them. "What surprise?"

He smirked. "Ah, curious?"

"I'm not listening to you. Jean, what surprise?"

"Stu's home."

"Stuart?" Her voice rose. "Home now?"

Jean nodded. "He's at the mill, talking to Father."

"Well, why didn't you say so? Come on, then!"

Annie hurried down the remaining steps past them, forgetting Colette.

"Come *on!*" she said again, waving at them. Jean turned to catch up with her.

"I'll make sure your guest gets home and catch up with you at the mill," Manason called after them.

"Oh, good grief!" Annie hollered as she and Jean hurried down the street. "Colette can get herself home faster without you."

Colette still sat on the porch swing.

Laughing, Manason turned to her and held out his hand. "Coming?"

She stood, and a warm flush accompanied her quick smile. She tried to ignore his outstretched hand, too conscientious to take it when it meant so much more to her than it did him. "Really, Nase, you don't have to. Go ahead with Annie and Jean. I know you're anxious to see Stuart."

"Nonsense. I just saw him a little while ago, and I'll have all evening with him. Besides, don't you know Annie's going to monopolize him for the next hour? I'll walk you home. Anyway, I saw this man, Eastman, down at the mill today. I may be able to tell you something about the business going on at your house right now."

Colette stopped short and looked up at him. She would melt like a lump of chocolate in his dark brown eyes if his words hadn't startled her so. "You know something?"

He nodded and pulled back the squeaky gate. They strolled out into the street.

Glancing at him, Colette remembered being just six years-old, the first winter her father had gone to work in the woods for Mr. Kade. She remembered peering over the edges of their snow castle to admire the antics of eleven year-old Manason writhing in the snow.

"You'll never defeat me!" he had shouted as he rolled to one side, brandishing his wooden sword at an invisible foe. "I'm the great dragon slayer. I'll save you, Princess! *Aah!*" He leapt to his feet and swished at the air, crying out in pretend rage, pain -- and with a final thrust -- victory.

"I've found the weak spot in the dragon's scale armor. He's dead! You're safe to come out of the castle, Princess."

Dark-eyed Annie, two years older than Colette, stood next to her and giggled. "If I were a princess, I'd sure want a better knight than you to save me."

"Who is it that speaks to me? Is it my lady's *maid?* Hark, fair Princess! Pay no attention to the ugly old maid. You are free to leave the castle and climb upon my mighty steed. I will return you safely to your father's kingdom."

Eight year-old Annie harrumphed and stalked away, but Colette smiled at her hero. He held out his hand for her while she pretended to climb upon his horse, then he took the imaginary reins and led her down the snow-covered street toward home.

"Lady, your castle."

"Thank you, Nase." She pretended to dismount and waved good-bye.

Now, with the memory of that time fresh in her thoughts, she glanced at him, taking in the sweep of his thick brown hair off his brow and the broadness that had grown into his shoulders from working at the mill.

"Tell me what you've heard," she said.

"Looks like you're going to be leaving us. Has your father said anything to you about it?"

"No. Not exactly. But I suspected. Are you sure? I mean, Papa has talked for a long time about starting his own mill, but he hasn't had enough capital. He's explained to me how terribly much it requires. It could be another ten years before he dare try it." She remembered the tall, astute looking man meeting with her father right this minute, the man who'd introduced the rumblings of change into her thoughts. Now Manason had confirmed them. "Is that why that man is here? Are he and

7

Papa making some kind of deal?"

"I'm afraid so." Manason slid his arm around Colette's trembling shoulders. His calm reassurance spread throughout her body as he continued. "His name's Eastman. He's an investor from Pennsylvania who's been doing some speculating in Wisconsin Territory. He has the money to start a company there, but he needs a man with know-how. He went to Detroit first, and someone there mentioned my father's mill. Then your father's name came up."

She tried to absorb the impact of Manason's words.

"Your dad really does have the know-how," he said. "He's the best mechanic and foreman my father's ever had. We hate to lose him. But it's his big opportunity, a chance to be more than just someone's hired help. Eastman's looking for more than a foreman. He wants a partner. He's willing to contract a part ownership in the new company for the technical knowledge your dad can bring to it."

Colette stopped walking long enough to think about everything Manason had said. *Wisconsin Territory!* Her heart pounded, and a million thoughts raced through her mind. How could she go so far away from this place? She'd spent the past seven years growing up with Annie and Manason. She didn't even remember her life on the farm near Detroit before Mama and Papa had brought her to this woods town. Jean was the only thing akin to a big sister she'd ever had. Annie was her best friend, even if she was self-absorbed and spoiled. And Manason -- she sucked in her breath -- Manason was the love of her life, only he didn't know it, and now she was going west to Wisconsin Territory. She shuddered. *I'll never see any of them again.*

Manason's arm slid from her shoulders and he grasped her hand, giving it a tight squeeze. "You okay?"

She gave a small nod. Thankfully, he didn't let go of her hand. It kept her from swirling away in a maelstrom of uncertainty.

"It's too bad you aren't older," he said in a way that made Colette know he was doing his best to cheer her. "Then you could stay, and I wouldn't have to chase after the likes of Margie Baker."

"Oh, Nase, you shouldn't say that. You like Margaret."

"Sure I do. But in a few years, she won't hold a candle to you, Princess."

"Nase." She couldn't say anything else, despite her embarrassment. In only a few brief words, he had succeeded in driving away her heavy thoughts and set her heart to fluttering.

They stopped in front of her house, and Manason released her hand. "Well, you may as well go in and hear it from your pa. They should be all through with the hand-shaking by now."

Colette nodded and walked up to her door. Before turning the knob, however, she looked back. Manason was still there, smiling his crooked smile. He winked at her to encourage her, and she went into the house, out of the sun.

*****

Two Weeks Later

Side-stepping a coil of rope, Harris Eastman ran a hand through his hair and sucked in the clean lake air. Two weeks after sealing the deal with Eldon Palmer, Michigan was behind them at last. Leaning against the ship's rail, he closed his eyes.

The rhythm of his body moved with the ship as he mentally recounted his months of planning and preparation. Trips to file claims, to hire builders for the house, to purchase equipment and find a surveyor had claimed his time. Besides all that, the speculating and dealing with the attorneys and the search for Eldon Palmer to sign him as a partner added to the travel and the waiting. But it had all brought him to this day. Yes, he was relieved to be on his way to achieving his goal, and almost as relieved to be up on deck, away from Helen's big-eyed tears.

The anticipation of settling ran faster than blood through his veins. The long journey ahead would be hard-pressed to keep pace with it. He doubted Helen would fare any better with what was to come: a river trip, then rutted trails that could hardly be called roads, a creaking wagon ride through dark, dense woods, and then another river to paddle and pole against. He would have to make a serious effort to be on his best behavior just to keep his wife from dissolving into a complete breakdown.

Tired as he was, he couldn't wait to put the Lake Michigan shoreline behind him and head west into the interior. First, they would spend two days in Fort Howard. Two more days...

He opened his eyes and stared at the water. It was imperative they not waste an ounce of time. Harris had only limited confidence in the man he'd left in charge back at the mill site on the Wisconsin River. Once Harris arrived, he would fire the man and put things in order, running them on his own from now on -- with Eldon Palmer's expertise at the mill, of course. That was the only way to grow his empire.

It was a shame Helen had to be so difficult about the move. Why couldn't she see how important it was to them? Remembering her sobs made his temples pulse.

Harris glanced up and recognized the Palmer girl standing on the deck a ways off. Why couldn't Helen be a little more adventurous, like that one? The girl had been full of questions and enthusiasm since the moment her father told her the news. Then again, Colette Palmer was just a child and had no idea what it would mean if their venture failed.

Harris ground his teeth. It was best he had left Helen in the cabin for a while. The time alone would help her to come to her senses.

*****

Colette walked across the deck and hugged her shawl across her shoulders. Could it be she was only hours from setting foot into the dark green mystery called Wisconsin Territory? A mere two weeks had passed since her parents, while introducing her to Mr. Eastman, had informed her of their decision, yet here she stood, on a packet slipping into the big finger of water called Green Bay.

Stopping to rest against the rail, Colette swept her gaze over the dancing expanse before her. A tendril of her bright curls escaped from the ribbon at the nape of her neck, and she pushed it out of the way as she took in the sparkling blue world. *The world can have its oceans. Nothing could be more grand or wild than the Great Lake.* She'd heard lumbermen, those who'd worked on the schooners, talk about how the Lakes could be meaner than any ocean. But today, serene blue stretched as far as she could see in any direction -- dark, chalky blue waters lapping against the bright, aquiline sky. Now and then a spray of water shot high against the prow of the boat and a sheet of moisture dampened her face.

Her thoughts reeled backwards, coming to the day that had changed everything. Back to the panic she'd experienced walking into her house and her papa had told her they'd soon be leaving for Wisconsin Territory, hundreds of miles away. She could still hear the resonant, business-like voice of Mr. Eastman telling them about the small log farmhouse awaiting her family in the wilderness. She remembered feeling easier after learning he had a young wife named Helen who seemed like a fine lady, but Colette had barely spoken with her thus far.

Harris Eastman himself must be nearing middle age, Colette decided, perhaps about thirty-six or thirty-seven. A spray of water shot into the air, and Colette turned her head. He stood further down the deck. *He is a striking gentleman.* The fine lines of his suit defined his broad shoulders. *He always wears a suit, and he's always well kempt, even here on the boat.*

His black hair, normally swept back in a thick wave with a hint of gray at the temples, was now mussed loose in the wind. He wore a trim mustache, and dimples creased his cheeks. Taken as a whole, his handsome face was long and square, and she'd noticed earlier that his dark eyes twinkled whenever he'd chuckle at some remark from either her or Colette's mother. *I suppose we shall all know one another quite well before long.*

A brisk wind switched at Colette's hair and shawl, despite the sublime sunshine, and she shivered a little as her thoughts turned once more to the Lake Michigan vista. One could hardly tell it was still high summer. Just four days ago she had been saying to Annie that she wished they had time to go swimming before she went away. Annie had sighed one of her deep, dramatic sighs and declared how she would simply have no one to talk with once Colette left them. It didn't seem to occur to Annie that she still had both Jean and Manason, and even Stuart as her allies. Colette, on the other hand, had no siblings, no friend with whom to share the trip, no companion. No, that hadn't fazed Annie in the least. Of course, she had promised to write Collette, but Colette knew that after one strained effort, Annie would give up her enthusiasm over it. Jean, however, was more likely to correspond faithfully. She would ask about Colette's new life in Wisconsin Territory.

Their last conversation had taken place during a farewell dinner hosted by the Kades for Colette's family. As they'd passed around platters of beef and potatoes, Jean had seemed to want to reassure Colette. "I don't suppose it will be so very different than it is here. Just a lot of trees and a lot of fellows anxious to cut them down," she remarked.

Colette's pulse stirred as it always did when they talked about the woods. "I read the pine are sometimes 180 feet tall and more than 400 years old. The green of their branches can block out the sun, even though their trunks might not have a single branch for 100 feet."

Manason fixed his gaze on her and smiled. "Yes, that's right. In fact, Father has had surveyors tell him of an occasional tree reaching 250 feet and nearly seven or eight feet in diameter, breast high. I suppose it all feels rather primal when you're under them."

"Papa calls them the aristocrats of the forests. Right, Papa?"

Eldon Palmer nodded. "Yes, indeed. Wisconsin has more of those virgin aristocrats than anyone has ever seen standing in one place. Please pass the gravy."

"Here you are, sir," Manason said. "I wish I were going with you."

Yes, so do I. Colette forgot about her food.

"Maybe in a year or two, I'll join you, Mr. Palmer."

"With Eldon getting started in Wisconsin, maybe I'll cut you loose to follow him before you know it, son," Manason's father, Grayson Kade said. "But I need you here for a while yet. You've still got a lot to learn."

Manason glanced at his father and nodded. In her heart, Colette knew she would have been just as anxious to make a start as he, if she were a man.

Jean spoke up. "Well, Colette has promised to write us, haven't you, Colette? We can all visit the big woods in Wisconsin Territory vicariously through her."

Colette frowned. "I'm afraid I won't get to see you marry Virgil, Jean."

"Has it come to that?" Lavinia, Colette's mother asked.

Jean blushed. She was never so pretty as when she blushed, with her dark hair framing her fair face and gray eyes.

"Not yet, Mrs. Palmer."

"Jean is learning what it means to have patience," Stuart said, flashing a grin that was a twin to Manason's.

"It's all very well for men to talk about patience," Jean answered, her fork poised in the air. "They have complete control over their destinies. Meanwhile, we women can do nothing but await their good pleasure."

"Sounds as if your patience is wearing thin."

Jean mashed the potato on her plate and harrumphed. "I'm only glad Virgil isn't here with us tonight to be any more encouraged by my own brothers to avoid the question. I don't intend to wear my patience like a badge of honor. You gentlemen can keep us ladies waiting all you want, but someday you may be sorry for it. Mark my words."

Her brothers laughed, and the others around the table grinned at Jean's dire warnings. "Maybe it would be good if Virgil were here after all," Manason said. "You just might frighten him into action."

"It isn't Virgil I'd hoped to motivate with my words, Manason, however appropriate they might be," she added. "You fellows are so caught up in your grand adventures that sometimes you fail to recognize the adventures under your very noses."

Colette's mind raced back into the present on board the packet bound for Wisconsin Territory. She didn't want to think about what adventures might be under Manason's nose. Margaret Baker, that's what.

She gazed down into the water's wake and realized it wouldn't be long now. Wood chips and sawdust washed along in the waves. She almost thought she could smell the pine.

*****

The journey took the better part of a week, traveling from Fort Howard down the Fox River by keel boat to Fort Winnebago, then up the *Wisconsin.* Lastly, they drove up the path others kept referring to as the *Pinery Road,* with the wagon sticking and jolting and lunging them into the deep interior of the pinelands.

Manason had told Colette the *Wisconsin* was sure to become the hardest working river in the nation, and that one day she would discover it felt like home. "You haven't seen the last of me, you know. I'll be coming to the Wisconsin pineries one day to get started on my own. Maybe in a year or two. Course, you might forget all about me by then."

"No, I won't, Nase. Not ever." She hoped he saw in her eyes what she wasn't saying. *I'll never stop waiting for you.*

"We'll look forward to that, then," he said. Manason always seemed to know the right thing to say to settle Colette's anxious thoughts.

The minute she stepped on the steamer to cross the Lake, she had already begun looking forward to Manason's promise to join her. She would wait, even if it took years. Maybe the next time they met, Manason would see her with different eyes.

She thought of that day now, with every mile of the painful ride to their new farm below the village of Grand Rapids, just a few bends above and across the river from the settlement they called Frenchtown, only a mile or two below the falls where the new Eastman-Palmer mill would be located.

Even when they ferried across the river and loaded their belongings onto another buckboard, even as they drove through the hamlet of Grand

Rapids and out to the cabin they would call *home*, even as she stood before it, and even as she strolled around the cabin and down the path that wound more than a hundred yards through trees, brush, and grass to sit on the banks of the unknown, dark, swirling river -- she looked forward to Manason's coming.

Someday.

Chapter Two

Joe Gilbert stirred quietly in the woods behind the trees as the girl stretched out her legs and dangled her toes in the current. She threw her head back to the sky with her eyes closed, so that her pool of flaxy hair picked up pine needles and grass. Joe smiled to himself. It was about time another girl settled around here. Only three young women lived in the whole area. Four, if you counted Fat Sally. A mere dozen if you counted the old grannies and the married women. This one wasn't too young. He'd seen her parents coming and going from their wagon, laughing between themselves. Then they had disappeared inside the cabin.

He supposed he could wait to meet the girl tomorrow when he delivered the sow from the man in Grand Rapids. But a five hundred pound sow carrying a litter didn't always behave, and he sure didn't want to make a fool of himself with a fat, obstinate pig when he was meeting a girl like that one for the first time. Maybe it would be better to walk over and meet her now. Besides, by tomorrow, some other fellow might be barging in already.

Joe stepped out from behind the big, knotty trunk of a white pine, his hands stuffed deep in his pockets, and sauntered along the river bank until he stood over her. She never heard his footfalls on the soft needles covering the ground, and she startled when she opened her bright blue eyes,

She jumped to her feet and swallowed, but quickly found her voice. "You scared me."

He grinned.

*****

The boy, almost grown, stared at her through eyes that sparkled with secrets. A mischievous, lop-sided grin spread over his handsome face, framed by wild, dark curls. He leaned back against the trunk of a great, tilting tree.

"Sorry. Name's Joseph Gilbert. What's yours?"

She brushed the pine needles off her hands and looked him over closely before deciding to forge ahead. "Colette Palmer."

Joseph seemed comfortable in the long pause that followed while he gazed at her. At length, he said, "I live just down the river. If you stay on this path, you can't miss it. Work in the woods with my pa. Logger. You know."

Colette knew. It's what all the boys did every place she'd ever been, log or farm. That was about it. Papa said there were a lot of miners in Wisconsin too, down south.

"How old are you, Colette?"

She hesitated for only a moment before lifting her chin and deciding to answer his bold question. "Going on fifteen."

"That's what I figured. I'll be seventeen in December." Joseph was tall and lithe, with an easy laziness in his movements belied by his muscled forearms. "You'll have to let me know when your birthday comes. We all like a party around here. Maybe I'll get you a present." He smiled again, flashing a double row of straight white teeth.

His green eyes and lazy smile drew her in. She took a deep breath and relaxed a little more. "I usually celebrate my birthday with my ma and pa. 'Sides, you don't know me. Why would you get me a present?"

"'Cause you're the newest, prettiest girl on the east side of the river," he stated flat out.

Colette flushed. No one had ever flirted with her before, and now here was this boy -- Joseph, tall and handsome and brash as could be -- trying to make her blush, and doing a passing good job at it.

"Oh."

Joseph laughed. "What? You didn't know? They got that many pretty girls where you come from? I'd like to go there if they do. I heard you come from Michigan. That true?"

She nodded.

"Well?"

"Well, what?"

"Do they have pretty girls there?"

Colette could see that he was teasing her now, but she didn't quite know how to extricate herself from the situation other than to simply answer the question.

"Yes, they do." She thought of Jean and Annie, and unfortunately, of Margaret Baker. She wished Margaret Baker would meet a boy like this. "There's a girl named Margaret you'd find especially pleasing. She takes a great deal of interest in flirting with boys," she said, a little shocked at herself, but unable to keep from smiling back.

Joseph laughed again. "Why, if you don't sound a little cross with Margaret. I'm sure you're prettier than she could be."

Colette steeled herself to change the subject. "Aren't there other girls around here?"

"Only a couple. But don't worry about it. I'm more fun than a cord of girls stacked up." He straightened up to his full height and stepped closer. "Say, you like to swim?"

She loved to swim, but only shrugged. "Is it safe?"

He chuckled.

"The river, I mean."

"It's got some strong currents, but it isn't too bad. I'll show you later."

She didn't know what she thought about swimming with Joseph Gilbert, so she just avoided saying anything that might sound like a commitment. Joseph went on to another subject.

15

"You can catch some dandy fish along through here. Like to fish?"
She did like to fish, and she said so.

"Good, I'll come by later and take you fishing, okay?"

"I guess it would be all right. I'll have to check with my ma and pa first, though, to see if they need me."

"All right. I guess I'd better go, but I'll be seeing you." He backed away. "Don't worry;" he said with a final glance, grinning again before starting off down the path, "I'll come by the front door and introduce myself proper."

Colette thought a lot about Joseph the rest of the day. Worrying about his teasing nature made the time go by quickly. She helped her mama wash the quilts and hang them on the line to dry. She helped her pa get the stall bedded for their horse, and a pen erected. Papa said that by next week, he hoped to have a new milk cow.

By evening, Colette was tired and hot. She felt like swimming, but didn't want to risk getting startled again by Joseph and having him invite himself along. She had just about given up on the idea that he might really come to take her fishing when he knocked on the door. His smile was still fixed in place, but he came with all sorts of good manners to introduce himself to her parents. Her pa took quickly to the idea that they might have fish for breakfast, and her mama only smiled and gave her that silent glance that said *watch yourself,* and let her go.

Colette hadn't had such a good time since her last picnic with Jean and Annie. Manason had come by later to spit watermelon seeds at them and toss them each into the mill pond.

She and Joseph hauled in a respectable stringer of fish while Joseph talked steadily in his easy-going manner. She learned he had two older brothers, *handsome devils* like himself. He told her stories about his work with his father, about how he'd shot the biggest buck in the logging camp last winter, about the other girls in town worth mentioning, as well as their families. He told her about the other boys, too, warning her how they'd be swooning around her before long, promising he wouldn't let them become too bothersome.

She was quick to assure him she didn't want them to bother her, and Joseph, raking her with a glance, merely grinned.

*****

Jean set a tray of lemonade out on the porch and lifted her head just as Manason and Stu came through the gate.

Manason dragged himself up the steps and dropped down on the top one, unlacing one of his boots and taking it off to shake out the sawdust. More sawdust clung to the sweat on his arms and the back of his neck. His collar felt damp and itchy.

Stu took a chair and sighed. Jean handed them each a glass. "Here, Nase, have something cold to drink. Looks as though you could use it.

Hard day?"

Manason ran his tongue over his parched lips. He shrugged and drained the glass in seven or eight long slugs. "No harder than most." Setting it beside him, he stared into the street.

Stuart took a couple of sips from his glass and looked over at Manason. "Going to the big doings at the Bakers' tonight?"

"Margaret's expecting me."

"And that means?" said Jean.

"You know Margaret. She'll have her brothers calling me out if I don't show."

"You ain't scared of them wildcats, are you?" Stu asked, laughing a little.

Manason glared at him. Scared? Hardly. "I just don't want the fuss."

"What's eating you Nase?" Jean asked. "Is it Margaret?"

Manason didn't answer her. Instead, he unbuttoned his filthy shirt.

"Do you love her?"

He peeled off his shirt and rubbed it over his arms. "Love who? Margaret?" Manason shook his head and turned around to face them more directly. Stars were popping out in the chalky blue of falling dusk. A shiver crawled up his back along with the cool wind that dried the sweat of the day off him. He pictured, for a minute, Margaret's dark, flaming hair and her cool, glassy blue eyes. She had lips shaped like a little beating heart and she used them willingly, like a stamp of ownership. "Margaret's okay."

"But you don't love her."

"I didn't say I did, didn't say I didn't. What's with the inquisition, anyway? You don't see me probing you about Virgil. Why haven't you married him yet?"

Anger clouded Jean's face, making her gray eyes look momentarily black and fierce. Then, just as quickly, the emotion dropped away and her face fell into a mask of vulnerability. Stu cleared his throat and regret stabbed Manason. It wasn't Jean's fault she wasn't keeping house for Virgil. That man was dragging his feet, plain and simple. Suddenly it dawned on Manason that Margaret thought he was doing the same thing. Manason had never said anything to Margaret about love, yet she kept pushing herself at him, waiting for a proposal.

"I'm sorry, Jean." He ran a hand through his hair. "You know, I'll tell you what it is." He looked both Jean and Stu squarely in the eyes. "Listen... hear it?" He shifted, tilting his head. The wind was slowly churning up a gust that washed along the waving tree-tops and gently picked up the tendrils of hair on their heads. "It's the pine. I like the work at Pa's mill. I really do. But every time the wind blows, and I see the tree tops swaying like a green ocean, it's like they're calling out to me. I want to be in them, listening, moving, gauging every board foot."

Stuart smiled and leaned forward with his elbows on his knees. "Sounds like it's time Pa sent you up north to do some cruising."

"I want to, but if he needs me here, well... I can't do anything about it."

"I'll talk to Pa. I'm foreman now. You aren't doing anything at the mill that one of Margaret's brothers or even ol' Patterson couldn't do. No offense. But you've got the mind for cruising pine, and if Pa wants to get something going up north, then he should put you to better use.""You think so, Stu?"

"I know it. 'Sides, if you hang around here, it's only a matter of time before you're stuck. Margaret's staking claim, if I don't miss my guess, and she's staking deep and for keeps."Later, at the Baker's, Manason thought about what Stu had said and knew it was true. If he stayed another season, he'd get married, and somehow he just never had it figured that in the end he'd marry Margie Baker. She was a pretty handful, and saucy, too. Tantalizing enough for any man, but he wasn't ready for that yet. He wasn't ready for a house and a wife and kids when his whole life still spread before him like an uncharted map. Manason started plotting the grid of that map as he tapped his foot to Abel Nelson's fiddle.

Margie strolled across the room toward him. Utter confidence rode in the sway of her hips. Green eyes beckoned beneath raised brows."Going to ask me to dance?"

Nase gave her a warm smile -- no sense getting her all riled up -- and reeled her onto the floor. But his head was full of white pine and tamarack swamp and the borealis dancing on a carpet of stars rolled out across the purple and jet night sky. When the music finally paused and they caught their breath, Margaret leaned against his shoulder and sighed. "You're looking awfully far away tonight, Nase. Didn't you want to see me?"

Holding his face close to her hair, he breathed in her scent. "Who wouldn't want to see you, Margie?"

"Where are you, then? What's going on in that handsome head of yours?" She gazed upward and placed a fingertip on his temple.

"Nothing pressing. C'mon, let's take a walk."

She smiled a beguiling smile and led him out the door and down the porch steps, but he stopped and looked up into the sky.

"Can you smell the air changing? Fall's here. Winter will be right behind it."

"Don't depress me," she said, sidling up beside him and then around to face him, her voice all soft and warm like dusk. "Course, then we'll have to work mighty hard to stay warm."

He lowered his eyes to her, taking in the moonlight bouncing off her shoulders and hair. "You're a catty girl, Margie, all willingness and wiles," he said softly.

A little fury settled into her eyebrows, and she raised her hand as if to slap him. He caught her wrists.

"It's true, isn't it?" he said, as the false anger left her eyes and surrender came into them. Her velvety gaze tugged at him, and he almost kissed her. Instead, he dropped her hands and looked past her. "I might be going away this winter."

"What?" Shock and dismay played over her face. That was obviously not part of her plan. "Why?"

"Stu's going to talk to Pa about me cruising for him next year. I think I might like to start by spending a season working in one of the camps up in the Au Sable pineries."

"You don't mean it, Nase. You're just saying that."

He didn't answer; he just looked at her.

She turned away. "I don't see why you'd want to waste a whole winter in some old camp if you're going to be gone next year, too. Wouldn't you rather just wait until spring? We could have the whole winter together, you and I." Her voice shook a little. She sounded genuinely alarmed.

Manason placed a hand on her shoulder and turned her to face him. "Margaret, I'm going to say something, but I'm not sure you'll understand it." Suddenly he knew he cared more for her than he'd been willing to admit. The fire had gone out of her eyes and sadness had crept in. Still, he forged ahead. "I've been working for my father, and that's okay, even though Stu's managing the mill. He has a great future there, but I've got plans of my own. I never planned on staying around and working at the mill forever. I want to branch out on my own. There's stakes to be made, and I want to be in on it. Cruising is part of it, too. But in a couple of years, if I'm careful, I'm hoping to go into Wisconsin Territory."

Her lip trembled and her eyes widened. "I don't understand. What about *us*, Nase?"

"What do you want me to say?"

"*What do I want you to say?*" A little gasp of exasperation escaped her mouth. "You mean, you don't know? Do I have to say it for you?"

"I'm sorry, Margie." He shook his head and rubbed his cheek to keep from reaching for her. "I know you believe I've led you on. I let you think that maybe there was more to our relationship than there is. I'm just not ready to think of settling down yet."

Big, glassy tears pooled in her eyes. Manason wasn't sure if they were real or not, but he knew they were brewing up a storm.

Her jaw quivered, and she took a little step back. "Manason Kade, if you walk away from me, you'll regret it. I promise you that."

"Don't say that, Margie. 'Sides, am I walking away? Maybe I'm just trying to get my life settled out. Then there'll be time for the sort of thing you're wanting of me."

She jerked her shoulders and stepped away from him. "Oh, you're walking, all right. I can see it even if you won't admit it. Do you think I'm going wait around for you?"

He tried to be calm, reasonable. He shrugged. "I kind of hoped you might."

"Humph! I bet you do!" Fire lit up her eyes. "You hear me on this,

Nase. I'm not waiting. If you leave me for a whole year, you just wait and see." She charged past him and up the steps, her skirts swirling around her. "You just wait and see!" she shouted again, before storming into the house. The door banged shut behind her.

Manason let out a sigh and swept a hand through his hair. His gaze trailed the stars down the street to the place where they disappeared into the black tree tops. Walking out into the sawdust on the road, he kicked his way along, following the glittering overhead trail toward the woods where the black night, swallowed him like the maw of a yawning cave.

*****

The mornings that greeted Colette when she climbed out from under her quilt each dawn were crisper now. The sun came up more slowly, hanging like a burst of citrus on the edge of the sky, radiating through all the russets and ambers of autumn. Even the pines had changed. First the pale green bud tips of springtime had changed to the solid deep green of summer. Now, the heavy, dark greens of coming winter dripped with long, narrow brown cones. Sprays of red-brown needles dropped away to increase the depth of the padded forest floor. The few good frosts that had chilled the air merely accentuated the pungent smells of leaf mold and dry wood stacked up for winter's fuel.

Colette rubbed her arms and gazed up in wonder at the light filtering through the feathery boughs like a veil, muting the world around her. The green veil made the long, dark trunks appear like the columns of some grand cathedral where the choir of voices were those of geese calling orders as they headed south, and the profuse flocking of pigeons pummeling their wings against their breasts. Daylight flickered above the veil as they passed by.

Primal, Manason had called it. And indeed, it was.

The forest was gloriously primal, and Colette wanted to run barefoot and singing across the cushy needles down to the river. But she only smiled, thinking about how they'd hear her clear over in Frenchtown, and how it was too cold to go barefoot anyway. She was fifteen today. Maybe that's all this silliness was.

Still, she skipped out to the barn to feed the animals, giving special care to a little runt that couldn't reach a teat on the sow and was likely to be crushed. She'd have to sell it once it was big enough, she supposed. She was already too attached to the little fellow, but she would refrain from naming it anything but Pork Chop in case it ended up in their own smokehouse someday.

She spent the rest of the morning with her mother storing beets and carrots in the root cellar. There hadn't been enough season left to plant much more than lettuce in their garden this year, but they'd been able to buy some bushels of produce from a farmer further south, for which Lavinia thanked the Lord.

Colette thought God must be something like her father, by the way He took care of them and helped her own father's dreams come true. Papa had always warned Colette to keep her out of trouble, like the time when she was nine and he told her she shouldn't climb over the log pile. It'd been sitting there most of the summer and most likely contained a nest of bees. But she didn't listen, and sure enough, she paid for it with more stings than the river could cough up mud for packing them. Pa didn't scold her, though. He just held her and comforted her, and she figured out she should've listened to him in the first place. Pa said folks learned by their mistakes, and she figured God sometimes allowed the same thing. Papa said failure was only a temporary setback. Maybe that was how he could hold onto his dream of owning a mill for all those years.

When Annie turned fifteen, Jean had said she was at that "wistful age", and that idea stuck in Colette's mind. Now, maybe she was going to get wistful, too. Maybe she should ask Helen about it. Maybe Helen would be able to tell Colette whether or not she seemed wistful.

Colette had grown grateful for Helen Eastman's company after finally getting to know her. Even Harris Eastman seemed inclined to enjoy Colette's visits to his and Helen's lovely home. Always curious about the work of the lumbermen and her father's business pursuits, Colette found she could ask Harris questions about the lumber empire he hoped to build, and he graciously took time to answer her. Sometimes he seemed surprised by her questions, like the time she'd asked whether it might not be wiser to hire family men like his housekeeper's husband, Heinrich Shultz, whose wife depended on his living, than to hire some of the single lumberjacks passing through who might just as easily move on at any given moment.

"Families planting roots are what will make Wisconsin grow and reach statehood someday," she'd asserted. "Not simply clearing the woods and turning them into cash. If families don't settle here, the towns will empty as soon as the trees are gone."

She still believed that, and Harris had seemed to consider her opinion, but it did make her wonder. *Will Manason come someday, and will he and Margie start a family here?*

Yes, she must be getting wistful. She sighed. With Papa away downriver, it would just be her and Mama for her birthday supper.

But those plans changed when Joseph appeared just before mealtime. Colette answered the knock on the cabin door to find him displaying one of his handsome, impish smiles.

"I remembered you told me how you always celebrated your birthday with your family, and I figured you'd probably be wishing your pa was here. I heard he's gone downriver with Mr. Eastman to get some equipment for their new mill."

"That's right. Goodness, Joseph, I didn't think you'd remember my birthday."

"Well, that's not all I remembered. Do you recollect me telling you I was going to get you a present?"

"Well, yes, but..." Until then, she hadn't noticed how stiffly Joseph was standing, and that he had one arm tucked inside his coat to make a decided bulge.

"Well, I didn't forget." Gently he pulled back his coat and withdrew his arm. Cradled on his forearm was a fat, yellow puppy.

"Oh, Joe!"

Her mother bit back a smile, her eyes twinkling at Joe.

"Mama, look!" Colette picked up the puppy and lolled him around in her arms. Lying on his back, he stretched his black nose upward and licked her chin. Colette laughed. "Joseph -- a puppy. I can't believe it."

"Well, old Bess had another litter at the end of August, and if I don't find them homes it'll be the river for them."

"Oh, no!"

Joe laughed. "Aw, Lettie, don't worry. I already got takers on all of them. My pa's even taking one up to the camp. It'll keep the scavengers away." Colette squinched her eyes while the pup licked her face, and Joe laughed again. "I swear, you'd save a cricket it you thought it looked desperate enough."

No one had ever called her Lettie before she moved to Wisconsin Territory. Harris Eastman had started it the first time her family visited his and Helen's new home. Now, it seemed, only her mama and papa ever called her Colette anymore. She cast Joseph a smirk and turned her attention back to the pup. "What'll I call him?"

"Why don't you call him Killer?"

She rolled her eyes.

"Well, how about Dandelion? He's yellow."

"C'mon, Joseph, you can do better."

"I think I'll let you figure it out. I only bring the presents. I don't name them, too."

She lowered the puppy from her neck and looked steadily at Joe. "Thanks so much. I never would've thought -- I mean, I never would have guessed that you--"

"Forget it," he said. "It's just a puppy." But the lazy smile and the spark in his green eyes told her it was much more than that.

Chapter Three

Harris Eastman strode across the puncheon floor of the government land office, tapping a rolled up map against his palm. Thoughts creased his forehead as he spread the roll open across the table in the center of the room. Where was that clerk?

Weighting the map with a book on one corner and a chunk of ore on another, he held down the lower edge while he scraped back a chair so he could sit and study the chart closer. The broad expanse of white paper was broken only by the ragged lines of rivers -- rivers to the world -- and by the long looping shapes of Lakes Michigan and Superior.

Harris hunkered more closely over the map and traced his hand down the lines that spread across the territory, fingers of wealth dipping into the heartland, dropping rich deposits of fertile earth along the way. Land abundant in natural resources; timber that was sure to produce a new class of overlord, deposits of lead, iron, and copper, and even the black loam itself, able to produce crops and raise herds. Rich land. More than any man could imagine possessing.

But he did plan to own it, getting richer and richer along the way. For the past two years, since the government lands had first been opened for both sale and settlement, Harris had been buying it up in such quantities as he was able. He already had nearly 13,000 acres to his credit, acres he planned to mortgage out to settlers at exorbitant rates of interest. Many sections he would see logged off first, thus doubling or even tripling his profits. Of course, plenty of other land barons, logging kingpins, and speculators were out there with the same idea. Every day more surveyors cruised the forests. A race would be on before long.

Harris was no woodsman himself, and he was more than happy to give a man like Eldon Palmer a leg up if it meant claiming a reward for it in the end.

Harris leaned back in the chair and stroked his clean-shaven chin. People clamored for land these days. Always moving west, the hordes were hungry for it. But the rabble couldn't do it alone. They needed someone like him to help them get their start.

Fortunately for Palmer, even with his intelligence, he didn't have broader ambitions. Eldon didn't see past owning a simple mill, running a modest little farm with his provincial wife, or settling his daughter into a comfortable marriage someday.

Harris rubbed his chin again and thought about Lettie Palmer. Now, there was a godsend he hadn't expected. Helen would have had even more difficulty adjusting to this backwoods settlement if it hadn't been for the Palmer girl. Besides, not only was Lettie Palmer a lively companion and a distraction for his wife, but she was also intelligent in her own right.

23

Harris found himself replying with interest to Lettie's shrewd questions about the business. Sometimes she even showed insight enough to answer them herself. Occasionally -- and at this, Harris chuckled -- Lettie Palmer even had the gall to challenge his plans. Yes, she had a good head on her pretty young shoulders, and Harris had no doubt that Eldon's daughter would make some lumberman a happy man someday. Whoever it was would probably not deserve her.

Harris reined his wandering thoughts back to the map in front of him. He sat forward quickly and pulled an envelope from inside his coat. It contained all the names of would-be settlers who owed him money. They'd come to his agents eagerly enough, begging with their hats twisted in their hands, hoping for a chance. Well, he'd give them their chance, and he'd line his pockets in the process.

Why not? After all, there would always be those who rose above the rest and made claim to empires. Harris tapped the envelope against the map and waited for the clerk to return, thinking hard about his prospects.

Wisconsin Territory. A place to build those empires -- a place to fashion kings.

*****

Colette tapped her pencil against the blank sheet of paper again, then smoothed the page. She hadn't written any of the promised letters to Annie or Jean, but now she thought she must. Jean would worry if she didn't hear from her soon. Colette sighed, steeling herself, then began to write. She would address the letter to Annie and Jean. They would read it to their family. It would be inappropriate to include Manason's name in the greeting, so she only imagined what she would say to him if she could. She would tell him about the pine.

Dear Annie and Jean, and everyone,

You must wonder at my long delay in writing to you. It has been quite rude of me.

The wind through the branches is just as you described it would be, Nase.

It's just that so much has changed so suddenly, I hardly know where to start. Our trip went well, though it was long and tiring at times. Crossing Lake Michigan was heavenly, and the weather quite fine.

The forest is like a veil drawn back when you reach the water's edge, and the sky reveals itself like a blushing bride. The tall trunks of the trees line up like a congregation, and the branches sway and sigh at the smile on the sun-kissed cheeks of dawn.

I have gotten to know Mrs. Eastman quite well now. We have made friends. She is such a delicate lady, so in need of my companionship, that it quite helps me keep my mind off how much I miss all of you.

I miss you, Nase.

How are you all?

Can you still hear the woods calling?

I guess if I had written sooner, I would have heard something from each of you by now. That teaches me a lesson.

Is it Wisconsin you hear?

Jean, do you have any news to share about Virgil? Annie, they tell me there is a man in Frenchtown who can play the fiddle beyond anyone's imagining. I hope I can hear him play sometime. I'm sure you could teach them all how to dance if you were here.

Please come before long.

I hope you won't forget me. I think of you all every day.

Don't forget your promise, Nase.

Sincerely,
All my love,
Colette P.

Colette took the letter to town the next day. She felt a little guilty that after all her excitement about the puppy, she hadn't mentioned it. How could she, though, without mentioning Joseph -- and wouldn't that have Annie's tongue wagging? Jean, too, might think it sweet and be filled with nonsense. The next thing Collette knew, Manason would believe she was just a fickle little girl who didn't mean anything by what she'd tried to convey in her eyes.

Well, she'd meant it. She'd always mean it.

*****

"How are you feeling today, Rose?" Colette asked the Eastman's

25

young and very pregnant German housekeeper who greeted her at the door. Rose Schultz's husband worked at the camps most of the year and as a river hog who rode the masses of logs down on the currents each spring. Rose's position allowed her to live with the Eastmans while he was away.

"Sehr gut." She swayed into the room ahead of Colette where Helen sat with her knitting.

Helen glanced up from her clicking needles. "Look what I have here," Her blue eyes shone like an angel's as she held her project aloft, a soft, yellow garment that was starting to take the shape of an infant-sized sweater. "Oh, Rose, don't strain yourself with the laundry on the line. I'll take care of it for you."

Helen didn't often cook or clean, but she was a good seamstress. She'd already produced quite a stack of tiny garments and linens for Rose's baby.

"You're keeping yourself busy these days," Colette said when Rose left the room.

Helen glanced up from her work with a wan smile. "Harris has hired old Mr. Stowe's wife, Etta, to help with the cooking so Rose doesn't overtax herself. I had to appeal to his masculine sense of honor, of course."

It didn't hurt, either, to know that Mrs. Stowe was also an experienced midwife, and was able to keep an eye on Rose's condition.

"Poor Rose."

"Why do you say, 'poor Rose'?" Helen asked as she turned another row on the tiny garment.

"She must long for Heinrich to be near. Especially now."

"Yes." Helen's voice sounded soft and far away.

"I don't know how she bears it, or how you do when Harris is so often away."

Helen sighed.

"A married woman must come to depend upon her husband as though he is her other self. Isn't that true, Helen? Aren't you and Rose more content and restful when you know your husbands are near?"

Helen smiled, while her needles clicked.

"Always just a heartbeat apart in thought, in longing, in understanding... that's how it must be," Colette added dreamily.

That's how it was for her parents, Eldon and Lavinia, and how it would be for her and her own husband someday, Lord willing. Could it be any different for Helen and Harris and the Schultzes?

Helen abruptly set her work aside. "In some ways you're right, Lettie. But every couple is different. I hope you marry someone someday, who's - - what did you say? Only 'a heartbeat apart'?"

She stood and beckoned to Colette. "Come with me. We'll take the clothes off the line before Harris comes out of his office and catches me 'ruining my hands with housework', as he puts it. Our understanding is quite different as it relates to that, I can assure you."

"When did he get back?"

"Yesterday afternoon."

She'd never seen Rose interact with Heinrich, but Colette often had the chance to observe Helen and Harris. Helen was never talkative when Harris was home, willing instead to listen to him recount his adventures in the woods and towns scattered about the territory. But when Colette asked her why she didn't simply throw her arms around him and chatter his ears off whenever he returned, Helen said simply that Harris liked his home to be sedate, and that it was her job, as his wife, to make sure he found it that way.

Colette marveled at the way it worked, so different from her parents' home. Harris would sit back and light his pipe after the evening meal, sending a thick, sweet smell wafting through the house. A smell that had been markedly absent over the last few weeks in a home filled with women. Helen would then pick up her knitting and wait for him to speak.

At home, Colette and her mother regaled her father with everything that had happened on the farm, in their home, in the community, and even at the Eastman's while he was away. Why, after his recent jaunt to camp two, they'd told him how they'd teased Helen when she made a dish that didn't turn out right -- an all too frequent occurrence -- and about how they'd seen a whole party of Indians pass by down near the river, which had encouraged Colette to keep a closer eye on Pork Chop. She'd showed her father the new things she'd taught Dandy, the name she'd eventually chosen for the yellow puppy. Simple things, like not nipping her heels when she walked away from him, and how to stand by the door when he wanted to go out and do his duty. She'd also told her father that Mr. Kromer, who ran the company store in town, was finally getting some bolts of fabric besides calico blue and red -- she'd seen the Indians wearing that, too. And lastly, besides the snippets of information she wheedled out of him about how many million board feet of pine might be coming down the river in the spring, or if he'd seen Joe at camp number two, she told him Rose was so big she was probably going to have twins, and about the layette of clothing Helen was creating.

But Helen chattered nothing like that when Harris came home. As far as he might be concerned, nothing of consequence ever happened while he was away. Life just went on, always the same, like the deep, dark river curling along between its banks. Unchanging.

After supper, Rose came into the room to help Etta clear the dishes.

Colette noticed Harris' frown fall on Rose's burgeoned form. Rose seemed to be trying to avoid his brooding gaze.

"What are your intentions, Rose?" he asked abruptly.

Rose stopped in her motions, balancing a stack of plates precariously as she fumbled to answer him. "Excuse?"

"What do you plan to do, you and your husband, when the baby comes?"

Her shoulders lifted slightly, but the plates looked heavy. "I work. I work hard for Herr and Frau Eastman."

"Yes, Rose, you work hard. But what about the baby? What will you do then?"

Her brows furrowed. "I work with baby."

"She's trying to say she will keep working hard, even after the baby comes," Helen said softly. Colette shifted soundlessly, wishing for something to ease the growing tension in the room.

"She can't work with a baby." His harsh voice rang out, too loud for the room, even though he hadn't really shouted.

"What would you have her do, Harris?"

He drew three hard little puffs on his pipe and crossed his arms. "Where's her husband?"

"Heinrick is up at camp number two. In the springtime, he'll come down on the drive. You know he hasn't been able to afford a place for them. Here Rose has a roof over her head, and the baby will, too, when it comes."

"Are you daft, Helen? She can't work with a baby to care for."

Rose's eyes darted back and forth at the discourse. The plates drooped. Colette tensed. "Go ahead to the kitchen, Rose," Helen said. "We'll discuss it later."

"I'll help," Colette jumped up to relieve some of Rose's burden. But even in the kitchen the Eastman's voices carried, and Colette's heart hammered at their discourse.

"What can you be thinking, Helen?"

"She has no place else to go. You know she depends on us. Why can't she stay at least until Heinrick finds them a place?"

"So now you make all the decisions for our family?" he chided her.

"No, not all the decisions. But you've been gone, and of course it's occurred to us--"

"Us?"

"To me, Harris. To *me*."

"To you and Lettie and Rose, you mean. Maybe old Mrs. Stowe, too. I can't be everywhere at once. I can't be in the camps to keep them running, at my office, and here, too, to make sure you don't make these idiotic decisions."

"Idiotic? You think I'm idiotic?"

"You have too much time on your hands." His voice deepened. "It isn't Rose who needs a baby. It's you."

The dining room hushed. Colette's insides curdled. Helen would have no retort to such a remark. She wouldn't be able to keep her tears at bay.

Rose stood still. Her eyes, too, swelled with unshed tears. Colette set down the bowl she was drying and went to her side.

"Don't be afraid. Helen will find a way."

Etta hobbled over unexpectedly. She put her arms around Rose's shoulders and looked her in the eyes. "You are a good worker. God will take care of you and Heinrick and your baby. If you cannot stay here, then you will stay with Mr. Stowe and me."

Rose wiped her eyes with her apron and whispered, "Danke."

The door burst open and they all looked up, guilt on their faces as if they were involved in some conspiracy. Helen stood before them, her own eyes red with crying, but her back stiff.

"It's all right." She looked directly at Rose. "You will stay here when the baby comes."

Relief at Helen's unexpected firmness eased some of the tension between Colette's shoulders, but even so, she doubted the substance behind it. Only the new day would tell. Her thoughts wandered to Harris. All her earlier conviction of his and Helen's oneness of mind blew away like tufts of milkweed on the wind.

*****

Shortly after Christmas, an envelope containing two letters arrived with the post. One was from Annie, the letter Colette had expected out of obligation. In it, Annie talked about the fun she'd had at the last party before all the fellows left for the woods, and how a certain Hank Pratt had taken a shine to her. Then she went on to supply a few snippets about how boring winter was going to be, and about how she was going to have to sew some new dresses during the long, dark days. The other letter from Jean was the one that told Colette the news that most mattered to her heart. She took a deep breath and curled in a chair by the fire to read it.

Dear Colette,

We were all so happy to hear that you arrived and are settling into your new life in Wisconsin Territory, that we simply wore out the pages re-reading your letter. I must say that it was quite short, however. Certainly you must write again and tell us all about the town of Grand Rapids and the people you've met. It's so good to know that you've become close to Mrs. Eastman. You thought you weren't going to have any friends, and look how the Lord has provided.

Colette thought of Joseph, and a pang of shame slid through her.

You are probably wondering what we have all been up to since you left. We had the usual last minute parties before all the jacks left for the woods. They worked mighty hard before they left, laying up wood for winter stoves, while we ladies quilted and canned, as usual.

Stuart is working hard as foreman now, and my father is relieved. He was unsure if he would ever find someone as capable for the job as your father, so imagine his pleasure at finding such talent in his own son. And we have other news on that front as well. Manason has gone up to Dad's number five camp to make his way in the woods. Come spring, he'll work with Dad's cruiser, Tom Durant, and a surveyor, Pete Nuchols, to get his real education. Mother had a hard time seeing him go, but she realizes he has his own dreams.

A little thrill passed through Colette, as if her own joy was bound together with Manason's aspirations. She sat there imagining it. Imagining *him*. Finally, she pulled her attention back to Jean's letter.

As for me, I shall address your question, though I am reluctant to write about Virgil and me. Yet, there's nothing more to it than to come out and say that Virgil has decided he cannot marry me at this time, and I take it to mean that he has no intention of ever doing so, but has obstinately avoided admitting it. I feel quite foolish for ever having wasted so much time on him. How long was it? Four years? Five? He seemed like such a gentleman, so proper, finishing his education and joining his uncle's law firm in Detroit. I was so fooled. But Mr. Holcomb has become quite full of himself, in my humble estimation. Recently, word has come to us that he is spending a great deal of time with a certain Harriet Brill, who is said to be a well-situated young woman with "favorable connections". I guess the daughter of a lumberman from the rugged north woods is no match for such society. I will say no more about it, lest I become morbid.

Mother and Father both send greetings and best wishes to your family. Stuart sends his regards as well, and as for Nase, the next time we hear from him, I will write again and tell you how he is faring. I'm certain that his vision of the future is wholly centered on the Wisconsin white pine, and that you will all see him again someday.

Loving regards,
Jean

Chapter Four

One February night, as Colette huddled deeper into the cocoon of her blankets against the plummeting cold soaking through the log wall above her pillow, Rose Shultz delivered a healthy baby boy. She called him George Herman, after first her father, and then Heinrick's. When Colette saw the baby the next day, she declared George to be the sweetest thing she'd ever seen. But to her surprise, not even such an avid declaration seemed to warm Harris toward the child.

Colette visited the Eastman's nearly every afternoon after completing her chores at home. She coddled George to her shoulder, cradled him on her lap while she sang, and explained to Helen for the hundredth time how important it was to knead the bread longer, while winter slowly passed into March. Harris' mood didn't lighten until nearly time for the spring drive when he came home with the news that he was taking both Helen and Lettie on a sleigh ride to visit camp number three.

"It's about time you ladies got to see what goes on in these Wisconsin woods," he said.

The sun had barely risen when they found themselves in the sleigh with Harris tucking furs around their legs and putting warm stones from the wood stove at their feet. A humid winter frost had settled over the landscape during the night, and the gray dawn appeared to be iced in ghostly white. Rime covered the horses' backs, and their breaths came out in wispy rags as they stomped their feet and shook their heads, their harnesses and bridles jangling. Dandy snuggled up on the fur robe covering Colette and Helen, adding an extra layer of warmth.

As they drove eastward, the sunrise crept over the horizon. The world glistened and sparkled. The branches of the trees, swooping over the track of the tote road, cast dancing, lacy shadows that flickered against their eyes.

"Your father headed up to camp three yesterday," Harris explained. "He's got to get a notion from the walking boss when to expect to see the head of the drive. Soon as that water opens up, he's got to make sure the booms down here can handle the logs."

Colette listened eagerly, anxious to understand everything about her father's work.

"Helen, the men don't know you girls are coming. They'll be in the woods when we get there. So don't be surprised at the looks you get when they start coming in for their evening meal." He cast them a devilish grin. "It's been a few months since they've seen any women."

"Oh, Harris, they won't be gawking like school boys."

"They might. Some of them are only school boys. Take it in stride. Lettie will, won't you Lettie?" He glanced past Helen to Colette.

Colette smiled back. She wasn't worried about the fellows at the camp. She'd put up with Joseph long enough to know they meant no harm. She and Helen would probably be treated like queens. Besides, her papa was there, and Harris would be, too. They'd make sure there was no funny business.

They rolled into the camp at a little past eleven o'clock, shivering and hungry. The camp cookee, wrapped in his white cook's apron, set them down in the cook shack, called the wanigan, to a lunch of biscuits and gravy. He topped off their meal with apple pie made fresh from apples dried over the summer. He even gathered a big plate of scraps for Dandy.

They washed down their meal with coffee and an endless stream of stories from the cookee while Harris went over to the camp office to look at some reports. They learned about the boys in the woods, how the hunting had been, and why they didn't make girls with good appetites like these gals from Wisconsin as he offered them donuts and more coffee.

Later they met up with Eldon. He wrapped Colette in his long arm as he showed them around. Finally they put some extra cots in the office, where they would later spend the night. The camp boss planned to bunk up with the men.

As the afternoon passed and darkness fell, the lumberjacks came in, some singing songs, others work-weary and hungry. Lettie and Helen, having eaten earlier at Eldon's suggestion, looked on in surprise, their cheeks reddening as the startled men halted, eyes widened in awe, some trying to hide their grizzled chins in their wool shirts, but unable to tear their eyes away. Others stared openly and gave them big, brazen grins if they managed to catch their eyes. Lettie's skin burned, but she smiled back politely, as much as she thought seemly, and turned her attention to her father as a means of escape.

"All right, that's enough, you bunch of woods oxen!" he bellowed. "These are ladies, and one's my daughter. So stop staring like you was a bunch of coyotes sizing up a pile of raw meat."

Most of the men sat down. A few of those who were likely unmarried lingered, letting their eyes take in the women.

Colette tried not to let them catch her gaze but shook off the discomfort as best she could, certain Helen had attracted all the attention. Why not? She was beautiful and sophisticated. A refined, golden chalice in the hand of a king. And there was no mistaking that Harris was king here.

"Gentlemen, I'd like you to meet my wife, Helen, and Mr. Palmer's daughter, Lettie," Harris said. "I'm certain you'll show them the highest regard and gentlemanly consideration while they're here." He let his words migrate toward their brains for a moment, drilling them with one of his most severe looks. "Though I'm sure you welcome their company, I trust you won't make them feel... uncomfortable."

The rest of the men sat down. Nobody talked during mealtime. Hands moved quickly as biscuits, pork, and beans were consumed. Coffee and tea flowed in gallons, and all Lettie heard was the scraping of forks, the clanking of cups, and the slosh of coffee they swilled it down, followed by the occasional belch.

"You can retire to your quarters," the camp boss barked as soon as they were done. The men slowly dispersed, their caps in hands as they shuffled by muttering, "Evenin', ma'am," or nodding at Lettie with a "Miss." One or two younger men about Joseph's age smiled openly and ducked their heads with a "Goodnight, Miss Lettie. Hope to see you in these parts again," while her father watched closely.

By the time they'd cleared out, Helen expressed how tired she was.

"You can't escape that easily, Helen," Harris said, chuckling. "The men are sure to fire up a fiddle, and they'll hope you can spare a dance or two."

Her blue eyes widened. "You want me to dance with them?"

"Only a little, if you will." He stroked her cheek. "You needn't worry. They'll all be thinking of their wives back home. I'll be right there."

The jovial tones of the fiddle drifted through the pines as they walked over to the men's bunkhouse half an hour later. As they came into the building out of the darkness and snow, warmth rushed out to wrap around Lettie. Heat, steam and the smell of unwashed men and wet socks assailed her nostrils. Helen put a hand delicately to her nose, then pulled it away. Lettie took a deep breath and stepped into the midst of it, smiling. In only moments, one of the younger fellows who'd spoken to her after dinner rustled up the courage to stride over and ask her to dance. He took her out into the center of the room, not far from the fire pit and reeled her around the floor as men sat around on the bunks that hung off the walls and stomped their feet, clapping and yelling to the tune of the fiddle. An older man with graying hair and a long beard sidled over and smiled at Helen, creases showing in the corners of his eyes. Colette glimpsed her friend taking his arm and heading out onto the floor.

Someone crowed like a rooster and other men stood up to dance, some alone, and others grabbing the arms of other woodsmen to swing them around the floor.

"You sure can dance, Miss Lettie," more than one fellow told her that night. "Hope you'll come visit us again sometime, or maybe we'll see you down in Grand Rapids or Frenchtown."

"Maybe," was all she'd say.

"Ain't you Joe Gilbert's girl?" another young fellow asked her.

"Where'd you hear such a thing?"

"Joe told everybody he knows to lay off. Won't he be surprised." He laughed, spinning her around.

"Well, as far as I know, I'm only my papa's girl," she said, laughing back, "and won't Joe be surprised indeed."

Her head spun to the rollicking tunes of the fiddler even after she fell onto the cot that night, exhausted, but too filled with the day's excitement to go right to sleep. Dandy whined at her side, and she let him clamor onto the cot with her. He licked her, and she scratched his head.

"I swear, Dandy," she whispered so as to not disturb Helen, who had already fallen asleep, "you're getting too big for this, especially on this skinny cot."

Still, she hugged him close and turned her thoughts to *what if?* What if Nase had been in camp tonight instead of the Au Sable pineries in Michigan? What if he hadn't seen her in all those months, and she walked into the room? Would his eyes light up like Paul's and John's and Wilbur's? Would he swing her around the floor and hold her a little too tight and tell her he was going to look her up and marry her someday like those teasing young men she'd danced with had tonight? Except they didn't know her, and Manason did. She thought she knew him pretty well, too. He would never say such a thing unless he meant it. She tried to picture him living in the woods camp, dressed in his mackinaw and boots, his breath coming out in warm ribbons and his teeth white in the snowy sunlight. How handsome he was.

Her prince...

Chapter Five

By the end of March, the ice was booming on the river. A week into April, it burst out all over, and the drive had begun in earnest. Three days into it, Colette finally met Joseph's brother Robin. He came to the Eastman house with word for Rose that Heinrick had been killed.

All winter long, logs of massive girth had been skidded out of the deep forest by the power of horse and ox and decked in long piles along Iron Creek, waiting for the day when the ice broke free and the melting snow turned the river into a wide, dangerous highway, with water gushing down in a flood tide able to sweep the winter cut first to the *Wisconsin*, and then down to the mills. On each side of the rollways, men pried at the bottommost logs with the iron points of peavies. One by one they cascaded into the water, a tumbling, thudding, jumbled thunder, and some hit the river only to upend and shoot full length into the air. Others landed with full-bodied force, sending out leaping sprays of brown foam.

Tossing and dipping, clotting and knotting, the logs soon moved en masse into the current. Sure-footed drivers, Heinrich Shultz among them, found their places with a pike pole or peavy. Riding the churning torrent, bobbing and leaping along on the backs of the scaly beasts or running along the bank, they unhooked snares.

"Ride high, you hogs!" a man shouted. Calked boots clutched to bark, shoulders heaved with the dual effort of prodding and hooking the logs while keeping upright. Water boiled up around their calks; some men stood in the icy stream up to their waists, fighting to keep the logs from hanging up on mud banks or pooling up in mud flats and pockets. In some places, the water overflowed the banks, tearing away mud and uprooting saplings and brush, adding to the snaring, writhing mass.

"She's wheelin'!" Heinrich hollered, the word coming out as "veeling" as he leapt from the back of one thick trunk to another, using his peavy like a balancing pole as he birled, his feet moving in total rhythm and perfect time with the direction the log spun on the current.

A man in a bright red mackinaw ran along the crooked bank, yelling at the others heading his way.

"She's jammin' up in the bend past the rapids!" another fellow hawked out to the men on the water.

In the twist ahead, logs had hooked along the bank, and more soon piled up like perfectly woven wreckage, locking and creaking, water sloshing and sluicing between them.

"Get that head free!" the boss driver running up the trail shouted.

Heinrick moved with the logs, doing his best to keep them separated and free flowing, hoping the small tangle ahead would be cleared before a big jam happened. Then he hit the rapids, not big ones, but with a current fast enough to require all of his skill and attention. He whipped a black lock of hair out of his face and smiled at the challenge, like a bronc rider, ready to ride down a stallion. It made him feel like a man. Proud of the job he did. Proud of his wife and son. Anxious to see them again, and holding them high in his thoughts as he coursed along.

At first, things went smoothly. The men ahead unknotted the logs threatening the passage, and Heinrich moved with adroitness in his feet the way a woman might weave silk thread with deft fingers. All around him the logs snaked and bounced along, and sprays of water shot over his legs and waist. Carefully, he made his way to the center of the main flow to shoot through the gap, ready to pry with his peavy if needed.

Then a log to his right hooked a boulder, and the force of the mass behind it pushed it up into the air like a pike. It crashed down with the force of tons and hit the section on which Heinrich was footed.

"Shultz!" His name echoed above the foaming tumult as he lunged sideways, trying to find footing on another beam, but he slipped.

As suddenly as it had begun, he disappeared beneath the pile.

*****

Joseph told the story to Colette as he'd heard it from his brother Robin, who had witnessed the tragedy. Even though she'd already known what had happened, hearing it straight and raw from Joseph's mouth made her sorrow fresh.

It was summer, and the accident was long since past, but the subject arose again as Joseph and Colette paddled a canoe up the river.

"I know it's dangerous and that someone has to do it," she said at last. "But I hope you'll never become one of the river men."

Joseph flashed her a lazy smile when she glanced back his way. "Nice to know you'd worry about me."

"Course I would. Just as I worry about my papa when he's in the woods, or the other men out there, the sawyers and swampers and skidders. They all have dangerous jobs."

Sun sparkled like diamond points on the water as Colette dipped her paddle languidly and watched little swirls spin off in the wake of each stroke.

"Hmm. Well, how's Mrs. Shultz doing now?"

Colette thought of Rose and baby George up at the farmhouse with her mother. Shortly after the funeral, Rose had moved in with the Palmers. She did little but rest and help with light tasks there, and she still went over to the Eastman's once a week to do cleaning and laundry. They paid her a small stipend for her effort.

Helen took delight in having to do more of her own household duties, and Colette helped out where she could.

"Rose is doing admirably. She carries her grief inside. Mama says she's young, and that she'll probably marry again someday. I don't think she wants to think of that right now, though."

"She's pretty enough."

Colette turned and gave Joseph a look, winking against the sun. "Rose is pretty. I bet lots of men think so."

"Did I disagree?" He paddled a little harder, and they grew quiet. Then he stopped paddling, and she sensed him looking at her.

She laid her paddle across her lap and twisted her head around. "What's the matter?"

"Nothing." He grinned, his white teeth gleaming and his eyes sparkling.

"What is it?"

"You look different than when you first came here." He studied her. "Did you know that?"

"What do you mean?"

"Well, for one thing, your hair's getting darker."

She shrugged and turned her eyes to the tops of the trees waving idly as they drifted by. "Mama says so, too. She says it happens to lots of people as they grow up. Used to be corn silk yellow when I was little."

"Looks pretty, Lettie." His voice was low and slow, like the current. She looked back at him again, and then turned to hide her smile.

"What else?"

"You're taller."

"So I noticed last time I outgrew my dresses."

"You ain't so skinny as a rail."

"What?" She turned again and fumed. "A rail?"

"I mean, you're shaped nice all over."

"Joseph, you're something." She dipped her paddle in the water again and watched the droplets dribble off. "Are we going to fish, or what?"

"Nah. I changed my mind."

"You mean you got me out here to take me fishing, and now you're just going to keep me trapped so you can pour drivel into my ears?" She grinned, eager to hear his next retort.

"Something like that," he said, and dashed the paddle against the surface of the water to splash her.

"Hey!"

She struck her paddle at the water and splashed him back. He returned the favor a bit more forcefully, and soon their war turned wild. Then, just as suddenly, the fragile bark canoe flipped over. Colette squealed as she hit the water, but she came up laughing. In an instant Joseph, too, surfaced and was at her side, supporting her against the canoe as they drifted along.

Water ran down his face and dripped from his black curls. "Hanging on?"

She nodded, and he let go of her waist.

He kicked around to the end of the canoe and pushed them to shore. There, Joseph turned the canoe, emptying out the water, and pulled the craft up the bank. Together they staggered onto the grass and collapsed, laughing. Colette wrung the water out of her skirt and Joseph peeled off his shirt.

"My papa probably won't let me go fishing with you anymore if you're set on drowning me," she said with a smirk.

"Who was drowning whom?"

"Say, Lettie?" He leaned back in the grass and let the sun warm him. "Want to do something fun?"

"What do you have in mind?" S never trusted Joseph's suggestions intrinsically.

"I was thinking of going across to Frenchtown tonight for a little dancing." He looked over at her with his dark eyes shining. "Want to go?"

"You pick a fine time to ask a girl to go dancing, right after you toss her in the river."

Joseph kept his eyes on her, steady, smiling.

"I've never been there. I don't know."

"Awe, c'mon, Lettie." He inched over next to her. Slowly, he lifted her chin and stroked it with his thumb. "You'd be the prettiest gal there, and that would make me feel real good."

Colette turned her chin away from his fingers. She was thankful her hair was getting darker, so Joseph might not notice the pink cast of heat warming her cheeks.

"I won't go dancing with you if you're going to keep up with this manner of yours," she said, finally.

"Sorry, Lettie." His voice grew husky, and he sat close enough for her to feel his warmth. "I can't help it." He leaned in toward her, and she scrambled to her feet.

"I've got to get home. I promised Rose I'd watch George this afternoon so she can visit Heinrich's grave. I have to get some things together to take over to the Eastman's tomorrow, too."

Joseph brought his long legs up and stood. He balled up the wet shirt and looked again at Colette. "Well, what about tonight?"

"If it's okay with my folks."

"You know it will be."

"Don't be so sure of yourself, Mr. Gilbert. My mama knows how to keep an eye on boys like you."

"You saying she's had lots of experience because so many of them have been knocking on your door?"

"Maybe."

Joseph laughed as they climbed back into the canoe to head upstream. "I know good and well there aren't any fellows left around these parts when I'm in the woods. Just a few grandpas and little kids. I haven't seen anybody else prowling around."

"You aren't looking all the time."

"Still, I know they aren't coming along."

"How could you know that?"

"'Cause I told them they'd better not," he said, and fell into a good hard push with his paddle.

*****

In the soft fullness of the evening, moonbeams scattered across the water and crickets sang in the grass. Joseph promised Colette he'd get them to Frenchtown high and dry. They were silent as he dipped the paddle with strong, rhythmic strokes and skirted them deftly across the water. Then he took her hand and helped her up the bank on the far shore.

Colette found it odd to look across the water from the west side, to see the pinpricks of lamplight that marked the homesteads on the eastern shore. She couldn't see all the way to Grand Rapids, but she did wonder what Helen and Harris were doing tonight. Maybe she'd go to town tomorrow. *Maybe I'll have something to tell Helen about this evening.* Then her thoughts drifted farther east, into the black beyond, past the miles and miles of woods and rivers and small villages, over the big lake called Michigan, to the woods there. To the town where there could very well be another party, another fiddler rosining up his bow. To Manason. Would he dance with Margaret tonight, or would Annie be wooed by Hank Pratt?

"I hear music. Do you?"

Joseph's voice called her out of the stillness, and her heart lurched. He wrapped his fingers around her hand, and she let him lead her toward town.

They followed the sound of the fiddle to the center of town where a string of lanterns marked off a square. People were already laughing and stomping and twirling about to the tune of the *violineux*. It reminded Colette of the men at the winter camp, only here they danced with wives and daughters and a number of young Indian girls dressed in calico skirts, sashed blouses, and tall moccasins.

Joseph fell into the swing of it right away, his hands tapping his hips with his thumbs hooked in the corners of his pockets, his feet itching with the rhythm.

"C'mon Lettie, let me swing you around the floor. It isn't fair that those bully boys up at camp three got to dance with you before I did." He gripped her hand, and she fell along with him onto the square. With his hands on her waist and hers on his shoulders, they whirled among the dancers.

Colette hadn't had such a good time since last winter, and she had to admit that dancing was so much more fun with Joseph. Time after time he pulled her out onto the rough wooden planking and spun her about.

"Joe!" a voice called out of the crowd in the semi-darkness. Colette and Joe turned as one to see Robin and Joseph's other brother Michael striding over to greet them.

"Lettie, you remember my brother Rob from that day..." They nodded at one another and Colette recalled the day she'd heard the news about Heinrich "And this is my brother Michael, whose face we hardly ever get to see. He spends all his time down in Saratoga courting an Irish lassie named Carrie Sullivan."

"I see you're doing some courtin' of your own now, Joe," Michael said. "Watch out for my brother. He's a good looking charmer."

"A charmer, I'll grant," Colette said.

"Ah, see how well she knows you already, Joe?" Rob grinned.

"Right. And I can assure you she thinks I'm good looking, too." Joseph gave Colette one of his sparkling gazes.

"If you want to dance with someone handsome, you should dance with me," Rob said. "May I?" He out held his arm. She took it and cast a prim look at Joseph.

"Well, Robin, it's nice to finally get to know Joseph's brothers." Colette raised her voice above the crowd.

"My friends call me either Rob or Robbie. You can do the same, if I can call you Lettie." He took her hand, and together they reeled across the floor.

As Colette smiled up into Robbie's warm brown eyes, it occurred to her that everyone she'd met lately called her Lettie, the nickname of Harris' making. Nobody seemed to know her real name anymore. That was fine. It made her feel as if she'd found her place here in Wisconsin Territory -- and that her old name, her true name, was reserved for her family and old friends. For Mama and Papa and the Kades.

Joseph's brother Robbie was indeed a handsome man and a good dancer. He had to be in his mid-twenties, but he didn't look at her as if she were a little girl. He reminded her of Manason, and she immediately liked him.

Michael was older, striking in the way they called black Irish, with the same dark curls and masculine jaw that ran through all the Gilbert men. Miss Caroline Sullivan was a lucky girl. Lettie figured Joseph would follow in Michael's likeness in a few years.

The evening wore on. Someone cracked the head off a barrel of liquor, and it flowed freely. Joseph helped himself to the offerings and didn't seem put off by Colette's frown. Her parents wouldn't like to know he'd been drinking while she was with him. To signify her displeasure, she denied him several of the next few dances, agreeing instead to dance with some of the young Frenchmen from town. She rather liked their manner of dialect and the way they bowed over her hand.

Finally, she sensed Joseph was getting mad. He stalked off out of sight and came back with an Indian girl on his arm.

Colette's current dance partner was lanky and awkward, and he spoke hardly a speck of English. Not that it mattered as he whisked her dizzily and none-too-gracefully around the square. She paid little heed to the happy way he gawked at her and rattled on in French. Instead she watched Joseph and the Indian girl. She was beautiful. Joseph wouldn't have wasted time on her if she wasn't. She lavished Joseph with a brilliant white smile that shone out of her coppery face. Her black hair glistened bluish even in the darkness, and several tendrils flitted over Joseph's arms as he first twirled her around the floor, and then pulled her close.

The boy dancing with Colette noticed her observations and tried to direct her away, pulling her over to the barrel for refreshment. She declined and sighed, unable to keep from watching the other couple. *I'm not jealous, but Joseph knows better than to try such a cheap trick with me.* With a strange stinging in her heart, she purposed harder to ignore him.

When she looked for him and the girl again, they were gone. Disengaging herself from the French boy's company, Colette searched for her escort. After some grim minutes, she finally bumped into Robin. Her heart settled.

"Rob, have you seen Joseph? I seem to have lost him in the crowd."

He pointed into the shadows near a grove of trees. "I saw him over that way just a while ago. He didn't lose you, did he?"

She shook her head, hardly feeling like jesting. "Thank you," she said, and wandered toward the trees.

A man with a harmonica played a melancholy tune, and couples embraced out on the puncheon dance floor. Colette moved out of the vicinity and looked around, bypassing a group of Indians sitting in a circle and a French trapper who leered at her with a yellow-stained grin, until she finally saw Joseph's familiar lanky form, his arm outstretched against an oak.

She stopped short. Joseph wasn't alone. The girl was with him, and he was kissing her.

She sucked in her breath, a bitter taste forming on her tongue. Exhaling calmly to control the erratic beat of her heart, she approached them.

"Joe?" She cleared her throat. The two broke apart, and Joseph's lips curved up slightly, but guilt was spelled on them as well.

"I have to go," he murmured to the black-haired girl.

The girl melted away into the shadows.

"So you've come looking for me." His voice hitched with a slur.

"It's what you expected me to do, wasn't it?"

"Now, Lettie, don't be mad." He tried to put his arm across her shoulders, and she shrugged him off.

"I want to go home, and I'm not mad."

"Oh, yes, you're mad."

"You'll make me mad if you don't stop talking. Maybe I should have Robbie take me home."

"I brought you. I'll take you home."

"Are you sure you're able?"

Joseph's face went high with color, his eyes dark and brooding, as he said sulkily, "You came with me, remember?"

"I'm not the one who seemed to forget."

"Come on, then." He took her by the arm and pulled her along.

"Let go. I won't have you handling me, Joe. Not that way."

"Have it your way."

He stalked on ahead and Colette trailed after him.

I'll not talk now, Joe. Your moodiness will get us nowhere. They would have to wait and straighten out everything by the light of day. She would have to trust he could get them home safely across the water, and he did.

He beached the canoe and held out his hand to help her onto the bank. She almost declined, but knew he would think she was more angry than she'd admitted if she did so. Or worse yet, that she was jealous. She took his hand, and he hoisted her upright. Once her feet found the shore, he tightened his grip and looked into her eyes.

"That with the Indian didn't mean anything," he said.

"I know, Joe."

"I was only--"

"Let's not talk about it now." She put her free hand on his shoulder and gently disengaged the other one. Then she backed up a step. "I can make it back to the house. Good night."

His shoulders slumped as she turned to go, but she went ahead. Finally, she glanced back to where she could just make out his shirt diminishing to a light, cottony patch in the darkness. She caught her step, and he answered.

"Good night, Lettie."

Chapter Six

Manason's return from work at camp six lasted only a few days. Long enough to reassure his ma that her boy was still doing all right, and that he hadn't lost any weight or been hurt or needed any clothes mended. Time enough to commiserate with Jean over her break with Virgil. A few hours to spend down at his pa's mill, helping with whatever odd tasks Stu found for him to do. Still, restless energy chewed at him.

In the summer, not many men hung about the camps. Those who did constructed new buildings, built road beds, collected wild hay for the oxen logging teams, dynamited boulders and built dams in the rivers, placed log cribbings around bridge piers to protect the bridges during the drives, and stacked lumber in the sawmill yard. Manason could have gone back to doing any of that, but he itched to learn to read the woods themselves.

Then one day his pa paused where Nase stacked a pile of fresh-sawn boards for curing. Nase sniffed and brushed a gloved hand at the sweat on his skin, then picked up another board, laying it crisscross over the previous layer. "Something bothering you, Pa?"

"I think it's time you got to cruising, son. You've spent enough time making your family feel good.".

Pa must've seen his restlessness, because he meant those words. Manason thought about the time since as he pulled a wrapper around his shoulders against the rain. Thanks to his dad, he had been walking the timber with one of his father's best cruisers for three months now. Tom Durant could read a tree down to an exact number of board feet. He could look at a 160 acre section and come up with an amount within a few dollars of its future profit. He never went over. Tom Durant was the woodsman Manason wanted to become.

He moved along the line of trees, his feet silent on the floor of wet, spent needles, counting his paces, notching his father's mark as he went. Tom walked along the western boundary doing the same, using his compass to run his lines. Manason took a small notebook out of its oilskin wrapper and wrote down descriptions as he went: of the terrain, where he'd found running water or intercepted an oak ridge, how many board feet to the "forty", occasionally applying a rule to the girth of a tree to help him estimate with greater accuracy.

His father had told him, "Learn as much as you can, son. If we do well this season, I may be able to help you get your start in Wisconsin Territory next year. It'll take all the know-how you can possess to get a foothold in that country. But the time is ripe. Men are clamoring into that great, green, lumber country, and if you can find the pine and get hold of it you'll have something to build a future on when all the trees in

Michigan are spent."

Well, Manason aimed to learn, and learn fast. He figured he was doing okay, too, because after most days of cruising, when he and Tom and surveyor Pete Nuchols sat around their fire eating what they could find in their packs, or chewing on a rabbit one of them had shot, Tom would look at Nase's descriptions, kick his crumpled hat back a notch, and nod appreciatively.

"Doing all right, Nase," he'd say, a big grin splitting his face. "Doing all right." Big praise coming from a man like Tom Durant.

"When are you thinking of making it big in Wisconsin?" Pete asked that night. The rain had stopped, and the earth smelled sweet and damp. They had to work to keep the fire alive. It hissed and spit. "That's a pretty big chaw to be sinking your teeth into."

"I'm hoping to do it after another season with you and Tom."

Pete whistled. "Wouldn't mind heading west myself. But I got the wife and a new little one on the way."

"How many does that make now?" Tom asked.

"Makes number four. But who's countin'?"

Tom smiled and chucked a small bone into the fire.

"You willin' to give up girls to satisfy a hankering after those big trees?" Pete asked. "I thought you had some pretty thing waiting on you back home."

Manason shrugged with a laugh. "Well, she says she isn't waiting. I don't know. I'll just have to see. I'd like to have something more to offer a gal than what's coming to me from my pa and Stuart."

"Spoken like a man," Pete said.

"So what's this gal's name? I'm going to stick around close to the mill this winter. Maybe I'll see if she takes a shine to me," Tom said.

"You go ahead." Nase gave a nod. "Her name's Margaret Baker. She's the headiest girl in town besides my sister, who doesn't know she's something to look at. You'll know Margie when you see her, 'cause she'll be looking back at you."

"So that's the way of it?"

"That's the way."

Manason let his mind soak on Margie for awhile. Sitting by the fire with his socks not quite dry and the ground still wet against his slicker from the earlier rain, he wondered if he hadn't made a mistake walking off on her like that last fall. He hadn't seen her at all when he'd been home in the spring. Annie had said she was visiting relatives in Detroit, and that she'd be madder that a wet nanny goat to learn she'd missed Nase's return.

"So she's been waiting for me after all?" he'd asked.

Annie harrumphed. "She'd like to say she hasn't. Truth be told, big brother, she's been flaunting herself around with Jack Sprague and Mitch Donnelson. But I think she's only playing with them. She'll be madder than a wet nanny goat that you weren't here to see it, that's all."

Manason laughed and ruffled Annie's hair.

"I'm not your pet," Annie scoffed, spinning away.

That Annie. She was one hot streak herself. How that goofy Hank Pratt thought to keep rein on her, Nase would never figure out. But then maybe Hank didn't have any intention of keeping rein on her. Maybe he'd just follow in her wake, keeping on her scent like an old hound. Every little while Annie might condescend to reach back and scratch his handsome, goofy head.

*****

In late September, Nase and the others returned with the land descriptions from their summer's work. Nase went with his father to the land office to make the purchase and file the deed. Then he returned home. It was good to be with family again. Good to feel the months of accomplishment tucked away inside him, knowing how proud they all were of him. He'd been gone less than a year, but he'd come back changed. If he'd gone away with a sense of his desires, he'd returned with his goals and dreams rooted even deeper -- and he'd developed the knowledge and skills to back those dreams. All the nights he'd lain there, staring up at the stars flickering under the lacy canopy that shrouded him, he'd dreamed about his big chance, and the days had gently clicked away, like raindrops, one by one, until the summer was over. If all went like he hoped, he had only the winter to ready himself before heading west.

"Where do you suppose you'll find good land once you get there?" Jean asked. They had just finished breakfast and come out onto the porch to sit together on the swing, waiting for the rest of the family to come out and walk to church.

"That's what I aim to find out. I've been studying on it, and it seems that while some companies are growing like wildfire up and down Green Bay, I'd like to prod into the interior of the territory."

"Like where Eldon and Lavinia went?"

"On the *Wisconsin*?" He nodded. "Maybe. But there're other great rivers there, too, all flowing out of big pineries. The Chippewa feeds directly into the Mississippi. The way folks are moving into the prairies, won't be long before you'll be able to walk down the Mississippi on the backs of pine boards, if I don't miss my guess." He looked out over the distance, across the sky. "They'll be crying for lumber out west."

"I'm afraid you'll go so far away we'll never see you again."

Manason laughed. "Ah, you'll see me from time to time. We big lumber men get used to traveling."

Jean laughed, then suddenly sobered. "I thought maybe the day was coming when I'd be getting to see some of the country."

"With Virgil, you mean."

"Mm-hmm." She twined her fingers in her lap, and Nase covered them with his square hand. She sighed and looked at him. "I hate to say it, but I miss him."

"Of course you do. It's no shame to admit it."

She blushed and tried to look away, but he squeezed her hand. "I told Tom Durant my sister was the headiest girl in town to look at."

She ducked her head, and pushed against his shoulder. "Oh, Manason Kade! You didn't say any such a thing."

"I told him you didn't know it."

She pulled her hands away and covered her face. "Of course I don't know it, because it isn't true."

"Sure it is." Manason gave the swing a little push and draped his arm across the back.

"Headier than Margaret?"

"Let's not go there." Manason wrapped his arm around her and pulled her against him in a bear hug. "Okay, Sis?"

"You've changed, you know. You seem older. As if I'm the younger of the two of us now. You've grown confident."

"Isn't it strange," he said, "since all I've done is spend time learning from Tom and Pete, men who know the woods. It's not as though I've done something great on my own."

"You will. That's the confidence you have inside you. You know you will."

The door swung open, and Annie came prancing out on Stuart's arm.

"Let's get going before the wind comes up and musses my hair," she said. Her parents stepped out behind them.

Manason's mom gave him a warm smile. "Everyone at church will be glad to see you back, honey."

In church, they filed into the same row they'd sat in every Sunday since Manason's childhood when they first got a preacher and built the church. Used to be they could look across the aisle and see the Palmers holding their hymnals and hear Eldon singing loud and clear. Now a family Manason didn't know sat there.

Just back of the new family, Manason usually saw Margie, flanked by her big, brawny brothers. Out of habit, he cast a glance in that direction, and there she sat, boring a hole through him with her penetrating green eyes, telling him she wasn't done with him yet. He gave her a smile, but she only stared. Rebuffed, he turned his eyes back to the preacher.

Later, he caught up with her outside, but she crossed her arms and looked at him coldly.

"Hey, Margie." He held his hat in his hand, and the wind picked at the ends of his hair over his eyes.

"Hello, Manason. So you've come back."

"For a spell."

Her chin came up a little. "A spell?"

"Winter's coming. Might stick around the mill and see what Stuart can find for me to do."

"What, and not go to one of your precious woods camps?" She arched

46

a brow.

Manason couldn't mistake the derision in her voice, but he decided to ignore it. "No, just here. Maybe I'll enjoy the snow, the winter nights, a few parties." He smiled at her, waiting out her mood.

Just then a tall, able looking fellow with lank blond hair combed back off his lean, tanned face walked up and took Margaret by the elbow.

"Nase," he acknowledged.

"Mitch," Manason said, nodding in greeting. His eyes went back and forth between the tall Scandinavian and Margie. He couldn't deny the burn of indignation that crept up in his craw at the proprietary way Mitch held Margie's arm.

"I see you two haven't forgotten each other," Margie said. "Well, Nase, you'll never guess what. Mitch asked me to marry him." She flirted a quick glance at Mitch and finally smiled at Manason. "Course, I haven't given him my answer yet," she added teasingly, but she let big Mitch put his arm around her.

"Guess I'm a little slow, then. Right Margie?"

She sniffed, so softly Mitch didn't notice, but her defiance wasn't lost on Manason. She seemed to be waiting for more.

"Congratulations, Mitch," Manason said. "Looks like the better man won the fair Margaret." He tipped his head and turned to leave, poking his hat back on.

Finding his family, he looked back once and found Margaret staring at him, angry, sullen, ignoring Mitch who tried to turn her away. Manason wanted to forget about it so he walked off down the road toward home with his brother and two sisters a little ahead of their folks.

"Margie won't really marry Mitch Donnelson," Annie remarked as they strolled.

"You don't think so? You don't know Margie."

"What do you mean? She's set on you."

"She's set on me, all right. Set on getting even."

"We'll see," Annie said.

"You sure you'll be able to take it? I mean, being around the entire winter?" Stu asked.

"She's not the only girl in town."

"Besides your gorgeous sisters, you mean?" Jean said wryly.

"Exactly."

Surprisingly, Annie didn't add a response.

*****

Colette's birthday had come and gone by the time Annie's letter arrived. Colette tucked it in the pocket of her skirt as she went about her tasks, occasionally pulling it out to reread the part about Manason.

You should have seen them after church this morning. Why, the air was just absolutely like lightning bolts! Now, Colette, you know I don't write much, and I've been too busy to apologize for it! But I promise I'll try and be better about it. I'll let you know how things progress between them. Isn't it simply divine?

Meanwhile, I wonder if maybe we might have two weddings in the Kade household next year. I speak of myself, of course. Hank Pratt has been ever so attentive, and my, but he's just the handsomest boy.

Speaking of weddings, it's a shame about Jean. I don't think she'll get over Virgil -- dirty rat that he is -- for a long time. Maybe never. She might wind up an old maid, considering she's practically one already.

Do write to me and Jean when you can. Oh, and have a lovely birthday.

Your friend, Annie

Next year... two weddings... Little George beat his fists against the paper while Colette rocked him on her lap, her mind wandering over the images in the letter, her heart heaving a little sigh that slipped past her lips. It was terrible news, yet not surprising.

The worst part was a niggling of another sort down inside her. She hadn't seen Manason in over two years. Suddenly he seemed more like a figment of her imagination that a real, live person. She had changed. She knew she had, just as Mama and Joseph often pointed out. Why, even Helen and Harris had commented on what a young woman she'd become.

So she must assume Manason had changed, too. They all had. But it niggled at her that she could only picture Nase the way he had been. In a good way, yes, but not the *true* way. Not the way he was now -- a man.

Knowing she didn't have an accurate image of him to dwell on frustrated her. *What's more, he doesn't have one of me, either. Just my baby cheeks and corn-colored hair.* She glanced at the coppery tan on her arms. Her hair, too, had gotten darker and richer. "A fine sienna", Mama called it.

Colette didn't know what color sienna was, but she'd take Mama's word on it. She twined a strand of hair around her finger, ignoring the beating her letter was receiving from George as he happily slobbered over it. Her hair didn't coil around her fingers the way it once had. These days, only a little curl remained in the ends, like she remembered Manason's. Just a little loop where it touched his neck...

Well, that might be gone, too.

Mama whisked around the room with a broom. "Is that your letter, honey?"

"Oh, my goodness. I guess I wasn't paying attention."

Rose came into the room and relieved her of little George while

Colette tried to rescue the damp, wrinkled letter. A small sigh escaped her.

Mama slowed with her broom. "Everything all right? Missing your old friends?"

Colette leaned against the rocker and nodded, crinkling her brow. "Mama, can I ask you something?"

"Sure, sweetheart."

She gazed out the window. "It's about marrying."

A smile brushed past her mother's lips, as if she had wondered when her daughter might think about such things.

"I just want to know whether God has a right someone planned for each person. I mean, instead of someone just deciding to marry this one or that one, random like, did He create a special someone for everybody?"

Lavinia and Rose exchanged looks. "Well, some people think so."

"What do you think?"

"I think God certainly cares about who you marry. Maybe He even has someone unique in mind for each person. Then again, maybe He gives us the freedom to choose, within a range of His will."

"What do you mean? You're saying two different things."

"No. I'm saying that while some things are clearly God's will, others aren't spelled out for us. But He always gives us principles to guide us. He has many godly servants, and sometimes He lets us make our choice among them, guided by those principles."

"You mean as long as Christians marry other Christians?"

"Something like that. However..." Mama's eyes grew soft, and she smiled. "I like to think your papa never would've gotten along without me; or I, him."

"I always believe Heinrich and me meant only for each other," Rose added, a sad, peaceful smile flitting across her face.

"Is Joseph getting serious?"

Colette's thoughts had been so far flung with the letter she was startled by such a question. What else was Mama to think, though, with Colette spending so much time with him? Wasn't he her best friend, even better than Helen? Mama never knew what had happened last summer at Frenchtown, how her friendship with Joseph had suffered. Colette hadn't meant for it to, of course, but it had. She'd been mad at him for deserting her, but hadn't been able to convince him it wasn't because of jealousy.

Joe had cracked the reins lightly over the back of the mule pulling them in the buckboard. "How long are you going to be mad at me, Lettie? I told you it didn't mean anything with Kasheawa."

"That's a silly thing to say."

"Kissing only means something if you want it to. If it had, I'd tell you."

"You think it didn't mean something to her?"

"Why should it? She's an Indian."

"Joseph Gilbert! She's a girl! She has feelings!"

"So do you, obviously."

Colette's shoulders rose and fell in a heavy sigh. She stared at the road ahead. "I just didn't appreciate your running off on me like that. It made me uncomfortable. I didn't know anybody, and with all the drinking..."

Joe's voice dropped. "I won't ever do it again. I'm sorry, for Kasheawa and for the drinking." He took her hand. His touch reassured her more than she wished for it to. "You have to admit," he said, a cozy smile creeping into his voice, "you seemed to be having a fine enough time without me, dancing with all those French fellows."

"I was just being friendly."

"What about that big, stringy looking one, with the pockmarks all over his face?"

"I didn't want to act stuck up."

"Aw, Lettie, admit it," he said, squeezing her hand a little tighter, "you were on one of your rescue missions."

She jerked her hand away. "Unlike someone I know, I don't always have to favor the prettiest flower on the wall."

"All right, I deserved that. You're not jealous any more, though, so can I hold your hand again?"

"I declare, Joseph." She pushed her shoulder against his and laughed. "You're incorrigible!"

She was glad they'd worked it out, after a fashion. Her thoughts turned back to her mother's question.

"No, Mama, you can rest your mind about Joseph. If God truly has someone for me, I don't think he's the one, even if he is my best friend."

"But he's very handsome, that Joe," Rose added, bouncing the gurgling George on her knee.

Chapter Seven

Colette slipped through the front door and found Helen asleep in the parlor, the house dim in the late afternoon light, the ticking of the mantel clock unusually pronounced. Colette hummed softly as she arranged a bouquet of freshly picked flowers in a vase on the side table.

"You're so steady, Lettie," Helen murmured, coming out of her drowsiness. "Nothing bothers you."

"That's a nice thing to say. Did you have a nice nap?"

Helen nodded groggily and sat up. "I must look a mess. What time is it?"

"Time to wake up. You promised that when I got here, you would tell me about you and Harris and how you met, remember? You also promised to teach me how to fix my hair like yours. I want to wear it up next Sunday."

Helen sighed. "I'm not sure I feel like telling romantic stories today."

Colette laid a hairbrush and pins on the table and sat in a chair. "Well, you promised, so you have to try." Helen smoothed her skirt as she came over and picked up the brush. Slowly she pulled it through Colette's hair.

"Such a pretty color."

"Not as pretty as yours." Colette closed her eyes, relaxing beneath the massaging, smooth strokes.

"Prettier, I think. So many different shades, and it's getting so long. Thank you for coming over today, Lettie. I needed the company."

"You need to get out more, Helen. You spend too much time alone in this house."

"Harris worries if I venture from home when he's away."

"Worries?"

"Oh, it's nothing serious. Don't sound so shocked. He suspects I'll do something silly like slip and turn an ankle out in the snow, and no one will be there to help me, or -- I don't know -- maybe he thinks I'll get run down in the street or something."

"*In Grand Rapids?*"

Helen laughed softly. "It's hard to explain." She sighed. "I believe it's best if I humor him, though. It makes him happy."

Colette frowned, finally daring to ask, "But Helen, what about you? Isn't he concerned that you are happy?"

Helen's long brush stroke paused. Colette waited; perhaps she had overstepped. Finally Helen continued, sweeping Colette's hair up high into a twist.

"Oh, you just don't understand Harris," she said, her voice a little airy. "All of his concerns are for my happiness. Just look around you."

Colette didn't need to do that. Harris had provided for Helen's every wish. From the moment they'd arrived in town, she had been well cared for, and she had the loveliest wardrobe Colette had ever seen. She thought about the time Harris had taken them both to the logging camp. He had done that in their interests, certainly.

"I guess you're right, Helen. Maybe I'll understand better once I'm married. Now, tell me how you two met."

Colette could tell by the way in which Helen swiftly undid Colette's hair, pulling it up again in a different way, sticking in pins and adding ribbons, that her mood had lifted, or she was waking up more, one of the two. Her voice took on a girlish lilt as she told how Harris had swept her off her feet while she was a student at Mrs. Vanderhorn's Academy for Young Ladies.

"You can imagine how excited all the girls were. After all, there was Harris, not a boy, but a man with experience and standing in the world. Of course, he's so handsome, no one cared that he was already over thirty while I was just nineteen." Helen set her pins and combs aside and patted Colette's hair.

Colette rose. "You don't seem so separated by age."

"That's because you're used to seeing us together, and we've been married for seven years. I'm no longer the naive child I was at nineteen."

"My friend Jean, who was supposed to marry Virgil Holcomb, is twenty-two." The two strode into the kitchen to prepare tea. "They were nearly the same age, but he jilted her. Maybe you were smart to marry someone older, a dependable man who is can truly take care of you."

"Maybe. How is Jean now?"

"Well enough, I suppose. But I received a letter not long ago from her sister Annie. She says Jean might not get over it."

"Hmm."

Colette's mind flitted on toward Jean and Annie and Manason. All the doubts and thoughts she'd fretted over as mere shadowy substances in her mind boiled to the surface. She opened the tea tin and looked hard at Helen.

"So you must have known right away Harris was the one for you."

"Yes," Helen said. "I knew."

"But weren't there other young men who courted you? You're so pretty and poised, Helen. I would think so many fellows would have wanted to marry you that you'd hardly have been able to make up your mind."

Helen chuckled and sat at the table. "Oh, it seemed pretty clear to my heart the first time we spoke, Harris and me. Are you worried about finding the right young man, Lettie?"

"Well…" She didn't answer outright. "Helen, do you mind if I tell you something?"

"Anything."

Colette took a deep breath. "I don't think I ever told you that Jean and Annie have a brother named Manason." Her heart beat a little harder when she said his name, somehow making him real again. Helen's expression showed no change, only sincere interest. Colette couldn't keep from saying his name again. "Manason Kade. I've liked him since *forever*."

"Why, Lettie. I didn't know." Helen beamed at her. "All this time I thought maybe Joseph was on your mind."

"That's my problem. Sometimes Joseph *is* on my mind. We spend a lot of time together. He's been good to me. Sometimes I feel confused about him, but Manason has always been in my heart. I know it sounds silly. I may never see Nase again. In fact, Annie says he's going to wind up marrying Margaret Baker. Yet, it makes me wonder, you know, what God has in mind? Maybe He does want me to marry Joseph, or someone else altogether."

"I wish I could tell you something that would help."

Colette shrugged. "I know there's nothing, really, you can say. I guess your question may have struck it on the head. Maybe I am worried about finding the right fellow. I hope when it happens I'll just know, like you did with Harris."

"I'm sure your parents will help you decide what's right. You shouldn't have to worry."

Colette gazed out the window at the drifts piling high against the trees. Her thoughts rambled off. Did Manason ever think of her? Did he remember calling her princess, or Juliet, or lady? "I talked to Mama," she said softly. "She thinks sometimes God has the right one picked out, like Isaac and Rebekah in the Bible, I suppose. Other times, He lets us choose within His guidelines. What do you think, Helen?"

"I think your mama's a wise person. Oh, Lettie, I can't say when I married Harris that I ever thought about whether God wanted me to or not." Helen paused, looking far away, wistful. Then she reached across the table and laid her pearl white hand across Colette's. "It could be that you will meet Manason again one day."

Colette looked back at Helen, her hope surging until the other woman added, "Could be, though, that he'll be married to someone else when you do. I'm sure God will help you get him out of your heart if He's trying to put someone else in it."

*****

Harris Eastman pushed his plate away and pulled the coffee saucer closer. He tapped his fingers on the edge of his cup, considering his future as he sat in the dining room of Milwaukee's most posh hotel.

Harris' business instincts would have left him comfortably well off by the time he'd reached his mid-twenties even if he hadn't already inherited a tidy sum from his father who'd speculated in transportation and the "black diamond" coal industry. Even now, some might have wondered at his decision to invest in a new business while the country was barely recovering from a panic. Yet, because of that very panic, Harris realized that prices would probably remain low for a number of years. He had spread his investments far and wide enough not to worry overly much, and thus had decided the shadowy time following the panic of '37 was not the time to cut and run, but to buy. He didn't mind offering pecuniary assistance to Eldon Palmer, helping the man make something of himself. He would gain back many times over what he had invested in Palmer's mill. But that was where the partnership ended. Harris Eastman had other irons in the fire.

A gambler at heart, Harris took risks he deemed necessary. Lately he had been buying small pineries bordering the much larger Indian pine lands. With the right connections, which Harris had, he'd been able to secure permits issued by the Secretary of War to log on those Indian lands, regardless of the risks such illegalities involved. He could be dispossessed, true; but the fact that there were parcels of land belonging to the Indians which might well put out 1,500,000 board feet per acre made the risks negligible.

He sipped his coffee. *And I've found the right kind of men to do the job.* Though doing so had frequently kept him away from home. Between meetings with land agents and lawyers, all of whom could be kept comfortably in his pocket for a price, he had scoured the territory for some of the toughest, brawl-able lumberjacks and woods bosses he could find. Men who were able to accomplish with fists and cant hooks what couldn't be accomplished with paperwork and lawyers. They could keep another crew from claiming a section ahead of them, or stop them from getting their logs downstream. At the same time, those men could work like steam engines. They were men who loved the raw life of adventure, and Harris was willing to pay them their price. He also turned a blind eye to the liquor and crude establishments which sprung up to keep the men content during their long months in the woods. As long as they were sober and working when Eastman needed them to be, they could have their drink and debauchery.

Harris Eastman couldn't squelch the troubled feeling that continually laid hold of him even with his current success, however. He found himself wondering more often than he cared to admit what might finally satisfy him. At one time, he'd thought Helen was the answer. Winning her hand was like wearing a pin on his lapel. She decorated him. She belonged to him.

Helen had come from an old Philadelphia family, and her father, a well-known doctor, had expanded his income by lending money. Employing various means at his disposal, most of them surreptitious, Harris had discovered many people were indebted to the old doctor. To Harris, finding Helen was like discovering a jewel among the coal pits. He knew other society women, but none so perfectly suited as Helen, with her youth, her beauty, and her naive desire to please him.

How, then, did that allure fail to keep him satisfied? Certainly it was not that he wanted other women. Harris scoffed. He had no desire to look elsewhere for womanly charms. Yet Helen lacked her own interests. She was dull. She lacked the ability to challenge his intellect.

Harris Eastman sipped his now tepid coffee and puzzled over it. He had no reason to complain. He hadn't married his wife for her intellect, after all, and he'd never tried to reason otherwise. He admired her more for carnal reasons. Still, one would hope that after seven years of marriage, the two of them would have found a commonality, a real partnership. That she would engage him. *That she would understand my true nature without holding an ounce of recrimination against me.*

Why did Helen harbor such an unreasonable desire to have the Shultz woman and her fatherless whelp so near? Perhaps they were the real reason for his unrest. Perhaps he'd not be truly satisfied until Helen produced an heir. A son to succeed him. A child who would make his striving worthwhile and live as testament to his memory.

Harris sighed and threw back the last dregs of his cup. He found it utterly incredible that she'd not yet born him a child. She'd had not one, but *three* miscarriages -- and he was angry with her, though he knew such feelings were unreasonable. She seemed to want to bear him a child as much as he wished for it. So why had such a normal function of life become so difficult?

He tossed some bills on the table and unfolded his long legs to retire to his hotel room. He passed a handsome couple on the staircase and nodded at them cordially. He noted the way they smiled at one another and spoke softly as they descended behind him. Did they have a child to complete them? Or did they share some other oneness missing between Harris and Helen?

Harris climbed into bed early that evening. His discontent made his head ache. He needed to still his thoughts. Tomorrow's ugly business required his full attention. He was going to have to evict some squatters off the land he'd just purchased. If they wished to stay, they had to pay a price. Women's tears and squalling children, or no.

Chapter Eight

Summer arrived lush and full. The green veil of treetops closed over the woods, dappling the undergrowth in a beautiful vibrancy of sunlight and shadow. Colette inhaled every smell, every nuance of the outdoors, absorbing it into the pores of her skin and the strands of her hair.

Helen said the closeness of the woods made her feel as though she couldn't breathe. But, to Colette, it felt like a great, protective embrace from God.

Ever since her talks with both Mama and Helen, Colette had grown a great deal more confident that God would figure things out for her. She no longer troubled herself over thoughts of love and marriage. Fact was, Manason had grown further and further away from her thoughts. He still came to her in a pleasant way, but Colette knew her imagination would never produce the relationship for which she'd wished when she was younger. Colette did feel much older these days. She'd learned to accept life's unknowns, and she refused to waste time mulling over questions that couldn't be answered.

She turned her mind instead to the realities of each day that stretched before her. First there was Rose and little George, who toddled about and needed constant watching. Then there was the garden to tend and the house to keep clean. With three women to do that, Colette found time to walk about the woods and go to the mill to visit her father. She had time to read when she was able to acquire something new. Her knowledge of the territory had increased like the spreading branches of an oak. Her father allowed her to explore the records he kept of the mill profits and expenses, the journals recording land descriptions, and his ideas. She studied his maps and knew the routes of the rivers and layouts of the area's best pineries. She was attuned to the nature of the industry and kept in her head the names of other millwrights and lumbermen on the river.

Someday, if God kept her in this country, she would need to know these things.

Sometimes Colette would share something of interest she'd learned with Helen, but usually Helen only looked at her with a puzzled expression, a little amazed that a young woman would care about such things. Joseph couldn't understand a girl who was so interested in a man's industry, but he said it was okay as long as she didn't talk about it all the time. He worked at the mills all summer and in the woods during winter, and didn't want to discuss his job with Lettie when they could be fishing or dancing or throwing sticks for Dandy to fetch.

Sometimes Harris was receptive to hearing about her interests, but only her papa's eyes lit up when she talked about all he'd taught her. He treated Colette as his equal, and the two of them discussed the logging business for hours.

"One day, you'll have her taking over the mill for you," her mother joked to her papa.

"What would be wrong with that?" he said, his eyes twinkling. The thickening crow's feet at their corners crinkled. "Look around you, 'Vinia. Lumberjacks, millwrights, and land barons. That's what makes up this territory. Someday she'll be the wife of one of them, and she'll make him as proud as she makes me."

He pulled Colette into a tight hug as they rode home from town in the old buckboard. Still smiling, she disengaged herself from her father's embrace and straightened her skirt.

"Is Harris a land baron, do you think, Papa?"

The wagon bounced and creaked. Eldon cast her a quizzical glance and clucked at the horses to pick up their pace. He shrugged. "I'm not sure if that's a question I should give my opinion on, daughter. There are rumors."

"Hmm. Yes, I've heard. Is it true he's going to be as rich as Mr. Mead?" she asked, referring to one of the better known lumbermen of the area.

"Well, now, Colette, time will tell." A small frown bent her father's eyebrows, a look of concern she recognized well.

"Is he doing something wrong?"

"That I don't know. I've only heard rumors without facts to back them up. Just gossip. So I won't cast doubt. Every man has a right to make his way. I do know that if Harris has done anything amiss, it'll catch up with him in the end, and he's been more than good to us. He's my partner, after all, and I brought nothing to the partnership except a strong back and the same experience many men possess. He's helped me see my dream become a reality. I won't fault him for trying to see to his own when I have no good evidence."

Colette laced her arm through her father's and rested her cheek against his shoulder.

The next evening, Eldon brought her a surprise. He reached into his pocket and pulled out a folded envelope. He'd barely held it up when Colette snatched it from his hand, recognizing the script on the outside as Jean Kade's. She ripped the paper out of the envelope and raced over the words.

Dearest Mr. and Mrs. Palmer and Colette;

By the time you receive my missive, it will be too late for me to change my mind, for I will be well on my way to your house in the beautiful Wisconsin woods. I had initially decided to write to see if you would be willing and able to receive a visit from a friend, but knowing how long it might take to reach you, and then the time it might take to receive your reply, put me in a mind to come without waiting. I won't deny that I've been feeling lost here at home. I admit, regrettably, that I haven't gotten over Virgil as easily as I'd hoped, and I have decided that if I am to vanquish any of this melancholy that's descended over me, I must have a change. Do you mind so very much that I shall be imposing upon you?

There is another reason I have made up my mind to come right away. Manason is going to Wisconsin. If I am to have a traveling companion across the lake, I must go now. He will be there for some months, and I didn't want to have to wait until his next trip -- if, indeed, you did decide to send for me. We will travel across the lake as far as the Winnebago settlement called Portage. We will then part company, as he will be gathering supplies and maps to cruise his precious pine up north. I wish he could come all the way to Grand Rapids with me, and he would like the chance to see you as well, but you, of all people, understand how a lumberman must take advantage of the weather and the seasons while there is time.

I shall see you soon, I suppose. I am so excited! It is the first time in months that I've found myself looking forward to what lies ahead!

Cordially,
Jean Kade

"Oh, Papa!" Colette threw her arms around her father. "Jean's coming!" She twirled and laughed. "Wait until I tell Helen and Mama and Joe!"

The next few days spun away in a whirlwind of preparations. With the time it had taken for the letter to reach them, chances were good that Jean might arrive at any time.

"Tell me more about her," Joe said as he helped Colette rake hay in a small clearing near her home. "I've only heard you mention her once or twice a year or more ago. I thought you'd given up on your old friends in Michigan."

Colette paused and brushed an arm across her forehead. She leaned against the rake, thoughtful. "Jean's the most wonderful friend I've ever had."

"Guess I know, then, what you think of me."

"Oh, Joe, don't pout. You're my best friend here, but you're not Jean. You're not even Helen or Sally."

"You're not even friends with Fat Sally."

"Don't call her that. Besides, I am her friend. We just don't get to see each other much beyond a meeting in the dry goods store or at a town picnic. Girls have to have girlfriends. It's just the way of it. We understand each other."

Joe frowned and set aside his rake. He took up the pitchfork stuck in the ground nearby, pitching hay onto the cart behind them. "Someday you're going to get married, Lettie. Then you'll have to give up your girlfriends."

"Give them up? Never. It'll just make things a little different, that's all."

"I say you'll give them up."

"*You* say?"

"Yes, *I* say." A mischievous look lit his eyes just as he pitched a forkful of hay into her hair. "You try and act coy, but you're the type that falls hard once you fall in love. You'll gladly give up your girlfriends. Wait and see."

Colette shook the hay out of her dress and hair, sputtering a little as pieces of chaff caught on her lips. "I ought to get even with you for that, but I won't. Leastwise not now while you're expecting it." She continued with her work, unperturbed. "Really, wait until you meet Jean. You'll like her. She's pretty, too. You'll probably fall in love with her yourself, only she'll think you're too much a youngster." She smiled wryly.

"Youngster, you say? I'm man enough."

"Then why am I raking twice as much hay as you're pitching?"

"You think you are?" He cast her a challenging glance.

Joe tossed more hay into the cart, and Colette raced ahead with her rake. After a few breathless moments, Joe caught up to her, dropped the fork, and wrapped his arms around her waist. She squealed with laughter as he tossed her into the cart.

"Did I prove my point?" he cried, lifting the end of the cart and heaving it forward. His muscles strained as he pulled her across the meadow to the edge of the tree line and down the lane to her cabin.

Joe huffed for air. Still laughing, Colette slid off the cart covered in grass and clover, unaware the front door of the cabin had opened and someone had stepped out.

"All right. I concede your point. If indeed you had one," she said as she plucked shafts of hay from her hair and clothes.

"No more questions about my manliness, then?" Joe's breathing calmed, but the grin remained indelible on his face.

"Not at the moment. I--" George's coo made Colette lift her gaze. Her mother, Rose, and another woman stood on the porch watching her and Joe with serene smiles. Excitement bubbled up in her chest. "Jean!" yelled Colette, scampering away from Joe. She flushed as she came face to face with her old friend, suddenly embarrassed at her frolicking arrival with Joe. "You're here! I want to hug you, but I'm so full of dirt and hay..." She couldn't help glancing over at Joe for just the briefest, guilty moment.

Jean laughed and pulled her into a warm embrace. "I don't care if you are dirty. It seems forever since I've seen you, Colette."

"Have you been here long?" Colette asked as they drew apart.

"Not at all. In fact, your mother knew you'd be upset if we didn't come get you right away. We were on our way to find you."

"Oh. Jean, I'd like you to meet a family friend." Colette turned to Joe, who was approaching slowly, the kind of smile on his face Colette wanted to wipe away. Wasn't he ever concerned about the impression he made? Did he have to insist on creating a sensation? He'd like Jean to think exactly what she was, no doubt, thinking -- that she, Colette, had a beau. "This is Joseph Gilbert. Joseph, I'd like to introduce you to my good friend Jean Kade."

"Miss Kade," he said, shaking her hand. "Colette's told me *so* much about you."

Colette threw him a wide-eyed, *must you?* look which, for all practical purposes, was lost on him.

"Only good things, I hope," Jean said, lowering her hand to her side.

"The best. And I have to agree with everything she said."

He didn't enlarge on that, only left Jean agape while he continued with that flirtatious manner of looking at her.

"Oh, Jean, I can't wait to have a long visit. But I'd like to clean up first. Do you mind?" Colette turned her hands over, glancing at the dirt under nails, hoping Joe would take a hint and go home.

"Certainly not," Jean said. "After all, we have all the time in the world. Isn't it wonderful?"

Joseph went through the motions of brushing dust off his overalls. "Yes, I suppose I'd better go home and wash up, too. I must be a sight." He grinned lopsidedly, a trickle of sweat hanging on the edge of his temple where his black hair glistened in a loose curl. He didn't need Colette to tell him his manhood was intact. She was certain he was aware of every bit of it. "Nice to meet you. I'll see you again soon, no doubt, since Colette and I see each other often. Good afternoon, ma'am. Ma'am," he repeated, nodding to both Mama and Rose before he stuffed his over-sized hands in his pockets and sauntered away down the road, whistling.

Jean held her hand to her chest and let out a small laugh as he disappeared around the bend through the trees. "Colette! You never mentioned..."

"That I knew such a rake as Joe?" Colette rolled her eyes. "There are some things you just can't explain in a letter."

Colette could tell Jean was more than a little curious about Joe. Wasn't it just like him to make himself the center of her and Jean's first conversation? They walked to the pitcher pump, and Colette thrust the handle up and down. Water gushed into a pail hanging off the spigot.

"I doubt I ever would've recognized you if I didn't know who to expect coming up to the house on that cart," Jean said. "You certainly have changed."

"That's what everyone says. '*Oh, Colette, you're getting so grown up,*'" she mimicked, and laughed at herself.

"It's more than that. Yes, you've grown, taller than I. You've filled out in a way I envy, as well. But there's also another kind of maturity I see that wasn't there before."

Colette glanced away. "How can you say that after I've just come flying up to the house in a hay cart?"

"I'm thinking of the nature of the flight," Jean said softly. Her hint at Joe's cavalier behavior wasn't lost on Colette, and she spent more time than she needed rinsing her face.

"Have you looked at yourself, dear?" Jean continued. "You're a full grown woman. Even squealing in a hay cart, you have a certain poise. You've come out of your shell, too, I think."

Colette reached for a towel hanging on a stump. She buried her face in it, gathering her breath. "Enough about me," she said as they strolled back toward the other women. "Come on, Jean. I'll take you down to the river and you can tell me all about your trip. Do you mind, Ma?"

"You girls go ahead. Rose wants to put George down for a nap, and I'm going to rest for awhile before dinner, too."

Colette picked the final bits of chaff from her hair, wound it into a knot at her neck, and led Jean toward the woods.

"Did you enjoy the ride on the boat?" Colette asked, finally diverting their conversation.

"It was a wonderful trip. We had perfect weather the entire way. I don't know who was more excited, me or Nase. He's sorry he couldn't stop to visit."

"Maybe another time." Colette hoped her answer didn't sound as hollow as it felt.

"Yes, maybe some other time. He's gloriously excited about getting a start here, as you can imagine. He learned so much last year with Mr. Nuchols and Mr. Durant. Our pa and Stu certainly seem to have confidence in him. He'll probably go home in the spring for a bit. Then he'll be back for good."

"For good?"

"Yes, I think so. As long as things go well, anyway."

Questions filled Colette's mind, questions she didn't dare ask.

"I'm to send love from Annie. She says she'd write, but Hank takes so much of her time." Jean laughed. "Of course, Annie doesn't give him an ounce more than she wants to."

"No, I'm sure she doesn't."

They laughed and strolled beneath the trees to the edge of the Wisconsin. Jean had a big double needle from a white pine in her hand, and bit by bit broke off little pieces of it, tossing them into the swirling water. "So are you going to tell me anymore about your friend Joseph?"

Colette started. She'd fallen peaceful. Now she caught Jean's sideways glance.

"Ah, Joseph. You mustn't mind him, Jean. He's a terrible flirt and very full of himself."

"Is that all you think of him?"

"He's a good friend, and I do like him, even if most of the time I find myself putting up with him in one way or another."

"Is that all?"

Colette looked steadily at Jean. "I know what you're thinking. You know I'm not like Annie. It doesn't please me to have someone admire me so I can... you know."

"What?"

"Tease them." She stooped to twirl a branch in the water's edge.

"I don't know if Annie means to lead anyone on. I think she's really serious about Hank."

"Oh, I didn't mean that. You know I love Annie."

"I think you mean you don't want to behave like Margaret Baker."

Colette jerked up her chin and swung her glance toward Jean.

"Yes," Jean said. "Now I see what you mean. But don't you care for Joseph? I thought you must."

"No one's been a better friend to me since we've come to Wisconsin Territory, except for the Eastmans, of course. Joe would like us to be more than friends. At least, he seems to want that. But I can't."

Colette stood and fiddled with her hands, running her gaze up the river.

"Why not?" asked Jean softly.

Colette shrugged. She wished she could be certain of what it was she wanted -- what it was she waited for. "I'm just not sure that he's the one. Joe *is* charming. He brought me a puppy last year for my birthday. You saw Dandy." The sun had turned orange above the tree line on the other side of the river. Its wavering sheen on the water mesmerized her thoughts. Her question was real. "But what if God has a plan, like my mama says?"

Jean sighed. "I do understand. In truth, I wish I'd been a little more patient when I first accepted Virgil. Now look what's happened."

"I'm so sorry about that, Jean." Colette's heart filled to overflowing. She turned and hugged her friend again. "Will you forgive me for being so thoughtless and unfeeling? I should have written more often. A better friend would have, to help you get past what happened."

"You couldn't have said anything to make it easier. Being here now, that's the best thing."

They sat in the grass, and Colette undid her shoes to put her feet in the water. Jean followed her lead.

"Remember the mill pond?"

"Just left it only last week," Jean answered, smiling.

Colette took a breath. "We had good times there, you and me and Annie... and Nase." Her voice softened toward the end. She couldn't hide her thoughts completely.

Jean must have sensed something of them. She swished her feet in the water and glanced at Colette. "Nase has been almost as much a brother to you as he's been to Annie and me, wouldn't you say?"

Colette nodded. "The best I could ever hope for. Thank you for sharing him."

Jean reached over and tucked a strand of loose, wind-blown hair behind Colette's ear, offering her a smile. "Nase is good at making others know they're cared for. These days it's only Margaret who doesn't seem to be able to keep him in her grasp entirely."

Colette met Jean's gaze and bit down to halt the questions on her tongue.

"She's trifled with him a bit hard. I'm not so sure he hasn't given up on her."

"But Annie said--"

"Annie isn't always right." Jean's gray eyes sparkled at Colette. "Then again, we'll have to wait for spring to see."

Chapter Nine

"Today we're going to draw," Colette announced as she and Jean took off their sun bonnets and tossed them on Helen's settee.

Jean and Colette's friendship had deepened during the days and weeks they'd spent with Rose and Lavinia canning summer vegetables, picking wild blueberries, taking care of household tasks, and mending clothes. Often as not, once their chores were done, they would go to town to visit Helen.

Afternoons were always quiet at Helen's home in Grand Rapids. She assured Colette that Mrs. Stowe came by from time to time to do some needlework with her, but still Colette was conscious of the fact that the ticking of the mantle clock was the only noise to invade most of Helen's silent times when neither she nor Jean were there.

Helen, however, seemed cheerful, and she was always eager to try new things when Colette and Jean stopped by.

"What a good idea," Helen said. "I used to draw a lot when I was in school. I wasn't the best, but I managed a likeness or two. Where shall we do it?"

Jean glanced about the room. "The lighting isn't very good in here for drawing."

"How about the back porch? It's a nice day, and the outdoors will inspire us," Colette said. "We'll find pens and paper in Harris' study." She headed toward his office near the foyer.

Helen followed her. "I hope he won't mind."

"Why should he mind?"

"Well, you know Harris. He doesn't like his things being bothered."

"We won't bother them. We'll just borrow them." Colette looked through the cupboard contents on the side of the room.

As always, Harris' office was tidy. Colette gathered a spare inkwell and pens, then glanced at Jean as she closed the cupboard. Her friend's glance roved the room. Her eyebrows rose a notch as she looked at the painting of a ship on the wall, the carved miniatures of a dog and a hunter on a bookshelf, and a newspaper, folded in half on a side table.

"It's been weeks since I've seen a newspaper," Colette said. "Bring it along and we'll read it together."

"We can't forget to return it," Helen said.

The three of them took the supplies and set themselves up comfortably on Helen's back porch. The afternoon breeze was gentle, not enough to disturb their paper, but enough to play with the topmost branches of the two oaks and a majestic white pine standing between them in the Eastmans' back yard.

"I'll draw the trees," Colette said, "and add some flowers, too. You need a flower garden, Helen. Next spring we'll plant one."

"Do you draw people, Helen?" Jean asked as she sketched with deft strokes.

"Sometimes. If you want, I'll try and draw a picture of Harris. It won't be very good. Colette can remind me to throw it away before he comes home. What are you drawing?" she asked Jean.

"You'll have to wait and see. Colette will tell you."

Colette leaned closer for a look, but Jean turned her paper away. "Not yet."

They each sat quietly, their pens poised silently from time to time, then scratching away again.

"Here's mine," Colette said at last. She held up her drawing. It was a fair likeness of the landscape in Helen's back yard. "I rushed a little, and left out lots of detail."

Jean smiled. "You never were very patient at detail work, if I remember right."

Colette sighed. "You're thinking of my embroidery. Well, I can't argue with you. Rose will tell you the stitches on my seams leave a lot to be desired, too. What have you got there?" she asked, walking over to look over Helen's shoulder. She recognized the face on Helen's paper immediately. "Why, it's Harris. Very good, Helen. You shouldn't throw it away. He'll like it."

"Do you?"

"Yes, except--"

"What? What don't you like? Tell me. You know Harris almost as well as I. What is it?"

Colette studied the portrait, thinking that was a strange thing for Helen to say. "Well..."

"What is it?"

She tilted her head and narrowed her focus on Harris' features, and then it came to her. "It's the eyes. Something's not quite right." Colette stroked her chin. "They're too far away. Too empty. No humor." She placed her hands on her hips. "Yes, I think that's what it is. No humor. No sparkle. He sparkles when he looks at you, Helen."

"He does? Still? I guess I haven't noticed."

"Oh, yes. He sparkles."

Jean was still busy sketching. Colette stepped closer. "May we look now, Jean?"

"No snooping yet. Just a minute."

Colette sighed, and Helen laughed at her while they both waited for not one, but several more minutes before Jean finally turned her art toward them.

"Well?"

"Who is he?" Helen asked.

Jean turned her eyes to Colette, but Colette only stared at the drawing in Jean's hand. Her mouth went dry. "Can you tell?" Jean asked softly.

Colette flitted a glance toward her friend, afraid that if she didn't say something soon, her feelings would be entirely exposed, feelings she'd thought were lost.

"It--" Her voice sounded tight and small, even to her own ears. She cleared her throat. "It's perfect, Jean. I didn't know you could draw so well. He's... perfect."

"Who is it?" Helen cried.

"It's Manason," Colette said, wanting to touch the drawing, but clasping her fingers together so she wouldn't.

"Now I see," Helen said, and Jean's expression settled on Helen in a knowing way that made Colette want to cringe.

She found it impossible to quiet the pounding of her heart. *I'm just being silly. I'd nearly forgotten what he looks like, that's all. I shouldn't be so affected. He's never even cared for me.*

Helen continued looking at her, and she determined she wouldn't talk about it here, now, or ever. Jean was suspicious enough, and Collette cared for her too much to ruin it by telling her about her ridiculous infatuation with her brother.

Yes, an infatuation. One she must give up, as she had the other remnants of her childhood.

If Nase ever gave her more than a passing thought, he would've come to visit with Jean, just to say hello on his way north. But he hadn't. She didn't have any part of his heart, and she never would. Regardless of what Jean had said about Annie being wrong, Colette knew Nase's heart belonged to Margaret Baker. He'd go home in the spring, and when he returned again to Wisconsin, he'd bring Margie with him.

So that was that. She tried to breathe normally.

"Well," the word came out like a gush of air, not at all the way she'd intended it. Both women stared at her.

"Well," she said again with a little more control. "Who knew you were such an artist, Jean? To think you've been hiding your talent all along." Her hands shook. She needed to find something to do with them. She couldn't keep looking back at Nase -- at the drawing. So she picked up the newspaper.

"I think you should draw another one. Draw Helen, Jean. We can leave it on Harris' desk as a gift. Won't he be surprised?" She looked at Helen. "You sit there, Helen; and Jean, you draw. I'll read the news to you."

She ignored the way Jean's look flitted to Helen's, then Helen's to Jean's. She plopped into a chair and flipped the paper up in front of her face to hide from them both as she cleared her throat and read the latest headlines, some ten days old.

She paused momentarily and was satisfied when Jean's pen again scratched on the paper.

"Let's see." She scanned for a likely item to read. "Ah, *Wisconsin*

Becomes Nation's Largest Wheat Producer," she said, and continued with the article and then on into the next: *New Roads May Connect Portions of Territory.*

"New roads? Next there'll be a stage line," she commented after reading the piece. "Wouldn't that be something? Think how easy it would be to travel around."

"Maybe they'll build roads over some of the old Indian trails. Some going clear up north," Jean said.

"You should read to me more often," Helen said. She'd gone inside to bring them some fruit, and now set a bowl down on the table near the picture of Jean's brother. "Then I'd be able to talk to Harris about the things he's interested in."

"Why don't you just read it yourself?" Colette reached for an apple, careful to avoid looking at the handsome image of Manason.

Helen shrugged. "You know me. I just wouldn't. Harris enjoys talking to Colette," she added, turning to Jean. "She keeps him on his toes with these political goings on and the logging and all that."

Jean raised her eyebrows. "Really?"

"Oh, yes. You should hear them argue."

"Colette argues?"

"About land rights and tenant farmers' rights and the safety of the loggers. All those things."

"I don't argue. I simply tell Harris what I think. He lets me go on and on out of courtesy."

Jean laughed. "I wish Manason could see you now."

Colette bit into her apple and looked away.

*****

By summer's end Jean had gotten two letters, including one from her parents telling of Annie's official engagement and plans for a spring wedding.

"She won't put it off," Jean said. "She'll be thinking she won't let him get away, like I did with Virgil."

The second letter was from Manason, who wrote to let Jean know he wouldn't be able to come that way and accompany her back to the boat as he'd planned. He hoped she would either find another way to travel to Fort Howard, or would consider staying with the Palmers until spring. He said he hated asking, but wasn't sure what else to do.

Jean's immediate response was that she'd stay in a heartbeat if not for Annie's engagement. "I can't miss my own sister's wedding. Not if there's a way to get back. We'll have to see." She looked at Collette. "Manason sends his good wishes to everyone."

Colette hid her thoughts. Manason wasn't coming until spring, and only then to collect Jean. And Jean wouldn't be here if she found someone going to Green Bay or Fort Howard with whom she could travel. For

Jean's first priority was getting home for Annie.

Oh, Annie! You always-- Collette cut the thought short. Blaming Annie was ridiculous.

Of course someone would be going in the direction of Green Bay. Many people came and went, and Jean could safely travel most any time.

Jean had given Colette the drawing of Nase. Colette tried to turn it down at first, but Jean had insisted. "You were friends. You should have something to remember him by."Colette could not refuse.

Sometimes she looked at it. Other times, she wouldn't let herself. He was the past. *My childish past.*

What was the future, anyway?

Chapter Ten

Harris helped Helen down from the carriage and was caught for a moment by her fragile beauty. *Why can't I always be pleased with her?*

Helen might be a bit of a bore at times, but lately she'd been going a little beyond herself. She'd seemed especially intent on pleasing him, and with a good spirit, too. Well, tonight he was pleased. He supposed he might as well make the most of it as it came to him.

This party was a good idea. *One of the few good ideas Helen has ever had.* It made them look good to everyone, at every level of society. Looping her arm through his own, he kissed her temple with a light peck. "Do you feel like dancing, or would you like to have some punch first?"

"I certainly intend to dance, Harris, but let's say hello to some of the others first."

Around the mill's open-sided pole building, spirits soared high. The autumn smells of leaf mold and wood smoke filled everyone with the impending sense of time running on from one season into the next. In a matter of days the men would leave, and many wouldn't see their wives, daughters, or sweethearts again for weeks. Rollicking music set the pace as wagons rolled up to the mill. A few canoes and other small barks full of revelry-makers had come clear across from Centralia and Frenchtown.

Harris spied Lettie spinning about the floor with Joe Gilbert. She was an interesting girl, quick-minded in a way that went beyond the norm for girls her age, and getting prettier every day. He hoped Gilbert wasn't taking advantage of her. Harris caught her eye and inclined his head with a smile. She smiled back, and in a moment swung near him and Helen. Her chest rose and fell in a rush as she tried to catch her breath. Her cheeks were flushed with happiness that only intensified her growing loveliness.

"You finally made it!" she said. "Helen, don't let him keep you sitting by the wall all evening."

"Oh, I won't," Helen said.

"I've promised to be light on my feet tonight," Harris said.

"Good!"

"If I'm not mistaken, you just had a birthday, and I'd like to claim a dance with you, as well."

"If Joe doesn't wear me out."

"I'll be sure and spare you," Joe said, "and that will give me a chance to dance with Mrs. Eastman. If it's okay with you, sir," he added, looking to Harris.

"She'd love to dance with you, I'm sure. Helen's a wonderful dancer, though I'm afraid I'm a bit of a clod."

"You are not," Helen said. "But I would indeed love to dance with you, Joe."

With nods and a quick curtsy from Colette, she and Joe headed back into the fray. Harris watched them swish away, thinking that one of these days Helen was going to lose her young friend to some rutting buck like that Gilbert fellow. Lettie had a way with Helen, and as much as Harris didn't like to admit that he couldn't be everything Helen needed, he was grateful for Lettie and the spark of life she'd brought into Helen's life, and -- heaven help him -- into his life as well.

*****

Colette smiled at the people she knew as Joseph twirled her about the soirée, through one song, and then another. They finally paused near Jean just as Joe's brothers walked over. Joseph introduced them to Jean. Michael escorted the green-eyed Caroline Sullivan, whose braids looked like burnished copper wrapped around her head. Rob looked as handsome a dark Irishman as Colette had ever seen.

Joseph drew Colette a little closer to speak into her ear. "I see a look in my brother's eye." Louder, he said, "Robbie's come to ask you to dance, Jean. Haven't you, Rob?"

Without waiting for a response, Joe tugged on Colette's arm. In a moment, they lost themselves in the crowd of twirling skirts and stomping feet.

"Will he bandy with her heart?" she asked, trying to catch a glimpse of Jean through the crowd.

"Not Robbie."

"She looks so pretty tonight." Colette spoke between breaths as the fiddle suddenly picked up the pace of the tune, and her feet switched rhythm. "I hope she has a good time with Rob."

"I'll be glad if you have a good time with me." He flashed her a devilish smile.

Colette rolled her eyes and pulled him off the floor. "I need to rest. I'm winded."

"Let's get something to eat and drink."

They went to the table spread with food and ladled their plates full. Gathering cups of punch as well, they went outside and found a place among some tables and chairs set up for the occasion. Light flooded out of the open-sided building enough for them to see.

Joe wasted no time putting away his food, while Colette watched and giggled and picked away at hers, making comments about his appetite.

"It's your fault; you wear me out," he said.

"You've more energy than Dandy."

"Well, I'd better store some up for all the work I'll be doing in a few weeks."

"I don't want to think about it."

"You'll miss me, won't you?"

"You know I will."

Joe's expression grew serious. He swallowed and laid down his fork; then he reached over and placed his hand on hers.

"You don't believe it, Lettie, but you know you are my girl."

She shook her head. "No, Joe."

"We can't be friends forever."

"Why not?"

"It just doesn't work that way. I want you to be my girl, Lettie. I want to know I'm coming back to that."

"But I'm not your girl, Joseph. I'm just--"

"Just what? My best friend? That's fine... fine. But think about it. We're growing up, Lettie. Things change, whether you want them to or not. You must see it. You're seventeen. I'm almost twenty."

Colette gently tugged her hand free and tucked it in her lap. She tried to change the subject. "I never got you anything for your birthday last year, and now you've got another one coming in less than three months. I wonder what I should give you."

Suddenly, Joe leaned close and kissed her lightly on the mouth before she could object. "That's for last year," he said, his face inches away, his green eyes burning. "For this year, I want a letter, on my birthday, telling me you miss me and that you know you're my girl. A couple of months should give you plenty of time to figure it out."

Her heart thudded, and a flush burned through her. Joseph calmly rose from the table and picked up their plates. "Should we go see how Robbie and Jean are getting on?"

Colette nodded silently, picked up her cup, and followed him.

*****

Over a hundred miles away in the deep green Chippewa River country, Manason lay looking up into the night sky and listening to the rhythm of his heart. A few weeks back he could listen to the crickets. Now the nights were getting too cool, even for them. He rolled onto his side and tried to fall asleep, but his thoughts kept chasing themselves in circles.

First he wondered how Pa and Stu were getting on with the mill back in Michigan. Then he worried over the coming season and whether he'd be able to get enough board feet down the river to break even. He'd cruised plenty of pine and filed claim on a good section. He'd spent the last few weeks trying to find enough men with the brawn and the brains to get it cut and skidded out. That hadn't been an easy task so late in the year. Most men were already hired out elsewhere. He didn't want to steal men from other gangs; that just didn't sit well with him. But he had to admit there were days he felt tempted.

Then he'd come upon a man named Purnell who'd lit out of an outfit the previous spring saying he would never again work for a man who required his soul. He'd gone out looking for honest work instead. He'd been hoping to find a different woods gang to hook up with when he ran into Manason. Then, through Purnell, Nase met with some others who decided to throw in with him as well.

"Any chance we'll cross paths with your old employer out here?" Nase asked.

"Naw. He's moved one of his crews east a ways."

"I heard there's been some log poaching off Indian lands farther upriver. Any chance you know anything about that?"

A couple of the men threw each other sheepish glances as Purnell gave a curt nod. He spat a squirt of tobacco juice into the grass and looked squarely at Manason. "We can't say anything for sure, but somebody's skinnin' trees off the Injun lands upriver, and if Seamus Boggs has got men thereabouts, then you can pretty well guess he's in on it some way or other."

Manason turned over to his other side, thinking more about Seamus Boggs and the rumors of men stealing pine off the Indian lands. Purnell had told him Boggs was a common woods boss and a ruffian. Manason knew his type well enough. They didn't have the cranial capacity for solid, honest business dealings, but they could motivate a woods crew into bringing in a cut with their own marks on it. How those marks got on the logs was another matter. Beating, bribery, and theft were the most common tools of their trade, and they weren't against committing murder now and then if someone got too nosy about their business. The main thing about men like Boggs was that they didn't work on their own. They always worked for someone else, someone with brains and money and a quest for power.

Nase flung an arm over his head in frustration and stared up at the stars again, unable to hold his eyes closed. The constellations were laid out in the same pattern as the night he'd walked off on Margie Baker. Or had she walked off on him? He remembered the bang of the screen door slamming shut and the muted sounds of the party fading away as he'd headed out of town.

Nights like tonight when he couldn't sleep and the stars made him think of Margie, he wondered if he wasn't missing something. She'd been so willing. He could've had her in his arms for good. He could've sealed it. The thought left a hunger in his core.

But he didn't really love Margie. Hadn't he been all through that? He merely wanted her the way he'd seen men want a shot of whiskey.

Quick, in his heart, burning his gut, and then he'd be done with her.

That wasn't right.

Their relationship should have more to it.

He knew that's how it should be. But on nights like tonight, reason escaped him, and all he could think about was her soft, white arms around his neck and her eyes smoldering into his.

He had to stop thinking about her, so he turned his mind to Jean. Purposefully, painfully pulling away from Margie to wonder how Jean was doing. What was she doing right now? Was she warm in bed at the Palmer's house? Was Virgil invading her thoughts the way Margie had invaded his? He hoped -- oh, how he hoped -- she would soon get over that dirty snake Virgil Holcomb. Jean deserved so much better.

He thought about her resolve to go off to Grand Rapids and visit the Palmers. His sister needed a lot of courage to do such a bold thing. He regretted now that he hadn't taken her the whole distance himself. He had been so close. The old trailhead from Point Basse he'd followed to the Black River wasn't even a half day's ride from Grand Rapids, but time had been of the essence. Still, now, he wished he'd taken the time somehow, to see the Palmers and Colette.

Little Colette Palmer. How was she? Her letters to Jean and Annie didn't tell much, yet she was older now. Almost grown up.

Hmm. He'd once told her it was too bad she wasn't older, so he wouldn't have to chase after the likes of Margie Baker. Now the time had come.

Wonder what she's like? His eyelids drifted up and down. *I wonder what little Colette Palmer is doing now.* The stars winked at him, and he finally dozed.

*****

Colette concentrated on the dance steps as Harris Eastman led her in a waltz. It would be awful to make a mistake now. When she danced with Joe, it didn't matter. They made it up as they went along, dancing and tripping and laughing over each other. But even that wasn't going to be the same since what he'd done outside.

Harris didn't fling her around like Joe did. He moved her as effortlessly as if she were a dandelion puff. He didn't laugh or tease or tell funny stories while they danced. He was all very proper and mature. It was different even than when she had danced with some of the timberbeasts at camp number three. It just felt so... adult.

She glanced across the room at Joseph and Helen waltzing about, Helen's pale green dress spinning elegantly, and Joseph's shirt sleeves rolled up, revealing his muscled forearms.

Looking the other direction as she made a turn, she spotted Robin and Jean talking quietly in the corner. She wasn't sure if Jean had danced with anyone else all evening.

"Has the party turned out to your expectations?" Harris' deep voice drew her attention back to him.

"Oh, yes. So much so."

"Good. I'm glad."

"I mostly wanted it for Jean, to make her feel welcome."

"Miss Kade has been here for most of the summer. She must feel quite welcome by now."

"I think so. I wish she could stay all winter, but she'll leave soon. November is no time to be on the lake. She'll have to be across before then."

"You'll miss her."

Colette nodded. Though Harris was only a few inches taller, Colette had to glance up to look at him. He was smiling, his dark eyes sparkling.

"I'm sure she'll miss you too, Lettie. And if my eyes do not deceive me, I believe Miss Kade will be back again soon."

They both looked over to see Robin Gilbert taking Jean by the hand and leading her out into the starlight. Colette let out a little laugh.

"I see what you mean. It would be very nice if you're right."

The music stopped, and they walked toward Helen and Joseph. Colette seldom saw Helen flushed from such exertion and happiness.

"It's been such a fun evening," Helen said.

"So Lettie and I were just saying." Harris took Helen's hand. "It gives me an idea. I have to go to Milwaukee on business in a couple of weeks. I wonder if you ladies would care to come along and do some shopping. You both need new dresses. Helen's told me about Miss Kade's predicament, and I was thinking we can escort her to Fort Howard to catch her boat so she won't have to travel with strangers."

"Really?" Colette said. "That would be wonderful. I'll go find her and tell her."

"It may have to wait until tomorrow," Harris said. "I don't see her anywhere around."

Colette looked about and saw that it was true. Jean and Robin had disappeared. She turned back to see Harris giving her a conspiratorial smile.

"Oh! You're right." Colette laughed. As much as she hated to think of Jean leaving them, the future suddenly seemed filled with possibilities.

Chapter Eleven

Manason uncoiled his legs under the plank table and wiped his chin on the scrap of linen Mrs. Sandowski had handed him to use as a napkin. He didn't have much money to spare these days, but with what little bit of extravagance he'd allowed himself, he decided to leave a portion with this pleasant farmer's wife who'd spread out such a fine breakfast for him. He didn't intend to appear on the Palmer's doorstep looking like some dirty, hungry beggar. The Sandowskis had allowed him the opportunity to clean up, so he'd trimmed his beard and his hair, and washed his clothes out at their pump. He no longer smelled like a logging camp or as if he'd spent the last three months hiking through woods and swamps and up and down the banks of rivers.

Land sakes, if I don't smell human. I might even look it, too.

He left coins on the table so the missus wouldn't protest and went out to saddle his horse. A pack animal, really, but one that put up with him climbing on its back when he had to. He didn't have far to go, and he couldn't wait to see the look on Jean's face when he surprised her.

Manason hoped she hadn't headed home yet, and figured she'd choose to wait out the season if she didn't miss Ma and Pa too much. From what Jean had told him on the trip over from Michigan, he didn't figure a few more months away from the past would really bother her.

He wished now he'd never sent her the letter about travelling on in the first place. He'd been premature thinking he couldn't get down here before the season started. Suddenly a window of time had presented itself.

He would enjoy getting away from woods life for a few days and reconnecting with old acquaintances. He'd been thinking more about it ever since the last night he'd worked so hard to put Margie out of his mind and fallen asleep wondering about Colette.

The princess.

He smiled and chewed on a piece of timothy grass as his horse cantered along in the autumn sunshine. He wondered if Colette even remembered him calling her that. He might just have to refresh her memory. Too bad the cold weather was coming on; otherwise, he'd find a pond to toss her into.

Nah, she's too old for that now. Wouldn't like it anymore, probably.

Hard to tell. Jean and Annie were both putting on airs by that age. Maybe Colette would be, too. He'd just have to take a look and see.

He finally got into Grand Rapids and inquired after the mill of Eldon Palmer just past three o'clock. Wandering down the trail to the mill site, he wondered if Jean and Colette could be behind one of the doors he passed. The smell of pine resin soaking the air and the whine of the saw reminded him of home. He could almost believe time had stood still.

With only a word or two, he located Mr. Palmer. Manason could tell Eldon wondered who this stranger was who was looking for him. Three years had passed, after all. Then, as he drew closer, recognition and a smile settled over Eldon's face.

"Manason Kade! Well, well. Welcome, my boy. Welcome." He pumped Nase's hand and offered him a cup of water. "If you aren't a sight for sore eyes. What brings you our way? Your sister, I bet. Well, if it isn't just a fine thing to see an old familiar face. How's your dad? And Stuart -- is he still running things in my place? My, but you're looking grown."

Manason could do nothing except nod and smile as Eldon laid his long arm across the younger man's shoulders and showered him with inquiries. As one fellow or another walked by on their way to complete a task, Eldon called them over and introduced Nase.

"Yes, sir, ol' Stu's keeping things running for my pa, and everybody's doing well so far as I know," Manason replied.

Eldon snapped his fingers. "Jingo! I bet you haven't even heard the news about your sister up there in the Chippewa country."

"Jean?" Concern twanged at Manason. Eldon brushed it away with his big paws.

"Nah, not Jean. Your sister Annie. Jean received a letter saying Annie's getting married. Bet your ma and pa are pleased as pudding."

So Hank Pratt had finally won Annie's heart. Well, she'd done better than her three older siblings. So had Hank. Nase had to smile at that. *Well done, Hank.*

"No, I hadn't heard. Guess I'm pretty hard to track down these days."

"Oh, there'll be a letter waiting for you somewhere, no doubt. It'll turn up eventually."

"I suppose it will."

"So, everything going okay for you up north? We hear tales of trouble now and then, but we hear there's some mighty good pine up there, too."

"Things are going very well. I've got myself a crew. My pa's backing me on that, of course. But we might be able to skid half a million feet this year if the snow holds out and the ice doesn't let go early."

Eldon let out a whistle. "Mighty fair stakes for a first cut. Mighty fair."

"I can't complain. Course, there are always the unknowns."

Eldon stood with his arms crossed over his flannel-covered barrel chest. He was a thin man, built for endurance. He tapped his foot and nodded thoughtfully.

"You take care up there. Can you count on your crew?"

"Yes, sir."

"Good, good. Got to have that first. Take care of your crew, and they'll take care of you come high tide or the devil."

"Yes, I was fortunate to find them so late in the year."

"God must've been blessing you."

"I can't deny that."

Eldon lifted his hat between his thumb and fore-finger and scratched at his disheveled scalp. Suddenly, he slapped his leg with the hat.

"I'll be -- you've come to see your sister!" He wagged his head as though it were a dismaying thought. "Why, you just missed her. She left with Colette and some friends yesterday. They were taking her to catch the packet over at Fort Howard. It leaves day after tomorrow. Here I am rattling your cage while I should be telling you that first."

Gone? He was too late. And now, not only had he missed Jean, but he'd missed his chance to reacquaint himself with Colette. Energy siphoned out of him. He tried to mask his dismay.

"Oh, I thought I might, since I wrote her and told her I wouldn't be coming. But I had to give it a shot. It's too bad I missed Colette, too."

"Yes, it's too bad. Sorry you had to come all this way."

Manason forced cheer into his voice. "It's not for nothing, though. I needed a break, and this way I get to see you and Mrs. Palmer."

"We have a nice young woman and her little boy with us at the house, too. We'll be glad to have you. Can you stay until Colette and her friends get back?"

"When will that be?"

Eldon admitted it wouldn't be for almost a week, depending on how long Harris Eastman's business kept him in Milwaukee.

Manason shook his head, and his disappointment grew more acute. "I need to head back north before then. Cutting's started. But I'll be happy to stay until Saturday. Maybe I can give you a hand here at the mill."

Eldon slapped him on the back. "And a welcome hand you'll be, son, as ever."

While Eldon brought out his wagon and hitched up the team, Manason looked around the mill yard, all the while berating himself for letting his thoughts grow to such outrageous proportions, and calling himself all kinds of a fool.

*****

Colette thought hard about her feelings and the measure of her disappointment. Finally she'd come to one conclusion. She was not meant to see Manason. Not yet. Maybe not ever.

She stared at the likeness Jean had drawn. "You're only a figment of my imagination," she murmured, "and it's time I let you go." She folded the paper into small squares and tucked it away inside the pages of a book. Then she put the book with several others on a shelf beside her bed and turned away. As though she had been reading his story, and now she had finished. The ending wasn't satisfying, but she couldn't do anything about it except move on. She wouldn't be tormented into focusing on unanswered longings again.

The next morning, she went out into the cold and cleaned the animals' stalls, pitching them fresh bedding, while Rose darned socks by the fireplace and her mother sorted out spoiled potatoes in the root cellar. Then in early afternoon, she walked into town to see Helen and was surprised to find Harris at home.

"Well, Lettie, I'd assumed you'd be tired of us by now. Come inside. Helen's in the sitting room."

Colette flushed. "I'll never tire of the two of you. I'm sorry to intrude, though. I didn't think you were home."

"I've already been upriver and back since our trip."

Colette took off her scarf. "That was fast. How did it go?"

"I had to let Mr. Woolly go."

"Mr. Woolly?"

"Yes. Unreliable chap. But don't be disheartened -- I've found a replacement."

She nodded in understanding. "I won't stay long. I just want to say hello to Helen."

"Nonsense. Stay as long as you like. I'm afraid we've gotten so used to having you with us, we find it much too quiet now that we're home alone."

Colette found Helen in the next room.

"I've missed you, Lettie." Helen rose to give her a hug.

"So Harris just said."

"Oh?"

"It's kind of you both to say so. I wondered if you've heard the news."

"News?" Helen sat and picked up her embroidery. Colette moved over to the fireplace to add a piece of wood to the small blaze.

She spoke with her back to Helen. "Yes. Manason Kade came to call while we were away. He just missed Jean."

"What a shame."

Colette turned and looked at her. "I knew you'd hear, and I was afraid you'd worry about me. I just wanted to let you know that it's okay. I'm over my infatuation with him."

Helen gave her a warm smile. "If you are, and you're glad about it, then I'm glad, too. He didn't leave a message for you or anything?"

She shook her head. "No, just he was sorry he missed us. I guess I'm old enough now to be mature about the whole thing. You won't hear me talking so foolishly about him again."

"Come." Helen patted the sofa next to her. "Sit by me."

Colette came to her side and watched Helen work in companionable silence for a while. Finally, she sighed and rose.

"You're not going so soon, I hope."

Colette shrugged. "I'm restless. Too much to do before, and now too little, I guess."

Helen agreed. "Between planning the party and then going on the trip with Harris, it is a bit hard to slow down and get used to the idea of winter coming." Helen rested her embroidery in her lap and gazed out the window. "Ah, look. It's snowing." Tiny snowflakes spun against the backdrop of trees.

"I thought it might. It's getting cold."

"Yes. I don't know how you stand walking all the way to town."

"I was thinking so hard I didn't really notice."

"About missing Jean's brother?"

Colette nodded. "But now I'm thinking there's a certain letter I need to write."

"Not to Jean?"

"No. To Joe. I promised him a letter for his birthday."

Helen smiled. "Oh?"

"It's not to be what you're thinking, Helen. Nor what he's thinking, either. If it's time I grew up, then it's time he grew up, too."

"You're planning an official rebuff?"

"I'm planning to make him understand our friendship is important, and I don't want to lose it or waste it."

"I see." Helen went back to her embroidery, her voice old and insightful.

"No, you don't. You think I'm being foolish about Joseph. You think because he's handsome and good to me that I'm making a mistake."

"I'm not the one who's saying so," she said, never lifting her eyes from her work.

"Well, I can see you don't understand."

"I've never been able to understand a man and a woman who are friends. I barely understand it between two people as unlikely as you and my husband. But between two like you and Joe, I find it impossible. In such circumstances, I find that friendship for one is something entirely different for the other."

"You're reading a lot into what Joe thinks."

"Am I? I've watched him, too. Enough to know he loves you."

"What Joe loves and what Joe wants are hard to discern. He's selfish, you know. Or didn't you know that about Joe? Sure, he's all sorts of fun, but he's self-centered to the core. Maybe he thinks he loves me, as far as Joe loves anything."

"You're being hard on him, don't you think? Do you need to be so hard?"

Colette flashed at Helen. "Why are you defending him?"

"I'm not defending him, Lettie. I'm trying to help you see whether or not you feel more for him than you think you do. Your emotions have been in a turmoil since we've gotten back."

Colette couldn't argue with that. She paced the room, her arms folded across her chest. Why did life contain these entanglements? Why couldn't God just send someone, the perfect someone, so she'd know for sure and would never have to deal with these questions or worry about hurting a friend?

"I'm sorry I raised my voice," she said. "I think I'll just go home." She forced a laugh. "Maybe more cold air will be good for my head."

Her body grew warm from walking, but her fingertips were numb by the time she arrived home to find her mother and Rose at the cook stove and little George upon his stool eating the mush in his bowl.

"Colette, I'm glad you made it home early." Mama helped her out of her coat. "I was afraid you'd get caught in a storm."

"It's really coming down in a fury." Colette dabbed a clean cloth at the baby's gooey cheeks and then kissed the top of his head.

"Supper won't be ready for another thirty minutes or so. Why don't you pull a chair up by the stove and get warm?"

Colette hesitated. "I'm fine. I think I'll just go to my room and write a letter or two before supper."

"It'll be chilly in there. You'd better leave the door open to let some heat in."

"I will," she said, but in the end she didn't. She closed herself off and cocooned herself in a thick wool blanket as she pondered over the sheet of paper. She was getting low on the small stack of sheaves her father had gotten her last year, so she could not afford any mistakes.

Dear Joe,

I wish you the most wonderful birthday ever. I know you're smiling; you always are. I'm sorry I can't add to the birthday greeting you asked me to give you. You truly are my best friend, and I wouldn't want to lose that for the world. But I cannot be your girl, not in the sense you've asked me to be. I'll be your girl in every other way. Can you understand? I've done a lot of growing up lately, Joe, and I'm going to tell you a secret. I've had someone else in my heart for a very long time, longer than I've known you. Just lately I've grown up enough to realize there will never be anything between that someone and me. It's been hard to accept. I need time to get over these silly feelings. Please don't laugh at me for having them, and don't be mad. I think I'll know now when I've met the right man and it's the right time. I've asked God to make it obvious to me. Can you understand all I'm saying, Joe? Will you forgive me for not sending the words you wanted me to send?

Winter's only just begun, and I can't wait to see you in the spring. We can go fishing and swimming like we used to. We'll do those things again, won't we? We'll always be...

The best of friends,
Your Lettie

Chapter Twelve

The snow settled soft and mushy beneath the bright January sun. A perfect winter's day. Helen wore a simple pale blue gingham dress, with her tresses coiled up in loops atop her head. She looked queenly, nonetheless, as she served the women tea and cakes. Her color was high for mid-winter, and Colette supposed the excitement of having company had made her so beautiful, if she could possibly be more so today than any other time.

Colette read to the four women who had gathered at the Eastman's. The paper she'd found was already weeks old and carried news of ongoing unrest and savage frontier fights in the republic of Texas, a situation that seemed an eternity apart from them here in the woods of Wisconsin Territory. The story was accompanied by an editorial expressing the ideals of "manifest destiny". On another page was an article about a missionary gentleman named Marcus Whitman who'd successfully lead the first "Great Migration" to the west, guiding a wagon train of a thousand pioneers up the Oregon Trail. Included in the story was a brief biography of Marcus and Narcissa Whitman during their time as missionaries among the Cayuse Indians in Oregon, and of the tragic drowning of their two year-old daughter several years past. The women breathed a collective sigh at the sadness of it.

"Well, that is indeed news," Helen said after Collette closed the paper. "But I have some news of my own I'd like to share with you all." Her eyes glittered, and the sadness they'd felt over the Whitman child evaporated into anticipation over Helen's announcement.

"It is now a certainty, as Mrs. Stowe can tell you, that Harris and I are expecting a child near the end of summer."

After a moment of stunned stillness, Lavinia and Rose jumped up to hug Helen. A tingle of both delight and dread convulsed through Colette. She couldn't help but remember Helen telling her she'd miscarried on three previous occasions, but she followed the others into the foray of well wishing just the same. Helen couldn't be very far along; she didn't show at all.

"I feel confident we have truly been blessed this time," Helen said, as though she could read Colette's thoughts. "I've never made it a full three months before. This time I have, and I feel wonderful."

"I'm so glad," Colette whispered, leaning close to Helen's ear as she squeezed her tight.

"I couldn't wait to tell all of you. You should have seen Harris when I told him. He was so thrilled. I think he was afraid it might never happen again. But both of us feel sure this time we will see our little one in our arms. Of course, Harris is certain it will be a boy."

Lavinia chuckled. "Men always think so."

Indeed, Harris walked with a lighter step in the following weeks. As Helen's belly rounded and grew, so did the light in Harris' eyes. Once, when passing Colette on the doorstep of his house, he picked her up and spun her around on his way to get into the house to see how Helen was feeling.

Helen's own glow could not be denied. She basked as much in her husband's delight as in her own. Colette had never seen such love between them before.

In April, water rushed down the river, bringing with it a careening, jumbled mass of logs to the mills and the men to their homes. April brought Joe.

He'd never sent a reply to Colette's letter. But when he knocked on her door and she stepped out to meet him, a warm smile quickly melted over his face, and she knew everything was okay. He whistled to Dandy and took her hand, turning with her to walk beneath the trees.

"So you're not my girl, but you are my girl. Do I have that right?"

She grinned. "I think so."

"I see. Any luck getting *Mr. Someone* out of your mind?"

"Some."

"Then there's hope." His smile clutched her heart.

She couldn't help but lean into his shoulder affectionately. "Glad you're not mad at me."

He stopped, dropped her hand, and faced her. He opened his mouth to speak but then closed it again, turned away, and resumed walking.

"So what else is new?" he asked, seeming to deliberately change the subject. He bent to pick up a stick and threw it for Dandy. The dog charged after it.

"Did you know Helen and Harris are expecting a baby?"

"I might have heard something about that."

"I'm so excited for them."

"Women and babies. What's to be excited about? They're messy and time consuming."

"You won't always think so."

"I won't?" He glanced sidelong at her.

"You know what I mean." Now she changed subjects. "How was it this winter?"

"Same. Long. I did pretty well, though. Matter of fact, I've got some money burning a hole in my pocket right now. So might I take the fair Miss Lettie into Mr. Kromer's General Store to buy her a present?"

"You may," she said with a smile. "A not-too-expensive present, anyway."

"You let the Eastmans buy you expensive presents."

"That's different."

"Is it?"

"Harris and my father are partners, and Helen's my friend."

"And you're mine, as you so kindly pointed out in your letter. It's not as though I'm your beau buying you expensive gew gaws now, is it?"

Colette flushed, then looked him boldly in the eye. "All right, Mr. Moneybags. Let's go."

On the long walk to town and Mr. Kromer's General Store, they talked about easier things and what they'd do with the summer ahead. "I would buy you a new fishing pole, but I don't want you to have an unfair advantage," Joe said, eyeing a couple of cane poles in a barrel as they came through the door.

"You could buy one for yourself."

"Nah. I'm looking for something different."

"Here are some nice wool socks. I could use those. Mine are kind of worn, and you know how I don't like mending or knitting."

"Aren't all women supposed to like knitting? My mother does it for fun."

"Not me. Ask my mother or Helen or Rose. I don't have the patience for it."

"Well, no socks today."

"Paper, then? I hardly have any left."

"Nope. I don't need any more disheartening letters from you. Ah -- there we are. Just the sort of thing I had in mind."

Colette turned to see what had caught Joe's fancy. He stood off to one side, fingering a blue silk shawl fit for a princess. She'd seen the shawl in the store weeks ago. It wasn't the sort of item most loggers' or farmers' wives could afford, nor would they have a place to wear it.

"Not that, Joe. It's too expensive, and I've no place to wear it."

"It would look pretty with your yellow dress." His voice was subdued, almost mesmerized.

"No, Joe. It's too nice."

"No, it isn't. It's perfect." He took it off the stand and laid it against her shoulders.

"I think you should put it back."

"I think you should put it on." He pulled it around her just as the door flew open and Harris Eastman burst into the store.

"Lettie!" His voice came out in a quick rush of breath. "You need to come quickly. Your father's been hurt. He's at home with your mother."

Colette blanched, and her hands fell to her sides. Joseph drew back the garment.

"Come. I'll get you there quickly."

She hardly cast a glance at Joe, but hurried out of the store after Harris. He lifted her onto his horse and flung himself into the saddle behind her. They tore off down the road and onto the tree-shadowed trail toward home.

Colette's heart pounded hard against Harris, drumming in time with the horse's hooves as they sped on. He'd seen the fear in her eyes when he'd put her on the horse, too much fear to ask what had happened. How could he tell her the devastating truth? At the moment, he simply wanted to shelter her with his strength and speed their flight home.

Eventually the trail narrowed and they had to slow down, for the horse's safety if not their own.

He had to tell her. "You know the boys have been building a dam downriver."

Colette nodded.

"They were dynamiting boulders in a spot that's been giving us trouble all along. The trees snag up on it." Harris would never tell it like this to Helen. He wouldn't bother to explain the details of why they were dynamiting, or the problems the men had faced time and time again. Colette, however, would want to know. She would understand. "You know... the place where we had the big jam last month."

She nodded again. "Papa got hurt in a dynamiting accident?" Her voice sounded small and forlorn.

"I'm afraid so."

"H-how bad is it?"

"Well..." He didn't want to say, but further delay would strike more fear in her heart. "He's lost a leg, Lettie."

Her hand flew to her mouth and her shoulders convulsed in a sob. He wished he were able to comfort her, but he could do nothing.

"I'm sorry. We'll do everything we can to help him." He tightened his arms around her, gripped the reins, and nudged the horse back into a trot down the lane.

Colette's father had fainted in agony by the time they arrived, but groans escaped his lips as he came around again. Lavinia's face was ashen. Men moved about the room with bandages that looked as if they came from someone's old petticoats. Rose rinsed blood-soaked rags in a tub of scalding water and took them to Lavinia and the others, returning with another sodden batch to wash.

Harris tapped Lavinia's shoulder and drew her aside. Reaching into his breast pocket, he withdrew some forms. "Some time ago, I purchased these vouchers from a physician in Milwaukee. I'd like Eldon to use them; he can get the care he needs."

Lavinia's eyes filled with tears. "Oh, Harris."

He drew her into his arms and shushed her. "I know it's hard to think right now, but we have to get him out of here as soon as he can be moved. The sooner we get him proper care, the better his chances of surviving."

Lavinia sobbed, and Harris held her tight. She was a strong woman, making it easy for him to see where Colette got her determination.

"I don't know what we'll do."

Harris recognized the words of a woman torn with distress. "Everything will work out. Trust me. I know people in Milwaukee. I can contact them and help you find lodging. Money is not a problem. You know that, don't you?"

"But his days in the woods and mills are over."

"Perhaps. Perhaps not. We'll talk about that later. For now, let's figure out how to get Eldon to a place where he can see a doctor. A surgeon, even."

Lavinia nodded and laid her head against his shoulder, weeping softly.

*****

By evening the bleeding had been stanched and Eldon rested, but with a small fever. Colette handed rags to Rose and knelt on the floor beside her father. She dropped her forehead to the bed and closed her eyes.

She hadn't shed another tear since her initial shock at Harris' explanation of the accident, but her body was depleted. Half an hour later, as the moon rose into the night sky, she left the cabin and found her way through the thickets to the river. She spilled her heart as moonlight played across currents.

"Please let Pa survive this, God. If you can see us and understand our pain, then please spare my pa."

"Lettie?"

She turned sharply, hardly recognizing Joseph's voice, then relaxing at the sight of him.

"How is he?"

She shrugged. "He's bad, Joe. His leg..." Colette hung her head. "Why would God allow such a thing?"

"You're shivering." He walked up beside her and gently wrapped the blue shawl around her shoulders.

"Oh, Joseph."

"What will your mother do?" His voice was soft, muted in the night shadows as though they were alone in a room with only breathing space between them.

"I don't know. Harris says there's a doctor in Milwaukee. She wants to take him there."

"You'll be going, too, I suppose."

"Oh, Joe, I don't know. I suppose so." He put his arm around her, and she rested her head on his shoulder. "I don't know what's going to happen."

"Lettie, I don't want you to leave. I know it's selfish of me. I know your father needs you, and your mother probably more so, but I don't want you to go." He stroked her hair, drawing it back behind her ears. She hadn't had it down in a while. She wore it up like a grown woman these days. "You must be tired."

Colette nodded.

"I'm just so sorry about your pa."

She looked into the green cushion of his eyes. They'd never looked so soft and warm before. Gone was the sparkle of mischief, and in its place was a reflection of her grief. Tears pooled in her eyes again, and Joseph became a blur.

"Shh," he murmured, kissing her forehead. "It's all right."

His lips on her skin cooled her fevered thoughts. The tension and sorrow within her loosened, gave way.

"It'll be okay," he whispered again.

The moon outlined his face and broad shoulders, and she sank into their succor. Slowly she turned her face upward, even as he lowered his lips to meet hers.

The kiss was everything she'd ever thought it should be, especially her first kiss. Not like the stolen peck Joe had challenged her with last fall. This was a real kiss, and Joe deepened it.

"I don't know what I feel, Joe," she murmured as he drew back.

"I hope you figure it out soon, because I'm pretty sure it's the same thing I feel for you."

"I can't be sure. I want to be sure."

"I want that, too," he said, and he drew her lips to his again.

Chapter Thirteen

Manason stood by the gate out on the street, gazing up at his parents' home. A rush of memories assailed him, reminders of the good things he'd left behind. A soft May breeze washed up the hill, carrying with it the wispy scents of damp earth turned to plow in small garden patches, and wet pine dust soaking up a spring rain from earlier in the day. In the next instant, the scent of warm pie wafted from an open window.

An unexpectedly shrill voice pierced the calm, "Nase! Is that you?" Nase looked up to see the shadowy form of Annie calling down to him from a window in the turret room.

"It is," he called, "so come on out and bring me some of that pie I smell cooling in the kitchen."

The window slammed down and, moments later, all three Kade women poured out of the house, with Annie in the lead. She ran down the steps and threw her arms around him. "This might be your only chance to kiss a married woman."

"That's what I came for." Nase returned her hug and kissed her soundly on the cheek. "I see Mr. Pratt must be working on your temperament, sister. I'll be sure and thank him when I see him."

"You don't have to give him credit. He takes too much as it is. Did you see our house up the street when you came into town?"

"No, I came from the other direction. I'll go see the grand Pratt castle as soon as I get settled."

"Welcome home, Nase," Jean said, giving him a more decorous embrace. "It's so good to see you."

"I'm sorry I missed you in the fall." He squeezed her tight. "I've been feeling bad about that all winter."

"It worked out. Besides, it gave me more time with Colette. She and the Eastmans took me to Fort Howard to catch my boat."

"So I found out when I got to Grand Rapids."

"You went there?"

He nodded, still holding her in his embrace.

Jean leaned back, beaming. "Then you got to visit the Palmers and Colette. How happy she must have been."

"No, I missed Colette. I arrived while you were gone."

Her face clouded. "That's a shame. I know she's sorry to have missed you."

"Are you two going to keep talking about Wisconsin, or are you going to hug your mother, too?"

Nase released Jean and hurried up the steps to the gray-haired woman smiling at him with luminous eyes. She smelled of sweet softness and golden warmth and baked things. Her wet cheek met his, and he held her in his arms for a long moment.

"You've come back to us."

"I'm sorry it took so long, Ma."

"It couldn't be helped," she whispered, patting his shoulders as he straightened.

"Ma, you're beautiful."

She slapped his arm. "You sound like you want some pie."

"I just want to look at you." He took her arm and let her lead him into the house.

Later that evening, his father and Stuart came home and continued the joyful reunion. Hank and Annie came to the house after supper, and Manason had the opportunity to congratulate his new brother-in-law on winning his tempestuous sister.

"I thought it well worth the effort," Hank said with a glance toward his new wife that earned him a promising smile.

"Well, here's to effort." Manason raised a glass of cider in their honor.

"It was a beautiful wedding," Manason's mother, Eleanor, said.

His father winked. "She was a beautiful bride."

"I had my work cut out for me on that mark, didn't I, Pa?" Annie cut in.

"Well, two pretty girls marrying in a fortnight in a small town like this..."

"Gray!" Eleanor admonished. "Are you saying someone else can hold a candle to our Annie?"

Grayson Kade chuckled. "Now, Ellie, you know Annie likes a good challenge."

"Two girls?" Manason glanced between his parents.

Jean looked over at him and said softly, "Margie Baker married Mitch Donnelson a week after Annie married Hank."

"Guess she got tired of waiting for you, brother," Stuart said with a forced laugh. "When you didn't come back for Annie's big shindig like Margie expected, she must've got it in her head to get on with her life without you."

"Stu," Jean said. "Really."

"It's all right." Nase gave a shrug of indifference. "The girl's got a right to live her life."

"Still, that's no way to hear about it."

"It's okay, Jean. Nase can take it," Stuart said.

"Course he can," Annie piped. "He knew it was coming. I told him so last year."

"Actually, I believe you told me just the opposite. But that's all right. Don't worry about me," Manason said, clearly seeing that although everyone said they thought he could take it, that wasn't the message coming from their eyes. *They all feel sorry for me. They're afraid I'm going to cry over Margie Baker,* Not wanting them to dwell on it, he hurried on to a different subject. "So what else is new?"

Stuart cleared his throat. "Pa and I are thinking on expanding the mill."

"Thinking on it?" Grayson said. "We're going to do it. It's no secret; we've had a very good year. Our cut was nearly two million feet."

Manason let out a whistle. "That's big stakes."

"How about you, son? Tell us all about your year in the Territory."

"Well, I had a bit of a late start, as you know, but I had an earnest working crew. They got the job done. I'm planning on doing more next year. I've put in for another section of stumpage farther up the Chippewa, and right now there's a fellow working on getting me another crew. It should go pretty well, except for one thing."

"What's that?" asked Jean.

"I've had a little trouble with a ruffian named Boggs. Some of my men came from his outfit, and he's tried to make trouble. Not because of the men, though. He wants to keep me out of that piece of timber, close to Indian land. My theory is that he's snaking cuts off that land illegally and putting his mark on other men's logs, but I haven't been able to prove it."

"That can be a dangerous game, son. Watch yourself."

"Boggs is a heavy who works for someone else, I suspect."

"I know the type," Stu said. "Wish I could do something to help you."

Hank leaned forward. "Sounds like the sort of action I'd like to be in on, too."

"Oh no, you don't, Mr. Pratt," Annie said. "I won't let you get any ideas in your head about going off to that godforsaken country. We just built a new house, and you're going to stay right here in it with me. Stu's got all the work you need to keep you busy."

"And Annie will provide the action." Stu laughed, and they all joined in.

Sunday morning, Manason was relieved to see that Margie and her new husband were not in church. He knew it wasn't a gracious thought, but it was the truth. He wasn't up to facing one of her scornful smiles while she flaunted her new husband in his face. Still, he wasn't completely off the hook. On Monday he went into the company store for his mother and almost ran smack into Margie while she was carrying a pile of packages out the door. One of the packages slipped from her grasp and Manason bent to catch it before it hit the ground.

"Oh, Nase!" she said, surprise fleeting through her wide green eyes. In only seconds, however, she regained her composure. "Why… when did you get home?"

"Only a couple days ago. May I help you with those?" She was about to drop another package.

"Yes, thank you."

Manason took the three largest packages and left her to carry a small one she could easily carry by hooking her finger through the string on the wrapping.

"Where would you like them?" he asked, peering out on the street for a wagon or some other conveyance.

"Would you mind? I just live around back. Over the store, actually, in that little pair of rooms. I don't usually buy so much at once." She laughed, leading him around the side of the building. "But I just got back from -- out of town," she said, her words catching, "and I'm out of everything."

"You must be." He followed her up a narrow flight of steep steps to a slim door.

Margie opened the door and stepped inside, moving out of the way to allow him to carry the load of packages inside. She closed the door.

"You can set them over there on the bed."

Manason dropped them on the new, hand-stitched quilt. *You little spider,* he thought. But when he dropped the bundle of goods and turned to face her, she looked almost sheepish.

"That do?"

"Mm-hm." She nodded. "It's good to see you again, Nase. Oh..." Her hands fluttered, and she moved to the cook stove that still emanated heat from the morning's breakfast. "May I get you some coffee or something?"

"No, thanks, I drank half a pot at Ma's this morning."

"Nase, I..." She turned to face him and took a hesitant step in his direction. "I don't know if you've heard..."

"I heard."

"Oh."

Suddenly she rushed toward him, only to stop short inches away. She lifted one long, tapered hand and glided it down the front of his shirt. "It doesn't matter, Nase."

Shock momentarily took his tongue and immobilized his thoughts.

In his moment of stunned silence, she moved closer. "I mean, me marrying Mitch, well... it doesn't have to change anything." The warmth of her breath bathed his cheek as she leaned in closer still, and he nearly lifted his arms around her. Then his mind awoke like water dowsing a flame, and the fire running up his flesh turned cold. He braced his hands against her arms and stepped back.

"It's not the same, Margie, and we both know it."

"Are you sure?"

Her sheepishness had disappeared. The Margie who'd been surprised to see him and was maybe even a little bit ashamed at having made a spitefully quick marriage to Mitch had been replaced by the Margie Nase remembered best. The hot-blooded, quick-tempered seductress who'd always claimed to love him, and was now freely offering herself to him, despite belonging to someone else.

"Don't you love your husband?" Nase asked, reminding her who she was.

"Love Mitch? He's been a dear. He took me to Detroit for a wedding trip. Spent every cent he'd saved. That's why we're living in this little room now that we rent from your father and Stu." She laughed. "I guess you could say we're renting it from you. That makes you the landlord, and everything here is yours..." Her green eyes pulled at him, and he fought everything inside himself to keep from giving in to them.

"I have to go," he said at last, not trusting his voice. "I've got work to do. Stu's waiting for me."

Moving around her, he headed for the door.

"Will you be in town long?"

"A month, maybe," he said, his hand on the door latch.

"Maybe you can come by and see us while you're here, and stay longer."

Nase didn't answer, and he dared not look back. He went outside and clicked the door shut behind him.

The sun was bright and warm and penetrated his skull, waking him from the drowsy drug of Margie. *Margie Donnelson*, he reminded himself. He could never feel for her what he once thought he might, but that didn't make the battle against her allure any less difficult. Good thing he had plenty of work to do with Stu at the mill. He needed to keep his mind full and busy.

"Where've you been?" Stu asked when he arrived. "You finished breakfast an hour ago. Did you stop at the store for Ma?"

"No, I forgot." Manason slapped his thigh. "Guess I got a little sidetracked, being back and all."

"No problem. We can run by and pick up her things later."

Stu went on talking about his plans and the work he and Grayson hoped Nase would help them with over the next few weeks, but Manason's mind kept going back to his encounter with Margie. *A month.* A month to have to keep his distance. Then he'd go back to Wisconsin and forget about her once and for all.

*****

That month passed slower than a sub-zero winter. Since their return from their honeymoon, the Donnelsons had been given to regular church attendance, and Manason feared the open looks of longing Margie turned his way in their place of worship would be noticed by all. He studiously avoided running into her in town, which was difficult given their close proximity and the fact she was likely hunting him.

Mitch was oblivious. He believed in his role as Margie's champion and was always friendly toward Manason, even if he did have a condescending spirit.

Toward the end of June, Manason made plans to head west.

"I hope you won't go until after the Independence Day holiday," Jean said.

"Why's that? My old friend Tom Durant is in town. He'll be here to dance with you. Can't wait, as a matter of fact."

"I wish you'd stop that." Jean blushed and slapped his arm. "Really,

Nase, I want you to stay a while longer."

"I can't much. Why's it so important anyway? It's just another picnic."

Jean walked over to look out of the window of Manason's bedroom. "Because there's someone coming I want you to meet."

Manason stopped fishing through his dresser and turned sharply at her words. "Who?"

Her gray-blue eyes glistened, and a flush spread down her throat when she turned to him.

"Jean?" His voice and broke into a laugh. "*Jean?* Who's coming?"

Jean reached into the pocket of her apron, pulled out a letter, and stared at it. "His name is Rob. I met him last summer."

"And he's coming here to see you?"

"To see me and meet my family. I think he's going to ask me to marry him. He's serious, Nase. Not like Virgil. He means it."

"And this makes you happy?" His smile warmed even more.

She nodded. "Very happy. He's a fine man."

Manason stepped over to Jean and touched her arm. "Of course I'll stay for the Independence Day holiday. I'd be happy to meet Rob."

*****

Robin Gilbert arrived on the second of July, and right up to the moment of the holiday, Manason's sisters kept Manason, Rob, Stu, and Hank busy carrying things here and there, setting up tables, hanging banners, devising games for the children, and whatever else they could dream up. Annie had Hank practicing his guitar whenever she could spare him elsewhere, certain he'd be called upon to lend music to the festivities.

Manason was sure the fireworks going off for Jean this year had to do with Rob Gilbert. Watching Rob court Jean filled Manason with a special warmth he had never experienced. He hadn't been around during Annie's courtship. This time with Rob courting Jean was different from the time with Virgil, or maybe Nase was just older and understood it better. Whatever the reason, he was glad of it, yet it left an ache inside him as well.

"So I see I probably won't get much chance to dance with your sister tonight."

Manason recognized Tom Durant's voice behind him and spun around. "Tom!"

"Hello, Manason. So you've come back to Michigan for a spell?"

"Been here since the end of May, but I'm going back in a couple of days. I can't run my company if I stay away too long."

"Your brother Stuart tells me you've had a little trouble."

"Nothing much. Some bully-boys trying to push us around, that's all."

"Any idea who the money muscle is behind 'em?"

Manason shook his head. "None. Not yet, anyway."

"Sure would like to have a look over there."

Manason's gaze narrowed. "You offering?"

A grin split Tom's face. "If you're looking for some extra help. You're dad isn't planning any new cruising this season. He's got enough timber lined up to keep him busy for the next three or four seasons."

"He's expanding at the mill."

"So I hear. What do you say?"

Manason stuck out his hand. "How about, 'welcome to Wisconsin Territory'?"

After a lunch of cold fried chicken, the three brothers-in-law joined in the three-legged races and arm wrestling matches. When the final wrestling match came down to Nase and Mitch Donnelson, a crowd gathered. For a moment, Manason thought about throwing the match, just to have it done with, but his innate competitiveness got the better of him until the two of them were locked chin to chin, sweat dripping down their furrowed brows, jaws clamped tight, their hands gripped square and solid in a deadlock.

"Come on, Nase. You can do it!" Annie cheered.

"Come on! Come on!"

"Take him Mitch!" Jack Sprague yelled in a gravelly voice.

"Put him down, Manason!"

"It'll be a draw."

"No, I think Mitch has him."

"There you go, Nase!"

"Don't give up, Mitch!"

Mitch's cheeks, red against the white blond of his hair, puffed in exertion, but strength surged through Manason pushing Mitch to the point of no return. With one final thrust, Manason settled the match. As cheers and guffaws rose from the crowd, Mitch released a deep breath and leaned back. Stu and Hank slapped Manason on the back.

"You'll do well in Wisconsin Territory," Rob said, stepping forward and shaking his hand.

"Thanks. Good match, Mitch," Manason said.

"Same to you. I'd like another try at it again sometime."

Nase nodded. "How about we get something cold to drink?"

He and Mitch rose wearily and made their way to a table of refreshments where they each let long slugs of lemonade slide down their throats. Manason took another glassful and excused himself from the group gathered around the table. Walking away from the crowd, he made his way toward the river that wound its way along the festival's park-like setting.

The day was hot. A good day. The water called to him, and he was tempted to leap into it. He thought about how fun it would be to have one more swim in the mill pond with his brother and sisters before he left them all for another long time, perhaps years. Realistically, his days of swimming in the mill pond were over. Annie was a grown woman now with a husband to think about. Before he knew it, she would probably have children. Jean and Rob would be next. Even Stu was behaving toward Ida Johnson, the new school teacher, in a way Manason had never seen him behave toward a young woman before, as though his interest went beyond casual perusal.

He strolled along the bank and sipped on his thoughts like his drink. Up the way another hundred yards, a group of young boys were fishing. In the other direction, several school age girls were having their own picnic under a cluster of shady trees slung over the bank.

This place was home, but his future lay in the great expanse of forest to the west. He was ambitious and ready to build on that future. That's what he had to focus on now.

"Lost in your thoughts, Nase?" Manason turned at the golden honey sound of Margie's voice. She sidled up beside him. "Willing to share?"

She gazed out over the water when he looked at her, her own glass of lemonade pressed against the small "v" opening at the throat of her dress.

He looked away. "Warm day. Perfect for the fourth."

"Mmm."

"Enjoying the festival?"

"It's all right. I hear you won the arm wrestling match against Mitch."

"He could've beaten me if he'd held on a little longer."

"You always beat Mitch at everything." Her voice had taken on a purposeful edge. Suddenly she slipped her hand into his. "I can't let you go, Nase. You understand that, don't you? You don't want to let go of me, either."

The sweet softness of her silky fingers entwining with his sent his senses reeling. Slowly he withdrew his hand, torn in wonder between her brazenness and the physical attraction that held him fascinated.

"Why are you doing this, Margie? Why now? Why not let it end like it should have? Like it did."

"I told you why."

"You're playing games."

"Not this time, Nase." She stiffened for a moment, then put her hand on his arm. "The truth is that I love you. I've always loved you. That hasn't changed with Mitch. I don't know why I married him." She shrugged. "I'm just a fool, I guess."

"The point is, you married him. You belong with him, not me."

"Don't say that, Nase. *Don't*. I belong to you. I always will."

"I never loved you, Margie." Manason knew his words stung. Her hand dropped away, and she stepped back.

"You're lying."

"I never loved you. I know that now. I don't think I've really understood anything about love until lately. We could never have the sort of thing my folks have, or what Annie and Hank have. And Jean."

"You're only saying that to be noble. You want to do the right thing for Mitch's sake."

He shook his head. "No, Margie. It's for your sake, and mine. You have to make what you can of your marriage. If there's nobility anywhere, it's going to have to be with you."

"Nase!" she cried, her voice bitter and tearful. She flung herself at him and held onto him. Nase kept his arms stiff at his sides, though he desperately wanted to put them around her. "I won't believe it. I don't believe it! I know you want me. I know you feel it right now -- the need to hold me. Do it Nase. No one will know. No one who matters. Hold me..."

Closing his eyes, he stayed as he was until she pushed away from him and fled, tiny, angry sobs ripping at her throat as she stormed away.

Chapter Fourteen

Manason stood by the river letting the minutes roll by. How could he go on fighting her? How could he get the hot blood of Margie *Donnelson* out of his system? He hadn't lied to her, not for a minute. But that didn't make fighting his desire for her any less difficult. *She's Mitch's wife,* he reminded himself. *No question about what's right. The only the question is about how to keep my hands off her.*

When he finally got the strength to look back again, his eyes fell on Jean standing a ways off, watching him. Sighing deeply, he walked toward her, and she met him half way.

"Where's Rob?" he asked, trying for nonchalance.

"Doing the three-legged race with Hank. I saw what happened, Nase."

Manason had a hard time meeting her hard gaze.

"You have to stay away from her. She's poison. Do you see that?"

"Of course I do." His control stretched to the boiling point.

"She'll chew you to pieces and ruin another man's life besides. Aw, Nase. I'm sorry now that I made you stay."

"You didn't make me stay. I wanted to stay. I wanted to meet Rob. Maybe I wanted this to happen, too, only I couldn't admit it to myself."

"Nason," Jean stepped closer and spoke softly, "I'm going to make a suggestion, and I don't know what you'll say, but I'm going to make it. You know I'm not the type of girl who goes around match-making. I never liked it when people tried it with me, so it's not a practice I make. But you need to see someone, Nase. Someone you need to be re-introduced to."

The intensity in Jean's dark eyes pulled at him. Jean wasn't a frivolous, giddy woman, but a serious one. "Re-introduced?"

"When you get back to Wisconsin, I want you to visit Colette Palmer. I want you to see her again. It goes without saying that when you do, it won't be hard to see that she's a woman now. She's changed."

Colette Palmer. She was the last person on earth he expected to hear Jean mention. Then again, she and Colette had spent most of last summer together.

"Little Colette?"

"No, Manason. Beautiful, grown up Colette. She's not like Margie. In fact, I don't even think she knows how pretty she is."

"I've said the same thing about you."

"You have, and that's nice. I don't want you to change the subject, though. Colette is so much more than Margie could ever be, Nase. She's not only lovely and charming, she's also got a good head on her shoulders. She's knows her father's business inside and out. She's going to make a wife an ambitious man will be proud of."

"It's hard for me to imagine Colette as anyone's wife."

"Go see her. Then you will. And I'm going to say one more thing, though saying it makes me feel like I'm betraying a confidence."

"What is that?"

"Colette hasn't forgotten you, little brother."

Manason's attention riveted in more closely. "What do you mean?"

"We're all idiots when it comes to the heart. I was an idiot for Virgil, and now I'm a glad idiot for Robbie. You've been an idiot for Margie, and I hope you're over it. The truth is that Colette's been an idiot for you, I think. In fact we've all been idiots not to see what you've meant to Colette. She may have had only a little girl's crush, but it's held. She still cares for you."

"I think you've imagined that. A woman's fancy."

Jean shook her head and her eyes held steady. "No. The woods are full of men in Wisconsin, and the ones who meet Colette take sharp notice of her. But there were things, not so much what she said, but how she said them that made me know. You're the one in her thoughts."

"After all this time?"

Jean nodded. "Will you go see her?"

Manason thought hard for a minute. Could Jean be right? Colette Palmer, all grown up... But what of it? So she had grown up with endearing thoughts of Manason. That didn't mean he wouldn't burst them all to pieces when she saw him through the eyes of a grown woman. He was nothing special, just another lumberman. Just another fellow who'd come to look her over as, no doubt, lots of others around Grand Rapids did.

Still, what if Jean was right? What if the sparks of their old childhood friendship could be rekindled? In a flash of moments, a hundred such questions ran through Manason's mind. What would she think of him now? Would she see him as being too old for her? She must be almost eighteen. Would their six year age difference be too much, or would they seem like peers? Had maturity really wrought such differences, as Jean suggested?

"You say she's changed."

"You might not recognize her," Jean said with a smile.

"All right, my wise, all-knowing older sister. I will present myself to the fair princess, Colette."

*****

Tom pulled out of camp and, soon after, Manason doused their breakfast fire and packed up the remnants of his gear. He sucked in deep breaths of summer air as he mounted and rode up the river path on horseback toward the Palmer's house.

The trip to Wisconsin had been uneventful. The weather ran in their favor and the trip up the Pinery Road into the heart of the wilderness was pleasantly free of its usual mire. Only days after getting off the packet on the Fox River, two weeks since their journey began, Nase and Tom camped just a few miles out of Grand Rapids. This morning Tom was headed north to Manason's primary camp, promising to get things in order before Manason's arrival and scout out Seamus Boggs' operation. Manason would follow in a few days, just as soon as he'd seen Colette. As his pack horse ambled along, part of Manason still couldn't believe what he was doing.

Before long, the cabin came into view, quiet and unspoiled. Tall grass grew close to the door, and stillness lay peacefully over the farm. Approaching the door with a gaze at the vacant-looking barn yard, he knocked. When there was no answer, he knocked again, harder. He tried the knob, but the door was bolted. Moving off the stoop, he peered into a dusty window, but saw only empty darkness inside.

He wasn't surprised to find the place deserted. Lots of people moved, and with Eldon Palmer doing as well at the mill as he had been last year when Manason saw him, he might have moved his family into a bigger house somewhere. Besides, the Palmers had that young German gal and her baby staying with them. They might have needed more space. He decided to go to the mill and inquire of them there.

Manason's mind filled with surreal possibilities as he headed toward town. Colette had walked these paths often over the past three years. Wandered beneath the shade of these trees and probably bathed here in the river. What would it be like to see her again? Would she really feel anything beyond brotherhood for him? Could he interest her in something more? Would he be interested in return?

The mill hummed with activity, turning the winter cut into boards, pails, and shingles to be floated on huge rafts downriver. Men worked in the heat of the sun, sweat and sawdust clinging to their arms and necks. Dirt lined the creases of their skin, and their muscles bulged with exertion. A sight Manason knew and loved well.

Approaching the first man who didn't have his hands occupied, Nase introduced himself.

"I'm looking for a family by the name of Palmer. Part owner in this mill. Can you tell me where I might find them, or if Eldon Palmer is here someplace?"

The man picked a dipper out of a bucket and sipped from it. "Hmm... Palmer, you say?" With a back swipe of his hand he wiped a dribble of water off his grizzled chin . "Sorry, friend, you're a little late to find ol' Mr. Palmer around here. He got hurt a while back and had to get himself mended by a doctor in Milwaukee."

"Hurt?"

"Lost his leg in a blast. Sold out the mill to Mr. Bloomer up there in the office."

Manason's heart thumped. "What about his family?"

"They went with him, naturally. Pulled up stakes here in the Rapids. Can't hardly lumber or farm without a leg."

"No, I -- I suppose not."*Eldon lost a leg.* He couldn't imagine anything worse happening to a man's dreams.

"Care for a drink?" the man held the dipper out to Manason.

"No, thank you." Then Manason remembered the letter Jean sent with him. "I have a letter for Mr. Palmer's daughter. Will it reach Harris Eastman if I leave it here? He'll know how to find the family."

"Sure thing."

Manason handed him Jean's travel-worn letter. "Thank you for your help."

"Any time." The man tucked the letter in his overalls and turned back to the pile of lathe he was stacking to dry.

Manason mounted his horse and headed into town, new thoughts exploding through his brain. *Gone. Eldon crippled. That's it, then. I don't have time to go to Milwaukee to see a girl, not with work waiting for me up north. Well, buddy, that's twice you've missed her now. Maybe it's for the better. Maybe that's how it's meant to be.*

The sun had lifted high in the sky, and activity hummed. From the clapboard building down the street., the sound of a hammer rang upon an anvil. An older lady and a boy stepped out of the general store. The strong, acrid stink of a tannery filled the air. Up the hill from the river, only about thirty yards away, a dark-haired man, possibly a few years younger than Manason, helped a young lady into a wagon. The late morning sun picked up tawny highlights in the girl's hair piled in a rich mound on her head, and even from the back she looked like a magazine picture wrapped in a blue silk shawl. Manason watched them long enough to see the young man smile at her and whisper close before he clicked his tongue at the horses. Then the wagon rattled off. Manason watched until they pulled out of sight over the hill.

Colette must not have been the only pretty girl to grace this town, Nase thought, turning his horse toward the nearest trail north.

*****

Joseph dropped Colette at the Eastman's house and declined an invitation to come inside.

"You know it's way too stuffy in there for me. I'm glad you like it enough to stay, though."

"It isn't a matter of liking it, Joe. I'm just grateful it's worked out so well. To know I can do something to help my folks is a relief to me."

"You aren't forgetting how much this means to me, are you Lettie?"

She smiled, glad he was happy, but when he tried to kiss her she pulled back. "Not in front of the house."

"Why not?"

"You know, Joe."

"Why don't we let the whole world know?"

"Know what?"

"How we feel."

"How do I feel, Joe? I still can't say that I know."

"Well, I'd like to convince you, but since you won't even kiss me, I won't start an argument."

"Thank you. Now, I'd better get inside and see if Helen needs anything."

Colette let Joseph help her down off the wagon, and she went inside. Hanging her shawl on a coat hook, she headed into the parlor.

She was thankful an arrangement had been worked out for her parents and herself. After her father's injury, their lives had turned upside down. Joe had made his hope that she stay in town clear enough, but that was beside the point in light of everything else. Helen had talked about how lonely she'd be without Colette during her confinement, and though her pregnancy was progressing normally, Colette worried over Helen's delicate condition.

Yet her biggest compulsion was to be with her parents at their hour of greatest need. In the end, Harris had come upon the idea to pay Colette to stay on as Helen's companion, with most of the money for her help to be sent to the Palmers. He even promised she could keep Dandy, a generous compromise indeed. Rose and little George, who had no place else to go, would move to Milwaukee with Colette's family and help nurse Mr. Palmer in exchange for room and board, just as she'd been doing.

Harris would lease the Palmer's farm as another source of income until Colette was old enough to decide if she wished to live there herself with anyone she might marry, or sell it. Who knew? Perhaps even Eldon and Lavinia might return there some sweet day. At any rate, Harris insisted the cabin was theirs by deed to do with as they wished. Lastly, Harris, Eldon, and Lavinia agreed to sell the mill. The resulting income would take care of them for a long time.

Their leaving had jolted Collette almost as much as the move to Wisconsin. Her maturity made all the difference now, however. She was setting out on her own. Even though she lived with the Eastmans, her true life had begun.

Chapter Fifteen

Harris arrived home from a trip to St. Louis to find Colette kneeling in a small patch of dirt in the front yard, carefully plucking weeds from between rows of beans in her small kitchen garden. He stood at the gate for a few extra minutes watching her work before making his presence known.

She's a good girl, that Lettie. Another reason to come home.

The excitement that tingled in his veins over the future arrival of his child had not waned. Never had Helen seemed more beautiful to him. Now, added to both of those things were lively discourses brought into their evenings with Lettie. She was smart. Harris had to grant he'd never known a woman with a brighter head on her shoulders. In another year or two, when Helen and their child were able, he'd take them all with him on some of his business trips. A beautiful wife and child, and an attractive single woman with brains accompanying them could open doors for Harris. Men were moved by beauty and loveliness, and surprised by wit and intelligence. Women were enthralled by children, and captivated by the thoughts of marrying off other women. Harris himself might even be able to assist in a future marriage arrangement for Lettie to benefit his growing empire. But for now, he simply admired her for the delightful companionship she brought him and Helen.

"Is this how you spend your afternoons while Helen is napping, floundering in the dirt?"

"Hardly floundering, Harris. Growing your next meal."

He chuckled and drew her to her feet. Casually, he swiped at dirt streaked across her nose. "You're a sight."

"Good hard work never hurt anybody, you know. Even Helen likes it."

"Yes, well, when you've a husband, you might take him into consideration. He might like to see you looking your best when he comes home at night."

"So my mother taught me. It is funny to hear it from you," she answered with a smirk.

"Indeed, I suppose it is. Oh, before I forget--" Harris reached into his coat and pulled out a dog-eared envelope. "Mr. Bloomer, down at the mill, gave it to me. Apparently it ended up there after your farm was vacated. Looks like it's from your friend Jean."

Colette snatched the letter from him, then apologized.

"I understand completely," he said. "I hope the news is good. I'll go in and kiss Helen now."

Colette ripped the letter open and raced through the page once hurriedly, and then read through it a second time at her leisure.

Dearest Colette,

I am so happy I hardly know where to begin. I'm writing this letter in a hurry because Manason is leaving tomorrow, and I want to send it with him.

This has been the most wonderful summer so far. Nase came back in late May and decided to stay through the Independence Day celebrations. We had such good times together. It has been like the old days, with all of us together again, except we missed you. Really!

You should see Annie. She's a real married lady. Hank just adores her, for which we are very thankful. But truth be told, she adores him just as well and has fallen into the role of housewife better than you may imagine. They have a new home just up the road from our parents. You remember -- it's the spot where the old Indian trail used to fork to the east. Annie is fixing the house up simply lovely.

Now, on to my biggest news. It is going to be a year of two weddings in our family after all. Oh, I am so excited, but maybe you've already heard. Maybe Joe has told you about his brother's plans. Robin came to see me, you see, and yes, he has proposed! We are going to be married in September, and we will return to Wisconsin for our honeymoon trip! Isn't it wonderful? Manason offered Rob a job on one of his crews up in the Chippewa River country. I know it is still terribly far from you, but we may cross paths again. I will be Rob's wife, and we will all live in Wisconsin Territory! I feel so blessed. I must remember to thank God daily.

We had another wedding this past spring, as well. Can you believe that only ten days after Annie married Hank, that catty Margaret Baker, who used to moon after Manason, walked the aisle with Mitch Donnelson? I'm so glad she's no longer a thorn in Nason's side!

I expect to hear good news from you soon, and plenty of it! Please, if I may be so boldly curious -- I'm trying not to be nosy, but I can't help myself. Won't you please write back and tell me how it goes?

All my love. Best regards to your parents and Rose, and hello to Mr. and Mrs. Eastman.

Your friend always,
Jean

Colette turned the letter over and back again, wondering about those cryptic lines. *How it goes?* What did Jean mean by that? She wasn't referring to Helen's baby, was she? Unless, of course, Joe had told Robin that Helen was pregnant, and Robin had told Jean. Hmm. That didn't seem like the sort of news Joe would find interesting enough to share with Rob, but who knew? Colette couldn't imagine what else Jean was wondering about. Colette's father's accident? No, that was unlikely as well.

She hadn't written to Jean since the accident. She was ashamed about it now, but she'd simply had too much going on, what with her parents' move and her own transition to living with the Eastmans. Then there was Joe. Joe, who consumed her time and attention like thirsty ground soaking up a rain.

She glanced over the letter again and considered Jean's news about Margie Baker marrying Mitch Donnelson. Colette couldn't put a face to him. Well, that was good news, indeed. Yet it didn't set her heart to pounding like it once might have. Perhaps, even though she knew her feelings might change if she got to see Manason again -- perhaps she was training her heart not to think of him as hers. Perhaps she was finally growing accustomed to the reality that she and Manason's lives were set on different courses.

She decided to wash her arms and face, scrub the dirt from under her fingernails, and write a letter to Jean. She had a lot to tell. Colette thought dreamily for a minute about Jean's news. *Jean and Robin.* What a glorious couple they'd make. She wished she could be at the wedding to watch Jean walk down the aisle in her white dress, her dark hair crowned on her head and her eyes sparkling with joy. *Mrs. Rob Gilbert... Jean Gilbert. Mrs. Joseph Gilbert... Colette Gilbert... What if Joseph and I...* She shook her head and pumped water into the bucket at the back door of the house. No, she wasn't ready to say God was leading her to marry Joe. *I'll know when the right one comes along. It'll be glaring and clear, and I won't be able to say 'no', or even think it. That's how it will be.*

Colette wasn't able to get right to the letter, but after supper she went to her room and let her pen flow with words back to Jean. She told her friend how thrilled she was to hear Jean's news. She told her about her father's tragedy, but how there was progress and hope. She told of her new living arrangements and how it felt to be making a life away from her family. She told of the spell of anticipation they were all under as they awaited the birth of the Eastman baby. She even told her about Joe and how their friendship had changed into something more serious than it had been before.

> *I should like to have your advice about Joseph, Jean. But as you're about to marry his brother, I'm not sure you will be unbiased... I'm only teasing. If you could tell me about Robbie -- how you knew, when you knew, whether you felt as if God was leading you, anything that might help me to know what to do about Joe, I will remain forever most*

grateful.

You are my closest ally, Jean. You always have been. So, you haven't been nosy or too bold to ask me anything. I hope with all my thoughts exposed, I've answered your questions. I don't know what else you could possibly have meant by "how it goes".

It all goes well, and I pray it's the same with you.

All my love,
Colette

*****

Colette rose early the next morning and tapped on the paneled door of Harris' study.

"Lettie, come in." His smile was a fine thing. Colette's heart warmed whenever Harris was in a good mood, as he had been a lot lately. He was often stern and impassioned, his jaw growing sharp and his brows narrowing like thunderclouds gathering for a storm. His displeasure would grow into a dark blaze that smoldered in his eyes, the fine lines of his face set like flint. Sometimes worry creased his forehead, making him look his rightful age. But lately, he'd been content, with a youthfulness about him that made his years fall away.

"Excuse me, Harris. I see you're busy, and I don't want to keep you. I have a letter I'd like to send and wondered if I may leave it with you to see that it's posted."

"That would be fine." He took the letter from her outstretched hand. "I'll take it with me to Kromer's store. He's sending out for a shipment, I believe, and he'll have other mail going downriver."

"Thank you." She turned to leave.

"Don't go, Lettie. I'd like to talk with you a moment, if I may."

She turned and settled in the over-sized chair he pointed out.

"Are you comfortable? Here, with us I mean?"

"Yes, very. Why?"

"No reason. I just wanted to be sure. I also wanted to reassure you about how glad we are that you decided to stay."

"It wasn't a difficult decision. Really, it was a relief. My father is getting the best care possible, and he and my mother and Rose have means and a place to live. Besides, I didn't want to leave Helen."

"Only Helen?"

Colette blushed and lowered her eyes. "If you mean Joseph Gilbert--"

"Actually, I didn't. I'm as fond of you as Helen is, Lettie. I'm glad you decided to stay because you're my friend, too."

"Thank you, Harris. I count you a friend as well," she said, her voice foreign, embarrassed.

"What about young Joe? He's been your friend a long time. Has he begun to press his suit?"

She nodded. Harris smiled. "Nothing wrong with that," A fatherly air infiltrated his voice. "Unless you don't approve, that is."

"I feel a little awkward talking about it with you."

Harris laughed out loud. "Then I won't embarrass you. All friendships have limits, don't they?" He leaned back, crossed one leg over the other, and tapped on the top of his heavy desk with his long, thin fingers. "I would like to see you increase your chances, Lettie. I think it's time we lease out the farm."

"Whatever you think."

"Oh, no." He chuckled again. "I want your input in this decision. I trust your judgment. I want to know what sort of people you want living in your home. Remember, it might very well be your home again someday, especially if you and Joseph decide to marry."

"Harris..."

"Don't blush. I may only be teasing about young Joe, but I am serious about your future. I feel responsible for you now, but I don't want to make decisions for you. You're too intelligent for me to do that."

"That's a very kind thing to say. I appreciate it. As for the farm, you're right. It is time. It's been empty long enough. It was Ma and Pa's plan to have it leased out, and I think we need to find tenants soon. Summer is going by quickly."

"Good. I thought that's what you'd say. I know of a family whose place burned down a couple of weeks ago. They've been getting by, but they need a solid roof over their heads so the man can get back to work. He works up at camp two in the winter."

"It will be wonderful to have a family in the cabin again."

"As you know, a steady influx of settlers has been moving into the area over the past couple of years. Demand for houses and property will continue. Towns like this one, French Creek, and Centralia are going to boom."

Colette's blood stirred as Harris spoke.

"Your folks are doing all right with the money from the mill. They should be comfortable for some time. You have an opportunity, Lettie, to do something for yourself. Such as take a portion of the rent from the tenants and save it for your own investment. Maybe buy some property yourself."

"But I'm a woman," Colette answered, stating the obvious. "I haven't the right--"

Harris stopped her with a hand. "I have attorneys who handle these kinds of things. I think you could do it without anyone knowing you're a woman. It's worth a try."

"But how?"

"Let me work out the details. I have some influence in these things."

Colette rose from the chair, too inspired to sit. "Where? Where will I do it?"

"Good land is all around us, some of it already in my name. And land further north."

North? Jean and Rob and Manason would all soon be living somewhere in the vast north. Later, when she wouldn't disturb Harris, she would ask to see some of his maps, ask him to show her the places up north. She would ask him to show her land in the Chippewa Valley.

"I've a lot to learn before I can buy any land," she said, trying to smother her excitement by sounding reasonable.

Harris laughed again. "I'm sure you'll learn quite fast."

*****

On Tuesday, as Mr. Kromer's brother-in-law mounted his nag with supply orders for the store, his pouch of letters and lists fell, spilling on the ground. Cursing his calamity, he hastened about in the sawdust and dirt, gathering them before the wind could carry them off or the horse could trod them into the mud. Jamming them back into the pouch, he made certain it was secure this time, and then he rode off toward the woods on his way to the Pinery Road.

So certain he'd not missed a thing, he never looked back or chanced to see the one thin envelope that fluttered against the hitching rail. It stayed there, caught in the dirt for almost an hour before another horse, hitched there, pawing at the earth, crushed it into obscurity beneath its hooves.

Chapter Sixteen

Harris' ideas about Collette investing in land settled deep in her musings as she swept the cobwebs from the corners of her old house. They had a lot of details to work out, but wouldn't it be something if she could really do it? Of course, in reality, no married women could legally own property, and anything Harris managed to purchase on her behalf would fall under her husband's authority someday. In that case, however, it wouldn't matter if twenty years passed by before she married. She would be a woman of independent means.

Criss-crossing her thoughts was the reality that someone else must soon take her family's place on this farm by the river. Part of her wished she had no need of means and could simply move back into the house herself. She would have Dandy and a pig or two, some chickens, and a milk cow. She would spend her days raising a garden, collecting fodder for the cow, sweeping the front step, and like now, admiring the sunsets like bright fingers of molten gold spilling through the trees. But that would never be. Harris had said the new tenants would arrive in a week. That meant Colette had a short time in which to think of the place as hers alone.

She closed up the cabin and wandered down to the river. The sun had moved into the western sky and now cast an orange sheen across the surface of the water. It was a late summer sun, big as a pumpkin, the kind that made her want to slip her toes into the water and splash at the color that played along the ripples and currents. For some time she just stood there and watched it while she threw sticks for Dandy. Finally, she knew she had to start back to town.

"Come on Dandy. Here boy!" He came out of the water and shook, showering the area around him. "Let's go, Dandy," she commanded, walking back up the crooked path. She turned onto the main trail home and had barely rounded the curve in the lane when there stood Joe.

Her hand flew to her cheek. "Joseph! You startled me. I thought you were a bear."

"Sorry. You surprised me, too. Come out to say hello to the old place?"

She nodded. "I miss it. Or maybe it's just my folks. I miss them something terrible."

"I bet they miss you too. Still, I'm glad you stayed."

"Me, too," she admitted.

"Can I walk you back to town? It's getting late."

"Yes, thank you." Letting Dandy take the lead, they walked in silence for a while, a rare thing with Joe. He'd changed a little lately, too. She grew pensive as they strolled along, mesmerized as ever by the beauty of

107

the late day sunlight rippling through the branches that shouldered their path. Finally, Joseph's hand cupped hers. She gave him a small smile as they kept walking.

His hand tightened, and in a breath his words boiled out. "Lettie, I want to get married. I've made up my mind. I'll wait until next spring if I have to, but if you're willing, I'd rather marry you right after your birthday. Or I can come back at Christmas if you want. It doesn't matter, but I want us to marry soon."

She stumbled.

He steadied her and turned her to look at him. "I'm going to leave in a few days to do some work up at the camp. They need men to build a corduroy road over some swamp, and we need to gather hay for the oxen and a lot of other things. They need help, and I need the money," he said, his deep gaze holding hers, "for us."

She stared at him. She'd put Joe off many a time. Still, in her core, she knew something was different this time. This time he wouldn't be put off. Yet, though she cared for him deeply, something compelled her to want to do just that. *If only Jean would write back and tell me what to do.*

He rubbed his thumbs across her knuckles, waiting.

She gathered her resolve. Still, her voice came out weak. "Why are you so anxious, Joe? What's the hurry?"

He pulled her towards him. "I can't wait anymore, Lettie. I just can't. I *need* you."

She looked down at their joined hands. "Don't talk nonsense, Joseph."

He let her go and grasped his chest as though he'd been hit. "It's not nonsense I'm full of; it's passion for you, Lettie. My body's about to burst with it."

"That doesn't sound like love, Joe."

He gripped her wrists and his green eyes bore into hers. "Don't say that. It's not true. I do love you. If Helen's tried to tell you differently, then--"

"Helen?"

"She doesn't know. It's you I want. What she saw with Kashe was nothing. I didn't mean a thing by it."

Colette narrowed her eyes, and a little arrow pierced her heart. *Kasheawa.*

"Helen's said nothing, Joseph." With effort, she turned her thoughts away from what Joe had just confessed. "It's too soon since my pa's accident." The trust in her heart seeped away like a blood-letting, and she could do nothing to stanch the flow. The plans she'd voiced to Harris rolled through her mind. "I have a lot of ideas, things I want to do. I can't marry and set up house when I have to think of my folks. They'll need my help for a long while yet."

"You think the bit of money Mr. Eastman pays you to be his wife's companion really makes a difference to your ma and pa? That they'd rather have you working to send money to them when you could be making a life for yourself? Who do you think you're fooling to believe such a thing? Do you even believe it? Or is it only me you're trying to convince?"

Her gaze flashed at him and she tugged at his grip, which only held fast as he pulled her closer.

"Kiss me, Colette. Kiss me like you did that night. You can't prove to me that you'd rather be working for old Harris Eastman than marrying me." He leaned toward her, but she turned her head away.

"I'll not be kissing anyone, Joseph, 'specially you."

"Why not?" His fingers gripped tighter, pinching her. "Who are you waiting for, Miss High and Mighty?"

She wriggled in his grasp. "Someone. Not a boy like you."

Joseph's expression changed to surprise -- genuine surprise -- and his hands fell away like rocks. He backed off, looking around him.

"Where is he?" he shouted. "Where is this *someone*? I haven't seen him. And I don't see you looking at anybody else more than me."

Colette's ears burned, and her face flushed with heat. For an instant, Manason Kade's face flashed before her, and she was embarrassed at how quickly his name came to her lips. Why had she said *someone*? And the rest of it... what did she mean to hurt Joe with such callous remarks?

Light filtered through the trees in streaks and shadows, and still he stood in her path. "I'm sorry, Joe. I didn't mean it. Really."

He grazed a finger along her cheek, but the light that had softened his eyes before was gone. "I think you did. I think you really meant it. I even *finally* believe you."

"I wish you wouldn't be angry, Joseph." Tears welled in her eyes. She couldn't help it.

"Don't cry, Lettie. It makes my blood heat up," he said, but he didn't touch her again. He just stared through her as tears spilled from her eyes and ran in rivers down her cheeks. He stared while she backed away and then rushed past him, leaving him standing in the growing darkness beneath the trees with his fists clenched at his sides.

Chapter Seventeen

Joe didn't try to see Colette again before he left. So she tried to only think of him the way she knew him best, with his dark, curly hair falling over his brow, a devilish grin on his handsome face, and his green eyes sparkling with secrets he'd only share with her.

Better to picture him that way than when she'd seen him last.

The first cool day hinting that autumn was on its way brought a circuit riding preacher to Grand Rapids. Folks from across the way in Centralia came over, as well as up from French Town and a number of other nearby villages in the region. The preacher intended to hold services in the new inn and boarding house that had been built on Grand Avenue just that year. Colette looked forward to Sunday like she hadn't since leaving Michigan. She hoped that somehow Helen might feel up to attending.

"I would be such a spectacle," Helen said, "and I could never sit through a long sermon. Why don't you go with Harris? He'll be glad to accompany you."

Again Colette was stung by the fact that had Joseph stayed true to her, either as her friend or something more, she would have no question as to who would accompany her to church. Colette had never known Harris to be a God-fearing man who would want to spend his Sunday morning in the Lord's house.

"I couldn't ask him," she answered Helen.

"Of course you can. He'll want to go with you. He'll do it for me."

"What will I do for you, dearest?" Harris came into the room unannounced.

"I told Lettie you'd be happy to take her to hear the visiting preacher this Sunday. It's a social event not to be missed."

Harris smiled, something they'd grown used to seeing for the past eight months. "Certainly I'll take Lettie to church. Wouldn't hurt me to undergo a good, old fashioned Bible-thrashing myself."

Helen laughed, but his words shocked Colette. "The preacher won't do any such thing."

"Are you sure? We live unfettered lives here in the wilderness. Why, there was another brawl over in Centralia just last night, I hear. And remember the shooting two months ago?" He paused, and Colette couldn't answer him. Then he smiled again. "I'm only teasing, Lettie. Not about the brawl, just the preaching. No need to worry. What time is the service?"

"Nine o'clock."

"Then we'll be ready to leave at eighty-thirty. Be sure to wear your prettiest dress. The blue one, I think."

Colette woke up on Sunday morning wondering if Harris would forget his promise. He hadn't mentioned it again. But true to his word, he was dressed in his finest suit with his black hair perfectly groomed and gleaming when she came down for breakfast. He looked her over with an appreciative twinkle in his eyes. "You are a sight to move even the most stone-hearted sinner to want to come to church and repent this morning, Miss Palmer."

Colette pirouetted and curtsied. "Why, thank you, sir. Will Helen come down to see us off?"

"I told her to rest a little longer. No need for her to get up early. She should save her strength for the day she'll soon need it."

Colette agreed.

"Shall we go as soon as you have your bonnet and shawl?"

"Yes."

Colette hurried to tie on her bonnet and drape Joe's beautiful silk shawl around her shoulders. Harris took Colette's hand to help her into his new buggy and, as she seated herself, she caressed the folds of the shawl fondly and wondered where Joseph was today. She wished he could be here. Not for her, but to be part of the community worshipping together. She didn't know if Joe had ever belonged to a church before.

Colette had nearly forgotten what it felt like to stand together to sing and pray. A tremor of joy ran through her during worship. Harris sang with a melodic, deep baritone, but he didn't seem as familiar with the hymns as Colette was. Sometimes the words fell away, and he merely hummed. To Colette, however, the verses to every hymn rose easily from her memory to her lips. She smiled fondly at Harris as she belted out the words to the old hymns.

The preaching was quite good, in Colette's estimation, even if the minister injected a little fire and brimstone. At one point, she let out a sigh as she took in the words, almost forgetting a room full of people surrounded her. She blushed and peered at those around her, but finally decided no one had noticed.

She wondered what Harris thought of the sermon. He sat with his arms crossed and his eyes settled directly on the preacher. *He likes it, too,* she thought. After service let out, she eagerly shook the preacher's hand.

"Thank you so much, sir," she said. "It was wonderful to hear good preaching again."

The preacher wasn't old, probably only in his thirties. He smiled warmly at Colette and accepted her thanks with a kind greeting. "I'm happy to have made it to your little town."

"Will you be staying in the area?" Harris asked, giving him a hearty handshake.

"Not this time. I'm going to visit some of the mill sites up the river. Just a short trip though. I should be back this way again in a month or so. I expect to spend the winter down at the Portage.

"We hope your travels go smoothly, then," Harris said.

"Yes, and that you can stay longer next time," Colette added as Harris led her out the door.

In the bright September sunshine, Harris and Colette rode home.

"Wish we always had a preacher," she said, her voice airy with contentment.

"Why is that?"

"I miss it. It just would make things right. To have a church meeting every week and hear the Bible read. To sing songs. You have a fine voice, Harris."

"Thank you. I guess we could all do with more opportunities to use our talents."

"God must be pleased to look down at this fine land He created and see us here in the wild, raising our voices to Him."

"Hmm."

Colette looked over at him and raised her brows. "Why do you say, 'hmm'? Do you disagree?"

"Not at all. I didn't know you were so devout, that's all."

"Devout? I could hardly be called devout."

"Religious?"

She shook her head. "No. I once thought I was. At least a little. But I believe religion is a poor word for what God wants of us."

Harris snickered. "You mean, after all the world has done to propagate its religions, they're not what the Almighty is concerned about?"

"Religion is man-made, to take the place of God, I think."

"You philosophize about religion? I had no idea you were a student of doctrine, as well, Lettie."

"Not a student, so don't tease. But is it wrong to want to know the truth, to want to weigh the issues of the world and God and discern the genuine from the counterfeit?"

"So you say religion is counterfeit. What, then, does God really want of mankind, do you think? If not piety and sacrifice and temples to His honor, what is it?"

Colette thought for a long moment. They rode on in silence, and Harris glanced in her direction only once. Finally, they turned into the drive where the Eastman house stood. Harris pulled the buggy to a halt and turned to get down.

"Obedience, I think."

Her voice halted him, and he faced her. "Obedience? Well, that's a tall order. Obedience in what? Isn't that what religion is based upon?"

"No, I don't think so. Religion is based upon doing. Making and keeping rules."

"Obedience."

"Yes, and no. Obedience to whom? Man? The church? No. I believe obedience to God is much more intimate. It's part of the faith that saves us, based on understanding even a tiny inkling of His great love. A desire to please Him, without being compelled to."

"You have no need of a preacher, Lettie," Harris said, stepping down and coming around to her side of the buggy. He took her hand. She alighted gently and looked up at him.

"I don't know all I should. I wish I had a Bible. Papa used to read to us every week from his. I took it quite for granted."

"Well, I can offer you a bit of consolation there. You can have the Bible on the shelf in my study. Helen and I received it as a wedding gift from one of her old teachers. It only collects dust. I don't think we've even put our names in it."

"Harris, really?" Colette's voice lifted in excitement, but then she drew back. "But I could never take it from you. It was a wedding gift to you and Helen."

"Please," he said, rolling his eyes. "If it's ever to be used, Helen would agree you should have it."

Lightness rolled over Colette. "It may seem silly to you, that I'm so happy about it. I've been wondering about things, and until the preacher came today, I never realized how much searching I need to do."

Harris laughed as he tucked her arm in his. "Then, by all means, go get the Bible and find what you need to know. You can correct both Helen and me on our confused theology."

"Oh, Harris," she said, laughing and blushing at once.

Once inside the house, Colette swept off her bonnet and shawl and followed Harris to his study. True to his word, there on the shelf with his books on surveying and land speculations and marketing and even railroads, was the promised Bible. Its crisp, tight spine was like new, and it weighed in her hands like a treasure when he gave it to her.

"I don't know how to thank you," she whispered, tenderly opening the black book and caressing its silky pages.

"No need to thank me for something so simple. For when you are happy, Helen is happy. You mustn't think me ingenuous. I derive great pleasure from seeing you smile, too, Lettie."

"And smile I shall," she answered, lifting her gaze to his.

"Come, let's go see how Helen is doing. We'll see if she's awake from her nap."

They found Helen in the parlor, quietly putting the finishing stitches on a tiny blanket. She looked up and gave them a wan smile. "How was church?"

"Hell-fire and brimstone, with the usual offering plate passed around," Harris said as he raised her hand and kissed it.

"It was heavenly." Colette laughed at her own pun. "Wish you could have been there."

"Are you feeling all right, my dear? You look a bit peaked." Harris reached out and put his hand on Helen's cheek.

She pushed it away. "I'm fine. It's just that--" She sucked in her breath, and her voice became airy as she said, "I think it has begun..." Her words fell out in a breathy trail, and she spoke no more for a moment.

Harris' eyes widened, and Colette came up beside him. "Shall I carry you back to bed?" he asked.

"No, no. It's all right now. I think it is quite early yet. These things can take hours, so I'm told."

"Can I get you anything?" Colette asked. "Some tea or something?"

"Just a sip of water, perhaps," Helen said.

Colette hurried to the kitchen and through the back door where the water pump stood just below the back porch. With a clean glass in hand, she deftly pumped the handle until the glass overflowed with icy cold water. *The baby is coming -- early.* She mentally counted the weeks to go. *Only two, maybe three weeks. Not so bad. Probably a good thing. Easier on Helen. I should go for Mrs. Stowe.* She carried the water to Helen and watched her take a small sip as both she and Harris hovered over her.

"I'll go for Mrs. Stowe," Colette said crisply.

"No, not yet. Harris can go later. It's all right for now. I want you to just sit by me, Lettie, and talk to me."

Harris moved across the room and Colette took a seat next to Helen.

"Both of you, stop fussing," Helen said. "Here, Lettie. Look at the baby's blanket. I just finished it. You know, now that I have so many lovely things for the baby, I should start helping you with your hope chest and trousseau."

"Whatever for?" Colette smiled, forgetting for the tiniest moment that Helen was in labor.

"Because you'll need them someday."

"Yes," Harris added, grinning at the two of them, "Helen is right. You are old enough now to find a husband, Lettie. I'll have to keep my eyes open for any likely candidates."

"Surely not!" Colette cried.

Helen sipped her water and handed the glass to Colette. They passed time talking about other things until finally, some fifteen minutes later, Helen closed her eyes with the steady, pressuring squeeze of another contraction. Both Harris and Colette waited silently until it subsided.

"I think we have a long wait coming." Helen sounded calm, but uncertain.

"You should try and rest more." Colette frowned. "You need to save your strength."

"I agree with Lettie. Come now." Harris rose. "I'm taking you to bed, whether you want to go or not."

Helen didn't disagree. She allowed Harris to walk her upstairs and tuck her into bed.

*****

Helen dozed, but grew restless when a contraction came, and after one or two, gave up trying to sleep. "Stay with me, Lettie,"

Colette sat in the chair by her bed. "Is there anything I can do?"

"No. Just sit. I'll want to get up and walk around some. Harris won't like it, but you can keep him in the study."

"If that's what you want."

"It is. He's too nervous. I could feel his heart pounding when he put me into bed."

Colette smiled. "He's so happy."

"Yes." Helen's gaze fell pensive. "At last." She focused on Colette with luminescent eyes. "Tell me about Joseph."

Colette sat back and looked out the window where the first red-gold leaves of autumn tapped against the pane. "I haven't heard from him."

"I know. Tell me how you feel."

Colette shrugged. "I feel..." She couldn't put a word to it, as though she'd taken that last encounter with Joseph and put it away in a place where she couldn't touch it with her heart. Now it tried to come out of that place. "I feel a bit sad."

"You loved him after all?"

"A few times I thought so. But my heart has never felt completely safe with him. I'm sad, because of what's happened to our friendship."

"You don't think he'll change his mind?"

"I don't know. He was so hurt and angry, Helen. He'll never trust me again."

Helen didn't reply, and Colette realized she'd been taken with another contraction. This one lasted longer than the others. When it passed, Helen smiled and asked her to go on.

"That's all I have to say about it, really."

"Why won't he trust you?"

"He thinks there's someone else."

Helen's brows rose. "Is there?"

"Of course not. But it'll do no good to try and convince Joe."

"Even if he's hurt?"

Colette thought of the Indian girl, Kasheawa, and of the other girls who passed through town and noticed lithe, handsome Joseph Gilbert. "Oh, Joe won't be hurt for long. He'll find a way around it."

"I hope you're not wrong. What about Jean's brother? What was his name?"

"Manason?" Colette knew she said it too quickly. It had risen to her thoughts with Helen's other questions. He was the *someone* who'd come to mind that day with Joe. She couldn't imagine why. She no longer even entertained thoughts of Manason Kade outside these trying conversations.

"Yes. Manason. Would he be a reason for us to fill your hope chest?"

"No. I doubt I'll ever see Manason again. It's wrong for you and Harris to tease me about marrying."

"Harris wasn't teasing; not entirely. Nor was I, as far as it goes."

Colette stood and paced over to the window. "Well, please don't be in too big a hurry to pack me off with a husband."

"Of course not, Lettie. I want you here with me and the baby. I need you," she said, as her voice dropped and another contraction brought silence.

The day waned on into evening, and evening fell into night. Etta Stowe fixed tea for Helen but would not allow her to eat anything. Colette joined Harris in his study and tried to distract him with conversation, even picking arguments when she could, just to take his mind off what was happening upstairs. The house was so quiet. So terribly quiet.

Finally Colette fell asleep in one of Harris' big chairs. She couldn't help it. When she woke, it was the darkest hour of the night.

Harris stood beside her, tapping her arm gently. "I've been with Helen. She's very tired, but she's asking for you."

His voice was gravelly and laden with worry, and it brought Colette to her feet. She nodded and went to Helen.

Helen's face was red with exertion, her forehead drenched in sweat.

"Etta says it's a stubborn child, much like its father," she said, trying to smile, but her voice shook.

"Shh, Helen. Don't talk." Colette rinsed a rag in cool water and stroked Helen's forehead. Etta left the room saying she would be right back. She'd no sooner gone when a contraction seized Helen, and Colette waited helplessly as her friend gritted her teeth and tears squeezed out beneath her closed eyelids. When the long minute passed, she finally relaxed, though not entirely, and patted the bed beside her. Colette sat down tentatively.

"I'm so tired," Helen said, her voice small.

"The baby will be here soon. Remember that. It has to end sometime."

The corners of her mouth twitched, but then Helen's brown creased in what could only be termed as fear while another strong contraction arched her up off the bed. For the first time Helen cried out, and Colette's own heart raced. Etta hurried back into the room.

"How do you feel, Mrs. Eastman?"

A ridiculous question. Colette bit her lip.

"Like pushing?"

Helen nodded, still in the throes of the contraction, a moan escaping her lips as it subsided.

"With the next one, you will push," the midwife said.

Colette bent next to Helen and took her hand. She wanted to offer comforting words but found none.

Then the pushing began. With the next several contractions, Helen pushed, but each time she seemed to grow weaker, and the babe was no nearer to being born. Even Mrs. Stowe puckered her brow with a look Colette hadn't seen before. The older woman lifted her eyes to Colette's and dropped them just as quickly. With a slight inclination of her head, Etta directed her to come to the side of the room.

"Don't leave," Helen whimpered.

"I won't. I'll be right there."

"It isn't good." Etta's tone was low enough for only Colette to hear. "The baby is turned, and Mrs. Eastman isn't strong."

"Colette?" Helen pleaded.

Colette rushed to her side. "I'm here."

"You don't have to whisper. I can tell. Something's wrong."

She barely got the words out before another contraction gripped her. She pushed, but not long enough. Afterward, she wept.

"Shh... shh. It's all right Helen. You can do it." Colette feared Helen would hear the dread in her voice. She wanted to run for Harris, but she didn't dare leave Helen's side.

"Lettie... Lettie," Helen moaned. Suddenly she looked straight into Colette's eyes.

Colette grasped for hope. "The preacher said this morning that 'perfect love casts out fear'. Isn't that wonderful? You and Harris have created this baby in love. 'Perfect love casts out fear'." She had no idea about the application of that Scripture verse, but she had to reach for something, anything to give Helen peace, and for a moment it seemed to have that effect.

"I don't think I can do it, after all," Helen said calmly, as though she merely longed for rest.

"Don't say that. You can do it; I know you can. You've waited so long for this, remember? Now do it, Helen. Do it!"

At last it seemed that Colette had said the right thing, and with the next exertion, Etta Stowe cried out, "That's my girl! Now, one more!"

With another agonizing wail, Helen gave birth.

"Helen! Helen you did it!" Colette squeezed her hand and leaned down to hug her, but Helen dropped her head back into the sweat-drenched pillow without acknowledging the accomplishment.

Colette looked to Etta, who was swaddling the infant and wiping its face. Silence engulfed the room. A tear traced a track down Etta's cheek, and Colette rushed to look at the baby. Then she whirled back to Helen, and for the first time, noticed the massive amounts of blood on the sheets.

"Mrs. Stowe?"

Etta shook her head sadly. She handed Colette the swaddled infant and quietly whispered to her, "She is bleeding too much. I don't know what will happen."

"Colette?" Helen's voice was weak, almost beyond hearing. "Can I see the baby?"

Etta and Colette exchanged looks before Colette lowered herself beside Helen.

"It's a girl, Helen. A beautiful baby girl. But--"

"Lay her beside me," Helen whispered, barely awake.

Colette glanced again at Etta, and then at the lifeless bundle in her arms before she obeyed. Helen smiled dreamily. "Look how she sleeps. Harris will love her. He must."

Closing her eyes, she sighed. "Please take care of my little girl, Lettie."

"I'll take care of her until you feel better."

"No." Her eyes fluttered open, steadying weakly on Colette. "I need you to promise me."

"All right, Helen, I promise."

Helen tried to kiss the little forehead in her arms. "So soft. So fragile. Poor Harris. Look after him, too. You will, won't you?"

Colette nodded. She glanced again at Etta working to stanch the relentless flow of blood. Etta shook her head. Colette struggled against the tears blinding her.

"Shall I get Harris for you?"

Helen's head drooped to the side. She murmured something indistinguishable, and Colette raced from the room.

Harris looked like stone. His face was ashen, his body rigid, his brows furrowed into great, heavy crags. He barely lifted his head to look at her when she flew into the room. Colette's breathing came in panicky rags, and she knew he feared the worst before she could say a word.

"My son?" he said, his voice low, reverberating.

"The child is a girl," she croaked.

He stirred. "A girl?"

Colette nodded, not even knowing if he noticed. He had to be told, but Colette could hardly make sound come out of her throat. "She was stillborn, Harris."

He rose and came around his desk, his movements slow and labored. He swam before her vision. "I'm sorry, Harris. So deeply sorry."

"And Helen?"

A sob rose in Colette's throat. She wanted to stop it; she tried to stay quiet. But it burst out of her, and through the tears spilling from her eyes, she could barely make out the change in Harris' own face, the anguish and uncertainty rocking him.

"Go to her," she sobbed. "Quickly."

Chapter Eighteen

Manason pulled his slicker closer around his shoulders and leaned a little nearer to the trunk of the red oak, taking what small shelter its leafy branches afforded him in the hard, gray veil of rain. Every verdant leaf, bough, and fern frond glistened and drooped in the deafening downpour.

He'd been walking the lines of his cutting for two days and had wandered over to have a closer look at the eastern section that butted up against the Indian lands. And lumber-rich though they were -- and tempting to the eye -- he knew it was time to turn back. Besides, he'd been pushing things since the clouds moved in yesterday. All the talk about someone stealing lumber off these Indian lands had made him want to have a look around. He also wanted to be sure the thieving hadn't stretched onto his own claim. Relieved it hadn't, Manason thought it might be wise to post a few men out here to walk the boundaries regularly, just in case.

Water ran from the brim of his hat each time he tilted his head. No telling when this weather would let up. He scanned the woods briefly. Maybe he'd have to break a few branches and put up a shelter for the night.

A quick movement about thirty yards away caught his eye. Then again. A man moved through the woods at a fast clip. Silently on the sodden forest floor, with the hard rain on the foliage still drowning out all other sound, Manason set out to follow him.

The man walked with his head bent against the sting of the rain. That made following him even easier. Nase, however, kept a careful eye all around. He was well onto Indian land, and doubted the stranger would be alone, unless he was just another curious cruiser like Nase.

Unlikely.

Then the man broke into the edge of a clearing -- not a meadow -- but land stripped of all its best trees with only mountains of tangled brush and tree tops left behind. He skirted the cut-over even as Manason's heart picked up its rhythm. The going was more tedious now for both of them. Discarded timber crisscrossed the way. Brush piles stretched over their path. More than once, tangles of branches and undergrowth snagged at both men. If the rain let up now, Nase would surely be seen or heard.

Suddenly the stranger stopped and Manason drew up short, ducking behind a scarred maple as two other men stepped from the wood's comparative shelter. They conferred with the man Nase had been following, talking loudly because of the rain. Still, Manason could not make out what they were saying because of the deluge. Then one of them turned to face Manason, and Manason recognized his wide ruddy face, even as he gestured at the others.

119

Seamus Boggs.

Manason's thoughts raced. He knew with certainty Boggs was stealing timber. But the question remained -- who did Boggs work for? If only he could confront the man then and there. *No.* Boggs' bullies outweighed and outnumbered him. They wouldn't likely let him go back to his camp alive. Nase crouched down to wait. Before long the men moved off, disappearing into the veil further east.

Not long after, the rain let up. Manason did a quick survey of the area, making notes of the specific violations he'd seen and wrapping them carefully inside an oilskin pouch. He knew roughly where Boggs' camp was located, legally on a claim, but just off Indian land. Manason had driven his own logs past Boggs' camp during the thaw, at which time his men and Boggs' had eyed one another warily.

For the next day and all the way back to his own camp, Manason turned over in his mind what he'd seen. He decided to assign the job of further investigation to Tom Durant. Tom would be able to scout out the country for other violations. Manason would learn what other claims Boggs had on record. Between the two of them, he hoped they might sniff out the real boss behind Seamus Boggs' operation.

Nase hadn't been dry in two full days, and with real affection for his small, warm cabin and the cookee's hot victuals, he finally returned to base camp. He discovered Jean and Rob waiting there when he arrived.

Stiff with cold, the sight of them warmed him. "Well, now. Look what came in on the current. When did you two newlyweds get here?" He shook water off his coat and stamped mud from his boots. After hanging his wet outer garments on a peg, he shook Rob's hand.

"Just yesterday."

"Yes, we came in looking just as much like drowned rats as you do now," Jean said with a laugh. "I hope you don't mind that we moved into your cabin. I promised Rob you wouldn't."

Nase waved off her comment and stooped to strip off his soggy boots and socks. "Are you kidding? It's good to have family here. I'm just wondering what took you so long."

Rob grinned. "I must admit, I didn't take comfortably to the thought of moving Jean into the bunkhouse with the boys."

"Most of them are gone already. You'd have had lots of room." Manason offered them a mischievous, lopsided grin. "You wouldn't mind, would you, sis?"

"I may have grown up with brothers, but that doesn't make the idea of a bunkhouse full of the male sex any less formidable,"

Nase and Rob laughed, and Rob said with a wink, "I can't say I'd like it any better either." Jean flushed, her pleasure at being treasured obvious to Nase.

Manason excused himself, and Jean turned her back while he went to the rear of the cabin, finished stripping out of his wet clothes, and put on dry.

"So, tell me about the wedding. I guess it must've come off okay."

Jean told him, her eyes still dreamy as she described her dress, the cake, their father trying to hold back a tear or two, their mother not trying at all, Annie as the maid of honor looking as beautiful as the bride herself -- but Manason doubted it. As becoming as Jean looked to him now, glowing from the love of his rugged Irish brother-in-law, Manason thought she must have been the most stunning bride in the world. Her satiny cheeks had the look of wild roses blooming on them as she talked about seeing Rob in his suit, and how they'd forgotten a word or two and giggled at the altar, and *almost* all about their trip back to Wisconsin.

"Wish I could have been there," Manason said. "But I have a surprise for you. I bought some land not far from here, on a tributary between the Chippewa and the Eau Claire -- with a beauty of a little spot for a house I'd like you to have as a wedding present."

"Oh, Nase, that's too much."

"No it's not."

"That's generous, Manason," Rob said, "but Jean's right. It's too much."

"What about your own house?" Jean asked. "I wouldn't feel right taking your land."

Manason held up his hands, fending off their arguments. "First, let me say it's really okay. It's just a little piece of the pie. I have another place in mind for myself, on an oak ridge overlooking the country where the Chippewa winds through like a silver ribbon. I've already got the better location. It's a big piece -- six hundred acres besides the forty I'm deeding you. What'll I do with all that? I need neighbors."

Prepared for Jean's protests, Manason also knew he'd win. Her shoulders relaxed and a conceding twinkle glimmered in her eyes when she looked at Rob, then back at him. She hugged him tight. "Thank you, Manason. I can't wait to see it."

"At last, a hug from the bride."

"And a kiss," she said, and pecked him on the cheek.

Rob shook his hand again, and Manason pulled him into a rough embrace. "I'm glad you brought her here."

"When do we get to see it?"

"I can get us a couple of horses and we can ride out there tomorrow if you like. Today I've got to see Tom Durant about some business."

"Anything I can help you with? I'm ready to be put to work."

Manason stroked his lower lip. Rob's brawn was not lost on Manason, and he figured that if Jean would have him, he must be intelligent, too. After what he'd discovered over the past couple of days, Manason was suddenly glad to know he was surrounded by men like Robin Gilbert and Tom Durant and a trustworthy, work-toughened crew.

"Actually, yes, there is. But I'd probably have to steal you from Jean for a few days."

"I'm a lumberman's wife, Nase. I know what that means."

"Some thieving's going on near here. Not my trees, thank God. I won't get into the particulars, but I need a few men to walk the lines and keep watch. Can I put you in charge?

"Point me in the direction."

Nase smiled. "You can come along when I talk to Tom."

The next day, Manason, Jean, and Robin walked over a parcel of the new property, and Manason promised he and a couple of his remaining crew would help them get the new Gilbert cabin up and fit by mid-summer. He admired Robin's genuine appreciation and the way he caught Manason's own visions with ideas of his own. Robin Gilbert stood head and shoulders above the Virgil Holcombs of the world any day of the week, and Manason believed Jean had finally found her true match.

Whether the same would ever be said for Manason was a question that nibbled at him when he was with them, and he couldn't be sure he'd build his own home on the oak hill until he had the answer.

*****

Two weeks passed. Rob went out on the lines with one of the other men. Manason had just returned from a trip to one of the mills near the Falls with the added jaunt of going to the land office in Clearwater to have a look at the books. He was surprised to find that, somehow, permits had been issued to harvest on Indian land. Of course, it was still illegal, and the person to whom they'd been issued risked dispossession and fines, but Nase knew that to some, the chance of substantial profit was well worth the risk.

Now he and Jean sat in the cook shack as she served him a plate of venison stew while he poured a cup of coffee. Tom Durant came in and slung one of his long legs over the bench, sitting down next to Manason, facing him. He cocked his hat to the back of his head so he could look at his young friend squarely.

"Tom, what's the news?" Manason asked as Jean pulled another cup off the shelf and served Tom. A peculiar shine in Tom's hazel eyes quickened Nase's pulse.

"Thank you, ma'am," Tom said as he drew the coffee close but didn't sip it. "Well, you're dead right about Boggs. He's skinning lumber, maybe ten -- fifteen thousand board feet a day."

"All from those Indian lands?" Manason asked, incredulous.

"Worse, or at least as bad. He's got a sweet little set-up going right in the middle of section sixty-seven. Government land. Cutting as fast as he can."

Manason set down his coffee while he thought hard. His venison stew began to congeal.

"But who's behind him? Boggs doesn't have the brain of a woodpecker. He's all thug."

"Well now--" Tom finally took a long draught of the weak coffee. "I might have the answer for that one." He drew letters on the table with his index finger as he drawled them out. "Do you recognize the mark 'EE'?"

EE. A range of identifying marks from different outfits coursed through Manason's brain. He tried to zero in on if and when he'd seen that mark while Tom continued. Something about it was familiar. He almost had it.

"That's the mark the logs get once they're skidded out to the river along with Boggs' legitimate cuts. Stands for 'Eastman Enterprises'." Tom held the coffee cup to his lips and waited on Nase's reaction. It was immediate.

The name had barely come out of Tom's mouth when it all fell together in Manason's memory. *Harris Eastman.* The Eastman mill where Nase had passed the time with Eldon Palmer during his first visit to Grand Rapids. He could clearly see the *EE* slashed into the logs being debarked and sliding through the buzz saw. He stared hard at Tom, trying to take in all the ramifications.

Jean sat down across from the two men, her eyes wide as she also reacted to the news. "What does it mean?"

"A lot more than we know, I'm sure. That Harris Eastman has been getting rich using thugs and no-accounts and dirty lawyers."

Jean's own eyes widened. "What'll you do?"

"Whatever we can to stop him. Men like Eastman don't back down unless someone stops them. He steps on a lot of honest people in the process of building his fortune."

"People like the Palmers."

"Possibly." Eldon and Lavinia had seemed to have souls of contentment when Nase had seen them last summer. It was hard to imagine their best interests could be in danger. But then, you never knew. "They seemed all right when I last saw them."

Jean nodded. "Maybe Mr. Palmer's accident was a blessing in disguise if it broke his family free of someone like that." She bit her fingernail. "Nase, if Harris Eastman is involved with more illegal activities than we know, and it comes to light, what will it mean to the Palmers? I mean, don't they still receive payment from Harris for their part of the mill?"

Nase shook his head. "They sold it."

Jean sighed in relief. "That's better. At least they're free and clear of all this. I wish I knew how to reach them. I'd like to write Colette. She never replied to my last letter. Too much change, I suppose. First her father's injury, and then a move. We've lost touch."

"Maybe the folks will hear from them sometime."

"I could write Helen."

"Helen?"

"Harris Eastman's wife. We became quite comfortable friends last summer. Maybe I could enclose a letter for Colette. Helen may know how to get it to her."

"Be careful what you write. We would be fools to trust Eastman or his wife."

Jean stood. "I doubt Helen has any idea what her husband does. She's the most naive creature in the world."

"Still, be careful, Jean."

"I will."

Chapter Nineteen

Grief suffused Colette's body with lead-like heaviness. Her head grew dizzy with weeping. Her bones melted inside her, unable to bear the weight of walking.

Harris' anguish seemed different, however. He went about the business of the funeral for Helen and the baby as though they were strangers. Then he locked himself in his study.

When those initial days of mind-numbing grief passed for Colette, she wondered if he were drinking or weeping, or just what he was doing in there. Wanting to help, she found no tangible means to do so.

Wonderful, kind Mrs. Stowe brought a bag and moved into Rose Shultz's old room off the kitchen, making sure they were eating and being cared for. By the time Colette was ready to take on some of the smaller day to day household tasks, Etta still remained, a quiet comfort.

"I will stay as long as necessary. When Mr. Eastman is ready to be left alone, you can come stay with Noah and me," she said. "But for now, we will take care of Mr. Eastman together."

Colette nodded and hugged her, missing her mother as she did so.

At last Harris emerged, unshaven and disheveled. He appeared to have slept in the same clothes for several days, and the gaunt whiteness of his cheeks evidenced that he'd eaten little. When he lifted his eyes to Colette as if seeing her for the first time since that night, all she could say was his name.

"Lettie," he said, his voice ragged, "would you be so kind as to ask Mrs. Stowe to draw me a bath? She's still here, I take it?"

"Yes." Colette nodded, choked with compassion. "She's gone home to collect some soap, but I'll be glad to get your bath ready."

"Thank you. It's very considerate of you."

"It's nothing," she murmured.

He just stood there, wavering, as lost as Colette ever hoped to see him, and finally she went to him and took his arm. She led him to the sofa where he sat, staring, rubbing his forehead with his fingers.

"I can't believe she's gone." Sorrow unmasked itself as he sat there. She perched beside him, wrapping her arms around his shoulders until he let himself rest in them. Tears crawled up her throat as he sobbed against her. Finally, he straightened and apologized for his lack of control. Colette wiped her eyes and pulled a handkerchief from her apron pocket, dabbing it at her red nose.

"I loved her, too."

"Yes, I know. You were a very good friend to her, and for that and many other things I shall always be grateful." Harris smiled at her, a weak, tentative smile, but an expression of release and even intimacy that spread soft fingers of relief through her.

"It'll be all right," she said, and he nodded, though she knew he didn't really think so.

After that, Harris went about his regular life again, eating his meals quietly with her and Etta, working in his office, and occasionally taking trips that lasted two or three days to collect his rents. But still there remained a new air of indifference about him, as if he were still lost, that slumped his shoulders, and an emptiness that haunted his eyes.

"I don't know what to do, Mrs. Stowe," Colette confided. "I've done all I can."

"Sorrow sets its own pace in a man's heart. He has to move on in his own way and in his own time."

"I know, but it hurts so to see it." Colette gave a hollow laugh. "He won't even argue with me."

"Perhaps it is time for you to move on."

"What do you mean?"

"What will you do now? You cannot stay in Mr. Eastman's home indefinitely. Summer is passing. I must go home, too. I have vegetables to put up from the garden."

Colette's heart churned with hesitancy. Could she really leave Harris to suffer through his grief alone? Yet what else could she do? Etta was right. He had to deal with his loss in his own way, in his own time.

"It is so hard to decide."

"You could go to your family."

Colette thought about that. It wasn't a new thought, but sometime during the past three years this part of Wisconsin Territory had come to feel like home to her, and she didn't want to leave it, didn't want her roots torn free like they'd been when she'd left Michigan. *I miss them dearly, but to go away and not come back... to leave Harris and Etta and Joe, even if Joe never wants to speak to me again...*

"You're right, Mrs. Stowe. I know you are. I'll stay with you if you're sure Mr. Stowe won't mind."

"He will not mind."

"Then perhaps, when Harris is better, I will go to Mama and Papa."

Then another idea emboldened her. Forgotten plans made in the haze of days prior to Helen's death came rushing back, plans to invest some of her money in land. Owning land would settle some of her disarrayed thoughts about her future.

It will help Harris to think of other things, too.

When he came home the next afternoon looking almost like the man she'd once known, she decided it was time to tell him her plans. She'd already packed the things she needed to take with her to Etta and Noah Stowe's. Her bag lay upstairs on her bed. Etta had gone home to bring supper to Noah, and Colette and Harris ate alone.

"How was your ride out to Saratoga?" Colette asked.

"Uneventful. I found squatters in the old Miller place and had to send them on. I need to get someone else in there soon or they'll be back, I wager."

"It shouldn't be a problem, should it?"

He shook his head as he spooned another serving of potatoes onto his plate.

"I see you've gotten some of your appetite back. I'm glad."

Harris cast her a smile. "Yes. It's good. It's hard not to eat with all the food Mrs. Stowe has been leaving for me."

"And my breakfasts."

His smile broadened. "Yes, and you. You're a good cook in your own right, Lettie. You're good at many things."

"Thank you. Which reminds me... is the land you told me about at Big Bull Falls still for sale?"

He chewed his food slowly, his fork poised in the air as he studied her. "You're still interested in the investment?"

She nodded.

"Yes, it's still for sale. That town is going to grow. More loggers are moving into the area. After they're gone, the farmers will clean out the stumps. The millers and tanners, blacksmiths, tinsmiths, and shopkeepers will move in right along with them. Ten years from now, little white houses with picket fences will line the streets. Twenty years from now, it'll be a city in its own right, with churches and schools and newspapers. The property you buy today can be surveyed into parcels worth ten times," he gestured with his fork, "maybe even twenty times its current value by then. What do you think of that?"

"I'm interested."

"You could become a rich woman, Lettie."

She recognized the spark in his eyes challenging her. She was certain her own eyes mirrored his.

"It's not that I want to be rich. But to be secure has its rewards."

"We can proceed with the paperwork after supper if you like."

"I would. Will I really be able to afford it?"

"The rent money from the farm alone wouldn't be enough, of course. But I owe you money for all the time you've been here."

"I don't feel right about that. Besides, I like to send it to my folks."

"Lettie, after all you've been to Helen, and now, what it's meant to me to have you here..." He paused, obviously struggling with his emotions. "Well, it's worth more than you could know. I'd like to help you with this. Please let me."

She gave a nod. "All right. If you really want to."

After their meal, they left the dishes and went into Harris' study to sign the offer on the property he had drafted earlier on Colette's behalf. A tremor ran through her. *Land. My own land.* To mark the occasion, Harris poured each of them a small glass of port and made a toast.

"To Lettie. May her days as land baroness be prosperous."

Colette laughed. "Land baroness," she mumbled. "Let's not get carried away." She sipped on the port as she walked across the room, pretending to look at the books on the shelves. "Harris, I do have something to tell you."

"What is it?" He had situated himself into one of the chairs nearby as she walked the perimeter of the room.

"Mrs. Stowe is anxious to be home. I'm going with her." She glanced at him to measure his reaction. "It's only right."

He lowered his glass. His brow furrowed. "Yes, I suppose it is."

"Then, whenever it can be worked out, I'll join my family. I miss them," she added.

Harris threw the remnant of wine down his throat with a toss of his head, as though it were something much stronger. Then he rose and went to the cabinet where he kept more liquor. Uncorking a bottle of brandy, he filled his glass. Colette tried not to watch him, but couldn't help noticing his hand was shaking.

Sadness overwhelmed her. "I'm sorry, Harris. I wouldn't go, but..."

"But?"

"I don't know what else to do."

Harris downed the brandy and set his glass on the desk.

"I'm sure your family misses you, too. It's only right that you should go to them."

She nodded, but couldn't shake the feeling that pinned her heart to her stomach. "I'm sure I'll be back to visit, or you could come to see us when you're down that way."

"Of course."

She knew he was only being polite. If she went away, she'd never come back to Grand Rapids. It was how these things went. She'd go away and the past would go with her, just like it had when she left Michigan. She wasn't only losing Helen. She was losing them all. She was losing this place and the past three years.

She wanted to mourn all over again. Promises to write often or visit were shallow sentiments. Joe, like Manason, was forever gone from her life. Next would be Harris. Mrs. Stowe and Noah would become memories. Friendships and acquaintances she'd made of the few new families in town would never have the chance to flourish. She'd never see the day that her parents' farmstead would either prosper or disintegrate back into the earth. It would be a place and time melted into a dream.

She hated it. She didn't want it to happen this way.

She turned toward Harris and discovered he had receded into the man he'd become following Helen's death. A black look had settled over him, all because of her. Mrs. Stowe was wrong. He wasn't ready to be left alone. He needed help to make it through. He needed *her*.

Unafraid, she walked over to him and stood in front of him so he had to look at her. "If there's anything I can do..."

A dry laugh escaped him. "You have to make your own way, Lettie, just like me." His eyes met hers. "It's just that I suddenly have no wish to be parted from you. Helen's little companion has, without effort, become my own."

Colette didn't know what to say, and she dropped her gaze. He took her hand and caressed it softly. "I'm sorry," he said. Then he dropped her hand and turned away, going back to the bottle in the cupboard.

She went that night to Etta and Noah Stowe's house. They'd prepared their son's empty room for her, and she quickly felt at home. It only made the thought of going away for good more intolerable.

Over the next few days she helped Etta pickle beets and dig potatoes. Some of these she took to Harris, reminding him to eat them, thinking she was beginning to sound like a mother hen, like Mrs. Stowe.

She wrote a letter to her family, telling them what had happened and that she would try to come to them soon. She couldn't guarantee just when, she said, trying to put off the inevitable, trying to find a way to become excited about such a change.

If only Harris didn't need me so. Then it would be easy.

She wanted to write Jean, but didn't know where to find her. Was she still in Michigan? Somewhere in the woods up north? Colette had no way of knowing.

She wanted Joseph to appear, to smile at her and tell her everything would be all right. They were still friends. She wondered, if he did appear, whether she might feel more affable towards him, might even say yes next time. Would there be a next time? She doubted it.

She wanted someone to tell her to stay.

All she could do, however, was wish it and drag out the days as long as possible. By early October, with her birthday not far away, she knew she couldn't do it any longer. She had to go.

*****

Harris wasn't doing well. He was lonely. To him, it seemed cynically humorous that he should feel this way. He'd never been lonely for Helen's presence when it was available. Now that she was gone, however, he missed it. Maybe, he reasoned, it was the *idea* of her presence that had been sufficient for him in the past.

Still, he had to admit, there was more to it than that. He liked knowing Helen was waiting to please him whenever he came home. He'd simply accepted it as his due. Then when Lettie came into their lives, bringing her intelligent challenges and bold ideas, his life had taken on a new and interesting dimension. With her gone, he was truly lonely.

He sat behind his desk, stewing over it as he shuffled through a stack of papers from his attorney and a couple of letters that had arrived. One stood out from the rest, and suddenly all his thoughts fled away.

It's addressed to Helen. Helen never got mail except a yearly post from her mother. This one came from Jean Gilbert. *Jean Gilbert.* Harris tapped the letter on the desk, his thoughts searching. *Ah, yes. That must be it. Miss Jean Kade, married now. Interesting.*

He broke the seal and tore open the thick envelope. Inside was a letter as well as another envelope folded in half bearing Colette's name. He set the second envelope aside and opened the first letter -- a brief account to Helen about Jean's marriage to Robin Gilbert, and a telling of how they were building a house up north on property their brother had endowed to them.

She went on to say more about this brother:

Manason and I wonder what's become of Colette and her family. When Manason came to Grand Rapids last spring, he heard about Eldon's accident and the family's decision to sell out and go for medical help. I've wanted to write Colette, but since I've no idea how to reach her, I wonder if you would address the enclosed letter and send it to her. I'm making an assumption that you have that information, but I hope I am correct.

Manason, too, had hoped to see Colette again. I think we both know how that would please her. I will tell you something -- I think it will please Manason, too.

I hope this finds you and Harris both well and enjoying your new baby...

Harris didn't read any further.

He picked up the other letter and stared at Colette Palmer's name written in feminine script on the envelope, wondering about this brother of Jean's who'd wanted to see Colette. Opening the desk drawer, he placed it inside.

Sorting through the other letters, he skipped one from someone who owed him money, begging for leniency, no doubt. He stopped to open an envelope which had no sender's name on it. This would be important.

On schedule, it said without introduction. *Done better than estimated. Suspect someone is looking in on the project.*

Harris understood what this meant, that someone might be on to them. And the B on the bottom of the page he recognized as Seamus Boggs' way of signing a letter he didn't want traced back to him.

He read on:

New man and crew in the area. Manason Kade. His man is Tom Durant, a cruiser from Michigan. Await instructions. ~B

Manason Kade. How could the same name crop up in both letters? Jean had seemed a bright young woman, and now it appeared she had an intelligent brother. Harris briefly wondered if Manason Kade might be a man who could be bought, but knowing Jean, Harris doubted it.

So Manason Kade was spying on his operations, and he was also probably more than a little interested in Lettie. Well, the two together just wouldn't do. In fact, either one alone just didn't sit right with him. He slid the desk drawer open and glanced again at Colette's letter. He'd have to think more about this before he gave it to her. He couldn't have her leave him for an enemy.

Harris closed the drawer and lifted his pipe from its cradle. After lighting it, he let the match touch the corner of Boggs' missive. He'd have to think long and hard.

*****

Colette made arrangements to travel along with an employee at Mr. Strong's Hotel who was leaving for Portage in less than two weeks to meet a supply boat. He was also bringing along his married sister, who had quilts to trade. From Portage, Colette would take a boat to Green Bay and a stage down one of the few territorial roads to Milwaukee to reach her parents.

"We were going to go this week," the man said, "but Martha wants to hear the preacher when he comes back through town."

"He'll be back this way?" Colette asked.

"*Jah*. We hear he is making his way downriver. Should be in Centralia and Grand Rapids by Saturday night. We'll have good preaching here at the hotel on Sunday."

Buoyant with the news, Colette hurried up the street toward the Stowe's home. Passing by the Eastman house, she slowed. She hadn't seen Harris in several days. She doubted he had been out in all that time. Her steps faltered. If she told him about the preacher returning, would it only remind him of that other Sunday, and how terribly it had ended?

Willing herself to be bold, she struck up the path to the house and knocked on the door. She waited, then knocked again. All was quiet. Her glance flicked past the little garden plot she'd planted. The peas and beans had dried on withered stems, and weeds had crept up between. Apparently she was wrong. Harris wasn't in. She turned to go when the door suddenly opened.

"Lettie?"

She turned, startled by sight of him. "I didn't think you were home. You surprised me."

"A welcome surprise, I hope."

"Yes."

"Come in."

She stepped inside and pushed the bonnet off her hair. He led her into the parlor and offered her a chair and refreshment.

As he went into the kitchen and out the back door to pump them each a glass of water, Colette marveled. She'd expected to find Harris looking withdrawn, but he was not. His dress was neat, if not immaculate, his hair freshly combed. His face wore only the beard growth of a day or two.

"Thank you," she said as he returned and handed her a glass.

"To what do I owe the pleasure of this visit?"

His smile encouraged her to plunge ahead. "The circuit preacher is coming back. He'll be here for Sunday meeting."

"Is that so?"

He appeared unaffected by memories of Helen and that other Sunday, so she went on.

"Yes. I hope you'll think of going to hear him again."

"You'll be going with the Stowes?"

She nodded. "We'd love for you to sit with us."

"Then I shall do my best to be there."

"Good." She tried to think of more to say. She sipped her water while he watched her, and wondered what his thoughts were.

Finally she said, "I've found someone I'll be able to accompany to the Portage. I'll be leaving soon after the preacher's visit. Perhaps he'll even travel with us for a while."

Harris frowned and swirled the water in his glass. "That's the real reason you've come then. To tell me goodbye."

"No. But I knew you'd want to know."

"Would I?"

She took another sip rather than look at him. He kept watching her.

"Well, I suppose I should be going." She rose to leave and turned to set the glass onto a side table. When she turned again, Harris was standing near her.

"Would you care to take a look at a new map? It concerns the property you purchased."

Colette relaxed. "Of course."

He led her into his study and picked up a rolled map that lay on his desk. Unrolling it, he spread it out before her. With his index finger he outlined the parcel in her name. "Here it is."

She came around the desk and stood beside him, using her hands with his to brace down the edges of the map, and together they perused it.

"I wish I could see the property. I want to see it," she said suddenly, turning her face toward him.

Inches apart, she couldn't help seeing that up close, the loneliness in his eyes, the hollowness was still there. Her heart tore, flesh from flesh. How she didn't want to go, didn't want to start over someplace else. She wanted to see this land, needed someone with Harris' insight to show her what to do with it. So aching inside, she hardly noticed his attention was entirely focused upon her, and not on the map at all. He spoke quietly, in a tone that would have told her without words that his mind was full of other things, drawing her.

"Been reading your Bible, Lettie?"

She stared back at him, unsure of the new direction their conversation was taking. "A little," she offered.

"I'm not much of a Bible man myself, but I know that somewhere in there it says it's not good for man to be alone." He placed his hand over hers where it rested on the map, and she trembled. "You'll think me foolish, and too old to be saying so, but I want you to stay, Lettie. With me. As my wife."

She gasped, and he drew her hand to his chest, collecting her other one there as well. "I need you, Lettie," he said, raising her hands and pressing his forehead to them.

Almost involuntarily, she stepped closer, drawn by pity and caring and her own need to stay. Did she love Harris? Did she care for him enough to answer his plea favorably? She didn't know, and she couldn't sort out any of the feelings coursing through her. She only knew she wanted him not to hurt anymore. She wanted to solve the problem of his need and his loneliness. She wanted to mend everything that had been broken.

Tears rose into her eyes, or maybe they'd been there all along. They tumbled out as she nodded her head and, strangely, bent it to rest her cheek on the crown of Harris' black hair.

"All right. I'll stay."

Raising his head, he stared at her again. She doubted he believed her, and she repeated herself. "I'll stay with you."

That settled, he pulled her into an embrace unlike any other she'd known.

Chapter Twenty

Young Frankie Kester was the first to see Tom Durant stagger into camp and slump to the ground. Leaping off a wagon piled high with skinned tree trunks, Frankie ran to him, calling out to anyone else nearby to come quick. Within moments, Manason heard the commotion and came to the door of his office just as the men were carrying Tom up the path. A brilliant red stain spreading across the side of Tom's white shirt was clearly visible even though he was surrounded by three big men.

Nase shouldered into the knot of men. "Does anybody know what happened?"

"Looks like he was shot," Frankie answered. "I had an uncle shot once when my other uncle misfired his gun. Killed him dead."

"Put him on his cot." Tom had been bunking with Manason since starting work. Gently as they were able, the lumberjacks laid him down.

Tom's face was chalk white, and he didn't make a sound. He looked dead. Manason knelt beside him and stripped off the bloody shirt, giving him a cursory examination.

"Go find Eb," he commanded, referring to one of the men who doctored the animals whenever they got sick or had a pain. He was pretty good at it, and most of the men revered him as they would a regular doctor.

"Louis went for him right away."

A bucket of warm water appeared, along with some strips of clean cloth. Manason stretched one dampened piece across Tom's brow to try and revive him and used another to wipe away the blood around the wound.

"Hopefully nothing vital was hit."

When Ebert -- Eb -- Smith arrived, he cleared everyone but Manason out of the building and rolled up his sleeves. Upon further examination, he declared the bullet was still in Tom's body and needed to come out. He asked for a hot knife and some brandy, then set to work.

Manason got out of the way, sitting on his own bed across the room, praying and listening to the rumble of Eb's concentrated breathing. When the clink of metal hitting the side of a bowl reverberated through the air, his head came up.

"Was that it?"

"Yep. Tom's lost a lot of blood. He's not come 'round. It's going to be touch and go for awhile, looks like."

Manason came over to his side. "Anything I can do?"

"He's got a fever. Got to keep that down. Let him drink a little brandy for the pain. Needs lots of rest and water, maybe some broth to keep his strength up. Should keep someone here with him if you can."

"Thanks, Eb. I'll check with my sister Jean. Maybe she can lend a hand."

"You do that," he said, wiping his hands on a towel before he bandaged Tom's side.

"Any deeper damage, you think?"

"I think it missed his vitals clean. But like I said, he's lost a lot of blood. If infection sets in, he's a goner."

Manason took that in with a bit of fear. He wasn't ready to accept that possibility. *God, I haven't been much of a praying man like I should be. But I'm asking for Tom... no, that's not even true. I am asking for myself. Forgive me Lord. Forgive me. Please spare Tom. I need him. Please.*

During the first few days Tom's temperature rose, and they all feared the worst. Manason prayed for Tom, but at the same time feverish anger raged inside him. The gunshot had to be Boggs' work, or that of one of his bullies. Why'd they do it, though? Did Tom get too close, or had he caught them red-handed? Maybe they had encroached on Nase's claim. Whatever had happened, it didn't really matter. The point was that Tom was lying there, possibly dying, and Boggs and his men -- and for that matter, Harris Eastman -- were all free to keep doing what they were doing. Well, it wasn't going to end that way. Not if Manason had anything to say about it.

The more Nase chewed on them, the more these thoughts caught like sand in his mouth. They gritted around his brain and made him spitting mad. At last, on the fourth day, while Tom moaned and tossed with fever and Jean, helpless but working tirelessly to try and bring it down, Manason collected his men. He called Rob and Purnell, and all the others except Eb and the cookee. He would have left young Frankie out of it, too, but there was no leaving a fellow who didn't want to be left out of his first fight.

Grabbing pike poles and peavies in their rocky fists, Manason and his men went to give Boggs and his bullies a little comeuppance.

"We won't use guns," he promised Jean before he left.

She paced in front of him. "You won't solve anything, Nase."

"It needs doing, and you're not going to talk me out of it."

"'Vengeance is mine, says the Lord'."

"Consider me a tool of the Lord, then."

She whirled. "I won't hear you blaspheme, Nase. And you're not taking Rob."

"He's already organizing some of the men."

She gasped.

"Jean--" Nase took her by the shoulders and lifted her chin. "Rob's a grown man, not a boy. He knows what he's doing. How do you think he'd feel if you demanded he stay here with cookee and Eb? Some of these other fellows have families, too. But they've got honor. Tom's got honor. Let them show Boggs that. Let them show *Eastman*."

"Can't you save your honor by calling the law?"

"What law? Out here? Do you know what'll happen if we do nothing? Boggs'll laugh."

"Is that so bad?"

"He'll mark us as pushovers. He'll move in and start taking anything he wants."

"He's already doing that, it seems."

"It'll get worse. We need to make him respect us."

"Respect!" She spat the word.

"You might feel differently if Rob was the one lying there on that cot."

Jean's eyes flared. She pushed his hands away. "How dare you, Nase? How dare you imply I would care less because it's Tom and not Rob or *you*? I don't want you to do it because I *care*. I don't want anyone else hurt."

"I don't want that either." Nase kissed her steely cheek. "That's why we have to teach Boggs a lesson now. Hopefully it'll be good enough to carry all the way back to Eastman Enterprises."

He turned and headed out the door, leaving her to worry after him and the rest of the men.

"You saw Jean?" Rob asked when they gathered together.

Nase nodded.

Rob grinned. "Got room for me in your cabin tonight?"

"You know my sister pretty well," Nase said, their long legs carrying them east into the thick woods.

*****

Nase's crew walked the five miles back to their own camp despite their fatigue, some limping, but not complaining, others feeling better after they'd drunk and bathed their faces from a nearby spring. At camp, the cookee and Eb had a pile of food waiting for them. They slung themselves into eating with the same enthusiasm with which they'd met Boggs' bully-boys. Then they swilled down several kettles of hot tea to boot, not caring that they were still dirty and bloody and aching as they sat at the cookee's tables.

Manason ate only a small portion, his rib cage too sore to absorb much before he headed back to his office cabin to check in on Tom. Rob was beside him as they headed up the short path. Neither were sure about their welcome from Jean, but she was too busy to think much about it. Tom was awake, and she was feeding him a bowl of broth when they came in.

Tom grinned feebly, and his voice was weak. "You look worse'n I feel. Pole cat get ya?"

Jean looked up at them then, her eyes flying wide. The bowl in her hand shook.

136

"We're okay, so don't go spilling that hot soup on Tom," Manason said. He limped over to Tom's side and pulled a stool next to his bed. Jean set her lips in a straight line, and Rob came over to whisper something into her ear. She set down the bowl and spun around to pull him into her arms, trying hard but unsuccessfully not to cry. Rob took her outside.

"Boggs?" Tom asked. His face was still pale, his cheeks sunk in so that his gray eyes looked big as lakes and not as steely as Manason was used to seeing them.

Nase nodded. "Don't wear yourself out asking questions. I'll tell you everything you want to know." He proceeded to tell Tom how he and the men had come upon Boggs' outfit building a sledge road through a stand of poplar just along the edge of an ash swamp, and about the fight that had ensued. "We finally forced Boggs into some kind of accounting."

"But you ain't quite satisfied."

Nase didn't counter for a moment. He had to think about it; had to reckon with the fact that Jean was right, that vengeance didn't content him. They might have paid Boggs back for the damage done to Tom, but they hadn't done a thing to settle the bigger picture with the pirating of logs and the long reaching arm of Eastman Enterprises. Boggs would recover soon enough, and he wasn't the kind of man who would back down just because of a few bruises and broken ribs. A crack across the jaw would have the same effect on Boggs as cuffing a mama bear across the ears. Nase shook his head. "Felt kind of good at the moment, though."

"Yeah, but you're too good a church boy to be happy with yourself."

"Maybe that's it." Nase gave a grin that made his face hurt. "Sure am glad to see you looking alive, Tom. I have to admit that coming back here to find you doing better gives me a whole lot of satisfaction."

"I suppose I have your sister to thank."

"Jean and Eb both. Frankie's the one who saw you hit the dirt."

"I don't even remember."

"I reckon you don't. You'll hear about it six different ways before winter."

Manason's vision had gotten worse. His eye had swollen to the point he had to cock his head sideways to look at Tom while he talked. On top of that, a wave of fatigue rushed over him along with relief at seeing Tom clear of danger. He had to go to bed, and soon.

Tom was starting to get drowsy, too, so Manason promised to talk to him later. He got up from the stool and dragged his calks across to his own cot where he didn't bother to remove them, but instead tumbled like a felled tree across his blankets, falling asleep almost instantly.

The next day Manason got back to the business of logging pine. Jean and Rob planned to go home to their new cabin, where she was going to make Rob rest up until the freeze. Meanwhile, she would send to Clearwater -- or Eau Claire, as most Frenchmen called it -- for some seed to plant in the spring. She chattered about the garden work she'd done with Colette and Helen the previous year.

"I wish one of them would write back," she mused. "Colette used to be so faithful about that."

"Does she know how to find you?" Manason asked as he tacked another chart to the wall behind the rough-hewn table he called a desk.

"I wrote her last month and told her where to write. Maybe my letter hasn't reached her yet. I had hoped Helen would reply, but she does have a new baby. Her world is probably quite full."

Manason didn't answer. His thoughts about Eastman Enterprises naturally meandered to the Palmers. He mulled over for the hundredth time the speculation Jean had planted in his head about Colette. He shared Jean's relief that the Palmers had gotten clear of Harris Eastman. He hoped to see that man cut down a few notches, even if it meant he'd probably never have the chance to see what sort of woman Colette had become. Even if it meant he'd missed out on his own best reason to build that house on the oak ridge.

Chapter Twenty-One

Colette lay staring at the rise and fall of the white curtain on the breeze. It lifted, lingered, and fluttered down in graceful waves. The days had grown steadily colder, and a hoary frost had covered the ground on a dozen different nights. But the return of Indian summer over the past few days gave her the opportunity to sleep with the window open just a little, to smell the fresh scent of autumn's glory one last time. Soon the days would lose their golden hue, and the gray cast of November would be upon them.

She rolled over, and another smell, not yet familiar, mingled with those riding the breeze. Harris' scent hovered where his head had lain on the pillow beside her. She reached out and felt the indentation, then leaned her face into it, breathing deeply, wondering over a myriad of questions that bounced like dust mites on sunlight through her thoughts.

I've married Harris.

A sudden, unexpected wave of panic washed over her, as if she'd completely absorbed, in a flash, the permanence of her decision. Fear tickled her arms and legs. Had she done the right thing? What if she hadn't? It was too late now if she had. The time for anxious questions had come and gone, and she had ignored it.

Yesterday, after the preaching service, she'd stood with Harris and vowed to love, honor, and obey him as long as they both lived. The service was a blur. So unreal. Yet real enough, she found, last night.

Home with her new husband, intimately together for the first time, she'd found what she'd always believed in every other way to be true. Harris Eastman was an exacting man. Yes, it was not the first, nor did she believe it would be the last time she would think of him that way.

Might she be pregnant? It had happened to women before, getting pregnant on their honeymoon. Why didn't that thought make her afraid, especially after what had happened to Helen? Colette splayed her hand across her flat abdomen and pressed down.

Where was Harris now? Why had he not awakened her? The hour must be late. Maybe he was hungry. Maybe, even now, he wondered why she hadn't risen to prepare his breakfast.

During the few fleeting days that had elapsed between the time he'd asked her to stay and be his wife, and the time the preacher came and made it so, she'd continued to stay with Noah and Etta. She'd thought little about the looming consequences of her decision; she chose not to. That was part of the unreality of it. She chose only to consider that her decision meant sparing Harris more agony, and that she would not have to abandon her life in Grand Rapids. That it meant so much more than that, and that she might come to regret any part of her decision, she chose to not think of at all.

The door opened and Colette turned her head to see Harris enter wearing a robe. Heat suffused her neck and face, and he smiled at her.

"Don't be embarrassed, Lettie. You look beautiful this morning."

His comment didn't assuage her, and she warmed even more. He slipped out of his robe and lay beside her. She looked away as his soft laugh tumbled over her.

"You're an amazing woman, Lettie."

She frowned. "How is that?"

"I think I've probably been falling in love with you for a long time. I just never realized it until you said you were going away. You've been in my life for such a long time that I didn't see how I'd come to depend on you."

Harris had never mentioned love as part of the equation before, and Colette had a hard time taking it in, even as he leaned across the bed and kissed her shoulder, causing her thoughts to flutter wildly.

"Helen was incapable of giving me what you already have, Lettie." His voice was warm and mesmerizing. He'd not mentioned Helen in days, and to say such a thing now seemed incalculably cold, seeming to Colette that she might have done something improper to warrant such words from him. But her senses were too on fire for her to be able to collect those random feelings into organized thoughts. His lips tugged at her ear. "You complete me, more than I've ever been."

Later, when she'd finally risen at an unbelievably late hour to find a bowl of something for Dandy, she tried to gather up what he'd said to her. Did he mean she had seduced him? What did he mean by saying she'd given him more than Helen ever had, or that she completed him? His words should make her feel good, she argued, knowing she'd become the wife he wanted, and so soon. But remembering them evinced an adverse effect, suggesting some sort of indecency on her part. She tried to shake off such foolish notions. She'd never done any such thing. Helen would have noticed and said something. She would have been hurt. Still, it was too late to hurt Helen now. Now all Collette could do was live up to her vows. She would have to be the best wife she could, and if Harris said she made him happy, then glad she must be.

*****

Harris, too, was giving this new turn in life a good deal of thought. He'd never expected to be drawn to Lettie in such a way. In truth, he'd not given her any untoward thoughts prior to Helen's death. His conscience was clean on that account. But as the days after Helen's death groaned on, the fact that Lettie Palmer had always been there for him, had always surprised and challenged him, had always tantalized him, came to the forefront of his thoughts. No question that she was a pretty girl. She suddenly became even more attractive, only adding to the way she constantly surprised him.

When Lettie had taken her bags and moved to the Stowe's house, he knew he wanted her. He wanted her not as a companion, or a confidante, or a housekeeper and friend. He wanted her body and soul. His desire for her had grown from a fledgling need to an insatiable hunger that demanded gratification.

From that point on he spent more of his days thinking about Lettie than mourning Helen. He'd cleaned himself up and prepared his own meals. He returned to his office not to drink, but to work. He fantasized about what a woman like Lettie could do for his career if she were his wife. She had charm and grace, as did Helen; but Lettie also had knowledge that would amaze the lumber kings. They would be flattered to have such a young, beautiful creature conversing with them at social gatherings, not about empty-headed gossip, but about their industry, and with understanding and passion. Important men would look up to Harris because of his wife. They would give him their attention and their money if necessary, because they would be bound under Lettie's spell.

Just as I am.

He shook himself. No, it wasn't a dream. She would need polish, of course. But Lettie was a natural beauty. Clothes were easy to come by and would only accentuate her charms. He would find her a maid, someone to dress her hair and scent her bath water. He, himself, would make her feel every inch the woman she was. He would sculpt her and mold her to suit him, should there be any flaws he'd not yet discovered.

He did truly love her, he decided. Yet, it was admittedly hard for a man like Harris to discern the line between love and longing.

He sat at his desk, distracted from his work by more thoughts of her, and smiled. He leaned back into his chair and tented his fingers across his chest. How gorgeous she'd looked when he'd left her in his bed. He was sorely tempted to find her again and take her back there. But she was delightfully shy, and he didn't want to overwhelm her with his desire on the first day of their marriage. Lettie was young, ten years younger than Helen, and he needed to be patient with her in many ways. He could afford that. In fact, he had more patience with her than with anyone in years. He took a deep, pleasing breath, just to enjoy it. No rush of adrenaline. No unnamed stress. She did that for him.

He spun in his chair and rose to look out the window. The leaves were blowing off the trees, and years had passed since Harris had taken time to enjoy the changing of the seasons. Later, if Lettie wished, they'd take a walk away from the houses and eyes of Grand Rapids. He'd romance her as though he were a younger man.

He smiled inwardly, pleased with his idea, as his eyes locked with those of Joseph Gilbert, who stood on the street with his feet spread apart and his hands in the pockets of his trousers. His eyes were set like stone, and the wind moved the black curls of his hair.

"Well, if it isn't Lettie's suitor, come one day too late," Harris murmured. He raised the window sash and was about to warn the boy off when Lettie stepped out the door and made her way down the walk to meet him.

*****

Sweeping away the falling leaves gathered on the stoop, only to be crushed to bits beneath their feet every time they entered the house, Colette startled when she came face to face with Joe standing in the street like a statue. "Joseph," she called, forcing a smile.

Her moment of delight dulled a split second later, when he squeezed his fists, working the muscles of his forearms. *He must know.* Joseph's eyes bore down on her as she approached him. He was angry by all accounts, yet Colette recognized the same pain in those flashing green eyes she'd seen there the last time they were together.

He continued to stare at her until she came to the end of the path.

"So, you've found him then?" He offered no preamble. Colette braced herself as the words seethed out between Joe's teeth. "This *old man*? Is *he* the someone you were waiting for?"

"Joseph, please..." She stepped closer, shaking her head. "I... I can't even explain."

"What's the matter, Lettie? Can't stand up to what you did? Sure, and you're not sorry now?" Joe glared at her, every muscle in his body taught and quivering. "Don't lie. You obviously got what you wanted. It's not what I would have thought of you, Lettie."

"It's not what you think."

"How's that?" Joseph sneered, but Colette glimpsed the wetness in his eyes.

Guilt settled over her. "It didn't happen the way you're thinking."

"Oh? What am I thinking? Would you like to explain that to me?"

She shook her head and moved her hands as though she, too, grasped for an answer.

"I'll tell you how I am thinking." He stepped closer to her and looked down into her eyes. "I'm thinking there is another fellow, somewhere, someone you might have met at the mills or here in town, and I can't figure out who it is. Then it becomes clear. It's not another fellow I can compete with. It's rich old Harris Eastman whose wife is beautiful but dull, and he's taken with you. I should have seen it, but I didn't."

"No, Joseph." She shook her head, unable to ward off the moisture welling in her eyes.

"You married him, Lettie. What more is there to think?"

Colette dropped her head and sniffed to try and stop the tears.

"Is it money you want? I would have worked 'til doomsday to make you happy."

"No."

"Is it his maturity, then?" Joseph's voice rose with each question that ripped out of him. He nearly shouted, "You seemed to imply often enough that I lacked in that area."

"It wasn't even *him*, Joseph." She choked, a sob catching like a fist in her throat.

"Not him?" Joseph laughed sourly. "How many others are there, Lettie girl?"

He grasped her shoulders as though he might shake her, but he didn't. Colette summoned the strength to look up at him at the same moment she realized Harris had come out the door. Still, Joe didn't back down.

Harris exited the house projecting calm and rationale. In the brief hours she'd been married to him, Colette had already recognized that it was forced. Perhaps Joe knew it, too.

"Joseph Gilbert? We haven't seen you in some time." Harris almost sounded pleasant.

Joe threw him a glare and freed Colette. She sniffed and widened her gaze at Joe. If she couldn't make him sense the danger, no telling what his intense emotion might produce.

"I seem to remember that you used to come to the door and knock when you wished to visit. I hope that if you have anything further to discuss with my wife, you will not forget to use that protocol."

"I've come to speak with Lettie *Palmer*," Joe said, never peeling his eyes from her.

"Well, you must realize that's impossible. However, if, as a gentleman, you wish to speak with *Mrs. Eastman*, please feel free to come at another time -- when we are both at home, of course. We're sorry we cannot entertain you today, as we are only recently married and are taking the time to better acquaint ourselves with one another. I'm sure you can understand how important this day is to us and why we wish to have it to ourselves."

Embarrassment rose in hot waves through Colette. She turned her eyes away from Joe and didn't lift them again until Harris glided his arm around her shoulders and turned her toward the house. Then she lifted her lashes only briefly at Joe as he stood rooted there, watching them go inside together.

"I expect he'll suffer awhile," Harris said, "but he'll get over it. Many young women are coming to Wisconsin Territory these days, and I'm sure any number of them would happily ease his distress."

Chapter Twenty-Two

Colette told herself Harris was right. Joseph had clearly been out of line in coming to her in such a manner. The act was so typical of him. Impetuous. Fire-headed. And yet... and yet, she felt terrible. Responsible. He must have been so shocked to learn she was married. How had he found out? His family, certainly. They'd all been at the preaching on Sunday, all except his brother Rob. Everyone knew.

When had he returned and been told? Just today? Yesterday, perhaps? Recently enough for his hurt and shock to brew into indignation.

Colette initially hoped he would come back later with a calmer demeanor, even though she had no idea what she might say to him that would change anything. Was she selfish to want everything smoothed over? That would cost her nothing, or would it? She wondered just how deeply her feelings ran for Joe.

Foolish question.

No wonder Harris had banished Joe afterward.

"I don't want you to receive him if I am not at home. In fact, I'd prefer you not speak to him in the street should you see him. I don't trust that young rogue."

"Why, Harris... I've spent hundreds of hours alone with Joe." Even as angry as Joe had been, she still trusted him.

Harris grazed her with a look she'd never seen him express. "I don't trust him."

"But--"

"I forbid it, Lettie. So let's just leave it at that, shall we?"

She had no other choice but to obey Harris. Perhaps it was for the best.

Trying to shake off her doubts, Colette finally wrote a letter to her family, framing her new situation as delicately as words allowed, explaining to them that she and Harris would arrange a visit the following summer. After taking several attempts to get it right, she finally sealed the letter and took it to the general store to be sent out with the next batch of mail. In her heart she was confident that once her parents got past the shock of Helen's death and absorbed Colette and Harris' age difference, they would see it was a secure match for her. Her father, especially, would be pleased. In fact, she remembered how he had schooled her to be the wife of someone important. Hints about that had never been lost on her.

"I can hardly wait to see them again," she said to Harris.

"The time will fly by, my dear. We have a lot to do between now and then."

"We do?"

"You'll be meeting with important people, Lettie. Wisconsin is moving toward statehood, and I want to introduce you to some of my associates who have a voice in the territory. I also intend to do some further speculating on your behalf."

"May I help you with some of your work?"

"No." He laughed. "Only things requiring a more *personal* touch." He looked her over in an intimate appraisal that still made her uneasy. "I intend to see that you are ready in every respect to meet these people. We will start with your wardrobe."

"My wardrobe?" She didn't know what he meant. "Is there something wrong with it?"

"Not for a small town like Grand Rapids or any other wilderness settlement. But we will be attending important dinners. Balls."

"Are you thinking of running for office in Wisconsin someday, Harris?"

"The idea has crossed my mind, but no. I only intend to make my presence known as an industry leader. You can help me with that because you are well-versed in everything related to the business. I hope you won't mind my saying so, darling, but you have a charm about you that will not be lost on these leaders any more than it was lost on the woods crew at camp three, the winter when you were still too young to realize your influence. Do you understand?"

Colette had grown up a great deal in the past two weeks. She understood surprisingly well.

"Now," Harris continued, "I want you to get rid of Helen's clothes. Don't look so glum. It's all right. I need it to be this way. I would rather it was this way." He reached across the table and squeezed her fingers.

"If you say so."

"Thank you. There is a box, probably in the back of her cupboard, containing four new dresses that have never been worn. I bought them last fall when we first learned of Helen's condition. They were for afterward. Something new for her, you understand."

"I think so. What do you want me to do with them?"

"Why, I want you to wear them, of course. Will you please stop looking so alarmed, Lettie? They hold no sentiment for me. Helen never even tried them on. She couldn't by that time. I've completely forgotten what they look like."

"So..."

"Wear them, so you'll become used to fashionable dress. I want you to enjoy nice things." He stood and leaned across the table to kiss her brow. "It will please me."

Colette nodded as he left the room, calling behind him, "I've been away from things for so long, I have a lot to catch up on. I'll be in my office for a couple of hours. I have to leave on business east of here for a few days. The clothes will be a pleasant project for you while I'm gone."

"Harris?" she called. "When are you leaving?"

"Tomorrow morning," he replied as his voice faded behind his office door.

*****

Tears came easily as Colette sorted through the former Mrs. Eastman's possessions. The yellow dress had made Helen look like an angel. The beautiful, creamy silk had been for special occasions. A blushing pink suited her best in summer. Colette distinctly remembered Helen wearing that particular dress the afternoon the two of them and Jean had sketched pictures while lounging on the back porch.

More difficult still was putting away the baby things Helen had so lovingly created. Collette couldn't simply get rid of them. She finally decided to put them into a box and store them in the attic where they could be used if she and Harris ever had a child. How wonderful if Helen could be a part of their lives by using the baby's layette she had so lovingly created.

Now, what to do with all of Helen's fine things? Colette couldn't just throw them out, although she was certain that was what Harris had in mind. They were simply too fine. There were so few young ladies in the area who could use them, or even fit into them, that deciding what to do was a bit overwhelming.

Finally she remembered Carrie Sullivan, the bride of Joseph's older brother Michael. Carrie was a slender woman, about Helen's size. She would be the most likely choice to get some use out of Helen's clothes. They might last her for many years, for where was a pioneer woman like Carrie going to wear these things? Colette decided it didn't matter. Carrie would simply have to enjoy wearing them around her own home if need be. She wasn't going to throw them out.

She couldn't go through all of Helen's things in one day. What wasn't physically tiring became emotionally exhausting. Every item brought back some memory: Helen fretting over Rose and little George, Helen laughing at Dandy's antics, Helen smiling at Harris from across the room, Helen's brow creasing with worry when Colette had insisted they rearrange the furniture, Helen knitting baby booties...

She was glad to do this while Harris was away. She couldn't imagine what trauma it might cause him to be here. Then again, Harris had startled her in many ways when it came to mourning Helen. Almost as though he had been able to store memories of her away in an attic in his mind, a room he now seldom visited.

Foolishness. Of course he thinks of Helen often. He wouldn't likely forget about her simply because he's married me. Still, she wondered.

Only one other troubling thought niggled its way into Colette's subconscious after Joseph's disconcerting visit, and it had less to do with

146

Harris than with an uncomfortable truth about herself. She realized that however staunchly she'd claimed to want what God desired for her, she'd never given Him a single thought before she'd agreed to marry Harris. She had no idea if God had wanted her to become the second Mrs. Eastman. She had never inquired of Him at all. She had merely stumbled on in a state of high emotion, doing what came naturally. Even now, feeling vaguely happy and content as Harris' bride, she couldn't help but wonder if she had made the biggest mistake of her life. She couldn't help but wonder if she had missed God's best for her, by somehow making the decision without Him.

Such thoughts kept crawling back, no matter how she tried to quiet them or justify her decision.

Finally, after two steady days of sorting, she finished with Helen's things. The room appeared barren. She decided to keep a couple of personal items to remember Helen by: a silver hand mirror and comb set, and a locket.

She dragged the trunk of Helen's clothes out to the shed where she would keep them until she had the chance to drive them out to the Gilberts' farm. She knew, naturally, that she might run into Joseph if she went there. If he'd stayed in town, it was probable. She also realized Harris would disapprove, but she told herself she and Joseph would not be alone. She needed to see him. She needed to speak to him one more time and try to make their parting right.

The next day, Harris came home. Colette was surprised at the brevity of his trip, fully not expecting to see him for at least a week. She was happy to see him, if not thrilled as she supposed most new brides would be. But she chose not to examine her emotions at the moment. She smiled and went to kiss him as he set down his satchel and removed his coat in the foyer. Her lips brushed the stubble on his cheek, and she smiled up at him.

"What are you wearing?"

Her smile fell, if only because she was thrown off by the first words to come out of his mouth.

"It's just my regular dress. Why?"

"Why aren't you wearing one of the new dresses from the trunk? That dress is old and worn. It needs to be thrown out with the others."

She knew he meant Helen's clothes, but couldn't really believe he meant it. "What for? It's serviceable yet. I need to have something old to wear when I'm working about the house."

"Nonsense. It's threadbare."

"Hardly that."

He rubbed the fabric of her sleeve between his thumb and finger. "Make it into rags. I told you I want you to get used to dressing more fashionably."

"But, Harris -- to mop the floors? Surely you wouldn't want me to ruin a new dress doing such things."

"If that's all you're worried about, I'll hire you a maid. Someone like the young woman Helen kept. Others can do those things. You're my wife, and I want you to look the part."

Colette flamed with defiance at Harris' reference to Rose. Then, just as quickly, another thought struck her.

"Are you worried I'll embarrass you, Harris?" she asked softly.

The hard look in his eyes relaxed, and he smiled at her. "No, Lettie, of course not. But it's important. You'll see soon enough. Then you'll understand."

She nodded, trying to understand now.

"Oh, my darling." He chuckled as he drew her into his arms. "Don't you worry. I'm not angry. I just want to help you. You're so lovely. I can't help but want to dress you up and show the world how lucky I am."

"Do you really feel that way, Harris?"

"Of course." He kissed her forehead. "It's wonderful to come home and find you here, waiting for me. I've been thinking about you all day, imagining our reunion. I knew I'd told you about the new dresses, and I just didn't imagine you'd want to keep the old ones. After all, I know you want to please me. Don't you?"

She laid her head against him and nodded. "Of course."

"Good. Run upstairs and change then, won't you?"

"Yes, Harris."

She did want to please him, didn't she? Then why did she hesitate? Slowly, she took off the old dress and donned one of the new ones, the simplest of the gowns, meant for day wear, but much more exquisite than she could imagine wearing at home. Still, wouldn't Carrie Sullivan Gilbert have the same thoughts when she perused through the trunk of clothes that would soon be headed her way?

I mustn't balk at this, she told herself. But her own defiant spirit rose above her thoughts. *It's ridiculous. I don't need a maid. I don't even want a maid. Someone to scrub my floors... I've been scrubbing floors my whole life. My mother would be ashamed to see me acquiring airs. I won't do it. I won't throw out a perfectly good dress. I won't be giving it to Carrie or anyone else, either. Besides, I'm tall. It would be too long for Carrie. The sleeves would hang past her wrists and get in her way. I'll keep it anyway.*

Revived anger boiled up inside her. And, then, like an arrow shot from hidden cover, another thought came into her head. She was as unprepared for it as a deer taken in the woods, unaware of the hunter who stalked it. *Manason would never make such demands of his wife, and I even doubt Joe would.*

She sat on the edge of her bed, every ounce of strength draining from her as the rebellious thought assaulted her. Caressing the fabric of her old dress, she fought to rid herself of such faithless thoughts. Harris was her husband. She must not compare him to anyone else, *ever*. She must not wonder why she wasn't any more excited to see him than if he were someone else. She must not ever consider what kind of husband another man might make. Such a root would choke her heart.

She would be with Harris for the rest of their natural lives. At times, he would distress her, as he had just now and as he surely would again, as he had even when they were friends. And over such a ridiculous thing as what she wore. She balled the old dress up in her fists and threw it across the room. Gaining her legs again, she stormed before the full length mirror and buttoned the new gown. Her cheeks were flushed, whether out of anger at herself or humiliation at having a view of her own perverse nature, she wasn't sure. She barely noticed. She pulled down her hair and brushed the dark brown-gold tresses. Harris liked it when she left her hair loose for him. Whatever it took in her marriage, *she would please him.*

She fought for controlled breaths as she exited her room and moved purposely down the stairs. He'd disappeared, probably into his office. She found him there, pouring himself some wine. He turned at the sound of her entry, and his eyes gleamed with delight.

"Ah." He set down his glass and came around to the front of the desk to take her hands. He turned her around, studying her with satisfaction. Finally he kissed her. Colette noticed how differently he kissed her this time. Not perfunctorily, but passionately. Funny how his response made her earlier thoughts melt away, and she didn't find it difficult now to give herself to his happiness.

*****

The following morning as she prepared their breakfast, Harris announced he would be gone again for at least two weeks. He thought they might have snow by the time he returned, so she should spend some time making sure she was prepared.

"I believe you'll have enough wood for the stove, but if you should run short, just let Noah know. He'll see to it that more is carried up to the house. If you've errands to run to the mercantile, be sure to get everything you need. If we should have a storm, I don't want to worry that you are lacking anything. You can charge whatever you need to my account."

She was perfectly capable of bringing more wood from the shed to the house herself, but knew it would be ill advised to say so. Instead she simply smiled and agreed.

He went on as he ate his eggs, "I'll have a surprise for you when I get back, I hope."

"What kind of surprise?"

"I can't tell you." His eyes twinkled. "You'll have to wait and see."

Colette pretended a pout, but he gave her no more information.

"I picked up a newspaper from some fellow downriver. It's in my study, and you may read it if you like. Just put it with the others I've saved in the cabinet behind the desk."

He got up, wiping his chin on a square of linen Colette and Helen had sewn into napkins last spring. He moved toward his office as he spoke, Colette following after him.

"I'll need to pack some things. Can you iron my shirts?"

"Of course, though I don't know how you'll keep them fresh."

"It's the thought. I'll feel better knowing they started out that way."

"Will you have a place to stay?"

"Not on the way. I have other clothes for outdoor wear though, so don't worry."

Colette promised she wouldn't and went to warm the irons on the cook stove in the kitchen. While they heated, she retrieved two of Harris' shirts. By the time she'd finished ironing them, he had come back downstairs with his bag packed. In a saddle bag were his papers, and beside it was a bed roll.

To Collette, it seemed that Harris was always on the go now, and while she didn't relish being without him for so long, she also wasn't about to give way to the kind of pathetic forlornness that had overcome Helen. She was even excited about reading the promised paper, and there was still the trip out to the Gilberts' to deliver the trunk of clothes. She and Etta would get together for tea and sewing, and she might even write another letter to her mother and Rose. She had plenty of ways to stay busy.

Once Harris left, she thought about the breakfast dishes in the kitchen, but decided to leave them until later. Instead, she went to find the newspaper in Harris' study. She poured the last cup of tea still hot on the stove and steeped to strength, then carried it with her and settled into her favorite chair.

Time droned by, but Colette was unaware. She eagerly read all the news in the pages of the *Madison Enquirer*. She read the latest in laws passed, a thought provoking article on Democracy and Religion, and some poetry. In those pages she sensed how the territory was growing, how even in the short years she'd come to be a resident here, the population had multiplied tenfold. The changes all pointed to statehood, as Harris had told her. She even found a discussion of a possible constitutional convention, and found herself growing just as excited at the possibility as Harris or her father might be.

At last, with her tea cup grown dry and the day waning on, she rose from her chair, shivering from the chill of the fires burning low. She hadn't lit a fire in Harris' study today, but instead had left the door open to draw heat from the parlor and kitchen. Still, the time had come to add more wood. She folded the paper and went to put it in the cabinet with the others.

The door was locked.

Hm. He must have forgotten to tell me about that, but then, he must have a key somewhere. Colette tugged at the front drawer of Harris' desk. It slid open easily, and was nearly empty except for a few papers and one envelope lying on top with her name written elegantly across the front.

Colette set down the newspaper and stared at the bulging envelope. That her name was not written in Harris' hand was obvious. His handwriting was elegant as well, but always done in bold, leaning strokes. This was feminine.

For a moment, she wondered if it was some forgotten letter Helen had written and never finished or given to her. But she was familiar with Helen's script, too, and it wasn't like this. This was familiar in its own way. It reminded her of Jean's handwriting. But surely it couldn't be.

Colette touched the letter, wondering. Was it truly hers? Obviously it was. Why hadn't Harris mentioned it? Had he simply forgotten about it? Or did he not want her to have it? She wondered when it had come and how. Had Jean run into Harris somewhere? Not likely. Had it come by post? It wasn't marked, or even addressed.

She knew only one way to find the answer, but she trembled like a thief as she lifted the missive from Harris' desk drawer. Even though the letter clearly bore her name, *Colette Palmer*, she felt as if she had invaded Harris' privacy.

That's silly. It's my letter. He should have given it to me.

Quickly, she tore open the seal and unfolded the pages inside.

Colette,

At last I've found you!

She sighed. As she read those words, it was as though Jean's voice bubbled audibly into the room. Her very presence exuded off the page, filling the empty corners of Harris' office with warmth.

At last I've found you! I didn't know how. I thought of sending the note directly to Milwaukee with the hopes it would find you and your family, but I feared it would be lost. I was glad to think I could send it with a letter for Helen, and she could foreword it to you if she knew how to reach you.

Ah. That explained why the envelope had Colette's name on the front but no address.

I hope your father is doing better. He has been so much in our prayers since Manason gave us the news of his accident and your family's need to move where he could find medical care. Did Rose go with you? Please give them all my love and regards.

Manason had given them the news about her father? Another mystery solved. Jean must have never gotten Colette's last letter.

I am so happy, Colette. I never would have believed how full my life could be until you introduced me to Joseph's brother. Rob is the man of my dreams. I'm not even embarrassed to say so. Annie might be appalled, but that's no matter to me. Truly, I think she's just as happy with her Hank.

Do write soon, now that you know where to find me. I'm so anxious to correspond with you, my friend.

We came back to Wisconsin Territory right after the wedding, and now Robin is working with Manason. You'll be surprised to hear that Nase has given us our own piece of land as a wedding gift. It seemed extravagant at first, as I'm sure it does to you, but he really seems happy to have us close to him. He has another place where he wants to build a home someday, but he hasn't begun yet. Something is stopping him.

Oh, I'm just rambling. He's so busy. Though he's young, the men here hold him in great respect. He's good to them in return, and I think that has a lot to do with it. They would do anything he asked, I believe.

Colette, I was so sorry to hear that Nase missed you when he went to Grand Rapids. You must have moved away only days before he arrived.

A strange thudding pounded inside Colette's chest. What was Jean talking about?

He was sorry, too. That's how we found out about your father's accident. Nase went there to see you. I mean, you particularly, Colette. I probably shouldn't say so, since you didn't get to see each other, but I guess it would be wrong of me not to admit to playing the matchmaker. I urged him to visit you, and so he did. That's when he heard you'd gone away. Will you forgive me, Colette? It's just that I think there might be real possibilities for you and Nase. I told him as much. Have I guessed wrong?

Colette swayed, then plopped back into the chair. The room no longer felt cold, or else she had become immune to any physical sensation, numb on the outside and numb on the inside. She kept re-reading those last lines.

Real possibilities... you and Nase... real possibilities...

Collette wasn't aware she was holding her breath until it escaped in a rush, and she crushed the letter with the weight of her hands falling into her lap. She turned her gaze to the window where gray clouds scudded across her limited view.

He went to see... you particularly...

She dropped her eyes to the wrinkled pages, lifted them again, grazed past the words, tried to absorb the rest of what Jean had written.

Maybe it's presumptuous on my part, but maybe not. At the risk of making you blush, I'll tell you I believe he's interested in meeting you again. Pray about it, will you?

Again she looked away. Again her heart raced, not with excitement or anticipation or longing, but with an unnamable sorrow. Then it plummeted with an indescribable sense of something lost.

Chapter Twenty-Three

Colette rose with purpose the next morning. She had several things she needed to do. First, she needed to go to God and tell Him she was sorry for plunging ahead without Him. After that, she needed to figure out a way to be the wife Harris desired. She needed to get to work on making her marriage a glorious thing.

Then she needed to take the clothes to the Gilberts' farm. Indeed, she hoped Joe would be there. She needed one thing, just *one* thing in her life, to be laid to rest in the right way.

She spent a long time praying. She read in the Bible Harris had given her. She'd never really needed Jean's advice. She'd ignored the advice she did have -- God's own letters to her. Well, she would seek His counsel first from now on. It was unfortunate she had learned this lesson the hard way, but learn it she had.

Refreshed and armored, she loaded the trunk and climbed on the buggy to go to the Gilbert farm.

Snowflakes swirled around her as she rode out of Grand Rapids. She wrapped her scarf around her neck, but her cheeks stung in the raw wind.

The road to the Gilbert's farm wasn't much more than a wide path, mostly tread by foot, but accessible to narrow wagons. Thankfully, the buggy fit along the trail, bouncing among the ruts and stumps. She ignored the turn to her own farm. Someone else lived there now. She tucked her treasured memories away in the pockets of her mind. Joseph's home was just ahead.

When the house came into view, her heart hammered. She wondered if he'd be there or far away at one of the camps that dotted the woods along the many waterways.

As she climbed down from the buggy, Mrs. Gilbert opened the door. The older woman's iron gray hair was pulled back in a bun, but a few loose wisps tickled her forehead. Her dark blue unadorned dress was covered with a full length apron, stained but meant for service. Mrs. Gilbert tended to look severe until she smiled. That's what she did when she recognized Colette.

Mrs. Gilbert held out her arms. "Lettie."

Colette hurried into them, thankful for the warm welcome. "Mrs. Gilbert, it's so good to see you."

"Ach. If I'd known you were coming, I'd have combed my hair."

Colette laughed. "You look wonderful."

"Come inside and warm yourself. It's getting nigh on winter."

Colette followed her inside even as Mrs. Gilbert called ahead, "Joseph! Put some wood on the fire and warm this old house up. We've got company."

The kitchen was bright and well lit. The log walls had been painted white. Warmth glowed from the wood stove, welcoming anyone coming in from the cold. But Colette realized she'd carried a draft in with her. Mrs. Gilbert shivered.

"Joseph!" his mother called again.

Then Joe appeared, looking every bit as brooding and handsome as ever, but with a questioning look in his eyes, tinged with worry.

"It's not cold in here, Ma."

"Fire's low. Get some wood."

He moved slowly, going out past her and coming back inside with his arms bulging with firewood. He dropped it with a clunk into the oak box in the corner of the room, then methodically lifted the lid of the stove and inserted several chunks. He took his eyes from Colette only when necessary, making her feel even more nervous. Finally, he rose and stared at her, his arms crossed over his chest.

"I'll pour you some tea. Have a seat, Lettie," Mrs. Gilbert said.

She went about the business of making Colette's tea and spreading jam on a biscuit, offering Colette the distraction of watching her and thanking her for her kindness.

"What brings you here, Lettie?" Joe asked.

"Well, I... a couple of things, really."

He lifted his chin as if to say, *go on.*

"I've some things for Carrie. Clothes and such."

"Helen's clothes?"

"Yes."

He studied her.

"That's very kind of you," his mother said. "Carrie doesn't often get new things."

"I couldn't think of anyone else they'd fit," Colette responded, her eyes going to Joseph who seemed to be weighing what she said. "She'll probably be afraid to wear them around the house because they're so fine. But tell her it's okay. She should enjoy them because Helen would want her to."

Mrs. Gilbert reached over and patted her hand. "I'll tell her. Joseph will get them off the buggy, Won't you son?"

"Sure." He nodded and turned away.

"You don't have to do it yet. I'm in no hurry," Colette said.

He halted and lowered himself into a chair. "What is it you've come to say, Lettie?" he asked suddenly.

Mrs. Gilbert pushed back her chair and rose. She offered to refill Colette's cup, but she'd barely touched it. Gently, the woman excused herself, saying she needed to do something, but Colette didn't even hear what it was. Laying a hand on her son's shoulder, the older woman murmured, "You're friends, remember?" before moving through the kitchen to another part of the house. Colette was faintly aware of a door closing somewhere.

155

They stared at one another in silence for another long moment as Colette screwed up her courage and searched for a way to say what she'd come to say. But Joseph spoke first.

"What is it, Lettie? Did you really only come to bring the dead wife's clothes?"

Heat flamed up her neck. Was that how he saw it? She reached for her tea cup and turned it around in her hands.

"No, Joe. Course not."

"Well?"

She still said nothing. Explaining what had happened was even harder than she'd thought. Then Joe dropped his head into his hands and all the fight seemed to drain out of him. He looked back up at her, his eyes pleading. Finally, she took a breath and said it.

"I came to apologize. You were right about a lot of things. I was wrong."

He straightened, his gaze intensifying. "You'd better explain yourself."

Lettie sipped her tepid brew and set down her shaking cup. "I was wrong. What I did was wrong."

"In what way?"

"In every way, Joe. I was wrong to say the things I said to you last summer. I hurt you the way I said it, and I never meant for that to happen. You're my best friend."

"Don't you mean that Eastman is your best friend?"

Lettie stared at him, silent at the remark. "When I said that, Joseph, *you* were my best friend."

"You know that now."

"I knew it then." She paused before proceeding, allowed her words to find their mark. "I was wrong in that I never once prayed about the man I should marry. I had a lot on my mind about that. I kept telling myself and others, too, that I wanted what God wanted. But I never even asked Him what that was."

"You're sorry now and turning to God. I know how that works."

"No. I was turning to God before, but I didn't turn far enough. Do you know what I mean, Joe?"

Perhaps it was the plaintive tone in her voice that made him drop his guard, or perhaps it was that her apology had reached through to him, she wasn't sure, but Joseph sighed and shook his head. His voice was steady as he told her he'd forgive her.

"Do you mean it, Joe? Really?"

"If you're sorry that you married Harris Eastman, how can I not? But you have to tell me what that means. Are you going to leave him?"

"No, Joe. I don't want you to even think something like that. I didn't come for that. I came only to tell you that I'm sorry because it hurt our friendship. But now I've made a vow, and I'll not be ignoring God twice. I'll stick to that vow."

He nodded. "I see."

"Do you forgive me for everything, then? Not only for marrying Harris?"

"That is the easiest part to forgive," he said, and Colette thought he bore a hint of a smile.

"Why's that, Joe?"

"Because you were doing what you always do, Lettie. You were saving the sparrow with the broken wing, rescuing the flower from being trampled in the dirt. You couldn't help it. It didn't matter that you didn't love him."

"Joe--"

"I know you don't, Lettie, so don't argue with me. It helps me to know it. But if you were going to marry someone you didn't love, and rescue someone with a broken heart, I wish it would have been me."

"Joe," she whispered, dropping her eyes away from him.

"Come on." He stood, taking her hand and drawing her to her feet. "Show me the trunk of clothes I need to bring in. Then you'd better be heading home. I think we may be in for a storm."

Chapter Twenty-Four

Manason stretched his legs and stood, letting his mind wander yet again from the ledgers and receipts scattered over his desk. Pacing across the small room, he stopped to look out the open door at the woods where the distracting garble of a pair of crows feeding their young echoed. He would pay wages for somebody to tell him why he felt so restlessness.

After all, work couldn't be going better. Little by little, sometimes even in strides, his small company kept growing. Over the winter he'd pulled out trees by the millions of board feet, and even Boggs' efforts to obstruct his operations had produced little or no adverse effects. He had accumulated new lands to cut, good, rich lands, without hardly trying. His bank account was comfortable, and already he'd paid back a liberal portion of what his pa had invested in him. Jean and Rob were doing well, and it had been a blessing to have them so near. He had little to complain about on any account.

Still, he couldn't seem to quench his disquiet, even around his family. Jean had noticed something was bothering him, and had questioned him about it more than once. He would have given her an answer, too, if he'd only been able to put his finger on the problem.

"Maybe you were just born with too much energy," she suggested. "Maybe all the newness of the enterprise has worn off, and you need to find something more to do."

"Such as?"

Jean shrugged. "Maybe you should start that house you told me about. Don't you ever get tired of living in your office?"

Manason stuffed his hands into his pockets and looked at the ground as they walked along the path toward Jean's house. "It doesn't matter."

"Seems a shame not to build up there on the oak ridge. I don't know what you're waiting for. You've got the money, right? You've got plenty of labor."

Spring had burst upon them in wondrous glory. The winter's cut was already long gone downriver to the mills. It would be a perfect time to start on the house.

"I guess I just don't see the need right now."

Jean grew quiet. Slowly a smile spread over her face. "You mean until you've found a wife, you don't see the need. It's springtime, little brother."

He bumped her with his elbow. "You would think that."

"It's logical. But you're making a name for yourself, Nase. You should at least have a place to live."

"Can't I just live with you and Rob?" He grinned at her.

"Really, Nase. You should find someone."

"Someone, you say. So you don't think I should still try to find out what's become of the fair Colette Palmer?"

"I wonder why she never wrote back." Jean frowned. "I hate that we've lost touch."

"Maybe she's trying to tell you something."

She raised her brows at him. "Meaning?"

"She doesn't want you to meddle."

"Meddle! What makes you think I ever mentioned you in my letter?"

He nudged her a little harder. "Knowing my sister as I do, why would I think that?"

Together, they laughed.

Maybe Jean was right, he thought now as he stared out the door across the green tree tops fluttering in the spring-blue sky. Maybe he should build the house. Still, something inside him urged him not to dwell on it. It did seem pointless. *Maybe later.* Maybe -- he finally admitted to himself -- maybe when he did find someone to marry.

He turned away from the door and strolled across the room. He stared down at the paperwork on his desk. In the pile was a note from Tom Durant congratulating him on the most recent rock he'd thrown into the spokes of Eastman Enterprises. Harris Eastman had been the recipient of fines and suffered forfeiture of property for his illegal cutting. Nase had learned by word of mouth that he hadn't taken the blow well, and that he'd had a hard time keeping men working for him ever since. Apparently, except for keeping a small hold on his logging interests, he was turning more of his investments into speculating in future town sites.

That was good for Manason and good for the interests of Wisconsin, but Nase couldn't help feeling pity for the sorry folk who found themselves paying Harris Eastman to live on one of his properties. He'd seen their like before. Settlers who came in, having bought land and farms from speculators without ever having seen it, but trusting the speculators' word. They would find their "farms" to be little more than hovels, and their land covered with stumpage that needed to be removed before any reasonable crop could be sown. Their houses were often quickly erected shacks or log huts with cracks between the logs through which the Wisconsin winters could easily drive the bitter winds and biting snow. Nase shook his head at the thought.

God spare anyone from men like Harris Eastman.

*****

Harris stomped wildly through the house, and Colette kept herself in the kitchen, out of his path, cringing every time he slammed a door. He wasn't upset with her, at least she didn't think so, but she couldn't help but reel from the impact of his fury over losing such a valuable piece of forest land, or over the fines that had been imposed upon him. She didn't know if he was angry because he couldn't afford to lose the land, or because his name had been publicly besmirched.

"Colette!"

She jumped, dropping the potato she was peeling so that it rolled across the floor. Ignoring it, she wiped her hands on a towel and hurried out of the kitchen. He only used her full name when he was upset, something she'd learned about him over the winter.

"Coming, Harris!"

He was breathing heavily when she found him in his study, papers strewn about his desk and a half empty liquor bottle sitting among them.

"Did you move the letter I left on the table in the foyer?"

"I put it here, on your desk." She moved to the spot and carefully slid the loose papers aside exposing the envelope.

"I've asked you not to move my things," he said, tearing the letter from her hands. It didn't seem to occur to him to thank her for finding it. Resentment snaked its head up inside Colette, and she turned to go.

"Pour me a drink, won't you?"

She stopped, turned back, and stared at him. He was reading the contents of the envelope and ignoring her, so she moved to the bottle and poured a small amount into the glass beside it.

"Fill it," he said, without looking up.

"Harris, I wish you wouldn't--"

A prolonged sigh escaped him, and his hand holding the letter fell limply to the desk top. "Must you insist on nagging me right now? Just do as I ask."

"I wasn't nagging. I'm just... concerned."

"Call it what you like, Lettie. You've become quite a nag lately. Haven't you noticed?"

Colette had long been apprehensive about Harris' drinking. Alcohol only exacerbated his growing rages, and she didn't understand why he drank. He had always talked to her before, telling her what he was going through. But since the forfeiture and fining, he'd bottled his thoughts away from her.

Well, he could keep his secrets if he liked, but she wouldn't as easily overlook his growing drinking problem. Harris had always seemed to drink more than was healthy or wise, but before they were married it hadn't been a problem. Now, with both his drinking and the most recent trouble, he'd become increasingly volatile. If he had been exacting before, he was intolerant now. Most despicable of all was that he seemed to slowly be relegating her to a place in his life reserved for less important things, ones he only drew upon when he needed them. For the first time in her marriage, Colette was genuinely unhappy.

Then, to add to her disillusionment, was the incident over the picture. Colette hadn't at first realized anything was wrong. She understood it only gradually, yet she didn't know why it should cause such a problem. Harris hadn't *known* Manason Kade had once meant something to her. He had been looking at the titles on the shelf in her boudoir when he pulled a book out from the others, and the drawing of Manason slid out of its pages onto the floor. Honestly, she'd forgotten all about it.

"Why, Lettie," Harris had purred. "I didn't know you had such a hand at drawing."

She had been seated at her vanity, brushing her hair. She looked up to see what he was talking about. At first, she didn't recognize what held his interest. So she rose from her little chair and peered over his shoulder.

Manason's face rose to life before her, shocking her. After a moment, she gathered her voice. "Oh, that. I didn't draw it. Jean did."

"Jean?"

"Yes, you remember her."

"Ah. This is a friend of hers?"

"No, it's her brother Manason." Colette went back to the mirror and pulled the brush through her hair again, hoping Harris would forget about the picture. Hoping *she* could.

"I see. He's your friend, too, then." He smoothed the creases and placed the picture on her nightstand instead of returning it to the book or simply throwing it away.

Later, she understood. Harris was jealous. He hoped that by leaving it out where she could see it, she might throw it away on her own.

But Colette didn't throw it away. She kept it. Not in the book where she'd kept it before, but in a letter from her family, a place where Harris would never bother to look. Not that she was trying to hide some secret longing. No. But the drawing was hers, and Manason had been her friend, as had Jean, and Colette wanted to keep the memory.

Remembering that incident, she decided that defending herself against his accusation of nagging would do no good. As she'd grown more and more used to doing, she would ignore his foul mood and hope to keep the peace.

Harris held out his hand for the glass and she gave it to him, standing beside the desk as he poured its contents down his throat.

"May I go back to cooking supper?"

"Of course. It's not as though you need my permission."

*****

The liquor warmed Harris, yet his thoughts swam in circles. His heart hammered in his chest like it always did when he was upset. He placed his hand over it. The alcohol would help him to feel calmer soon.

This logger -- this *Manason Kade* -- was responsible for all his recent trouble with the Indian lands and the fines, and he couldn't stop thinking about him. Lettie's picture of Kade came back to his mind. Lettie hadn't forgotten about the picture in the book like she'd claimed. Harris was certain of it. She was playing coy with him.

She purposely kept it hidden from me.

Perhaps she still had strong feelings for Kade. Perhaps she secretly wished she could see him again.

Then he remembered the letter from Jean which had come with Helen's letter, the one he'd kept from Lettie since their marriage. He'd forgotten about it himself, it was true. Pushing back from his desk, he pulled open the drawer. He would have to read the letter and see what else her friend Jean had to say about her brother. Harris regretted, now, that he'd burned Helen's letter. He would have liked to review it.

Now where was the envelope with Colette's name flowing across the front?

He'd tossed a few other notes and communications on top of it over the months. It must be somewhere beneath them, or maybe in the back. Harris shuffled through the items in the drawer to no avail. His pulse quickened as he searched a second and third time.

The letter was gone. *Lettie must have taken it.*

He slammed the drawer and stormed around the desk. He ran a hand through his hair as he headed toward the door, thinking to call her back. At the threshold he stopped himself. That wouldn't do. The letter was hers, after all. It had come before they were married, and he'd had no right to keep it from her. Still, he had to know what it said. He had to know if Jean had mentioned feelings expressed toward Colette from Kade.

His mind and heart burned with the wanting. Was Jean playing matchmaker? Had Colette written her back?

He rubbed a hand across his jaw and returned to the bottle for another drink. He had to think about this rationally. Perhaps she still had the letter.

He opened the door a few inches, then called her name, injecting his voice with calm. She appeared a minute later and Harris tried not to think that she looked hesitant, suspicious even.

"I'm sorry to call you again," he said with a little laugh. "I just remembered something, and I was afraid to let it wait in case I forgot again."

She stepped closer, and Harris reached for her hand. He walked her out of the hall and into the parlor where he pulled her gently onto the settee next to him.

"I'm afraid I have a confession to make to you."

She turned to him and pushed herself off the settee. "It's all right. I understand."

He pulled her back down. *She thinks I'm apologizing.* He would have thought it ridiculous, but then realized such a move might actually help his cause.

"No. I need to apologize. I was curt with you, and I'm sorry." He stroked her hands in his and kissed her cheek. "But actually I do have something more to say. It's just that as I was going through some things in my desk, it occurred to me I had something that belonged to you." He laughed at his apparent carelessness. "It was a pure oversight, I assure you, and I hope you'll believe me."

"What is it, Harris?"

"Well, it is, or *was* a letter. It came just after Helen died. I absentmindedly set it in my desk drawer intending to pass it on to you, but with my emotional state being as it was..." He let his words sink in for a moment, "well, I ended up forgetting all about it."

"A letter?"

"Yes. It came to you in care of another letter to Helen. Of course, I read her letter and set yours aside. I feel terrible about it, because now it seems I've lost it. I think that's why I forgot for so long. It wasn't there where I could see it to remember. I'm sorry, I--"

Colette patted his arm, agitated, trying to stop him. "No, no, Harris. You didn't lose it. In fact, I took the letter. I saw that it was mine, so I just took it."

There it was. Absolution.

"You took it?"

"Yes. I was getting the key to open the cabinet where you'd asked me to put the newspaper, and I found the letter inside. It had my name on it, so naturally, I read it. When I saw it wasn't something that would be important to you, I took it."

He laughed again, trying to sound relieved. "Well, then. I guess it isn't lost after all."

"No."

"And you've gotten to read it. I suppose it's long gone now."

"Well, it's put away. I kept it so I'd know where to reach Jean if I ever want to write to her again."

"Oh?"

"Yes. She's actually here in the territory with her husband. I don't think I ever told you that she married."

"Did she?"

"Yes. Remember when she met Robin Gilbert at the dance we held?"

He shrugged.

She hugged him and smiled. "Sure you do! We watched them while we danced. Remember?"

"I remember how you looked," he answered, trying to turn her thoughts elsewhere. "I recognized you as a woman that night."

"Oh, Harris. Helen was with you that night."

"Of course I was with Helen." He pulled her into his arms. "I'm only saying that you were enchanting. Everyone was aware of it."

He kissed her, and she melted against him. All the while, even as he allowed himself to enjoy the kiss, he thought of the letter. She'd kept it, and sooner or later he'd know what it said. He'd know if there had ever been, or still was, more in her thoughts about Manason Kade. But for the moment, he would do what he could to make sure that man was kept far, far from her mind.

Chapter Twenty-Five

Colette wondered at Harris' change of mood, and yet, such sudden shifts of temperament seemed to be the norm for him. She sighed. All his talk about the dance and how she'd impressed him that night came back to her again. Of course, he didn't know Joseph had declared himself that night. If Harris had known, he would never have mentioned the dance, she was sure. In fact, she would keep that a secret. She didn't need to give Harris another reason to be troubled.

For that same reason, when the "surprise" Harris had brought back for her after one of his trips turned out to be a young Indian girl of about twelve, whom he expected Colette to train as her housekeeper, she accepted the gift graciously. The girl called Onaiwah was the eldest child of a poor family near Point Basse, a few miles downriver. Harris told Colette the girl wished to avoid having to marry a certain trapper who'd been offering presents to her family for her hand. Colette agreed this was a preferable arrangement and quickly took Onaiwah under wing.

The girl was a quick learner and possessed more skill with a needle than Colette herself could claim, so it was easy to find things for her to do. Onaiwah was also an adept gardener, and when summer came she was not only a joyful help in the garden, but she also taught Colette how to forage for some of the earth's hidden fruits.

Colette admitted to herself that having Onaiwah's company was pleasant, yet she was largely still able to keep her own house. The only trouble the two encountered was an occasional barrier in their languages that could generally be gotten around. Talking with her was no more difficult than engaging in conversation with Rose Shultz. All in all, they got on well together.

Also, to Colette's great relief, Harris' business troubles passed. His lightning temper and high strung emotions were placated as others forgot his censure. Colette knew he only had himself to blame. After all, what he'd done was illegal. But she said nothing about it as he occasionally murmured that what he had done was not uncommon, and that the day would come when those who had "nearly brought him ruin" would live to regret it.

Toward summer's end, they were finally able to visit Colette's family near Milwaukee. Colette and her mother wept in one another's arms. Lavinia confessed her earlier fears that somehow they would not get to see one another again, but now she cried for sheer joy because they had.

Colette had to hide her shock when she saw her father. He had grayed in the year they'd been apart. Not only his hair, but his face and skin looked pale and fleshy. Lines and creases existed where Colette didn't remember them. He'd also grown paunchy being confined to his chair so long, though he was beginning to get around with a crutch.

"We had word from Grayson and Eleanor," Mama told Colette. "Annie's given them a granddaughter."

"She has?"

"Yes. They're hoping to hear news from Jean on that score soon, too. Have you heard from her?"

"No, not lately."

"I'm sure Annie would love it if you wrote."

"Annie and I have run out of things to say to each other, I'm afraid."

Her mother frowned. "What? With your new husband and the two of you starting families? Surely not."

"Oh, Mama. We aren't starting a family yet."

"You and Harris are a family now. Don't think otherwise."

"Mama..." Colette hesitated. "I hope you won't tell them about us. I mean... I'm not really ready..."

She ignored the look her mother cast her way, as well as the tone of her question. "Is everything all right with you and him?"

Colette nodded and looked at the pot she was stirring. "Yes, of course. It's just that I don't think Annie would understand. She would get so many notions about it. It would take pages of explanation to make her understand how it really happened."

Mama sighed and nodded. "I suppose you're right about that. She was always a girl who could get carried away with notions. I wouldn't want her thinking wrong thoughts about how you and Harris came to be together so soon after Helen's passing. It was hard enough for your father and me to understand."

Colette looked up sharply. "You know it was nothing -- untoward -- don't you?"

"Yes, yes." Her mother reached over and patted Colette's hand, then kissed the top of her head. "You've explained it all, and so has he. Rest your mind about it. I don't have to be the one to tell all your news. You can tell the Kades or anybody you want to when you're ready. Someday it'll all seem like such a small thing, this question of propriety."

"Thank you, Mama."

"Oh, my darling girl. I wish you could stay longer."

"Me, too. We only have this week, though. The convention in Belmont begins on the 25th. Even though Harris isn't a delegate, he wants to be there as a voice in the populace. The lead miners will have a lot of representation, and the loggers also need to play a role."

"The women, too."

"What do you mean?"

"Haven't you heard?" Mama fetched a newspaper off a chair in the corner of the kitchen. Colette's eyes scanned down the page to an article about the convention reporting several issues the delegates would address. They intended to propose that private banks be outlawed, that immigrants be allowed to vote, and that married women be permitted to own property. They also planned to address the question of black suffrage.

Colette digested the news with great interest. The outcome of this convention would have an important impact on her life. Even while Harris continued to invest money in her name, C. Eastman, she knew she had no authority over such an investment. Even the property she'd purchased prior to her marriage was now relegated by law to her husband's sole control. The outcome of the convention was something she intended to keep a close eye on, and if Harris intended to allow her to represent his interests among his social and business peers, then she would speak her mind to sway those who had real influence in the territory.

After a week with her parents, Harris took Colette to Belmont, where the convention would convene in just a few days. He said the arguments would likely go on for weeks into winter, but he wanted a chance to make himself and his position known.

Colette found herself caught up in a whirlwind as Harris introduced her to important men and their wives, some of whom would act as delegates to the constitutional convention, and others who were lawyers or wealthy investors. In circumstances such as these, surrounded by important people, as always, Harris was at his best. As Colette fell into her role as his beautiful and charming wife, knowledgeable in the logging industry, yet demure, Harris flowered back into the deferential gentleman and astute businessman she remembered him to be.

In the evenings, they dined either in the homes of prominent leaders, or in their hotel dining room together, she always looking lovely and refined, he always the dapper, handsome, and attentive husband. His actions toward her were most wooing.

"You must want something," she said to him one evening, laughing as he flirted with her.

"Nothing, really. You've already given me everything I need."

"And that is?"

"You see how these gentlemen are taken with you. You alone may be responsible for women's suffrage in the new state if you keep your wits about you."

She laughed. "You make me think of King Ahaseurus."

"Who was he?"

She paused momentarily, then seeing that he really didn't know, she explained. "He was a king in the Bible who had a comely wife named Vashti. He wanted to bring Vashti out to woo his guests with her exotic beauty and her dancing."

"Hm. Interesting idea."

"Of course, she was scandalized to be put on such display. She refused his request, so he sent her away. He took a new wife and made her queen in Vashti's place."

"Oh, yes. I remember now. Queen Esther, who saved the Jews."

"Yes."

"*Vashti.*" Harris grinned and winked at her. "My little Vashti."

Colette rolled her eyes.

"Yes," he said, "a fitting title."

"I think one nickname is enough."

"Lettie? It's not really a nickname."

"No one else ever called me Lettie until I met you."

"Well, Lettie it is. But Vashti will do, too," he said as he filled her glass with wine.

*****

Harris enjoyed Lettie when she acted as his enchantress. For a while, it took him back to those early days only a few months ago when being married was new to her. He had taught her and was adored by her. Later, he knew, he'd dropped in her estimation of him, but on nights like this he could ignore that. With her sitting here, watching him and flirting with him, he could almost forget all his troubles and especially her connection with Manason Kade.

He listened to her talk, imagining he was looking at her through the eyes of his enemy, and his jealousy was aroused even while he was filled with his own lust. Her golden brown tresses lay against her pale skin, and the dark blue luster of her eyes both teased and taunted him. Is this how she would appear to Manason Kade or even Joseph Gilbert if one of them were dining with her? He didn't worry so much about young Joe these days. He'd been scared off.

Harris believed, however, that he knew the ways of young women's hearts, how they held on to their fantasies. He had no doubt that Manason Kade had once been that kind of fantasy to Lettie. He also had no doubt that Kade was *not* a backwoods fop like Joe. The man had made his presence known in the great Wisconsin woods. He'd become a contender in the business. The fact that another man could actually compete for Lettie's interest and attention both stimulated Harris and raised his ire.

Then it occurred to him. A woman like Lettie might be such a distraction, might cause such a luscious diversion, that she could bring a man, a prominent man, any *natural* man to ruin...

Chapter Twenty-Six

Six weeks later, Harris leaned back in his chair as sunlight streamed through the window, reflecting off the amber liquid of the whiskey glass he turned in his hand, and indulged in a self-congratulatory smile. Just thinking of the ways Manason Kade would suffer brought him a perverse and well deserved pleasure.

Lettie still had no real idea of her allure. Yes, she really was his Vashti. And while she was distracting Kade, completely within Harris' control, of course, he would see to it that the man's foundling logging empire crumbled like dust. Harris wasn't the only man who could be fined or dispossessed. But he would be much smarter about seeing to his foe's destruction than Manason Kade had been. He wouldn't leave his enemy standing with enough leg under him to continue. *Lettie will see to that, and she'll never even realize what she's doing.*

Harris spent the winter preparing for his assault. He wrote letters. He visited mill owners and pine kings. He stirred them up to agree they themselves needed to convene in order to put forth the issues they wished to present at the next territorial convention. The convention in October had lasted for ten weeks, and in the end a majority rejected the constitution due to the controversial issues of suffrage for both women and blacks. The stands were simply too radical for the new state-in-waiting.

Harris had complimented Lettie's attempt to sway constituents. She'd written a long anonymous letter to the editor of the *Wisconsin Democrat* explaining the position of women and many of their men folk. She reasoned that property which had come to a married woman by inheritance, or that which was hers prior to marriage, shouldn't be appropriated by her husband without her consent and against her own wishes only because she had become his wife. She expressed her view that a woman allowed to own or keep property was unlikely to come into dissension with her husband over her dutiful role in the home. Furthermore, she agreed with another anonymous -- and most probably feminine -- author that in truth, almost every case in which a wife could derive income from such property, her husband would benefit.

Still, despite Colette's zeal and that of other women suffragettes, voters rejected the constitution the following April. Many opposed argued that men would use their wives to shelter their own assets from creditors, and even worse, the change would cause women to become speculators. To this last accusation, Colette had no reply.

"Don't fret, Lettie. The day will come when Wisconsin will not only claim statehood, but you and your women friends will become leaders of the suffrage movement in this grand country of ours."

"It's nice that you think so, but I cannot say I'm not disappointed."

"You showed remarkable ingenuity in writing to the *Democrat*, just as the other woman did. It didn't hurt that many of the men who will make these decisions got to meet you."

"They don't know I wrote the letter."

"Nevertheless, they know women like you are keenly intelligent and able to stand alongside any man on these issues while at the same time maintaining their own remarkable femininity."

"I hardly think the two need be separated."

"Of course." He put his arms around her. "I agree."

Sighing, she laid her head on his shoulder.

"I hate to tell you, but I have to leave soon. Men have returned from the spring break up, and I need to meet every jack, millwright, teamster, and lumber baron I can to convince them of the need to organize if we wish to have an impact at the new constitutional convention this fall."

"Oh," she said, looking up at him. "I thought you'd be home for a while. Summer's just 'round the corner."

He kissed her forehead. "You'll be fine. I won't be gone any longer than necessary. The garden will be up by the time I return, and I'm sure you and Onaiwah will find plenty to keep you busy."

"Keeping busy is never a problem."

"That's my gir.l" He kissed her hair again. "You're different from Helen that way."

Remembering how lost Helen had been without Harris, Colette winced. Today she might wish he could stay, but at times she was content to have him gone. He had the affect of turning her emotions that way. Maybe she just didn't love him deeply enough.

"I love you," she said, and he gave her a squeeze.

*****

Joe was reminded of the first time he'd stolen up on Lettie and watched her dangling her toes in the river. Now she straightened stiffly from her work in the garden, shielding her eyes from the sun when he called her name.

"Joe!"

He couldn't help grinning at her surprise. She brushed her hands against her dress and, knowing her, he was sure she wished she could do something about the sweat and dirt clinging to every inch of her, but it didn't affect her negatively at all. She looked just as beautiful with her hair in a bunting and dirt smeared across her cheeks and under her fingernails as she did wearing a blue shawl in the moonlight.

He was glad to have caught her out of the house. He wasn't entirely sure Harris wasn't around, and he didn't dare knock on the door, not even to share the news he'd come to tell her.

An Indian girl stood behind Lettie, watching them, and Lettie turned to her. "Go ahead inside and get yourself something to drink. We'll finish later." Then she hurried over to him.

She swung out the gate, and he reached his hand out to her.

"Hi, Lettie."

"Joe." Tears sparkled in her eyes. She threw her arms around him, and he hugged her in return.

"Two years," she said, drawing back.

"Almost."

"Where have you been?"

"Working up a ways. Didn't my folks tell you?"

"Well, yes. I've talked to your mother a few times. But for so long…"

Now was the time to tell her, but he had to soak in the sight of her a little bit longer. She fidgeted under his gaze, brushing again at her hands and the smear of mud on her cheek where a tear had slipped away.

"Are you just going to keep staring at me like that?"

He threw back his head and laughed. "Lettie girl, it sure is good to see you."

"You too, Joseph. Now tell me what's kept you away all this time."

"All right. But first I want to thank you."

"What for?"

"For putting me in my place."

She laughed, the sound of it like fresh, cool water. Joe's heart would always have a home for Lettie Palmer. Well, Lettie Eastman now. He'd accepted that.

"Is that what I did?"

He nodded. "You did. I'm grateful for it, Lettie. Is Harris home?" He glanced back toward the house and then at her. A frown crossed her brow.

"No. He's away."

"I don't want you to get into trouble for talking to me."

"Let's walk."

She slipped her arm through his and they walked up the street and turned the corner. They strolled down it under the shade of an elm, away from the other houses.

Joseph patted her hand and smiled at her again.

"I have big news to tell you, Lettie."

"Oh?"

Again they stopped and he turned to her, taking both her hands in his. "I'm getting married." He watched her reaction closely.

She blinked once and caught her breath. Then light came over her face. "Really?"

"Really."

"May I ask?"

"Kasheawa. You remember."

"Kasheawa… Kashe? The Indian girl?

"Yeah." Joe didn't expect the rush of heat that crept up his neck, and he dropped his eyes. He didn't like getting caught blushing, but he supposed Lettie knew him too well for it to matter. Then, for Kashe, he didn't mind.

"Joe..." Her voice grew soft. "Do you love her?"

He looked at her again, and heard the hopefulness in her voice. A pang slid through Joe, not over the fact that he loved Kashe, but because he didn't think Lettie loved her own husband. Not enough, anyway.

"Yes, Lettie girl, I love her."

"That's wonderful news." Tears filled her eyes. Joe dashed them away with his thumb.

"Thanks. My hands are all dirty." She laughed, then opened her arms. "Congratulations, Joe."

He pulled her to him in a tight hug. "That's what I was hoping you'd say. It means a lot to me, Lettie."

Releasing one another, they walked back to the house.

"When will I get to meet her?"

"Any time you like. I'll stick around for at least another month, maybe six weeks. Kashe's staying with us, helping my ma out at the house. Michael and Carrie are due with another little one soon, so I'd like to stay long enough to see the bairn."

"That's good news."

"Yes. Robbie and Jean will soon have a little tyke, too. Did you hear?"

"They will?" Colette grasped his arm. "No, I didn't hear."

"You should write her. I get the feeling she hasn't heard from you."

"No. No, she hasn't."

Joseph glanced at her, catching the pensive note in her voice. It made him wonder. Why hadn't Lettie written Jean?

"You know where to reach her?"

She nodded.

He wanted to say more, to ask why, but a niggling voice told him the answer, and thinking again of Harris Eastman made storm clouds move through his thoughts.

*****

Harris noted the affection in their glances and the way they held one another. Then he snaked his way through the trees to the shed butted up against the woods by his house and waited for Joe and Lettie's return. They were talking too softly for Harris to understand what they were saying at this distance, but the glow on their faces was clearly readable.

"Good-bye, Lettie. See you later, then." Joe held out his hand, and Lettie squeezed it.

Shaking hands. How nice. No more intimate hugs on the public thoroughfare where anyone might see. Harris stepped back out of sight as Lettie turned to come up the walk. She was smiling and humming, and it grated on his nerves.

*****

Inside the house, Colette found Onaiwah washing dishes and rinsing vegetables for their supper. Dipping warm water from the reservoir on the stove, Colette scrubbed her arms and face as her mind turned over Joe's news. She took the scarf from her head and shook out her hair, wiping the dampness and grime from her hairline and neck.

"I need to wash my hair. Maybe later I'll heat up enough water for a bath. We'll make one for you, too, Onaiwah."

Standing in the kitchen with just the girl, Colette stripped off her filthy outer garments and petticoats and left them by the back door to wash.

"I'm going up to change," she said, and Onaiwah nodded.

Feeling cooler and more comfortable in only her camisole, corset, and drawers, Colette strolled through the house toward the front hall stairs.

"My, my."

She stopped short, her heart lurching into her throat. Harris stood in the hall outside his study. His hand rested on the banister, and his eyes glittered.

"Harris!" Her hand relaxed against her chest where it had flown. "You startled me. My heart is pounding."

He raked a slow gaze over her and lifted one side of his mouth in a grin that matched the gleam in his eyes.

"When did you come in?" she asked, uneasy beneath his sensuous gaze.

"Only just now. Interesting costume. Do you always wander about the house like that when I'm away?"

"Oh, heavens, no." Her hand drifted up to her hair and down her front. "I was covered in dirt from the garden, and I thought I'd change."

He moved toward her, and she could tell he wasn't listening. He took her by the arm and pulled her to him, kissing her hard. One of his hands tangled in her hair, and he pushed her against the stair rail, caressing her.

"Harris--"

He ignored the soft pleading in her voice and loosened her stays.

"Harris!"

"Come, Lettie. I haven't been away long enough for you to have grown shy."

Dandy lay on the other side of the parlor. Now he abruptly raised his head and growled. His attention riveted on them, he sprang to his feet and barked.

Onaiwah stepped into the room and Lettie's eyes flew wide, embarrassment consuming her. Just as quickly, Dandy stalked toward Harris, his growl becoming more menacing.

"Send him out!" Harris demanded.

Onaiwah twirled to leave.

"Dandy, go!" Colette said.

"Onaiwah, call him!" Harris said.

Without looking up at them, Onaiwah turned and called to the yellow dog, patting her thigh. Reluctantly, as Colette repeated her command for him to go, Dandy pulled himself away and followed Onaiwah from the room. Colette tried to move out of her husband's grasp, but he pinned himself against her and pulled at her corset.

"Harris," she whispered fiercely.

"Onaiwah comes from a large family who live in a very small house. I'm sure she's neither shocked nor naive."

The corset fell away. Humiliated, Colette closed her eyes.

Later, in her room, Colette sniffed and brushed away her tears as she stared out the window. No love had been in what Harris had done, and even his desire seemed driven by something unknowable. He'd whispered no warm, tender words, and no caring, loving exchanges had passed between them. He'd only given her rude demands. His one real kiss had left her lips bruised and her heart shattered.

She didn't know if she could face Onaiwah. *What that poor girl must think.* Colette didn't recall having ever experienced such shame. The worst part of all was that Harris seemed totally unaffected. If anything could be said, it was that he had hardened toward her.

The sun set. Onaiwah was probably still getting their dinner ready, but Colette didn't feel like eating. She felt sick. Nevertheless, she tried to pull herself together to go downstairs. Her pain would be worse if she didn't face them both and get it over with.

She walked downstairs slowly in the half light. Harris' study door stood open, and she would have liked to walk past it and directly into the kitchen to apologize to Onaiwah, but Harris called her name.

She stopped outside the door. "Yes?"

He sat at his desk gently swabbing the barrel of his pistol.

"I want you to get rid of that dog. He's becoming a menace."

Alarm propelled her into the room. "What?"

"He's dangerous and likely to hurt someone."

"Dandy?"

He glanced at her and then tenderly rubbed down the gun barrel with a soft cloth, pausing for minute inspections, then polishing some more.

"If you find it too difficult, then I shall take care of it for you." He weighed the pistol in his right hand, then aimed down its length at some object on the far side of the room.

"But, Harris, he's my dog. You can't really expect me to just get rid of him. I love Dandy."

Harris set the gun down and leveled her with a no-nonsense gaze. "I do not intend to discuss it with you. As I said before, get rid of him... or I will."

He pulled open a drawer in his desk and gently laid the pistol inside, then locked the drawer securely and deposited the key in his pocket.

"Let's go eat dinner, shall we?" he said, smiling as he rose.

Colette stumbled over the rough terrain of her thoughts. Her heart heaved. Unable to speak, she turned and fled from the room.

Chapter Twenty-Seven

Manason swept the brush through a cup of shaving soap and dabbed lather across his face. He wanted to make a good impression on the men attending this meeting, especially the infamous Harris Eastman. The trouble with Eastman had died down some, although Boggs still tried to cause Nase problems just to be mean, Nase figured. One man couldn't simply force the bully out of another, not even with a good whopping.

He lifted his razor and carefully pulled the blade across his cheek as he listened to Tom. His friend was buffing a rag across the tips of his gleaming black boots.

"Well, do I look pretty enough to meet the famous Mrs. Eastman?" He straightened and tossed the shoeshine cloth aside.

Nase swished the razor in the washbasin. "You'll do. Course, she won't notice you once she sees me."

The source of their quips harkened back to a conversation Manason had shared with one of his crew before they left Chippewa country. On learning they would attend this conference, Fred Marsh had filled Manason in.

"Mrs. Eastman'll be there, of course," Fred said, scraping the edge of his boots on the doorstep as they came into the cookhouse. "Not a prettier gal on the whole Wisconsin River, maybe in the whole Wisconsin Territory."

"That right?"

"Yep. And not just pretty either, but Lettie Eastman's got a heart of pure gold, too."

"Lettie Eastman?" Nase tried to recall the name of Harris Eastman's wife from his conversations with Jean.

"Lettie's his second wife, a real doll. If you're polite and gentlemanly, then Eastman might even let you dance with her."

Manason's eyebrows went up. "Like a prize?" His sarcasm was lost on Fred.

"Whew-y! What a prize!" Fred gave his hands a cursory plunge into a pail of water sitting on a stand inside the door and wiped them on a dingy towel.

"Well, if she's all that, maybe I'll have a look at the fabulous Mrs. Eastman myself."

Now Nase, too, wiped his hands and face and turned to grin at Tom.

"You do look kind of pretty," Tom piped, and Nase threw the towel at him.

They made their way down to the hotel dining room where they would eat a quiet dinner with some of the other attendees, then go to the ballroom at the Grand Hotel to enjoy a relaxed evening of rubbing elbows and imbibing before getting down to business the following morning.

Entering the dining room, Manason was relieved to see that Harris Eastman was not present. After carefully questioning the hotel staff, Tom had confirmed that Eastman and his wife were staying at the Grand Hotel where the ball would be held.

Now Manason could relax and enjoy his dinner.

They arrived at the Grand promptly at eight o'clock. Walking up the steps, Manason grinned at Tom and straightened his tie. "Time to see what kind of party these lumber kings can throw."

Eastman and his cronies had spared no expense in helping contrive this event. Quixotic lighting graced the ballroom, and a small orchestra played in the corner. A maid in a cap and apron served them wine.

Manason and Tom recognized several well-known lumbermen and lawyers, as well as some of the statesmen and delegates to the coming fall constitutional convention. A quick glance around the room took in small groupings of well-dressed gentleman escorting their wives, who all looked divinely prestigious in their glossy, bejeweled evening gowns, their collars and their ribbons, their gloved hands poised on lacy fans. All very elegant and matronly, but not one Manason thought fit young Fred's description of the amazing Mrs. Eastman.

He tried to draw on what he remembered the man himself to look like. He hadn't actually seen Harris Eastman in the flesh in years. Not since that late summer day back in Michigan when he'd gone to Eldon Palmer's house. He was tall and slim and dark. Surely he hadn't changed so much in seven years that Manason would fail to recognize him now.

*****

Colette raised her gaze to her reflection in the mirror and once again dropped it. Harris, standing behind her with his hands on her shoulders, laughed.

"Very becoming, that blush. You may use it freely tonight, my dear."

His words chilled her even as they sent flames shooting up her neck.

She'd never dreamed of wearing such a dress. It should have been beautiful. It could have been elegant. But it was neither, in her estimation. It was too sensual, too risqué for that. Its brilliant red color alone would cause her to stand out among everyone in the room. Of course, that's what Harris wanted. Moving away from him to the armoire, she pulled out a black, beaded shawl and flung it over her shoulders. To say anymore about it would only make him angry. He'd already expressed his doubts that she cared enough to please him, and obviously this was what he wanted -- to parade his wife about in front of strange men.

"You won't be able to hide beneath the shawl all evening. You may just as well relax, Lettie, and enjoy yourself. I'm sure you know how."

Descending the stairs and making their way down the long hall into the ballroom, Colette was aware of glances turned their way. Once inside, the first thing she noticed was the contrast and cut of her red satin dress with the many soft-colored gowns worn by the other women present. The ladies leaned together to speak in hushed tones, their eyes following her as Harris removed the shawl and handed it to one of the attendants who whisked by them.

"I'm cold," she whispered.

"Posh. It's stifling in here." He reached toward a platter for a drink as another servant came by and handed a glass to Colette. She took it dutifully, but did not drink. Only a few minutes later, Harris' attorney came by and spoke to him. Others as well, drew him aside to converse, absorbing Colette into their greetings and asking her if they might reserve a dance.

"Of course," Harris always answered for her. "Lettie loves to dance. I don't mind sparing her a little tonight. After all, we're all gentlemen."

They all chortled agreeably and smiled at her. Eventually they would smile again and bow and hold their glasses up to Harris and move on, but they cast knowing looks at her until she felt swallowed up by them. It made her skin crawl.

*****

Manason stood on the veranda admiring the stars spangled across the sky. He was winding up a lengthy conversation with Francis Biron who'd purchased a mill northeast of Grand Rapids from Weston, Heldon, and Kingston only two years earlier. Finally, dry from talk, Biron moved inside. Manason turned to follow him and was met by Tom.

"There you are. Thought you might be out here. Orchestra's playing a waltz. Folks are dancing."

"Not you though?"

"Not many pretty girls. All married, anyhow."

Nase glanced at Tom in the moonlight, his question perceived. Tom gave a curt nod. "He's in there, all right. Ready to meet the man who probably hates you?"

"Are you ready to meet the man who nearly successfully got you killed?" Just thinking of it that way stirred Manason's blood. Oh, he'd be civil. But Harris Eastman would easily be able to read his thoughts. He wasn't about to hide them.

"I'm ready." Tom touched Manason's arm as he stepped forward. "By the way, about that wife of his... Fred was right."

Nase grinned and relaxed. "You should dance with her, Tom. While you're out there on the floor with his lady, it'll give me a great pleasure to let him know just who you are."

Tom shucked a laugh and they went in through the open doors where the stifling heat of the crowded room and dozens of burning candles pushed out the evening's fresh summer air. The music swirled around them while couples waltzed in its grip. Liquor had had an effect by this time, and the company had loosened. Laughter and the volume of even the most genteel talk grew steadily.

Nase gazed across the mass of people, recognizing this person or that, thinking about who he'd avoid and who he'd mingle with throughout the evening. Finally, as the music died and the sea of dancers moved apart, he could see the clusters of bystanders who stood on the far side of the room. Harris Eastman, looking suave and at leisure, stood among a conclave of men. Nase had no doubt that leisure was the last thing on his mind, however. Business was always at the forefront for a man like Eastman. A rustle of red moved in the circle, and Nase looked more closely as one dapper gentleman stepped aside and revealed its source. Manason had been about to lift a glass of water to his lips, but now he stopped, his arm poised halfway, his lips parted, and until he realized he was holding his breath, he didn't move.

Amidst the sea of black coats stood the most stunning woman he'd seen in many months. He knew she was stunning even though she had her back to him, even though he couldn't see her face, only the rich color of her hair piled high with just a few loose curls touching her bare shoulders.

Harris Eastman's wife.

Her figure in the brazen red dress taunted him, as he was sure such a wife of Harris Eastman's would mean it to do. Power was what Harris Eastman wanted, and he would be married to the kind of woman who could help him to achieve it. She was a beauty, but Manason had no doubt she would be cunning and clever, too.

Is that the sort of woman Jean would befriend? Jean said she was naïve... no... wait. That wasn't the one. Didn't Fred say something about Harris Eastman having a second wife? Nase decided to reserve judgment. If Jean was right, and the first one was naive, then this second wife could have been fooled, too. Suddenly, Manason softened toward her, a feat that wasn't difficult with such a lovely woman.

He didn't realize he'd stepped toward them. Drawn to her, he looked at her in the glow of the candlelight and laughed inwardly at the old trite comparison of a moth drawn to a flame.

Where was Tom? Hadn't his friend just been standing next to him? Manason didn't look away to find him. It didn't matter. He didn't need Tom to dance with Mrs. Eastman. He'd ask her himself, and he'd introduce himself to Harris Eastman in front of the others, challenging him to deny Nase the pleasure of the dance.

The color of her hair stirred a far off memory, and he tried to make sense of it in his brain. Finally it nestled into a crevice where he recalled a young woman wrapped in a blue shawl traveling up the dusty road in a wagon in Grand Rapids. This was the same woman.

Harris Eastman's wife.

Manason stopped mere feet away from her, his approach causing several heads to turn in his direction. Eastman looked up and stopped speaking. Did recognition flash in his eyes? How could it be?

Then the woman turned, and Manason consciously tried not to pull in his breath.

Trouble. A stumbling in his thoughts. His words unformed on his lips. *Familiarity.*

Could it be...

Shock in her eyes. Dread. Her beautiful, flushed face turned white and she swayed, but Harris Eastman's hand shot out, steadying her, as if he'd anticipated her response.

She pulled in her breath, telling Manason she was trying desperately to regain her composure. All the while, Eastman smiled as he wrapped his arm around her waist, no doubt keeping her on her feet.

Eastman held out his other hand and, his body numb, Manason shook it.

"I don't believe we've met. I'm Harris Eastman. Eastman Enterprises."

"Manason Kade." The grip on Nase's hand brought him back into the present, sent the searing blaze of a branding iron through him.

"Pleased to meet you, Mr. Kade. Allow me to introduce my wife. Lettie, this is Manason Kade. Mr. Kade, my wife, Lettie Eastman."

The coolness of the man's introduction struck Nase like an ice jam. Almost as though Eastman had anticipated this meeting. Which, of course, he had. He'd known Manason was likely to be here, just as Manason had anticipated Harris' presence. Like a pair of wildcats, the two of them measured one another before going for the other's jugular. Manason determined to match Eastman's coolness, despite his shock at seeing Colette Palmer as the man's wife.

"A pleasure, of course." He held out his hand to Colette. She took it tentatively, and trembled. "Colette and I are old childhood friends," he added, hoping the remark would somehow take Eastman by surprise. To what end, he didn't consider.

Harris gave a cordial laugh. "Yes, so you are. I'd forgotten. Lettie mentioned you were Jean Gilbert's brother."

So he knew Jean was married. And he'd spoken to Colette about Manason. Why? How many other things did Harris Eastman know about them?

Colette lowered her gaze to the floor and then shyly looked back at Manason. She seemed to feel a little better. He hoped so. For the moment, he didn't want to deal with Harris Eastman anymore. He only wanted to talk to Colette. He wanted to take her out of this crowd and look at her and find out how she ended up marrying a man like Eastman.

She looked so bashful. So beautiful and timid. But Manason knew the girl she'd been. Strong and smart and imaginative. Now she'd become this stunning woman standing before him.

Jean, you were right.

Manason sought the right thing to say. He settled for the obvious. "It's good to see you again, Colette. I wondered if we'd ever cross paths."

179

"It's good to see you, too, Nase."

So, she remembered his familiar name. He was still Nase to her.

"I bet the two of you have lots to talk about," Harris said.

"Would you mind?" Manason asked. He was asking Eastman's permission, but looking at Colette, and he didn't care what Eastman thought of it. Yes, Manason found her utterly fascinating, just as did every man in the room, no doubt. But Eastman must realize that. *He must even want it.* So, then, why pretend?

Her soft, delicate hand came into his, and he wrapped her fingers inside his and led her to the dance floor as the music coiled around them.

"Colette."

She smiled at him, a small, tentative smile that made her blush, and turned her face away.

"You're all grown up," he said lamely.

She laughed then, momentarily letting her forehead touch his shoulder and then lifting her face to him again. Now the strains of uncertainty were gone and she looked happy and at ease. He turned her around the floor another time before he thought about speaking again.

"You're different, too, Nase. But not much," she said, finding her tongue before he found his.

"I'm not fat, and I'm not bald. I'm not gray either, as far as that goes." Too late he thought of Eastman and feared she'd think he was comparing himself to her husband. "I mean--"

"No, none of that. But you've changed. I can tell." Her arms tightened on his shoulders, and he chuckled. Out of the corner of his eye, he spied Tom watching them, grinning. He didn't care what Tom made of it. Eastman stood on the other side of the room, and except for a slight change in Colette's demeanor when they swung past him, Manason didn't care what he thought, either.

Colette was a vision, and the only good thing likely to come of this conference. He wanted his time with her to last. He couldn't wait to see her again tomorrow, and he *would* see her. He was certain of it.

The music stopped, and he pulled her aside for refreshment.

"Would you care to go outside? It's hot in here."

"No, I--"

"Then we'll keep dancing."

"But I promised others."

"Let them cut in. I dare them."

She laughed at him. "Do you still slay dragons, too?" He looked at her, catching her blushing at her own bold question.

"Only for true princesses. Come, princess. They're playing our song." The music began again, and he waltzed her across the floor.

*****

Harris smiled benignly at the woman talking to him. As she rattled on aimlessly, Lettie and Manason Kade whisked by once again.

He'd hoped for this, and yet... maybe it was going a little *too* well. He'd have to govern his own emotions. He wanted Lettie to confuse Kade. To cause enough of a distraction that he wouldn't be able to see straight much less keep a keen eye on what was going on with his business up on the Chippewa.

For seeming so put off by his urging her to make good use of her charms, however, she certainly wasn't troubling her conscience over it now. His chest swelled as he recalled her desire to keep that detestable drawing of the man Jean had made. Yet he had to admit the likeness was incredible. He'd recognized Manason Kade the instant he'd crossed the room.

Yes, his plan would work, even if he had to let Lettie know in no uncertain terms that she'd played her role a little too well tonight. Besides, he wanted her to show some attention to the other important men here as well. She could lead Kade on, but if he used up all her time, he'd not be left wanting.

Harris turned his full attention now to the woman before him. What was her name again? Oh, it didn't matter. She was saying something about her son and safety hazards or some other such thing. He just smiled at her and patted her hand.

"Yes. This is why it's so important we have a voice in the legislature when Wisconsin achieves statehood, as we know it will before the year is out."

When next he looked across the room, Colette and Manason were gone.

Chapter Twenty-Eight

"I told you to *dance* with them."

"Harris, please, your voice."

"I don't care who hears me. If you think I'm going to stand by and let some no account woodsman manhandle my wife and then disappear with her--"

"Nase is a friend!"

He moved so quickly she didn't see the slap coming. He struck her across the face with such force she fell across the bed. Then, bending over her, he grabbed her jaw and thrust her head to the side in a second half-slap before standing up.

"Don't you think I know who he is to you?"

Colette hardly heard him. Stunned by the ferocity of his assault, she flinched. Tears filled her eyes. A muscle was pulled in her neck, and even her shoulders ached from the jolt of his blow.

"Why'd you want his picture so badly, Lettie? Did you hope he'd come to you someday?"

"I didn't want it."

"You did. I know you did. You have it now, somewhere, don't you?"

She buried her face in her pillow.

"Don't lie to me, Lettie. Don't think you can turn my mind with your tears. I've seen enough tears to last me a lifetime."

Helen's tears? Lettie tried to stop crying, but only succeeded in coughing.

He hurled something across the room. Glass broke in the fireplace.

"What does it matter?" The words moaned out of her.

"What? What did you say?" He came over and dropped heavily onto the bed.

"I'll never even see him again."

He grabbed her by the shoulders, picking her up and clutching her. The smell of liquor hung heavy on his breath, and his eyes were wild.

"You think so? Well, that's where you're wrong, my dear." Then, leaving the white imprints of his hands on her shoulders, he rose and stormed out of the room, slamming the door as fresh sobs tore out of her.

*****

When Collette awoke, light streamed through the windows, and she pinched her eyes shut against the agonizing intrusion. Pain clutched her, squeezing her head and shooting through it with rhythmic explosions, throbbing in the muscles of her neck and back.

She thought about the dress as it stirred against her skin, and she shivered.

She wanted to burn it.

Her eyes were swollen from crying, but it didn't matter; she couldn't force them open.

Why had Harris done it? Why had he put her on such display, demanding such despicable, coquettish behavior from her, only to be so angry when he got what he wanted -- envy? Wasn't that the sort of power that fueled her husband?

God, how could I have been so deluded?

She thought about God and wondered if He, too, cried over her heart's deception. She didn't want to awaken. She wanted the day to go away, for night to come again and bring back blessed sleep, sweet oblivion.

Blood pulsed against her temples like the surf on Lake Michigan, when she'd peered over the rail as a younger girl on her way to this dark place. Where once Wisconsin's pineries had seemed a glory, they'd now become a suffocating green veil. A trap. Like Harris' jealousy.

Oh, to return to that earlier time, to those lovely days when she was young. When she and Nase were children... She quivered as fresh tears squeezed from beneath her eyelids. Her body convulsed as she tried to stop them when the key turned in the lock on the door. She would pretend she was asleep. Harris came into the room. The tears obeyed and ceased.

He settled himself gently on the bed and touched her arm. She willed herself not to recoil.

"Lettie," he whispered hoarsely.

He leaned over her and kissed her cheek. "Lettie." He stroked away the dampness on the bridge of her nose with his thumb. "I know you can hear me, darling."

Endearments. What right...? Anger burned inside her, and she liked it better than sorrow. By what right did he call her *darling?* She shrugged away, spurning his touch and ignoring the raging headache that nearly paralyzed her.

"Lettie, I need you to look at me... Lettie, I'm sorry."

She cringed.

"Lettie..." What was wrong with his voice? Was he crying? He kissed her shoulder and stroked the hair back from her face. Tenderly he kissed the bruise on her cheek. "Please, Lettie. Won't you answer me?"

Resolve filled her. She sat up, facing away from him on the other side of the bed. The blood rushed from her head, and she wobbled.

"Please don't touch me," she said, when he reached out to her.

"Lettie, you must allow me to apologize. I'll never hurt you again. I promise."

Finally, she turned and looked at him, hoping she looked as horrible -- no, worse -- than she felt. Hoping he would see what he'd done. Wishing he were truly sorry, but doubting him.

"I wanted you to impress them last night. And you did, Lettie. You were wonderful. I never expected to be jealous." He paused, waiting for her, but she would not speak.

"Can you ever forgive me?"

He rose from the bed and came around to the other side, lowering himself on his knees.

"Get up, Harris."

"Not until I know it's all right between us." She looked away. He grasped her hands. "I need you."

"Why do you need me, Harris?"

He obviously hadn't expected her to question him. He'd expected her to respond in a dutiful manner. *Yes, Harris, I absolve you of all your sins against me. I love you, Harris. I could never want to displease you.* That's what he expected. But he wasn't going to get it.

"I -- I, simply can't get along knowing you -- knowing your happiness is in my hands and that I've failed you."

"And that is need?"

"Yes!" His voice rose and he sprang to his feet. A green pallor washed over his face. "Must I explain myself? Can't you just accept my words?"

A sigh escaped her. She couldn't put off the pain any longer. She rose slowly and tore off the hateful dress.

"I need some headache powders," she said. Harris turned to her trunk and sorted through it until he found them. He poured her a glass of water from the pitcher on the nightstand and offered her the medication. She swirled it in the water and drank it all, then continued to ignore him while she went to the armoire to find the plainest dress she'd brought on the trip.

"Is that what you're wearing to breakfast?"

She scorched him with a look and proceeded to dress. "I'm not hungry."

"I'll have something sent up for us."

"No. You go down. I'm not eating."

He turned his palms up in a half gesture, as though wanting to convince her. Whether to come and eat or forgive him or change into something more fetching, she wasn't sure. He never said. For once, he said nothing more at all.

She stayed in their room all day, happy Harris had gone to the conference without her. She slept some, soothed by the headache powders. In the afternoon, she ate an early dinner in their room. Harris returned, but never asked her to go down. Perhaps because the bruise on her cheek had turned a livid hue and he risked his own embarrassment. In the evening there was another gathering. Not a ball this time, but an opportunity for the men to gather socially yet again. Many would call it an early evening as most would be leaving in the morning. Some, like Harris, would stay as late as the evening demanded.

Collette called for a bath after dinner and resolved to write a letter to

Jean. They would all know soon enough that she had been fool enough to marry Helen's widower. She had nothing more to worry about on that account. And she needed her friend.

She would also write Joseph and ask how Dandy was getting along. She had taken him to Joe, gratefully knowing he would take good care of her beloved dog. She wished right now that Dandy were here so she could run her fingers through his coat and have him lick her hand.

Harris has taken every joy...

She rebuked herself, but it was true. At least it seemed so. Yet, he was still her husband and he would remain her husband. If what he said was true, that he wouldn't hurt her again, then possibly they could put this episode behind them when they returned to Grand Rapids. Perhaps there was hope.

A knock on the door interrupted her thoughts.

"Just a moment." Her long hair hung loose, and she brushed it down across the side of her face, hoping to obscure the bruise on her cheek. She didn't want even one of the hotel servants to see it. Rumors spread easily. She opened the door a crack, and her heart jumped. She swung it open wider.

"Manason."

"Hello, Princess."

She flushed warmly. "You have to stop saying that. Come in."

"Is it all right?"

"I don't care if it isn't." She knew she sounded harsh. It wasn't what she intended. "Have a seat." She directed him to a chair beside the table near the window.

"I don't feel like sitting. I wondered if you'd like to take a walk."

"Well, I--"

"It's a beautiful evening, and still broad daylight. Won't be dark for over an hour yet. I promise to keep you in discreet view of the hotel so your husband won't be offended."

She thought about Harris' sudden jealousy. He'd misunderstood Manason. She'd told him that Nase was Jean's brother, and that he was a childhood friend. Other men had acted more boldly toward her, and yet Harris hadn't been jealous of them. She thought he was probably jealous of Joseph, but that was understandable, as Joseph had actually courted her. Nase, on the other hand, had no real connection to her that should bother Harris. So why had he been so angry? Did he see something in Colette she wasn't even capable of seeing in herself?

Should she go with Manason? If Harris was truly sorry, like he said, then why shouldn't she? In the end, perhaps only the alcohol had driven him to react the way he had. It often had the effect of making Harris mean.

"All right. Let me get a wrap."

"It's warm out. I doubt you'll want one. Haven't you been out today?"

"No. I've slept most of the day. All that dancing last night, you know."

"Ah." She had pulled out the blue shawl and now tossed it onto the bed at Manason's assurance that she'd be warm. She discreetly wound up her hair and tied on her sun bonnet. Then she allowed him to lead her out into the hall and walk beside her down the stairs. She stayed to his right, knowing he was less likely to notice her bruised cheek if she remained on that side.

"I've seen that dress before," he remarked, "and the blue shawl."

"You have?"

"Yes. In Grand Rapids, I'm sorry to say. I came there once to see you, but at the mill they told me you'd gone away with your family when your father was injured. I was walking up the street and saw a girl climbing into a buggy with a man I thought was her beau. She was wearing that dress and blue shawl. I thought, *what a pretty girl*, and regretted I'd missed you."

Colette's heart thrummed with sadness. If only he hadn't missed her. Maybe she wouldn't have missed out, either. For somehow, she knew she had. She had missed out terribly.

"I wish I'd seen you, too." She glanced out the corner of her eye at him as they strolled out the doors and onto the boardwalk. He was watching her. She took a deep breath and sighed. "You followed your heart, and it brought you to Wisconsin. I followed mine… and look where it brought me."

"You are unhappy then."

She noticed he didn't ask her if she was, only that he had observed it.

She nodded. She'd never imagined she would admit such a thing to anyone, much less to *this* man. Perhaps it was a dangerous thing to do. She shouldn't say anything but good about her husband. By next week, she might regret it. If Harris lived up to his promise, maybe she would. But right now the pain was still there, physically, and the heat of the evening's tirade too close. She considered her current circumstances, but then accepted that she'd been unhappy much longer than that.

"Why did you marry Harris?"

She laughed. It was a laugh of derision. "I told you, I followed my heart. It's a treacherous thing to do, you know. There are always consequences. I might ask you, Nase, why didn't you marry Margie Baker? Do you regret she got away?"

He snorted. "*Margie Baker.* I haven't thought of her in over a year. No, I don't regret it a bit. Why should I?"

"She had her cap set for you."

He nodded. "I suppose that's true. But somehow I knew she wasn't the one for me."

"You did? How did you know?"

"I just had a feeling something better was out there." His voice was changed, and Colette wondered about it.

"The pine was calling?"

"I'm not in love with the pine. Say, why does everyone call you Lettie?"

"It all started with Harris and Helen and Joe. Pretty soon, that's who everyone knew me to be."

"Joe? Say, you don't mean Joe Gilbert."

She nodded and smiled. "If you saw me in Grand Rapids, that's who I was with."

They rounded a turn in the road and found themselves in the town square. A little park sat in the middle of it. They wandered down a path to a bench hewn from a pair of logs.

"Joe was courting me then," she told him as she sat and loosened the strings of her bonnet. She wanted to take it off and fan herself, but she was conscious of the bruise.

"Oh, I see... but he wasn't the one. Harris Eastman took your heart."

She turned at an angle to see him better, still protecting his full view of her face. "No. I wasn't sure about Joe. He and I were very good friends, but I just couldn't be sure, not the way you seemed to be about, you know... finding the right person. Then Harris lost Helen and... so did I. Our worlds crumbled, and our lives were so intertwined by then. It just happened."

She added, "What you're thinking and being too polite not to say is right, and Joe was right, too. I don't love my husband. Not like I'm supposed to, anyway." She hurried on, "Oh, I suppose I do feel some kind of love for him. We've made our efforts. But what I once thought was love seems to have dissolved because of Harris' supreme efforts to treat me the way he treated Helen."

"I don't understand how that could've happened."

"He treated me wonderfully once. He thinks he still does. Only he used to tell me about all the things I wanted to know about and understand. I used to help him, too. With business things, you know? But then he shut me out. Now he buys me things, like he did with Helen. Gifts to capture my heart, I guess. Like that dress last night..."

"I thought you were beautiful. I think you're beautiful now."

"Really, Nase? Or before you knew it was me did you think me merely cheap, like a... like a harlot?"

She thought she'd shock him, but he didn't appear moved. "You aren't used to being displayed like that?"

"Oh, I'm quite used to it, unfortunately. But he's never asked me to wear anything so tawdry."

"That's how you felt? Well, on you the dress didn't look tawdry. Believe me."

She looked at him squarely, more boldly than she'd ever hoped to in her life, forgetting the bruise, forgetting she had anything to hide.

"I believe it when you say it, Nase."

He drew in a sharp breath, reached up, and pushed back her sunbonnet, spilling her hair around her. Self-conscious now because he'd seen the truth, she tried to turn away. Gently he gripped her chin and turned her to face him again.

"He did this."

"Yes," she whispered.

"You have to leave him. Come with me. I'll take you to Jean."

"No, Nase. I could never do that."

"Why not?"

She wanted to cry because of the possibilities rolling over her like a spring flood, but she wouldn't follow her traitorous heart again. She'd made vows, and they were deeply ingrained. Besides that, she meant to follow reason this time.

"I made a marriage vow. A vow is a vow. I can never break it."

"I'm not asking you to. I only want you to get away, to be safe."

Trembling, she touched his hand. "Would I be safe if I went to the Chippewa country with you, Nase?"

He had to see what she was asking. She might be safe from Harris' angry tirades, but would her heart ever be safe with Manason? The answer was obvious.

Manason looked away. He leaned back on the bench and ran a hand through his thick hair. "You hope he'll change."

"He could. God could make him change."

"You believe it? God will change him if you sacrifice yourself?"

"I don't know. He may, or He may not. God doesn't count it as a promise. But He does promise me that what I do -- or chose *not* to do -- in my own conduct, if it's right, is very precious in His sight. That means something to me, Nase, to be doing something precious..."

Chapter Twenty-Nine

Jean wound her way up the hillside through padded layers of compressed leaves and hazel brush and around stately oak trees. Muffled thumping in the draw ahead drew her on in the right direction. Rob had told her she would find Manason on the ridge clearing scrub and marking out the dimensions of his house.

She'd been surprised to hear it, given Nase's earlier proclivity to put it off. She hadn't spoken to him since he'd returned from the conference, and she wondered what on the long trip had turned his thoughts. Maybe she'd finally convinced him to move out of the office. Maybe he was just getting tired of returning home to those cramped quarters after noting at the conference how Wisconsin's upper class lived. Either way, she was happy to see him doing something with the plot of ground on the ridge.

She discovered that the thumping came from her shirtless, sweaty brother wielding a small sledge hammer against stakes in the ground. At the moment, he was running a line diagonally between the stakes to see that the square he had created was just that -- square.

"So you're starting, then," she said. He lifted his head and smiled. "It's not very big, but I suppose it's better than what you live in now."

"This is just the kitchen," he said, rolling the string into a ball.

Jean raised her eyebrows. "Planning to spend a lot of time in there?"

"I might learn to cook something besides beans and side pork."

"Because you have so much free time, you mean," Jean said with a smirk as she perused the area. She turned away from the hillside and took in the view of a stream sparkling in the distance. "I have to say, Nase, I'm somewhat surprised. You seemed pretty adamant about holding off on the house. What changed your mind?"

Manason gathered up the unused stakes and carried them to the other side of the clearing. Dropping them on the ground, he eyeballed the area west of the *kitchen*, his mind bent on the project. He cruised the lot with the same focus and determination as when he set his jaw and cruised pine.

"What if I put the master bedroom here, and run a big front room the length of the entire south side, with a two-sided stone fireplace that faces both rooms? That would give me nice morning sun in the kitchen, and a southern exposure with an outward view in the sitting room." He nodded, clearly not expecting her to answer.

She dropped her arms to her sides. *The master bedroom? The big kitchen? Nase learning to cook?* Well, she knew he'd been joking about the last part.

"What's come over you?"

Nase finally looked at her. His face harbored such a serious expression, alarm skittered through her.

He sighed and settled his hands on his hips. His gaze fell to the lines of string and stakes, then rose back to hers again. "I saw Colette."

"What?" She stood up straighter.

"She was at the conference with her *husband*."

The flower of joy that had bloomed in Jean's belly contracted again into a tight ball.

"Her husband? But... really?"

His head moved up and down. "Her husband, *Harris Eastman*."

"No! Nase, you're not serious. Not him. Not really!"

"She sent you a letter." Manason picked up his shirt from a stump and reached into the pocket, pulling out a creased, folded envelope. "I was going to walk on down and give it to you when I finished here today."

Jean glanced at the smudged letter, and then back at her brother. "Tell me what happened. What about Helen?"

He shrugged. "She died in child birth."

Pity stabbed Jean's heart, marked by the fact that she must soon get back to the house to nurse her own infant son. Rob wouldn't be able to keep him quiet for long once he awoke.

Poor Helen.

"I don't understand. She always felt strongly toward you, and then there was Joe. They were close. We all thought that maybe the two of them would end up marrying."

"Joe knew."

She couldn't believe it. "He did? But he never said--"

"Colette didn't want us to know."

"Why not?"

Manason stretched the shirt over his broad back and buttoned it. He turned his head and spat before speaking again. Anger lit his face the next time he looked at her.

"Eastman's cruel to her, that's why."

"What do you mean? Does he hurt her?"

"Not always physically, or so she claims. But she's hurting; I can promise you that. She doesn't love him."

"I still don't understand how it could've happened. Their ages... oh, I know I shouldn't think that way, but--"

"She lived with Eastman and his wife after Eldon got hurt. When his wife died, Colette comforted him."

Jean closed her eyes, imagining how easy it would've been for someone with Colette's sympathetic nature to be led into such a relationship and even marriage. "So Joseph knew where she was all this time. Doesn't that upset you?"

Manason shrugged. "It seems like a waste to be upset now. It's too late."

"Nase--" She walked over and put her hand on his shoulder, looking him squarely in the eye. "What do you have in mind? Why are you building the house? Are you thinking of bringing her here?"

He shifted. "I wanted to. I asked her to come, but she wouldn't. She means to stick to her vows."

Jean sighed. "Then there's nothing anyone can do."

"If it weren't for what she said, I'd try to change her mind."

"What did she say?"

"It doesn't matter."

He turned away and gazed down the ridge again. Jean had never seen her brother so close to the brink of defeat before, and yet the fact that he was here, working on the house, meant he'd been inspired to fight for... what?

"Nase..." She looped her arm through his. "Are you in love with Colette?"

He flashed her an indecipherable glance and laughed mirthlessly. "This was the first I've seen her in seven years. Wouldn't that be a bit sudden?"

"But she's not really changed on the inside, is she? I mean, she's still Colette. Grown up, yes, but still her. You know her."

"Grown up... *ha*! That's putting it mildly." He ground his teeth. "She's the most memorable woman I've ever met." He bowed his head.

"She's beautiful, isn't she?"

He nodded.

"But she's still Colette. Our Colette."

"She wasn't shy. She said things I never imagined she might say. She stunned me in every conceivable way."

"Did she tell you he was cruel to her?"

"She didn't have to. The next morning she wore the marks he'd given her."

"Bruises? Are you sure?"

Manason threw up his hands. "What do you think I mean? First he flaunted her about all evening like she was some kind of ornament. He dangled her in front us like a steak before a pack of wolves. Then he punished her for it."

"That makes no sense. I don't understand."

"He used her to win favors. Told everyone they could dance with her. Ask Tom if you don't believe me. He saw how it was."

Jean measured what Manason had said. "What about you, Nase? How was she toward you when you first saw her?"

His voice softened. "Nervous." He smiled. "Embarrassed, shy, worried. But she got beyond it. We spent most of the evening together. Dancing. Talking. Laughing over memories..." He looked out past the tree tops and the stream, but Jean knew he wasn't seeing them.

"So you won the prize?"

His voice grew sharp. "What do you mean?"

"She spent the evening with you? Not with Harris? Not with anyone else?"

191

"Mostly me, yes."

"Don't you see, Nase? Harris was jealous of you. He knows you're responsible for the forfeitures he suffered, and then you come along and steal his wife for an entire evening. You men can be so thick sometimes. Don't you think he might have been taking out his resentment on Colette? He hates you, Nase! Heaven help us if you two have anymore conflicts."

"No... no." Nase shook his head. "Eastman wasn't surprised by it. He knew I'd be there. He even said he knew Colette and I were old friends. But you might be right about one thing."

She looked to him, waiting for him to tell her what that was.

He reached out and drew her to his side. "I think that maybe I do love her. I think that just maybe... I do."

Chapter Thirty

Upon examining himself, Harris felt truly sorry for having lost his patience with Lettie. She had, after all, behaved exactly as he had expected she would when thrown face to face with Manason Kade. Harris' personal failure had resulted from seeing how, despite his need to use her to destroy Kade, Lettie was genuinely affected by the man. The true Lettie had shown her colors with both Joseph and Manason, and had it not been so important for Harris to procure some measure of revenge against Kade, he would teach his fickle wife a lesson she'd never forget. Yes, he was sorry for what he'd done. Sorry for what it might have cost him.

He couldn't trust Lettie. That was certain. She was much more willing to share her affections than she had admitted. She'd run to Joseph Gilbert as soon as Harris had told her to get rid of the dog, hadn't she? Gilbert had become her hero when he'd taken the creature. Then there were her unbearable lies about Manason Kade. Harris had known she cared for the man the day he'd discovered the picture. To see the two of them carrying on at the conference had been both disgusting and satisfying, since he knew his plan wouldn't fail. No, he couldn't trust her. She'd married him for security. Months had passed since she'd told him she loved him. Apparently she'd shed any effort to propagate that lie.

His chest constricted at the thought of her perfidy. Even as he contemplated on it, a small voice inside his head argued that he might be wrong. He went to the liquor cabinet to pour a drink to chase that thought away, but his hand fell short of the knob, and he turned to gaze out the window instead.

Your so-called proof that Manason Kade was ever anything to her is thin. She hadn't seen him since she was a child. Joseph Gilbert, then. No need for proof there. He's been bitter about losing her all along. She once thought she might marry him. Helen confided as much. The two of them truly shared an attraction. And the way she'd hugged him that day...

Harris leaned against the window sill and kneaded the stubble beneath his lips. His thoughts rebuked him.

Remember the early days, how she blushed when you first held her? Joe hasn't been back here since that one day, and she never knew you saw them together. You could be wrong...

He cursed and turned to his desk. Yes, he could be wrong. Lettie might have been faithful to him since the beginning.

You're too old for her, you know. There will always be other men her age. Young, virile men who'll seek her out.

Why haven't we had a baby? Is there something wrong with her? Or is it me? No! Of course not. There was Helen... but you're older now. Maybe...

Harris yearned to go to the cabinet, but even he recognized how easily he lost his patience and self-control when he drank. He didn't need his wife nagging him to realize it. His hands shook as he shuffled through the papers on his desk. He paused and looked at them.

She's going to leave you if you aren't careful. Play this game with Manason Kade carefully, or you'll lose her.

He thrust his hands over his face. He couldn't take it anymore. Stiffly, he turned and opened the cabinet. His hands quivered as he removed the cork, and he poured himself a drink. The burning in his throat was a welcome balm. His heartbeat slowed, and his breathing calmed.

Make it up to her. Be her husband. It will be important for her to tear Kade's attention from his business prospects, but you must be careful not to drive her into his arms. She must never have a reason to leave.

Now his thinking cleared. His thoughts became rational and controlled. Pouring himself a second shot of brandy, Harris smiled.

*****

Colette braced herself for her husband's disapproval when he came into the room and saw her rearranging the furniture.

"What are you doing?"

She straightened and took a breath. "I thought I'd change things around a bit. I need a change in here."

She had expected his reproof. The memory of how Helen had fretted over such a simple activity was not lost on her. She understood that now. Harris needed to control every aspect of his world, including the part in which she lived. That she'd made this decision alone was a risk, but she was determined to not become Helen.

"Let me help you."

Here it was. He would tell her what could be moved, and what couldn't. Where each piece should go.

"You shouldn't be lifting these heavy pieces alone," he said. "Where's Onaiwah?"

"I sent her to the mercantile."

"Well, where would you like this to go?"

Colette opened and closed her mouth. He was asking her? "I, uh, well... over there by the window. I'm going to move the chair nearer to the fireplace."

"All right, then. Stand back. I'll do it for you."

Colette stepped back soundlessly as Harris shuffled the bulky pieces around.

"Thank you, Harris," she said when he had finished.

"Is there anything else?"

"Just that one small table. I can get the rest."

"All right. Here... you take one side, and I'll take the other."

Together, they moved the table.

Harris straightened and smiled. "You're right. It does look nicer this way. Very good idea." He kissed her on the forehead and smiled, then left the room whistling.

"I've always wanted to try it this way," she murmured to his back as he disappeared into the rear of the house.

Thirty minutes later, Onaiwah returned and set Colette's purchases in the kitchen. She entered the parlor exclaiming over the new arrangement. Her heart unusually light, Colette thanked her.

"Oh!" Onaiwah said. "I forgot. Letter come for you." She reached into her apron pocket and pulled it out. "Who it from?"

"Let me see." Colette took the letter and stared at it. She'd written Jean over a month ago. Now here was her reply. "It's from my dear friend, Jean."

She sat on the sofa by the light of the window and tore it open as Onaiwah went away humming into the kitchen.

Dear Colette,

Dear, dear Colette! How wonderful it is to say that again and know you will get this letter and read those words. I have missed our correspondence so very much. Why didn't you tell me where you were? Oh, I could scold you, but I won't. I know so much has changed.

Manason gave me your letter. It took some time for me to think over all the news you had to tell. Poor Helen. My heart is sick at losing her. It is such fresh news to me. And to think it happened over two years ago. Now life has moved on, and you are a married woman. Manason told me you married Harris. I know you will understand my surprise, but I hope you will also believe me when I tell you that I do understand how it could have happened for the two of you...

Colette set the letter in her lap and stared into the cold fireplace. Manason and Jean were the closest of siblings. He would have told her everything, not just that she and Harris had married. He would have told her of their troubles, too. Jean had picked her words carefully. Why? In case Harris intercepted the letter? That wasn't beyond the realm of possibility. She returned to Jean's words.

I only wish the best for you, my dear, dear friend. Now I will share my news. You will have heard from my brother-in-law, Joe, and from Nase as well, that Rob and I are proud parents. We have been blessed with a little boy, and we named him Stephen Kade Gilbert after Rob's grandfather and, of course, my family's surname. I can't wait for you to see him, and can happily say that you will before long. We are coming to Grand Rapids for a visit before the weather turns cold. Rob is so proud of Stephen, and his family longs to meet him. Rob misses them, too. I hope that if time allows, I can persuade my brother to come along with us. But we shall have to see; he will be getting ready to begin the new cutting season soon, and he is building a house.

Colette continued to read the letter telling her about Stu's upcoming marriage, and that Annie was already the mother of both a boy and a girl. The words flew past her eyes barely absorbed. *They are coming here.* Jean and Rob, their baby, and Manason. She didn't doubt he would come. She knew Jean knew it, too. She had veiled her words, but there was no question that after their long visit during the conference a month ago, Manason would come to see that she was safe and well. *He wants to see me again.*

Her hands trembled. She pressed the letter to her chest. Just then, Harris came back into the room. He stopped and looked at her, catching her by surprise. Too late for her to guard her expression.

"What's wrong?"

"Oh, nothing," she said, quavering as she held the stationary away from her.

"What is that?"

"A letter from my friend, Jean."

Harris looked quizzical, then nonchalant. "Ah, yes. Jean Gilbert. Good news, I hope?"

"Yes." He strolled closer, and she gathered her wits and her courage. She held out the letter, fully expecting him to want to read it. "She's had a baby. A little boy."

"How wonderful for her."

"Yes. She and her husband Rob intend to bring him here to meet his grandparents."

"Well, isn't that lucky. You'll get to see her again."

"Yes." She sighed, only partly relieved. "I am lucky."

"Is that all?" He looked ready to be on his way. She knew she should say more. She didn't want Manason to surprise them with a visit. She didn't want to put Harris in that position.

"She mentioned Manason. He may come along."

"Oh?" Harris stopped and absently fingered his pocket watch, his thick black eyebrows lifting. "Why is that?"

"I don't know, really. He and Jean are quite close. Just to come, I guess."

Harris drew a slow grin, walked around the small table that stood between them, and took her shoulders.

"Oh, come now, Lettie. He's coming to see you, of course. He was so entertained the last time you met. He's not quite full of you yet."

"Harris, don't say such things."

Harris laughed. "It's all right. I expected we might hear from him sooner or later. Now, don't look so aghast. Really, it's quite all right. We'll have them all for dinner. The entire lot of the Gilberts and Kades, if you wish."

She looked at him, uncertain if he meant it, but his eyes were clear and twinkling. She tried to smile. "That would be very kind."

He stroked her chin. "Think nothing of it," he said and kissed her.

"Thank you, Harris."

"No need," he said, and strolled out of the room.

*****

Harris sat in his study giving serious thought to the visit coming their way. He hoped Manason would indeed come along with his sister and brother-in-law. Better still if his man Tom Durant came as well. Harris knew Robin Gilbert had also become an important part of Kade Forest Works. Ah, well. At least two out of three of them would be out of the way.

Now wouldn't be the best time to strike at Kade's holdings. That would be in the spring, after they'd spent an entire season's labor and money only to lose it in the end. But this was just as well. Striking now would mean there'd be no season at all for Kade if Harris had his way.

He pulled out a fresh sheet of paper and wrote quickly, giving Boggs instructions.

Use any means at your disposal. I want the stakes to be high... I cannot overemphasize enough that a connection must never be made to either of us.

Chapter Thirty-One

Colette checked herself over once again. She didn't want to appear ostentatious, but unpretentious; the way Jean would remember her. Harris might wish her to dress with a bit more flare, but she was prepared to stand up to him if he said anything about it. She doubted he would. Lately he'd been less demanding about what she wore. In fact, he'd been less demanding about a lot of things. He hadn't questioned her all when the red dress disappeared from her wardrobe. She smoothed the simple checked gingham and turned before the mirror to have a look at the back. Satisfied everything fit properly and that her hair, but for two ringlets, was tucked neatly into the blue-beaded snood at the nape of her neck, she breathed in the pleasant aroma of the pork roast wafting up from the kitchen.

Onaiwah had become a remarkable cook, and the two young women enjoyed one another's company the most when they were cutting, peeling, boiling, and baking things in the kitchen. A quiet, lovely girl, Onaiwah would someday make someone a fine wife. Colette hoped that when that day came, she'd find a man who'd make her happy.

Sometimes she looked at Onaiwah and thought of Joseph. She hadn't seen him since taking Dandy to him almost two months ago. He and Kashe hadn't married yet, and she wondered if they had determined a date for their plans.

She left her boudoir and met Harris in the upstairs hall. He was still working at buttoning a fawn colored waistcoat over his shirt and expensive silk jacquard cravat.

"Let me help you," she said, pressing her hands against his vest and smoothing the cravat into place.

He smiled at her. "Thank you. You look lovely."

Surprise shifted her shoulders and she smiled back at him.

Harris had been behaving differently lately. In small ways that were almost imperceptible at first, and she'd hardly dared to breathe, hoping he wouldn't suddenly pull the rug out from under her. But in fact, he'd hardly spoken a harsh word to her in weeks. Yet it wasn't as though he was suddenly someone else entirely. She knew there were times he fought with himself over his temper and his need to control everything and everyone, including her. She knew, too, that he still drank a lot, even though he took pains to keep his excesses from her. Still, she was thankful for his efforts. She needed to believe he was trying, especially on this occasion.

"When will dinner be ready?" she asked Onaiwah as she and Harris walked into the kitchen.

"In one hour."

"Perfect. It smells heavenly."

Onaiwah's white teeth shone out of her brown face.

"Is there coffee?" Harris asked.

"I get some," the girl said, moving toward the stove.

He held up his hand. "Never mind. I was only wondering." He met Collette's eyes. "Perhaps your friends would like some wine."

"After dinner?"

"Whatever you think."

A knock at the front door called their attention.

"Your guests are here," Harris said, slipping into his jacket.

"Please, Harris, think of them as your friends, too. You always liked Jean."

"So I did." He cast her a pleasant smile. "Onaiwah, do you mind getting the door? You can show our friends into the parlor."

"Yes, sir, Mr. Eastman."

Colette followed Harris into the parlor and stood beside him, kneading her fingers together. Harris put his arm around her, and she was surprised by its calming effect. Then she heard their voices. Jean. And that must be Robbie. She twitched anxiously. She recognized Mr. Gilbert's deep Gaelic accent. A chilly draft from outside wafted its way across the floor into the parlor, and a tiny whimper reached her ears. It must have come from Jean's baby. There came a "tut, tut" from Mrs. Gilbert, and then there were no other voices before the door closed with a solid thump. Sharp disappointment momentarily punctuated Colette's joy in a way she neither expected nor found pleasing. Had she really wanted Manason to be there so badly?

Moments later, they came into the room. Colette's joy returned, and she slipped from Harris' side.

"Jean!" She tried to hug her, even with the baby between them. She looked down at the infant who seemed only slightly disturbed from his sleep, then back into the eyes of her friend. "Jean, you've come. I'm so happy." She beamed at Rob, welcoming him.

Harris shook hands with Mr. Gilbert and complimented his wife. They came further into the room, and then--

Manason.

He was here after all. She bit her lip and smoothed the fabric of her skirt. Then she reached to shake his hand.

"Nase, welcome." She turned to Rob and shook his, too. "Welcome, all of you."

"Is this it?" Harris asked. "We'd hoped that your brother Joe would join us."

"He's picking up some extra work over at Whitney's mill in Point Basse. He'll be sorry he missed it," Rob said.

"How are he and Kashe?" Colette asked, trying not to be drawn into Manason's gaze. Her heart pounded. *Harris was right...*

"Joseph? Why, he's the same as ever. It'll be a wonder if that little girl can settle him down," Joe's mother said.

"Oh, come now, darlin'," Mr. Gilbert said. "Look what you did with me. And wasn't I the image of our Joe?" He gave a boisterous laugh, and she grinned.

"So you finally admit it."

"A good woman can tame the wildest beast," Harris put in, smiling at Colette and causing her to flush.

"Come in and sit down, won't you, everyone?" Dizzily almost, she stepped back beside Harris again and motioned them to the various seats. "May I offer anyone coffee?"

They all accepted but Jean. Colette called to the kitchen, and Onaiwah brought out a tray with a coffee service and set it on the round table. Colette poured. Having something to do quelled her nerves and helped her avoid looking directly at Manason. She served them all, starting with the older Gilberts, then Rob, then Manason. Passing him the cup, her eyes fell into his and he gave her a small smile. The others were talking, and Harris commented politely on Jean and Rob's baby.

"You look well," Nase said softly.

"I am," she said, then pulled away to serve Harris.

Slowly, her heart stilled its fluttered racing. She stood close to Harris, looping her hand in his arm and tucking her shoulder behind his. Feeling safe... or maybe using him like a shield to cage her heart.

Good things are happening in my marriage. I can't let anything jeopardize that.

"Would you like to hold Stephen?" Jean's question interrupted her thoughts.

Colette stepped forward to cradle the baby in the circle of her arms, the folds of her wide sleeves draping his tiny form. "He's so precious."

Jean beamed at Rob. "He looks like his father, don't you think?"

"But a little like his uncle Manason around the forehead," Manason said, speaking up finally.

"I have to take Nase everywhere I go so he can tell people that," Jean said, laughter rippling her voice.

"You both know it's true."

"He looks like he's a fine, strong boy," Harris said.

"What about Michael and Carrie?" Colette directed her question at Rob's parents.

"Oh, yes. They had another girl. That's two for them now. Both just as pretty as peaches. I'm a spoiled grandma."

"Joe's sure to have a house full someday," Rob said.

"I expect he will, once they marry."

"When will that be?" Colette asked. She recognized the curious look in Harris' eyes, but thought nothing of it. She had avoided talking to him about Joe, a sore spot in their past, and had never mentioned he was engaged to Kasheawa.

"We haven't heard yet," Mr. Gilbert said, a look of parental consternation lifting his forehead as he set his cup on his knee. "I don't know why they're waiting. Joe seems certain enough of the lass."

"He only wants to make sure things won't be a struggle for them," the Mrs. said. "He's a good, hard worker, my Joe. He may like to have his share of fun, but I can't say he doesn't take his responsibilities seriously when the time comes." She took them all in with her declaration over Joe, but her eyes caught and held Colette's a little longer than they did the others. She sipped her coffee and smiled. "I think he's hoping for a big doings next spring, after statehood. People will feel like lots of celebrating then."

"If we've made it by then," Manason said.

"Oh, we will. I'm feeling confident about that," Harris said. "The delegates will meet again in two weeks. I think they're going to come up with a workable constitution this time."

"Let's hope so," Mr. Gilbert said. "We've waited a long time."

"We must keep out leaders in our prayers," Mrs. Gilbert added. Everyone murmured their agreement.

Colette made her way to the settee beside Jean, where they discussed the joys of little Stephen. Colette could not help but be drawn again and again to Manason's dark eyes watching her and Harris. After their day of camaraderie in the park, she would have loved to speak with him openly now, but even though Harris had been more than good about Manason and the others coming tonight, she didn't wish to lose the strides they'd made over the past few weeks. Memories of that other time were still too vivid.

At seven o'clock, Onaiwah announced dinner was ready. Colette and Harris guided their guests into the dining room and took their places as host and hostess at opposite ends of the table.

"We shall be informal tonight. You may seat yourself in any manner you wish."

Colette smiled at Jean and discreetly patted the chair to her left so that she might be close to her during the meal. As everyone else took their seats, Colette found Manason sitting immediately to her right.

"An empty chair," Harris said. "Too bad Joseph was unable to come."

Colette raised her gaze, gauging whether he meant what he said or not.

"Well, maybe next time," she said. "Harris, will you say grace?"

They never prayed over meals when they ate together, though Colette often did so alone; but Harris rose to the occasion as he always did when they entertained the more prominent of his acquaintances. His words were always eloquent.

Lifting their heads, they moved on. For a while the conversation was all inclusive, each bringing up this or that, and everyone discussing it in turn. Eventually, however, as the main course was served and consumed, and Onaiwah brought them a cobbler for their dessert, the conversations drifted apart into twos and threes. Jean leaned toward Colette.

"Has Nase told you about his house?"

"No. Tell me about it, please." Colette looked now at Manason, happy to be able to talk to him, glad there was something to say that had nothing to do with her.

"It's just a house."

A little puff of sound came out of Jean. Her gray eyes gleamed. "Just a house?" She looked sideways at Colette. "It's much more than that. When I first told him he should stop talking about it and start building it, I expected him to get on with it and wind up with a comfortable little place to hang his hat. Just something to get him out of that drab little building he calls an office, mind you. But if you could only see it, Colette. It's a dream house."

Colette looked expectantly at Manason.

"It's a nice house," he said, and smiled.

"Tell me," she urged.

"Well…" He took a sip of water, "It's built of both logs and planed lumber. It has a wide, open porch, and a stone fireplace in two rooms."

"It must be big."

There was a subtle, knowing look in his eyes. "Do you like to cook? I remember you and Annie baking pies."

She nodded.

"My sister here has laughed at the proportions of the kitchen. But cookee tells me a good cook needs elbow room, and I've always believed what he tells me."

"He's right. Go on."

Nase leaned back in his chair, letting his fork dangle over his barely touched dessert. He watched her while he explained. "It sits on the brow of a hill covered with straight, tall oaks. I like to watch the deer at night, coming up to browse the acorns. The Chippewa valley is a vast ocean of woodland."

"It sounds kind of desolate."

"I can see Rob and Jean's place when the leaves fall and the smoke of their chimney curls up. It's close to a little creek that feeds the big river. It gives me company."

His voice died away, but he didn't stop looking at her. In a pleasant way, she realized he was doing what he'd done ever since she was a little girl. Mesmerizing her with talk of the land, his love for the forest and the trees, their grandeur. She could see the mist rising from the river as he talked, feel the crunch of the acorns beneath her shoes. Smell the leaf mold and feel the autumn leaves brush her arms as the wind gusted and tore them loose from their tentative hold on the gnarled branches overhead.

"Tell her the bad part, Nase."

Jean's words called her back into the room, made her remember they weren't alone.

"There's no bad part."

"There is. Colette, he doesn't even *live* there."

"What?"

"It's not finished," he said, taking a bite of cobbler.

"It's finished enough to live in. It might be missing a few gewgaws, but he's worked like such a mad man for the past two months and has gotten everything in place but the furniture."

Colette looked again at Manason. He hid behind a prolonged sip of his coffee. *Two months. He's been working like a mad man since he returned from the conference.*

She stared at him until he lowered the empty cup.

"When do you plan to move into your house?" she asked.

He shrugged. "When the time feels right."

*****

After dinner, everyone moved back into the sitting room by the fire. Harris had embroiled Mr. Gilbert in a deep discussion on some of Grand Rapids' future prospects, and eventually Harris invited the man into his study to discuss some ideas over plat maps. Robin went along to try a glass of Harris' wine. Manason declined the offer, saying he didn't mind visiting with the ladies a while longer. Then the baby began to fuss.

Manason offered to go with the gentlemen anyway so his sister could nurse the child, but Jean asked to use Colette's bedroom, confessing it was liable to become complicated feeding the infant. Colette told her which room it was, knowing Jean was familiar with the layout of the house. Mrs. Gilbert went along, exclaiming over her desire to change and tidy her little grandson, and to lend Jean a hand. Colette thought Mrs. Gilbert might also like a little peek at the rest of the house, but was too polite to say so.

Suddenly she was alone with Manason. Seated on the opposite end of the divan, she allowed herself to look at him.

"Is this uncomfortable for you?" he asked. "I can join Rob if you like, and you can be with Jean."

"No," she said, a little too quickly. "This is fine. It's good to see you, to talk with you again."

His easy smile warmed her. "Are things better?"

She nodded. "Yes. Truthfully, they are. I don't want you to worry about me, Nase."

"I can't help it."

"You live too far away for that. Besides, I've been rambling along without my dragon slayer for quite a few years now."

"So you have. Are you absolutely sure, Colette?"

Suddenly he took her hand. She tried to pull away, but he leaned closer and tightened his hand over hers until she relaxed.

"Nase."

"Colette..." His eyes searched hers. "There's room for you in my house."

"Don't say that."

"I'm going to say it. I know you, Colette. I always have. It's not so surprising, is it, that even after all these years I should come back into your life and want to be with you?"

She shook her head, but he wasn't hearing the *no* screaming inside it.

"I don't want to live there without you, and that's the truth."

"Stop it, Nase."

Joe had talked to her like this, and she never knew what her heart wanted to do about it. This time she did. She understood her heart with the steel clarity of a cold, blue winter's day. But she'd have to suffer the consequences if she obeyed it -- always. Consequences she wouldn't know about until it was too late. They were heavier to bear than anyone understood. She refused to follow its leading. *Not this time. Not this way.*

He gripped her forearm, his hold strong, yet gentle. Even through the fabric of her dress, the heat of it seared her.

"Aren't we told that husbands are to love their wives and not be harsh with them? Things are better now, or so you say. But will it last?"

"I don't know. Heaven help me, I don't. But we're also told that whatever we do, we need to do it heartily as for the Lord, and not for men. Doesn't that mean in everything, Nase? Even marriage?" She swallowed with effort. Dare she say it? "If I were married to you, Nase, wouldn't we have times we'd have to work at it? Could we always live on our emotion?"

He didn't say anything.

She plunged on. "Why should I think I'd get through life without some great trial or affliction? Do I seek to escape it? You want that of me and, God forgive me, it's sometimes *exactly* what I want, too. But is that what God wants? Do I flee His instruction or discipline? I've learned, Nase, that I have no way of knowing what trials will come, but I do have a way through them."

"There has to be more to marriage than a stubborn refusal to divorce."

"No, there doesn't, Nase. Sometimes that's precisely what it is."

He let go and sat up. "I don't believe it."

"You have to, Manason... I can hardly believe you feel this way. It's -- it's everything I ever wanted. But I married Harris. I'm *married* to Harris!" Her voice was low but urgent. "I did it, and I can't take it back. I *won't* take it back. You can't fix what I've done. I'm the one who has to live with it."

"But I want to. I want to *more* than fix it."

"Nase..." She touched his face. A dangerous thing to do, she realized, as a tremor moved through her. But after just this once, if he could only understand, she'd never do such a thing again. "Thank you. I mean it. Thank you for coming for me. Thank you for remembering who I am. But I can't walk away from this. Not now. Not ever. I need to save my marriage. I'm going to do everything I can to save it."

Nase captured her hand against his cheek, closed his eyes, and nodded. Dear God, how she prayed he understood. He opened his eyes. His Adam's apple bobbed when he swallowed, and he said gruffly, "Make me a promise?"

She pulled her hand away and laid it in her lap. "Only if I can."

"That if he hurts you, you'll do something about it. You'll go away, to stay with Rob's parents, or someone else."

She didn't answer right away. She thought about that prospect. Would Harris hurt her again? Oh, she believed that in one way or another he would break her heart again, but would he physically hurt her? Would he ever be that kind of danger to her again? He had been so kind lately, and yet, she hadn't seen it coming the other time. Would temper come over him again like it had then? Like he'd fought it doing since then? Would he one day rip her heart wide open without a care and even damage her body? She knew it was possible, but she also knew that next time she wouldn't stay and wait for him to creep back into the room with his regrets. She would never divorce him -- not that the scandal it would bring would mean anything to her. Her will was stronger than that, and she believed God would give her strength. She'd never divorce, but she would go away if he hurt her again.

She sighed finally, satisfied she could answer him. "I will. I promise. But, Nase, you have to promise me you won't say or do anything to interfere. I mean it. I need that more than anything. I need you to help me do the right thing."

"You know how difficult that will be?"

She nodded.

Voices drifted back to them. Jean and Mrs. Gilbert, coming down the stairs. Colette scooted away from Manason.

*****

Except for the nearly indiscernible, slow pivot of Seamus Boggs' head, he could have been mistaken for just another black stump in the darkness. He stood outlined by the moonlight in the clearing beneath the shushing maples, poplar, and spruce, measuring the strength and direction of the brisk, dry October wind that lifted and swirled the crisp autumn leaves in its path. The sky was starry and bright, with no sign of rain.

A leering smile lifted the stubble on his grizzled cheeks. They hadn't had much rain all this season; this would be too easy. He called to the two other men who leaned back against the wall of the cabin behind them, balancing on the back legs of their chairs.

"It's time," he growled, and they both dropped forward and leapt to their feet. Together, the three men stalked off into the night.

Twenty minutes later, they crept like catamounts around the outer perimeter of Manason's base camp, making every effort to strike in a manner to make the destruction appear accidental. A stray spark from a piece of machinery, or maybe from an inattentive hunter's campfire, smoldering in the leaves. Fire was a common monster everyone both expected and dreaded in this part of the country where all the slashings -- the careless heaps of branches and tops -- lay parched as tinder. Boggs' men started the blaze far enough away from Manason's log works so it would chew its way naturally to the site, sent crawling along by the wind.

No one besides the cookee and two or three of the skeleton crew were in the whole establishment. Even that devil Tom Durant had left, headed off someplace to spy out more timber. He could spy out all the timber he wanted, but a long time would pass before Manason Kade would build himself back up to where he could start to harvest it -- not with all his equipment and his buildings and deeds burned up.

Seamus Boggs smiled to himself in the dark as he went about his work.

*****

"I'd like to see you again before we go back to the Chippewa," Nase told Colette as he buttoned his coat. The two of them stood a little apart from the others. "Will Harris let me come again?"

She glanced at her husband, who was helping Jean and Rob find their coats.

He sensed her hesitation. "I won't interfere. I promised already."

"Of course," she said, her voice winded, as though she were forcing her confidence. "Bring Jean. I hardly got to talk with her alone."

"I will. Thank you." He landed a cursory kiss on her cheek, the merest tribute of a gentleman to his hostess. He stepped back while Rob and Mr. Gilbert did the same and shook Harris' hand.

"Wonderful evening. Thank you so very much," Mr. Gilbert said.

"Fine meal," Rob said, smiling at Colette and then glancing at Manason before taking the baby from Jean's arms.

Jean gave Colette a hug, and Manason noted both girls' eyes were moist. "I wish winter weren't coming," Jean said. "It's going to be hard to leave in a few days."

"I'll come out to the farm to see you, all right?"

Jean nodded.

The others had said their farewells. Now Manason tipped his hat to Harris, but didn't reach for his hand. He could only give so much.

He glanced back once as he climbed up beside Rob in the front of the buggy. Colette and Harris watched them from the doorway, then Harris closed the door. Jean and the baby were nestled in the back between Rob's parents with a stone warmed on Colette's kitchen stove tucked behind them. The night was cool and clear as the wagon pulled away.

Manason gazed back toward the house where, through the square of lighted window, he spied the dark shape of Onaiwah adding more wood to the fire.

Chapter Thirty-Two

The golden October days remained warm and bright throughout the week that followed. The nights were cool, but not unbearable. Still, Rob's visit home wouldn't last much longer.

Breaking away from the work down at Whitney's mill was difficult, but Joseph got home as soon as he was able. In fact, he hadn't been to his parents' home for a couple of months, and he hadn't expected to find it such a barrel of activity. Now, besides Rob and Jean and their little one, he'd been surprised and curious to discover two extra men staying at his parents' home.

Rob had brought his brother-in-law with them to visit, and Joseph found that a bit odd. He'd met Manason Kade only once before, briefly and inconsequentially, the summer after Colette had jilted him, when he'd gone up north to see Robbie. But why had Manason come to visit with Robbie and Jean now? Yes, he was Rob's relative, and Rob worked for him. Was spending the better part of October jaunting off to meet his sister's in-laws reason enough to leave a prosperous, hectic logging operation just before the rush of the new season?

And then, last night, before Joe even had the chance to enjoy his first meal with his family, a new man had arrived. Tom Durant. What was his story? He'd created a disturbance when he arrived, though Tom and Manason both made an effort at nonchalance. They'd gone outside and talked for a long time. Later they'd pulled Robbie in on the discussion. Something had apparently gone awry while they were away.

Now, this morning, Tom Durant and Manason Kade were setting out for the Chippewa three or four days ahead of the others. Something was definitely going on, and Joe wanted to know what it was. As soon as he had a chance, he pulled Rob aside.

"There's been a fire," Rob told him. "Tom says everything is gone. All the buildings, the supplies, even the cook house and Nase's office where he lived."

"Your place?"

"It's okay. It's a few miles away."

"Kade can rebuild, can't he?"

"He can, but all the skidders and the pikes and peaveys, the buck saws, the wagons, blankets -- everything got burned up. It's all gone. Every last tea cup and kettle. Most of the oxen were in the barn, too. Tom says one of the men fighting the fire got trapped. First he was there, and then he wasn't."

Joe whistled. "That bad, huh?"

"Sounds like it." Robin sighed deeply.

"What are you going to do?"

"Wait and see, I guess."

"You're going to stick with him?"

"Course. I've got a family to consider, and Jean's his family, too. I can't go running off now looking for work with some other outfit."

"How'll you make it?"

"I don't know, but we will. We'll just have to see. I'm sure I can find work over at the Falls or in Clearwater. It's close by, and I can still be there for Nase. You saw the mill at the Falls. It's the biggest in the territory."

Joe nodded. "So you're pretty thick with Kade?"

"Yeah, he's all right. Like his sister." Rob smiled, and Joseph slapped him on the back.

"So, Robbie... I heard the lot of you had dinner with Colette and ol' Eastman the other night. How'd that go?"

"It went well. I'll tell you the truth, though, Joe. Manason and Harris Eastman hate each other."

"Why'd Manason go if he hates Eastman so much?"

Rob raised his brows and looked at Joseph, communicating in a way brothers understood. Joe leaned back as a new understanding lightened his mind. "Ah," he said. "Lettie?"

"He's known her a long time."

"You don't say."

Later, Joe watched the two men saddle their horses and say their good-byes. Shouldering a small pack, he sauntered up beside them. "Mind if I ride along as far as town? I've got to catch the ferry to Centralia."

"Sure. Climb on behind me," Tom said.

Manason looked at Tom and smirked. "My horse isn't as old as yours," he said. "Climb up here, Joe."

Joe came in between the two animals and leapt up behind Manason. He gripped the back of the saddle. "Thanks."

"You're welcome." Nase twisted around in the saddle to shake Joe's hand. "It's good to see you again. Sorry I didn't say so last night when you came in."

"Same here. Say, I hear you had some bad news."

"Sure did." He turned back, and with a flick of the reins urged his horse to canter off down the lane. Tom followed along behind.

"Wish I could help."

"I don't suppose there's anything to be done but to clean up and start over on one of the new sites."

"Before winter?" Joe's question was rhetorical.

"I reckon it'll take some time," Manason said, raising his voice so his friend could hear him. "What do you think, Tom?"

"We won't be cutting this year."

"I'm glad to have Tom and your brother Rob to help me out at a time like this. I'm afraid a number of my other men won't be back this year. Not now."

They'd just rounded the lane into the wider road leading into town when a buggy came toward them. Joe recognized Colette in an instant and jumped down off the horse's backside as soon as Manason pulled to a halt. He flashed Manason and Tom a quick smile. "Looks like maybe I'll catch that ferry later. Thanks for the ride," he said, and he strolled out into the road, catching Colette's horse by the bridle.

"Hi, Lettie. What brings you out of your warm house?"

She looked from Joe to Manason and back again. Her eyes flicked momentarily to Tom.

"Joe, what are you doing home? Where's Kashe?"

"With her folks. I'm heading over to see her. Say, I'm sorry I didn't make it to your big shindig the other evening. I would have liked to have been there."

"We missed you."

"*We?* I doubt your husband missed me at all."

"Well, I missed you." She looked away, giving her attention to Robbie's brother-in-law. "Hello, Nase."

Manason smiled at her, and the way he did it, with a warmth that reached into the depths of his eyes, wasn't lost on Joseph. Joe stroked the muzzle of Lettie's horse as Manason dismounted and walked over to the buggy, pulling off his gloves. Kade swung up beside her in one strong, easy movement.

Joe glanced at Tom to see if he was as surprised by the man's behavior as Joe was, but Tom clucked at his mare and moved off to the side of the road to let her browse the dying grass. Joseph wasn't as obliging. He watched the discourse between Collette and Manason with increasing interest.

"I have to head back up north," Manason said.

"You do?" Was that disappointment in her tone? She blinked. "So suddenly?"

"We'll have a freeze up before too many weeks. We have a lot to do."

"Were you even going to say good-bye?"

Manason hesitated, and Joseph wondered just how deep their friendship went. That it even existed was news to him. How could he have known Lettie Palmer all these years and not known anything at all about *Manason Kade* until now? She'd obviously known him all along. He was Jean's brother, after all.

"I'd hoped to tell you farewell, but not goodbye."

"You hoped?"

He didn't tell her about the fire. Yet if it had to do with the trees or the men who worked among them, those were the kinds of things that Lettie -- the Lettie Joe knew -- wanted to hear about. In the years he'd known her, he'd never dared keep a secret from her about something that affected the Wisconsin lumber industry. She was always too keen to know every bit of news. It was one of the things about her that had frustrated him as much as it marveled him at times. Kade must not know her well at all if he didn't know she loved to hear about the way the business affected her friends.

"Is Harris at home?"

"No. He went to talk to a consignment man about the company store at the Yellow River camp. He'll be home later."

"Good."

"Why?"

"Because I didn't want to see him again before I left. I doubt I could keep my promise to you if I did."

"Why, Nase? What's wrong?"

Were his fingers stroking hers? Joe couldn't tell.

Nase smiled an ardent but sad smile. The sort of smile Joe had smiled at Colette himself.

"I'm going to be gone a long time. I'll have to make a trip to Michigan in the spring to talk to Stu and Dad. Then Chicago. Maybe even all the way to Washington to the general land office. There's been a fire, Colette."

Her hand trembled against her lips. Joe remembered that hand well. He'd held it often enough, just as Manason Kade was doing now.

"Your house?"

"No. But the equipment stored at the base camp is gone. Everything's gone. The buildings and office. All the maps and charts -- the deeds. I have to go to Chicago and get copies. If not there, then Washington. I have to buy new equipment and supplies, and I may need another loan. A lot of the men will leave. I can't blame them. One of the men's wives is a widow now who'll need help with her farm."

"No, Nase! Someone was killed?"

"I don't even like telling you about it."

"I'm glad you did. Can I help you somehow?"

He sniffed. The cold air had reddened his nose, her cheeks. Joe detected numbness in the tips of his own fingers.

Manason shook his head. "I'll have to figure it out with Tom and Rob."

"I'll pray for all of you." They grew quiet for a moment, but Joe was too intrigued to intrude. "So this really is goodbye."

Had she ever looked at Joe like that? He tried to remember. He was sure she had. But still, it had been different. The look in her eyes when they met Manason's was deeper, sweeping him away, telling him things she'd never said to Joe.

"Remember what I said," Nase told her.

"I'll always remember. You can be sure of that."

"But you won't act on it."

She lowered her lashes and shook her head. Her face was hidden from Joe beneath the brim of her bonnet, and her voice had grown so soft he couldn't hear what she said. When she looked up again, there was a shine to her eyes, and a trembling smile. Suddenly she glanced his way. "Joseph, why didn't you ever tell me that you knew my friend Nase?"

Joe came around the horse and tucked his hands into his pockets. He smiled in return, ignoring Manason, warmed at the sight of Colette just as he always had been. "Well, Lettie, I'm sure it was for a different reason than the one you have for never telling *me* about Manason."

Chapter Thirty-Three

Manason had no way to prove the fire was arson, even though he suspected it. Even if he and his men did find proof, it pointed to no one in particular, despite the fact that all of them were sure of Boggs' involvement.

"All of Boggs' ties lead to Eastman Enterprises," Manason growled. "I would have killed him if I'd seen him."

"No, you wouldn't have," Rob said. "Much as you might have enjoyed it."

"The pleasure would've been mine as well," Tom said, resting his hand across his healed wound. His side still ached occasionally.

They all stood around Jean's kitchen table, wondering how they'd be able to get anything more accomplished this year now that winter's grip was upon them. The wind howled down the chimney, and the snow was piled up to a man's waist outside the door. Manason wouldn't be doing any traveling until spring. He'd barely had time to get to Clearwater and back with winter stores. He'd been nearly frozen when he'd returned home.

As soon as a thaw came, he intended to set out for Michigan, and then Chicago. He didn't know when he'd be back. The trip might take months. He advised Rob to stick to the work he'd found at the mill in Chippewa Falls until then. Nase patted baby Stephen on the head and looked at Jean. "You'll be all right up here while Rob's working?"

"I'm a lumberjack's wife. I'll be okay."

"You'd better be."

"Nase, what about your house?"

"It'll be all right without me."

Manason had finally moved into the house. He'd had no choice. During the cold weather when Tom was around, he stayed there, too. But neither of them slept in the master bedroom behind the stone chimney. Manason had set his cot in a wing of the upstairs loft that was slowly transforming into a make-shift office, and Tom preferred to sleep by the big window in the front room where he could look up and see the stars. The two of them rattled around inside the immense kitchen, not really cooking anything much beyond beans and side pork, and the occasional egg when Jean's chickens were laying. But it was enough.

Tom understood how it was, and he never needed an explanation. He knew the house was meant for someone else.

Manason knew Collette would never live there. She'd been adamant about her plan to keep her vows, as though the thing was settled for eternity. All Manason would ever have was the ghost of her, walking through these rooms.

*****

The long, cold season passed, and folks -- including Colette -- spent much of it trying to find out news about the constitutional convention and the legal proceedings taking place that would grant Wisconsin statehood. Finally, in May, Wisconsin was conferred the privilege to be numbered as one of the United States of America, and people danced in the streets. Parades, pie socials, speeches, and spectacles were the order of the day in towns with any significant population.

Grand Rapids was no exception. Several important citizens opened their homes and hosted grand parties, while in the country citizens held square dances, picnics, and every other sort of festivity.

Harris was out of town often during those early days of summer, and Lettie enjoyed tea and cake with Noah and Etta Stowe and their son Clem, who'd gone back to work at one of the new mills. She had a picnic at Mr. and Mrs. Gilberts' with Joseph and Kashe, as well as Michael and Carrie and their two children.

Joseph and Kashe still had not married, despite Mrs. Gilbert's certainty that they would have by now. Speculation on that front was futile. Joe's nature remained as unpredictable as the wind. Colette wanted to ask him about it directly, but they were no longer youths, and some things didn't bear talking about. He clearly loved the girl and was kind to her.

Likewise, Joe never questioned her about that day in the lane when she'd said goodbye to Manason. She'd driven Joe to town, and he'd listened to her brief, less-than-satisfactory explanation. His face had been clearly readable, though, and in it she saw he now understood about the *someone* from her past. Yet he hadn't chided her about it, and she owed him the same courtesy.

When Harris came home, they attended balls and dinners and other social events. The first was at the home of John J. Kuikshank, another at the residence of Daniel Whitney who lived downriver at Point Basse. Reuben C. Lyon, builder of the new mill at Hurleytown, invited them to a party at his home, as did Francis Biron. Mr. and Mrs. David Baker opened the doors of their long log house on the west bank in Centralia, where they and the Eastmans made toasts along with George Kline and Joseph Wood and Ira Purdy and other ambitious and prominent men.

Mr. Miner and Mr. Kromer, owners of the area's two stores, competed between themselves with long summer sales of dizzying proportions in honor of the state's new birth, and talk circulated on the streets outside these busy establishments claiming the real growth of the Wisconsin country would now begin. Schools, churches, and settlers would flood in like rafts of logs. Speculators who'd invested wisely would grow fat off their earnings.

Colette smiled at all this talk. She didn't care if she and Harris ever made another penny. It was enough for her that he seemed happy. His overbearing displays of disapproval seemed to have become a thing of the past. He continued treating her with greater kindness than ever before, and he shared his ideas and plans for new enterprises. Occasionally he was tender and loving, and it made her believe there could be lasting hope for them. Her heart yearned for it.

Manason did not interfere. She had not heard from him again, though more than ten months had passed since his visit. She had received an occasional letter from Jean mentioning where he'd been or where he was going, but she said Nase had not returned to the Chippewa country all summer, and she only hoped he'd be able to build again before fall. Then, in mid-summer, Colette received another letter telling the sad news that Jean's father, Grayson Kade, had passed away, and they would all be leaving for Michigan to spend the winter with her mother.

We don't know what the future holds. We may have to stay even longer. Perhaps everything that happened with the fire last year was for the best. Now Manason and Stu can be there for each other without the distraction of Nase being needed here. Rob will help where he can. Manason has closed up his house...

Harris showed understanding when Colette told him the news and offered to take her to see her family. Two years had passed since their last visit, and he went so far as to suggest she spend the winter there.

"I intend to travel a great deal in the coming months. I have to see my lawyers in Milwaukee and Chicago. Then I'd like to investigate some property further north in the Peshtigo and Marinette area. Now is the time to strengthen our claims there."

She understood why. Shortly after statehood had been granted, all Indian titles to lands in upper Wisconsin were extinguished by treaty. This opened the entire northern section of the state to settlers, and already speculators, land agents, woodsmen, and mining agents had sent in scouts to lay claims on the area.

"I'll hardly see you," she said.

"That's why I thought you might enjoy this time with your family. I'm sure it would be a delight to them."

"Thank you, Harris. I'd love to go."

*****

They arrived in Milwaukee in late August when heat and humidity lay like a heavy cloak across the region. Colette, limp and weary from the long trip, didn't look the way she'd hoped when she first saw her parents again after their long years of separation. Yet it didn't dampen their meeting.

Tears streamed down her mother's soft cheeks, and even her father had to dash a hand across his eyes. Colette wrapped her arms around

215

each of her parents one at a time, and then again.

Harris was welcomed affectionately with a hug from Lavinia and a handshake from Eldon. Eldon's face was alight with joy.

"Papa, you look so well," Colette said.

"Your mama takes good care of me. I have much to be thankful for, despite my injury."

"That's a positive way to look at it," Harris said.

Eldon waved him off as though it were nothing. "I've seen men killed in lesser accidents, their wives and children left with nothing. Don't go making me a saint or a hero. I've had my moments of self-pity. Still, sooner or later, a man realizes what he's got, instead of what he hasn't. That's the important thing."

Colette bent to kiss his cheek and rose with her arm draped over his shoulder. Her father caressed her hand.

"Just seeing the two of you is proof of that today," Eldon said.

"Yes, your words are filled with wisdom," Harris said.

Colette wondered if he meant it. Harris was hardly ever content with what he had, and still, he had changed.

"Why don't I show you your room? You can get cleaned up and rest a little while before dinner. Rose will probably come by this evening; she's anxious to see you again. Wait until you see how little George has grown. He's learning to read, and Rose is so proud."

Colette had been surprised but pleased to learn that Rose had remarried and moved out of her parents' home. "Will we meet her husband, too?"

"I'm sure you will sooner or later, but not tonight. He works in a mine, you know. Here is your room," her mother said, holding the door wide open. It was a small room, the one that used to belong to Rose and little George. It smelled of dried flowers and sun dried linen. The dresser, displaying a porcelain pitcher and chipped bowl, was covered with a hand-tatted runner. The room was quiet and cozy, with a feather ticking and lace coverlet over a well-worn quilt.

They brought their baggage inside and decided it would be nice to freshen up and lie down for a while. Colette quietly closed the door behind them.

"This is a primitive room."

Colette scowled at Harris' comment.

"I don't mean to offend," he said, laughing.

"I like it. It's romantic."

He put his arms around her. "If you think so, then I like it better than before."

She kissed him and laid her head on his chest. "Are you feeling well? You seem a little flushed."

"I confess to being a bit tired." He kissed her forehead and drew her down onto the feather ticking. "Not tired enough to sleep, however."

His voice was low and he kissed her again, and for a time Colette was happy. Here in this room, seeing her family again, and with the feeling that maybe Harris could love her if he tried, a quiet balm slid over her.

*****

Harris stayed with her and her parents for almost a week. Then he left for stretches of time lasting two weeks to a month. During his absences, Colette genuinely missed him. Those last summer days spent together with her family had impressed upon her heart that Harris really could change.

Then the weather turned.

A frigid autumn, colder than most, led to a winter that followed the same pattern. Long, bitterly cold days bit and stung.; The clear, frosty nights were punctuated by the busting sounds of trees splitting open. Colette thanked God each time Harris returned safely, and she dreaded sending him on his way again.

When the long winter finally ended, prolonged periods of heavy rain delayed their early return to Grand Rapids.

"Too bad I can't be out there," Eldon lamented. "This year we'll have a spring rush like no one's ever seen."

Colette figured Manason and Rob were probably thinking the same thing.

When Colette and Harris finally left Milwaukee, floods prolonged their return trip by two weeks. In places, the Pinery Road was bogged down in mud so deep anyone who dared try it with a wagon risked losing his wheels altogether, and river travel was no better. Water rose hundreds of yards beyond the banks in swift torrents and languid pools of brown muck. Farms and houses were damaged or lost. River men lost their lives riding the broiling currents on the tangled masses of trees that plunged downstream.

Those whose lives were caught up in the currents of the times hardly had time to take notice of a gold rush going on way out in California.

At last, Colette and Harris arrived home again, back in Grand Rapids.

*****

Home. Harris didn't know when the word had last appealed to him. *Probably not since the first year of mine and Lettie's marriage.* He remembered how it had been to come home and see her standing in the yard happily greeting him when he was still Helen's husband. *Home has been associated with Lettie as long as I can remember.*

He was glad the winter's business was over, even more glad it had included finishing his personal business with Manason Kade. He'd successfully avenged himself on that man for the damage caused him.

217

Harris had more than adequately requited himself, and Lettie was still his. The time spent in Milwaukee, away from this town and its memories and Lettie's friends, had secured that. He'd managed to keep her, despite Kade's more than adequate charisma when he'd come here more than a year and a half ago.

Well, Harris was done with the man, and according to Boggs' reports and Jean's letters to Lettie, the whole lot of them were once again swallowed up by the state of Michigan, perhaps for good. Wisconsin had rid herself of one more unsuccessful entrepreneur.

The trip to Grand Rapids was the longest he remembered. Lettie was right. She had told him it was time for a rest, and it was. He'd earned it after purchasing a number of new land tracts that promised to either bring in farm rents, a harvest of logs, or the platting of new town tracts. He could even afford to retire if he wished. But why?

When home was in sight, Lettie gripped his arm and sat foreword on the seat of the wagon hired to bring them up from the river.

"There it is, Harris! Oh, look at the flowers peeking through the snow. Onaiwah must have planted them in the fall when we left."

Harris tried to answer. The warmth of the sun was on his face. Youthful pleasure bubbled in the voice of the beautiful woman beside him as she kept saying, "Look! Look!"

Yet he couldn't respond. A powerful fist gripped the muscle of Harris' heart, the terrible shaft of pain moving down his arm, paralyzing his ability to move or speak.

*****

Joe Gilbert had just taken the ferry from Corriveau's store in Centralia, and now he was perusing the latest fashion catalog in Kromer's store in Grand Rapids. Mr. Kromer had two suits on hand, but neither reached past Joe's wrists or ankles.

"How long will it take me to get one of these?" He pointed to the catalog.

"It's spring. Everyone is going up and down the river. Now that I'm postmaster, I can say you'll probably get that suit in two months."

"Pretty fast. I'm getting married this summer, and I'm going to do it up right."

"So you should," Mr. Kromer said. "It's a big occasion."

The bell jangled on the door, and Joe glanced up as Onaiwah strolled in. He forgot the catalog. "Onaiwah, how are you?"

She looked up and smiled. "Good, Joe. Good."

Joe liked Onaiwah. He thought that bringing this girl home to Lettie was probably the only good thing Harris had ever done for her. Onaiwah seemed like a real sweet girl, someone Lettie could talk to since her husband was hardly ever around, and since she didn't dare keep up her friendship with Joe, as he might have liked.

He hadn't seen Lettie since last summer when she and Harris had gone away, leaving Onaiwah to take care of their home. "Have you heard from Lettie?"

"She good." Her smile fell, and her face pinched. "She come back few days ago, but Mr. Eastman bad."

Joe's interest quickened. He beckoned Onaiwah with a jerk of his head, and led her off to the side of the store, out of earshot of Mr. Kromer or any other patrons who might happen in.

"What do you mean?"

"He sick. Real sick."

"Is it something catching?"

She shook her head. "He work too hard, Lettie say. He hurt his heart. Very bad."

Joe's pulse sped up. "Has he seen a doctor?"

"Yes. Lettie say they lucky Dr. Hensley in town when Mr. Eastman fall down sick. He say he get better only if he rest. Lettie taking good care of him," she said, adding confidently, "He get better soon."

Joe thanked Onaiwah for the information and changed subjects to chat about his and Kasheawa's wedding plans while she made her purchases. Then he offered to carry them back to Lettie's house.

Onaiwah beamed her white smile. "That is nice, Joe. You come in and have some tea with Lettie."

He appeared with Onaiwah at the back door, hoping Lettie would be in the kitchen, but she wasn't.

"You come in, and I find Lettie," Onaiwah said.

"How about you just let her know I'm here."

"Yes, okay." She took the packages and left him standing on the porch while she went inside.

A few moments later, Colette appeared on the other side of the threshold. A smile lit her face. "Joseph, what a nice surprise."

"Onaiwah told me you'd gotten back, and I wanted to say hello since I was in town."

She came outside and grasped his hand. A gentle rain pattered the slanted roof overhead. "This is so unexpected, but so good. Let's sit down while Onaiwah fixes tea."

She sat with a sigh, and Joe took the chair on the porch beside her. She looked tired and older than her twenty-one years. Dark rings lined her deep blue eyes, and a look of weariness edged the corners of her mouth. Still, she was his Lettie, and beautiful just the same. Strange that seeing her would make him think of Kashe.

"I had to come into town to buy a suit."

Lettie fixed him with an expression of amazement. "A suit?"

"For the wedding."

"So you're finally getting on with it."

He grinned, then sobered. "Onaiwah told me about Harris. How bad is it?"

Colette turned her head to look out at the falling rain. "Oh, he'll be all right. It could have been much worse."

"It's his heart."

She nodded, still looking away. She was a strong woman, but when she spoke again, Joe discerned a catch in her voice she wasn't able to hide.

"He'll need time to recover."

"But he *will* recover?"

She looked at him, her smile weak. "I was afraid, Joe. I don't know if I've ever been so afraid."

He held her hand. "Harris is a tough old man. He'll pull through." He smiled at her, trying his hardest to help her fight through her worry.

She threw her head back and laughed a real, brave laugh. "You always make him sound like he's ancient."

"Compared to us, he is."

She swatted his arm with the back side of her hand. Then she laid her head back in the chair and took a deep breath.

"Smell that springtime. Doesn't it just go right through you?"

"I'd like it better without so much bloomin' rain."

"I don't mind the rain. It refreshes me."

"Lettie, I'm staying with my folks' for a while. Send Onaiwah or one of the boys around there if you need anything. I mean it. I want to help. I don't want you to be afraid. I'll help you if I can. If Harris needs anything..."

She turned and stared at him. *Yeah, Lettie, even if Harris needs anything. I'd do anything for you. Don't you know that?*

"Thanks, Joe. Thanks so much."

They sat for a while longer. Colette told him about her time with her family, and about Rose and George and how wonderful it was to see them all again. They talked about Rob and Jean and the news from Michigan. Colette hadn't heard from Jean in months, but Joe said she and Rob were planning to come back to Grand Rapids before summer, and that Rob and Tom Durant were going to try and get a new crew rounded up to start cutting again in the fall.

Joe knew Colette wanted to ask about Jean's brother but was holding back, so he offered what little he knew. "Manason isn't coming back with Rob. He's got other things to take care of first, I guess."

Her expression didn't change; she only nodded, accepting his information.

"Well, Joe," she stood, and Joe rose, too, taking her cue that their visit was over. "I'd better go inside and check on Harris. He may need something."

Joe nodded. This Lettie was different, yet she was the same. A mature, grown up woman he didn't know as well as he once had. He shook her hand again, holding it a little longer than necessary as he said goodbye. "Don't forget what I said. If there's anything I can do..."

"I'll remember, Joe. Goodbye."

"Bye, Lettie."

He carried himself down the porch steps and went home, forgetting all about his errand to find a suit.

*****

Colette sat beside Harris on the bed and carefully ran the razor over his cheeks, then wiped and patted them dry. He worked a slow smile onto his face.

"Thank you," he said weakly.

"Ssh. Rest now. I'll bring you some broth in a little while." She tucked the covers around him and let herself quietly out of the room.

Onaiwah hummed softly over the chicken stewing on the kitchen stove. "It smells good," Colette said. "I'm hungry."

"How is he?"

"Better today. He slept well."

"Good. Lots of rain. This broth warm him up inside."

"I'm sure it will. When will it be done?"

"Few minutes more."

"I'll be right back, then. Harris asked me for some paper. I think he wants to write a letter. I'm going to help him with it, though. I don't want him over-taxing himself."

She left Onaiwah and went into Harris' study to procure the requested tablet, pen, and ink. Setting them on a tray, she returned to the kitchen for the broth and tea and carried it all up to Harris where he waited propped up in bed.

"There she is," he said, smiling. "Thank you again for the shave, my darling. I feel like a new man."

"You'll feel even better after you have some of Onaiwah's broth."

"I can hardly wait."

She set the tray beside his bed and offered him his cup of tea.

"Careful with that. You're still a little shaky."

"From being in this blasted bed. I've just about had enough of it."

"Dr. Hensley said you need to stay right where you are and rest for as long as I can keep you in it. I might just be stronger than you are right now, so you'd better be careful." A smile broke her stern words.

He drank both the broth and the tea, and sighed. "That was good. Now, I see you remembered my writing supplies, so if you'll hand them to me, please…"

"No, sir. You are not to overdo. You may dictate while I write."

A momentary shadow of stubbornness passed over his expression, and she suspected words of rebuke formed on the tip of his tongue, but she was prepared to be more stubborn than he. She raised her eyebrows and pursed her lips, and he laughed.

"You minx."

She didn't relent. "Any time you're ready."

221

She sat poised, pen and paper in hand, but he only looked at her. After a bit, she grew impatient. "Harris?"

He motioned her to move closer him.

"What is it? Are you tired?"

"No. Come here." She scooted closer beside him, and he draped his arm across her lap. Gently, he reached up and brushed a strand of hair off her brow.

"I'm going to write my lawyer. I wish to make some adjustments to my will," he said. She tried to protest, but he held up his hand and continued to talk. "Other matters also need my attention -- personal things, business things."

"You shouldn't talk like this. You're worrying yourself--"

"It's necessary. I want to make certain you have everything you need, in case..."

"Harris, don't."

He placed his fingers against her lips, lowering them when she stilled. "I'm the greatest of fools," he said.

She caressed his cleanly shaved cheek but didn't say anything.

"I have wasted a great deal more than I ever deserved to possess."

"How can you say that? You are the most astute businessman--"

"That's not what I mean."

She waited. She knew it wasn't what he meant, but she didn't know what else to say. Harris didn't talk to her like this. He didn't call himself a fool. She looked down at his hands caressing hers. They were determined hands, hands as refined as they were strong.

"Look at me, Lettie. I have something important to say."

Slowly her eyes met his, and in them she found what her heart had craved. His eyes had held her riveted on the day he'd proposed. At other times, they'd inspired her and raved at her and smoldered intensely at her, but now the look that emanated from them fulfilled her.

"I love you, Lettie."

She sat like stone, but tears had already erupted, blurring her vision. He cupped her face, capturing each teardrop and cradling them like precious jewels.

"Did you hear me, my darling? I love you. I love you." His whispers fell like the soft touch of down around her, covering her.

She fell onto his neck and he held her there, telling her again and again the words she'd longed to hear for so long, and whispering his regrets. When night fell, she lay quietly beside him while he slept, and loved him.

Chapter Thirty-Four

Manason was happy to be working in his father's mill again. Or should he now say *Stuart's* mill? The fierce labor of cutting trees into planks and splitting shingles invigorated him. Sawdust clung to the sweat on his back and his muscles ached, but he didn't care. The drive of earlier days that had urged him to fight the confining nature of this type work and cruise the pine instead, now lay quietly at rest inside him. He was his father's son, and for the time being he was filled with the settled contentment of working side by side with his brother, fulfilling his father's legacy.

After all, his regrets chewed at him, what had his own achievements accomplished in the end? Nothing. He'd spent the past months acknowledging that the merits of his accomplishments were questionable at best without a greater purpose and call on his life. Why hadn't he seen that before now? Why had he wasted so much time chasing success? The realization drove the incentive out of him like a gust of sudden wind passing over a clear-cut. His father's death had brought sharp clarity into the murky view of his life's attainments.

Even Colette had somehow understood that call. When she'd stood rooted in her determination to save her marriage simply because she believed it was precious to God, she had understood that purpose. Manason never had. He'd never even once considered God's intent.

Now the death of his God-fearing father reminded him of that. Grayson Kade had always planned his way with prayer and guidance found beyond himself or any man.

Manason's chest rose and fell heavily as he lowered the maul to the ground and sat to rest. He'd been working hard, realizing finally, out of the turmoil of his thoughts, that all his planning for the future had to rest on discovering God's plan and call. True success lay in that discovery. For now, he'd stay here with Stu and do everything he could to comfort his mother and sisters. He'd put everyone else *first*.

Before now, he'd never put other people ahead of himself -- not really. He'd loved them and provided them support, but not as much as he should have. It had always been about *him*.

Again, Colette came into his thoughts. She was never very far away, no matter how many miles he put between them. Yet his love for her was selfish, too. It had been since the beginning. With chagrin, he faced the truth, and an honest man could act upon that knowledge in only one way. If he would love her, he'd support her decision to stay with her husband. He would provide genuine support this time, no longer merely biding his time until she called out to him.

Manason scoured his jaw with the palm of his hand. Nearly two years had passed since he made that self-seeking offer to help her escape, and she'd sounded no horn to beckon him back in all that time. He'd spent his days hoping and believing that Harris Eastman would fail her completely, and that she would need *him*. Then, like the selfish lover he was, he'd run to her rescue and provide her a place of refuge to satisfy his own need to love her.

Ha. Love her?

No. To really love her, he had to release that possibility. He sighed and planted his hands on his knees until, rested and filled with a vitality born of self-indictment, he rose and brushed his arm across his forehead. Then he hefted the splitting maul again.

An hour later, Annie found him stacking piles of raw, green boards to dry. Two small children tagged along at her skirts, and a third, an infant, nestled in the crook of her arm.

Annie hasn't changed. Manason watched his cheeky sister stroll over to him. "You're a pretty mother," he said, offering the compliment freely without any further remarks.

"Why, big brother, that's the nicest thing you've ever said to me. You must be getting soft in your old age."

"I hope I am."

"Mama wants you to know supper's almost ready. It's time to come home."

He took a rag from his pocket and wiped the sweat off his face and neck.

"Good. I'm hungry as an ox."

"Ssh. Don't go saying things that might offend your dinner."

"Beef, then?"

"Mm, hm. Mitch Donnelson sent over a whole quarter with his sympathies."

"You don't say. That was nice of him. How're he and his wife getting on these days?"

"What? Oh, you mean Margie. Didn't I ever tell you? Margie left Mitch a few years back. She hardly stayed with him a year. Last I heard, she took up with someone over in Kalamazoo."

Manason scratched his chin and thought about that as they strode up the hill. Then he bent down and hitched up one of Annie's tikes and lifted him onto his shoulder. *So Margie's unhappiness got the best of her.* It didn't come as any surprise, and a genuine sadness for Mitch washed through Manason. The man had been taken advantage of in the worst possible way by a girl who couldn't -- or wouldn't -- keep her vows.

That thought made him hold Colette even closer in his heart. It made him want her to get her prayers answered. Made him hope she could save her marriage.

Realizing the altruistic nature of his own thoughts, Manason smiled and roared up the hill with his little nephew bouncing on his shoulders, screaming in wild delight. Perhaps he might learn how to love in a selfless way after all.

*****

Colette awoke late the next morning. She'd stayed by Harris' side throughout most of the night, happy to lie in his arms. Finally, afraid she might be keeping him from getting sound rest, she had tip-toed to her own room and undressed, crawling sleepily between the covers where she curled up like a purring kitten until the sun was high off the horizon.

She sat up lazily, rubbing her eyes and wondering over the new day and the fresh direction her life had taken with Harris' words of love. As the sunlight streamed through the window she thanked God above for her husband's change of heart. Hers had broken in more ways than she had expected.

A soft tap on the door called her out of bed, and she opened it to Onaiwah, who held a breakfast plate she'd prepared for Colette.

"I think you probably awake now. I bring you breakfast," she said.

"Thank you, Onaiwah." Colette lunged forward and kissed her on the cheek.

Onaiwah giggled. "You are welcome."

"Is Harris awake?"

"I not see. I thought you with him at first. Then I figure you in your room. I have a plate for him, too. Just eggs."

"Run down and get it, will you? I'll take mine to his room, and we'll eat together."

Onaiwah slipped out, and Colette wrapped herself in a warm robe against the spring chill. She carried her plate to Harris' door and tapped on it lightly, then let herself in.

"Harris, sweetheart," she called as she padded across the floor. She set the plate on the bedside stand and knelt beside him. Bending to wake him, she kissed his pale, smooth cheek.

It was waxy and cold to her lips.

Chapter Thirty-Five

Colette barely registered the words Harris' attorney spoke telling her the sum of her endowment. That she would be able to continue comfortably in her financial position was a fact for which she was grateful, yet one on which she could not really spend any lengthy deliberation. She had bigger things to think about, shocking things, and yet her mind seemed unable to take in any of what was happening. A misty veil lay over her thoughts, similar, in part, as it had after her father's injury and Helen's death, except with even stronger poignancy this time.

For one thing, she had to think about the tenants, the poor immigrants who paid to live on some of Harris' properties. *My properties*, she realized, only slowly. She'd taken a day to ride out to some of the closest farms, never having done so, and saw they were dilapidated. The folk renting them had done what they could to make them sturdy against the elements, but Colette knew the interior walls would be covered in frost throughout the winter, and the dirt packed floors would heave when the earth froze. The women wouldn't be able to knit enough socks and sweaters to keep their children and men warm, no matter how much wood they burned in the small fireplaces with cracked mud, stick, and fieldstone chimneys. First, Colette reduced their rents so that they could improve their shelters if they wished. Then, if they desired, she would apply those rents to payment on the property if they aspired to make it their own.

She also had the dilemma of the town properties and the best way to manage Harris' investments. His lawyer seemed to think she was too ignorant to make any decisions about them on her own, but Colette put her foot down and spoke up. She wasn't sure what to do with those parcels, but she knew she could figure it out, and she didn't intend to be swindled or talked down to by a smooth lawyer. If need be, she would write her father and get his advice. She could talk to others, too, some of the businessmen she knew who respected her intelligence. She had Harris to thank for that -- for helping important men see that she ornamented Harris as much more than a bauble.

She dreaded the thought of going through his personal effects, and she silently closed the door to his bedroom, telling herself that as long as she was in mourning, she could avoid that unpleasant task. Still, she needed to go through his office. For, if she were going to manage her inheritance, she must become well acquainted with Harris' personal files.

Besides, dealing with the paperwork and other mentally demanding tasks that loomed before her also kept her mind occupied -- well enough so that she could avoid dwelling on the one thing that stood out as the most imminent of her problems. The problem she could not face thinking about... at least, not yet.

She stood in the doorway of the study, staring at the empty room. Her husband's scent still lingered, even after two months. She took a breath and closed her eyes, but when she opened them a moment later, nothing had changed. The room was still as vacant as before. He was not there.

"Here is tea," Onaiwah said. She had come up silently behind Colette.

"Oh, thank you, Onaiwah." She stepped across the threshold into the room, and for a second she thought she might swoon. She squeezed her hands into tight fists, then opened her fingers to stretch them, allowing herself to breathe again. She went to sit in the chair behind Harris' desk. The leather was cold even through the layers of her petticoats.

Onaiwah set the teapot and tray on the corner of the desk and offered Colette a warm smile. "Drink it hot. It good for you."

"I will. Will you have some?"

"No. I go outside to hoe potatoes. You get more work done without me."

Colette nodded, distracted, and Onaiwah slipped out of the room.

Colette opened the side desk drawer and pulled out a stack of files. Ledgers, deeds, bills of lading, receipts of rents, and letters all came out, one at time over the next several hours. She waded through them all. Some were resigned to the trash. She made brief notations on others. Some were in her name, the properties he'd purchased for her. Others were in her father's handwriting, from the time when he and Harris were partners -- letters and business receipts and so on. She found several letters still unopened, letters that had come during Harris' convalescence. Colette painstakingly tore them open one by one.

Most were from business associates, lawyers, some personal acquaintances, people and business names she recognized. But she discovered one she did not, from a man she'd never heard of before. Someone named Boggs. She scanned it only briefly at first, but taking in the postmark from a town on the Chippewa River, she sat forward in the chair. The leather had warmed, and she no longer felt the strangeness of the room.

Perhaps Boggs was a tenant. But, no. He must be someone in Harris' employ, perhaps someone on a woods crew. She certainly didn't know all of them by name. But unlike the other business letters she'd opened and filed or thrown away, this missive from Boggs seemed almost incomplete in its tone, a mere report of the briefest phrasing. Besides its being brief, it seemed almost portentous.

But that was silly. More than likely, Boggs was merely uneducated. Yet that didn't quite ring true either. Colette knew some of the things which had happened in remote parts of Wisconsin had been outside the boundaries of the law. She knew in her heart that Harris had not always stayed within such boundaries, probably not even after the heavy fines and losses he'd suffered only two years back. Even so, the wording itself bothered her, that and the postmark...

The job is complete. Expect no more interference from the party in question. He's finished. I've confirmed that he's gone back to Michigan. Payment expected as prearranged.

S. Boggs

Colette set the note aside, but her thoughts kept coming back to it. She rubbed the stiff muscles of her neck. Her temples throbbed, and her back ached. Time to stop for the day. Perhaps tomorrow, she would find something else that would give her a clue as to what job the man referred, and what payment he had expected. She would like to have a reasonable explanation for who in the Chippewa country might have gone back to Michigan.

Surely the man didn't mean Manason, she told herself. *The letter couldn't have anything to do with him. That's just impossible. Isn't it?*

The next day, however, nothing more presented itself in the way of an answer as to who S. Boggs might be. Colette restored complete order to Harris' office over the next week, and nothing at all turned up during that time to help her solve the puzzle. She had nearly decided to give up thinking about it until the man either appeared at her door or wrote again asking for his pay, when Joe showed up to see how she was doing, and to bring her a little surprise.

"Dandy!" she cried, as soon as she saw the yellow dog. "Oh, Dandy." She bent and buried her hands in the scruff of the dog's neck, even allowing Dandy to kiss her on the cheek as she laughed.

"Thank you, Joe." She welcomed him in and pointed out a chair for him to take as she sat across from him on the settee. Dandy lay at her feet as though he'd never gone away.

Joe leaned back and stretched his long limbs along the arms of the chair. He smiled. "You look well, Lettie."

She shrugged. "I'm doing all right. Can I get you anything? Onaiwah is making a pudding."

"No thanks. I just wanted to bring Dandy over and sit with you for a few minutes, see if you needed anything. I'm going to take a trip downriver to the Portage. Is there anything you need?"

"No. I'm well supplied. The garden is coming up. Besides, you've already brought me the most important thing." She reached down and patted Dandy's head again.

"Any business you want me to take care of down that way?"

"Well, now that you mention it, I have a letter to send to Prairie du Chien. Would you mind?"

"I'll be glad to take it."

She rose and retrieved the letter from the study. A cash payment, actually, for someone else owed money by Harris. She figured it would be safer to send it with Joe than to trust the mail. It also made her think of that other letter. She collected it as well.

"Joe, you've spent some time with Rob up in the Chippewa country, haven't you?"

"Sure."

"Have you ever heard of someone up there, maybe on one of the crews, named Boggs? S. Boggs?"

Joe hesitated. "Maybe. Why do you ask?"

She shrugged. "It's nothing important. Just a letter to Harris I'm wondering about."

Joe leaned forward in the chair. "Any trouble?"

"Should there be?"

Joe grinned, but Colette could tell it was less than natural.

"Do you know who he is, or don't you?" she asked.

Even more hesitantly, Joe nodded. "Yeah, sure. Seamus Boggs. He's a woods bull."

That makes sense. A woods bull. One of the toughs that keep crews in line and makes sure orders get carried out.

"Is that all, or are you refraining from telling me more?"

"He's a mean devil."

"So I imagine."

"Can I see the letter?"

Colette pulled it out of her dress pocket and leaned over to hand it to him.

His eyes rose to hers, then dropped again as he read the note.

"Well?"

He folded the letter and handed it back to Colette. "What is it you want to find out?"

"Apparently he worked for my husband."

"Yes, apparently."

"He did a job that's now completed, for which Harris owes him money. I guess that means *I* owe him money. Isn't that how you read it?"

Joe stood and moved across the space to prop an arm against the fireplace mantle. He stared into the empty hearth for a while. "I don't think I'd worry about it if I were you."

She stood. "How can I not worry about it? If the man is owed money, he obviously intends to collect."

"He'll have heard that Eastman died. He won't be looking for anything."

"You sound so sure, Joseph. But something tells me you're wrong."

He finally looked at her.

"What else can you tell me, Joe? If there's something you know, then don't leave me in the dark... please. Do you know who it is that Mr. Boggs refers to in the letter? It says someone is *finished.*" She stepped closer. "What did Harris hire Mr. Boggs to do?"

Joseph's eyes fired up. "Awe, Lettie, why're you asking me this? You

229

don't want to know."

She'd stumbled upon something ugly, surely. Joe worked his hands through his black curls like he used to do when she had frustrated him. He paced, if it could be called pacing in the tight little circle of the parlor. He brushed past her twice, stepping past Dandy, then turning around.

"Got any water?"

She gaped at him.

"All right, all right." He motioned her back to the settee, but he kept standing and paced a little more before he let everything out.

"Eastman hired Boggs to run his operations along the Chippewa. He's the one who was cutting timber off the Indian lands your husband got fined over."

"Well, that's not surprising. Why couldn't you have just said so?"

He threw her a sidelong look before sitting next to her. "Well, why do you think?"

"Joe, I'm not shocked or surprised that Harris has been involved in illegal activity. I've known about the cutting for a long time. What can you possibly tell me that would make it any worse? I know what kind of man my husband was -- at times."

Her voice faltered, and she waited. Joe looked at her closely now, his green eyes searching, worried.

"What is it, Joe?" she whispered.

"I'll tell you. Harris wanted to get rid of the man who gave him the most trouble over those lands. He wanted to get even. Several brawls took place between those men and Boggs' men. One man was nearly murdered."

Colette clutched her stomach. "Harris condoned this?"

Joe nodded.

"Then why were there no further charges?"

"Some men don't operate that way. They settle things on their own. That's what happened up on the Chippewa. But it wasn't over, even when the other outfit beat the devil out o' Boggs and his men."

"Go on. I can see by the look on your face that there's more. Are you going to tell me who this man was that Harris despised so fiercely?"

"I don't want to. I don't think you really need to know."

"Joe!" She stood and pulled away from him as he tried to restrain her.

He stared at her. "Don't you know already?"

"You knew all this because you knew the men it involved." She met his eyes as understanding poured over her like ice water. "It was your brother, and... and it was Manason who was *finished*." Her gaze fell away. "He's gone back to Michigan."

Joseph patted her arm. "I reckon he figured a woman shouldn't have to hear some things about her husband. I'm sorry I had to tell you."

Tears crept out of her, tears over Harris, the type she'd hoped to never shed again. Joe tried to help her dry them.

"Don't fret, Lettie girl. It's over now. And they're all right. Jean and

Robbie are coming back to try and get the work started up again with that fellow Tom Durant."

"Have you heard whether Manason will come, too?" She turned and made a gesture of pure exasperation. "I don't want to know for me. Don't think that. I just want to know if he's given up, like the letter says. It doesn't matter about me. They all think I knew what Harris was doing, I'm sure."

"Course not."

"I was his wife, and I knew his business. They must wonder, surely. Didn't you wonder?"

He shrugged.

"See?"

"No, it's not like that. I know you, Lettie. You'd never stand by and watch a friend go down like Kade did. Not even out of obligation to your husband."

"That doesn't make me sound like much of a wife."

"I could see what kind of wife you were. You were perfect."

Colette gave a bitter laugh, then fell silent.

Joe took her hand and led her back to the settee. "I wish now I wouldn't have come over here today. As it is, I can't leave you like this. What's Onaiwah making for dinner?"

She offered him a hollow little smile. So like Joe, always wanting to help her.

"The family living out on the old farm brought me a ham yesterday. We're having that."

"Sounds good."

"Joe?"

"What is it?"

She laid her head against the back of the settee. Everything he had told her swirled through her brain. She was exhausted, and now she had to deal with all this extra emotion. All of her crying and working and thinking during the past weeks lay like sacks of flour on her limbs. But the one big problem, the most difficult one of all, the dilemma her brain had avoided confronting was the only thing left. It wrapped chords of fear around her conscious. Dare she tell Joe about it?

He stroked her hand. "You've got something more to say? You okay?"

She closed her eyes, then looked at him, willing out the words she'd not yet said aloud. "I'm going to have a baby."

He stared at her. His eyes grew wide, and his face paled. He shot a quick glance at her midsection. She wrapped her fingers around his, sensing he might jump up and start to pacing again. As the shock subsided, anger filled his eyes.

"If he weren't dead already I'd--"

"Why would you say such a thing, Joe? Is it impossible for you to consider that I loved Harris?"

"Even now?"

"Yes. I'm just afraid, that's all."

"What are you afraid of, Lettie?" His voice grew softer, more understanding.

"I don't know. Just the unknown, I guess. The future."

She let go of his hand and stood, fanning herself.

"I'm all worn out from all the emotions, Joe. Don't worry about me, okay? I just needed to tell someone. Let's go see if we can help Onaiwah with dinner."

He followed her into the kitchen. "You haven't told anyone?"

She shook her head. "But I feel better now, having told you."

They talked of other things once they reached the kitchen. Onaiwah was always glad to see Joe, and she jabbered on about little things. He was amicable in reply. They ate the ham, though Colette mostly picked at her food. She didn't feel much like eating these days. She was sharply aware of how Joe's eyes followed her every move throughout the meal, worrying over her already. Maybe tonight she would tell Onaiwah the news. Telling would give her courage to face having the baby without Harris.

After eating, Joseph helped with the dishes even though Colette refused to sit by and do nothing, as was his intention. She laughed at him, telling him what a good husband he was going to make for Kashe.

"Now she notices," he lamented, and Onaiwah laughed, too.

"When is the wedding, Joe? Have you finally set a date?"

"I wondered if we could talk about that, actually," he said, his smile giving nothing away. "It's not dark outside yet. Can we sit on the porch for a few minutes and let our stomachs settle before I leave?"

"That would be nice."

Outside, a cool summer breeze washed over them. A twilight sunset blazed plum red across the western sky. Colette liked that about her house in town. She could see the sunsets. The forest didn't choke them out.

"Now," she said, settling herself in her favorite chair, "tell me about the wedding. You've been planning it for ever so long."

Joe stood with his hands in his pockets, gazing into the back yard. Turning suddenly, he squatted beside her and looked up into her face. "I want you to listen to me, Lettie. Listen to me good. You can't have that baby all by yourself."

"I don't have any choice about that."

"Maybe you do."

"How's that?"

Joe licked his lips, and a look of earnestness came into his eyes. "I do love Kashe. You have to believe that. I'm not being fickle-hearted. But you and I... well, I would do anything for you, Lettie. You know that?"

"I suppose." Silence lengthened between them, boring into her almost as deeply as the look he gave her. Until she dropped her voice, and answered again. "I know, Joe."

He moved closer. "So you know I want to be there for you now, with this little one coming?" Compassion filled his voice, and his eyes reflected tenderness.

She whispered back, "Yes, but you can't be, Joe. I won't have this baby until almost Christmas. You and Kashe have waited long enough. You can't wait anymore."

"Don't you see, Lettie girl? I'm not suggesting we wait. I'm suggesting that I marry you instead."

Colette sucked in her breath and tried to reckon what Joe had just said. "Joe... you're proposing?"

"I want to help you raise your baby, Lettie." He tightened his hold on her hand. "I want to give your baby my name and a home. *My* home."

"What about Kasheawa?"

He closed his eyes and shook of his head. "I'll explain it to her. She'll understand."

"She will?"

"Lettie, you don't have to worry about that. All you have to do is tell me. Will you marry me?"

Chapter Thirty-Six

Jean Gilbert looked at the family sitting around her table, and warmth and love washed over her. Her strong, handsome, dark-eyed husband rocked their little angel on his knee, while their big boy, Stephen, offered his daddy bits of mashed potato on the ends of his pudgy fingers. Tom Durant, who had become like a brother to her, made sour faces at the mess Robbie so fondly allowed and laughed at how grown men became putty in the hands of their women and children. She was comforted by Tom's companionship with Manason still away in Michigan.

Manason had said he'd be back eventually, but weeks and months had drifted by, and now, with winter upon them, Jean wondered if Nase had worked Wisconsin right out of his blood -- and why. Yet, she knew why. He'd confessed a little of it to her, right before she and Rob had left her ma's place in Michigan to come back to the big woods of Wisconsin. How he believed he'd failed God and his conscience. He'd told her he meant to start over, in every way possible.

"Sometimes, when a person is anxious, he makes stupid decisions," he said. "It takes a long time to right them, but I'm going to stay put until I learn how."

She missed Manason. Thankfully, part of Rob's family was here to fill the empty spaces in her house and heart. His brother Joseph had come up to work for the winter. She was thankful to have another reliable hand to help get the Kade operations underway again. She hoped Manason realized what everyone had at stake for him -- how they all believed in him.

"You like me to make more tea?" Kasheawa, the pretty young wife Joe had brought with him to their home, asked.

Jean smiled and nodded. "If you wouldn't mind. Thank you, Kashe."

"It is no problem."

Tonight was the first time Joe and Kashe had been able to come over for dinner since their arrival two weeks earlier. They had settled into a little cabin not far from the logging operations scheduled to begin in another week. The young couple had had a lot to do to set up housekeeping in the empty cabin. Besides rooting out critters, cleaning the place, and stocking the shelves, Rob and Joe had put new shingles on parts of the roof and cut firewood. Now they were cozied in, and had time to get together and enjoy the company of others.

"So, Joseph, I bet your folks were glad to see their last boy married off to such a fine girl," Jean said.

"They were beginning to wonder about him," Rob said with a grin every bit as lopsided as his younger brother's.

"They loved the anticipation," Joe retorted.

"Well, I wish we could have been there."

"It was real nice," Kashe said. "Joe make me a fine wedding. My parents and family come, too."

"That's good."

"Everybody loves a party," Tom said.

"Did Colette go?"

Joe's expression lost a bit of its humor. He'd brought them the news of Harris Eastman's death, and though Joe had assured them Colette was coping with widowhood as well as could be expected, Jean wondered how joy could ever be restored after such a shocking loss. She planned to write to Collette soon and send her condolences, but wouldn't be able to get a post out for a while. She hoped to find out more from Joe in the meantime.

Joe nodded. "She came. She was happy for us."

"I'm glad. She needs some happiness, that's for sure."

"Tell them," Jean overheard Kashe whisper to Joe. Jean looked to Rob to see if he had heard, but he was busy contending with an antsy Stephen. Joe's eyes jumped to Jean's briefly, then went back to Kashe's.

"So... I have more news," he said. "Lettie's going to have a baby."

"What?" Jean nearly leapt out of her chair.

"Yeah," Joe looked sheepish. "In about another month."

"Joe!" Jean wanted to shout and ask why he hadn't told them sooner, but that wasn't fair. He had just gotten married a short time ago, and was busy starting out a new life with his wife. The past two weeks had been so full, he simply must have forgotten, just the way that Rob sometimes forgot to tell her important things when his mind was otherwise occupied.

"I should've mentioned it sooner. She's doing fine," he added hastily. "She's got that girl, Onaiwah, with her. Kashe says Onaiwah's pretty smart, and she is. She helped deliver her own brothers and sisters. Then there's Mrs. Stowe, the old woman who helps the other women with their birthin' -- you remember her, Jean."

Jean scrambled to find her tongue. "Oh, yes... Mrs. Stowe. Joe, what's Collette going to do? Are you sure she's all right?"

"She say she going to be fine. She not afraid at all," Kashe said. "She not afraid enough to marry my Joe."

"What?" Tom and Rob said in unison, their smirks not very well disguised.

Joe blushed, and Kashe patted his arm with a teasing grin. "It's okay, I don't mind you tell them."

"*I* sorta mind," he answered.

"Awe, come on, Joe. You gotta tell us now." Rob laughed.

"I explained it all to Kashe after it happened," he admitted. "I thought she had a right to know."

Joe explained how he had proposed to Colette in his earnestness to help with her complicated situation. He had known in his heart she wouldn't accept, but at the time he couldn't think of any other way to help her.

"What if she had said yes?"

"I would have done it."

"You would have married Colette?" Jean asked, her gaze landing on the tranquil Kasheawa. She was strangely fascinated by the young woman who could smile over such a thing.

Joe was nodding even as Kashe said, "My Joe, he always love her. She easy to love. But he love me, too. Don't you Joe?" she asked with a giggle and a little dig to his ribs.

"Well, I never..." Tom said, and they all laughed, much to Joe's obvious chagrin.

"I'll have to write Colette soon," Jean said as she and Kashe cleared away the dirty plates and poured everyone more tea.

*****

Snow swirled in piles against the sides of the house, and wind blasted the window panes. Colette startled at the sound of someone pounding on the door.

"I'll get it." Onaiwah jumped up from her place by the fire. She set her mending aside and opened the door.

A cold draft caught at Colette's ankles as Onaiwah spoke firmly with someone who answered in gruff, less-than-pleasant tones. Suddenly the bulk of a stranger filled the parlor door. He was dressed in layers of wool and wore tall boots. Cold air fell off him, and Colette shivered.

"You Mrs. Eastman?" he demanded, squinting at her. His eyes moved over her speculatively.

She shifted her bulk in the chair and rose slowly. "Yes. I'm Colette Eastman. How may I help you?"

"Name's Boggs. Your man at home?"

Colette looked across the room and into the hall, following Seamus Boggs' gaze. "I'm sorry?"

"Not married again, then?"

"Pardon me, Mr. Boggs, but is that any of your business?"

He moved his arm in a half gesture toward her condition. "It's his, then? Eastman's?"

She stepped forward. "I find this to be a very rude form of questioning, Mr. Boggs. If you have a reason for coming into my house uninvited, to speak to me, then state it now, please. Otherwise, you may return the way you came."

He eyed her again and chuckled.

Colette's ire rose, but Boggs waved her irritation aside. "Never mind. I just come for the money that's owed me. Your husband owed me a thousand dollars. I need it."

Colette gasped. "A thousand dollars!"

Onaiwah stepped over beside her.

"Yes, so if you'll just get me the money I'm owed, I'll be on my way."

Colette reined in her shock at the sum and stiffened. "I don't have such a ridiculous sum of money in my possession, and even if I did, why would you expect me to pay it to you? You have no letter or invoice, nothing to show what work you've done for which my husband owed you. Can you produce such an invoice?"

He looked muddled for a moment, but rallied back. "Let's just say your deceased husband would boil up in his grave if I ever kept such a bill in my pocket. Someone might see it and connect him to mischief he'd not want to associate with his good name."

"Such as?"

Boggs drew his eyebrows and seemed to collect an inch or two more of height. He leered at her. "I ain't playing no games with you. I come for my money, and I intend to have it."

Colette got a cramp in her back, but stood her ground. "I have no intention of playing games, either, Mr. Boggs. I believe you expect me to give you money for criminal actions you have performed. Am I right?"

"If you call getting rid of woods scum like that Manason Kade's outfit criminal, then you go right ahead. Now get me my money."

"You might be interested in knowing, Mr. Boggs..." Colette's back arced with a twinge that forced her to take her seat again with as much as composure as she could, hoping Boggs would think her regally calm in the face of his dreadful demands. "I have already addressed the situation for which you have come."

"Oh?"

"Yes. Just last month, I wrote a letter to the proper authorities explaining what I have discovered of my husband's illegal activities in the Chippewa country. I told them I have evidence showing my husband hired a certain Seamus Boggs to commit arson meant to destroy both the acreage and personal property belonging to Mr. Manason Kade. I believe they are already looking for you, Mr. Boggs."

For a moment she had to make an effort not to hold her breath in the face of his raw anger and puzzlement. Slowly, however, he backed down.

"I might believe you. And then again, I might not." His voice rustled like sandpaper. "I can see you're not an ignorant woman." He gave her another cursory perusal. "I'll find out if you're lying to me. But even if you're not, you'd best keep in mind... I'll get what's owed me one way or another."

Seamus Boggs turned and stomped out of the house, leaving the wind to gust through the wide open door he left in his wake.

Colette drooped into the chair and let her forehead fall into her hands. Tears of anger and fear rushed out. After Onaiwah closed and locked the door, she came and put her arms around Colette, soothing her.

"Oh, Onaiwah, pray he doesn't come back."

"I will pray."

"I don't like to think what might have happened if he hadn't gone."

"You all right?"

Colette shook her head. "I think I'm going to have my baby tonight, Onaiwah. I'm having strange pains."

"You don't cry anymore, Lettie." Onaiwah smiled. "That bad man, he gone now. You smile. You are having your baby!"

Colette sobbed, then laughed, even while she wiped tears off her cheeks. "Yes, Onaiwah. I'm going to have our baby, Harris' and mine."

Chapter Thirty-Seven

Manason sucked in his breath. Spring air rushed into his lungs, filling him with energy and a new zest for life. Stuart reached out and shook his hand.

"It's been great, working with you these past two seasons, Nase. I hate to see it end."

"Well, we have a little time yet. Another month."

"It'll go fast -- too fast. But I think we both know it's time you got back to your own place." Stuart surveyed the lumber yard. "So... Tom says you made a haul last winter?"

"Not me. They did it all. And not really a haul, but it's a start."

"Well, anyway, it's good you have people you can count on."

"Yeah."

"Like I've been able to count on you."

"I was a slow learner," Manason said.

Stu slapped him on the back. "So, what will you do with the rest of the summer when you get back? Scout more pine?"

"No, Tom'll be doing that. I'm just going to get his claims filed, do a little work on the roads with the fellows, and spend time with our little nephew and our sister."

"Hug them for me."

"I will."

"I hope to come and see your house someday."

Manason thought about the house on the hill. "Yeah, I suppose I should go back and get the dust out of it. It's time to get on with living."

Stu grinned. "It is, little brother. It is."

*****

Colette gazed at the baby girl lying quietly in the cradle beside her bed. Five month old Elaina Hope was fast outgrowing the small bed Noah Stowe had brought to her last November. Elaina could sit up already, and Colette was afraid that before long she would be pulling herself up to things, including the side of the cradle box.

Colette looked out the window where Onaiwah was twirling in the sunshine, and laughed. The baby stirred, and Colette gave the cradle a little push to rock it gently and send Lainey back into an oblivious slumber.

She continued to be in awe over her tiny daughter. Waves of downy black hair covered her perfect little head. She had delicate, alabaster skin, and in all likelihood, would have Colette's deep blue eyes. She was a precious angel, and how Colette wished Harris could have seen her.

To think he had been gone a year already. She could hardly believe it. Her life had changed in that time in a way she would never have imagined with the arrival of Elaina. She had been calling her Lainey or Laina almost since the day she was named. *Elaina Eastman. How your father would have adored you.*

She tiptoed out and closed the door, then padded down the steps to her study. Once she seated herself at the desk, she sifted through a stack of letters and bills. Since paying off some of Harris' debts and then reducing rents paid by some of the tenants, her income had been curtailed.

Still, she wasn't hurting. Even though she might not be as well off monetarily, her good will had moved others to show their gratefulness. Tenants and neighbors often brought her produce and baked goods and cured pork or venison. Some sent their boys to do little projects to help her keep up the house and yard. Others, who'd managed to purchase their rustic homesteads after she'd decreased their prices, gave her gifts of quilts or honey, and one family even sent a new heifer. She had a lot for which to be thankful.

Ah, the letter from Jean.

Collette laid aside the other papers and turned the dog-eared envelope over in her hand. She'd gotten the letter in January, shortly after Lainey's birth, and she hadn't written back because she wasn't yet able to form the words she wanted to say. But the time had come. She needed to send them all her apologies for what Harris had done, for what she should have known. She read the letter again.

Dear Colette,

How badly I miss you. Joe is here with us, along with Kasheawa, of course. They make a fine couple. Joe has told us about everything. Oh, Colette, I am so sorry for what you have gone through. By the time you get this, you will have had a baby. I have been praying so much for you, that I trust you and the little one will be well.

Colette, Joe has told us you feel you must share the blame for what Harris did to Manason. Please don't. We could never feel anything but love and understanding toward you. Believe that.

I wish I could travel to see you this summer, but I simply have too much to do. I hope you will write. Even more, I hope that when you are able, someday, you will come here to the Chippewa. We will have a place for you in our home anytime you wish. You mustn't worry about meeting Nase. He's given us no indication of when -- or if -- he might return.

But I hope to see you again. Write soon.

Much love,
Jean

How well her friend knew her thoughts. Colette was touched Jean understood how difficult it would be for her to face Manason after all Harris had done, after the feelings Manason had expressed. She couldn't bear it, even if she did owe the apology to him more than anyone.

Her thoughts turned to the safe inside the lower cabinet. She had enough cash inside to pay Seamus Boggs, but she had no intention of ever doing that. Thankfully, he hadn't returned since the night before Lainey was born. But knowing the price Harris had offered Boggs, she had every intention of using that money to recompense Manason and Tom and Rob. Somehow, she would do it. When and how were the only questions facing her.

A fortnight passed before they were answered.

She had just kissed Lainey's head and tucked a blanket around her when Onaiwah went out the door downstairs. Twilight had fallen. The two of them had washed their laundry earlier that day, and she supposed Onaiwah was going outside to retrieve it from the clothesline before the dew settled. She thought that if she hurried, she could join Onaiwah in her chore at this peaceful end of the day. Then, perhaps, they could take a cup of tea on the back porch before nightfall. As she entered the upstairs hall, however, Colette heard movement below, the familiar creak of a footstep on the fourth step.

"Onaiwah?" she called, then stopped short and sucked in her breath. A man stood on the steps a third of the way up, looking at her.

He wasn't dressed in layers of wool this time, only a simple, plaid flannel shirt over his barrel chest, his sleeves rolled up over the trunk-like muscles of his arms. He looked some years younger than her last impression of him, with a trim hair cut and only a day's growth of red beard on his face. But the glint in his steely eyes made Seamus Boggs look every bit as menacing as he had the first time, and now he leered at her.

"So you *are* here," he said.

Colette breathed a silent entreaty for help and courage as she faced him, remaining fixed in her position at the top of the stairs. Slowly, Boggs lifted his foot as though to continue coming up. In that instant she resolved to hold the upper hand, and also not to let him anywhere near Lainey, whatever his intent.

Where is Onaiwah? Please let her not be in the house.

"Mr. Boggs!" Her voice came out louder than she had intended, even if she did mean to be firm. "Where are you going? Who let you in?"

She came down the steps slowly, but purposefully, intending to halt his progress, until she stood only two steps above him, her proximity hinting he should turn and go down.

His gaze slid over her in a way that made goose flesh run up her spine, but she returned it with an angry furrow of her brow.

"Please remove yourself from my stairway."

He snickered and held his ground, only long enough to make it clear that her asperity had no effect on him.

"I will gladly do as you ask, Mrs. Eastman, just as soon as you get me the money that's owed me."

She breathed deeply, harrumphing just a little. "If you think that coming in here and making demands obviously meant to frighten or intimidate me will help you gain what you request, then you are using the wrong tactic, sir." She stepped down closer to him, close enough to smell the man's personal pungency, and recoiled as he gripped her arm. Her heart flailed inside her chest as she tensed, trying to pull free.

He yanked her close enough to get in her face. "Get me the money," he snapped, his eyes drifting for a moment up the stairway past her, and back again.

Colette realized he had no way of knowing whether or not she was truly alone, but as his eyes drifted up to the place where her daughter slept, twin chords of fear and aversion twanged even more deeply inside her. She was sure he felt her trembling.

"Do I need to persuade you?" he snarled.

She shook her head. "No... no, I'll give you the money if you'll leave."

She nearly fell backward when he released his hold on her arm. Trying consciously not to rub the bruise that was rising where his fingers had pressed into her, she slid past him down the stairs. He followed her into the study and waited as she went around the desk.

Still shaking, she sat in Harris' chair and lifted her chin as though a normal business transaction was about to take place.

*****

Onaiwah set the basket of clothes on the stoop and pushed open the back door to the kitchen, catching it with her backside as she stooped to retrieve the load and let herself in. Long hours of helping Colette walk with a crabby baby who'd been woken from her sleep had taught Onaiwah never to let the door slam. Now she stepped in on soft, moccasin-covered feet and let the door ride shut against her until it made only the softest click.

She carried the load in through the dining room and parlor, and was almost to the downstairs hall when the voices of Colette and a man rang from the study. Colette hadn't told her of any company or business she had planned for this time of night. Who could it be?

Not wishing to disturb them, she planned to tiptoe past the door and up the stairs, but a certain charge in Colette's voice set Onaiwah's instincts on edge, and she gently placed the basket on the floor. Cautiously, she approached the doorway and saw Seamus Boggs standing with his back to her, and though Onaiwah hadn't caught his last words, his tone was not friendly.

"I don't know if I have all the money," Colette said. "I can give you some now, but you may have to wait for the rest." Colette's hand rested on the top drawer of the desk. She opened it slowly and withdrew the key to Harris' safe.

"What if I told you that unless I get *all* of it, I'm just going to stay right here? That is, unless you have some *other* way to pay me."

Onaiwah peeked around the corner. Fear blossomed on Colette's face, although she knew Colette was trying to hide it.

In that same second, Colette shifted her gaze just enough to notice Onaiwah. In the time they'd come to know one another, Onaiwah understood a lot had been spoken in that momentary glance. In seeing Onaiwah, Colette had registered both relief and worry in her intense blue eyes. She'd also registered urgency.

In the silent way Onaiwah had always been taught to move, she slipped away to the back door and out of the house to get help.

"You do realize, Mr. Boggs," Colette said, relieved to see Onaiwah disappear. She stood and turned to the cabinet housing the safe, keeping her back to the man as she twisted the key in the lock. "I wasn't lying the last time you were here. The law is after you, and they'll likely catch you sooner than later after your visit here tonight."

Her pulse quickened, and a thickening filled her throat as she swung the door halfway open. Inside the safe lay several bank notes, deeds, a stack of cash, and Harris' pistol. She swallowed and ran her tongue over her teeth as she looked at it. He'd always kept it clean and loaded with three shots, but locked it here in the safe when he was home.

She kept the breach in the door out of Boggs' sight while she reached in casually, pretending to remove the cash while her hand slid over the gun's cold grip. Moving smoothly, gracefully, she pulled back the hammer as she turned and leveled the weapon directly at her intruder.

Startled by her bold move, Boggs changed his expression dramatically. Then he made the error of stepping closer.

"Stop!" she shouted, not caring now whether her voice carried, or whether she sounded afraid, or whether Lainey awoke.

"Don't be stupid, lady. You'll kill yourself before you kill me."

"If you step any closer, I'll squeeze this trigger -- and I will not miss."

Boggs hesitated, clearly weighing his options and the chances he might have of appropriating the weapon.

His voice became smooth, oily. "Now look here. Wouldn't this be easier if you just gave me what's mine? I know you don't want blood on this nice carpet. You don't want to live with having shot a man either, 'specially when there's no cause."

"I won't shoot you if you leave now, or if you just stand there until the law comes."

He laughed. "Now you and I both know nobody's coming, so why don't you just put that gun on the desk before we both get hurt?"

The gun's weight pulled on her arm, and she braced her forearm with her opposite hand.

"You're wrong, Mr. Boggs. Men are coming now. My maid's gone to get them." She knew as soon as she said it that it was a mistake. A bull-like frenzy lit the woodsman's eyes, and the oil in his voice turned to venom.

"Why, you--" Without warning, Boggs shot sideways, crouching to the floor. Before she could re-gather her wits or her aim, he was on his feet again, springing for her. She swung the barrel of the gun and clenched the trigger.

A shot exploded, and as if in slow motion, Boggs tumbled forward, catching at her roughly. Colette screamed, and Dandy barked somewhere upstairs. As Boggs drooped to his knees, pulling her with him, the yellow dog lurched into the room and clenched the man's arm in his teeth, snarling, pulling Boggs back while he wailed and groaned.

Colette stumbled upright, disheveled. The pocket of her dress was torn, and blood laced the front of her skirt.

Boggs screeched in agony as Dandy thrashed at him until finally, Colette caught her breath and hollered at the dog to stop. "No more, Dandy! Dandy!"

Salivating, the animal drew away, growling and barring his teeth.

Boggs shielded his face with his arm and rolled onto his side, his wound gushing blood through the front of his shirt all over the rug. Colette had no idea where he was actually hit. She held Dandy back as the dog strained to lurch at Boggs again. The man struggled to his knees and crawled toward the door.

"You won't get far. You'll die," she said, her voice quavering even to her own ears.

"I've seen worse," he rasped. Making it to the doorway, he pulled himself upright and turned to look at her. "I'll get over this. Don't think I won't." Then he limped out of the house and into the night.

Colette fell back into Harris' chair and trembled in earnest.

Chapter Thirty-Eight

The house soon filled with men from town. Colette was still shaken, but Onaiwah handed her a cup of tea, and Mrs. Stowe rocked Lainey in her arms while Colette explained what had happened. A few of the men banded together to search for Seamus Boggs.

About an hour later they'd all gone away except for Noah and Etta and one of the mill workers who vowed to sit outside and keep an eye on her house so she could rest easy.

But she didn't.

All night long her nightmares kept her awake, and her thoughts while she was awake were no less unpleasant. Etta and Onaiwah had done their best to clean up the blood stains in the study, and Leo Johnson, out there in the moonlight, wouldn't let unwelcome visitors close to the house, but still she couldn't sleep. The look on Boggs' face and the surety in his words told her she wasn't safe here. She wouldn't be safe until he was either captured or dead.

How bad was his wound? He'd lost a lot of blood. But was he truly alone? Was it possible he had come here on his own, without any of the other rascals he usually worked with? Certainly, if he was with anyone else, they would help him.

She had to get away. In the morning, she would arrange it. She would go to visit her parents in Milwaukee. She would take Elaina and stay with them.

Or, I could go stay with Jean...

She sat up in the gray dawn and considered it. Seamus Boggs would never think she would go to the home of Harris' enemies, would he? On the other hand, he might consider she would go to her family. He would find her there. He would threaten her papa, or her mama.

If he returned to the Chippewa, which he certainly might, he would need a lot of men to face Rob and Tom's crew. They had their own reasons to watch out for Seamus Boggs. She would feel much safer there.

She could take Onaiwah.

If only Joe were here. Joe would take us to Jean.

But she knew other ways, other people who could help her.

Elaina stirred, fussing and sucking at her fist. Colette got out of bed and picked her up. She kissed the infant's velvety cheeks and pushed back her downy black hair. She laughed quietly at Lainey's little snorting sounds as she searched for her mother's breast. Colette tucked her close and crawled back into bed.

"It's a fine time of year to travel," she whispered. "The sun is warm, and I'll keep the mosquitoes from biting you, sweetheart. You'll see. So many people are waiting to meet you." She kissed the little girl's head.

That day she and Onaiwah packed their bags and drove the buggy out to the Gilbert's cabin. Colette didn't wish to spend another night in the house where the terror of her encounter with Boggs remained so fresh. She locked it up and gave Noah the key. She took the money and important papers to Mr. Gilbert, who promised to keep them safe.

She, Elaina, and Onaiwah spent a week at the Gilberts' before finally hiring someone to take them on the arduous trek along the overland trails up north. Then they thanked their hosts with hugs and promises to pray for one another, vowing to pass those hugs along to the Gilberts' sons and their wives in the Chippewa country.

*****

"You came, and without even a warning." Jean drew her three guests inside her house. Two weeks had passed, during which time Colette had seriously questioned her decision to make the difficult journey. But now, nearly drowning in a second burst of hugs from Jean, relief washed over her, the likes of which she hadn't felt in a very long while. Rob smiled while he and Kashe unloaded the luggage from the wagon after having retrieved the women and baby from a boarding house in Chippewa Falls.

"I'm sorry to surprise you. I didn't have time to write."

"It doesn't matter. I'm just glad you came. I never would have dreamed you'd come, at least with Elaina so young, and just you and Onaiwah to handle the trip."

"I'm kind of surprised myself."

"What made you do it?"

Colette shrugged. She would have to explain it all again later when the men came home, so she put it off. "It's a long story. I'll tell you about it later."

"All right. You don't have to even talk now. Just rest from the trip. We'll have hours and hours to catch up. For now, I'll do all the talking until you're ready to fall asleep if you like."

She told Colette about the latest changes in their lives on the Chippewa. She talked about the trip to Michigan and shared news of Annie and Hank, their children, Stu, and their mother's sorrow over the loss of Grayson, but also how she was bearing up under it with a great strength of faith. Jean never mentioned Colette's own loss, though Colette could see the hint of unasked questions in Jean's eyes.

Jean mentioned Manason in only the most casual manner, saying how supportive he and Stu had been of their mother, and how he had decided to stand by Stu at the mill for a time until things settled down.

"That's the last we've heard. Rob says Nase didn't want to rush things while Stu or Ma still needed him. He also said he might have to take a trip to the land office in Washington before he can even think of getting back here." She shrugged. "We just don't know. So, in the meantime, Rob and Tom will work the crew they put together for Nase, and do what they can. Tom's been scouting out new pine."

Colette only smiled and nodded in understanding while inside, her emotions were torn. Part of her breathed easier knowing she wouldn't have to face Nase yet, or maybe ever, but she couldn't quiet the part of her that wondered about him, either. *Would his feelings be vastly different if we meet again? What will mine be?*

She took an afternoon nap with Lainey, and when she woke feeling fresh, Rob and Joe were at the house with their wives. Supper was on the table.

"Well, look who's awake," Joe said. He got up from the table to pull out her chair.

She smiled her thanks as he seated her and gave her shoulder a squeeze.

"I never imagined this," he said as he sat back down next to Kashe.

"Did we wake you with all our clatter?" Rob asked.

"No, I didn't hear a thing. I think the delicious smell of this stew did it. My stomach was awake."

"Kashe made it," Jean said as she set a loaf of brown bread on the table near Onaiwah's plate and sat down.

"She's a great cook," Joe said, and kissed his wife's blushing cheek.

"You slept well?"

"Like a log."

They visited casually over their meal, but Colette sensed the curiosity thrumming in the room. Why had she come to visit so suddenly? What had inspired her to make such a difficult trip with a new baby and no husband to help her? She wouldn't keep them in suspense any longer. Feeling rested and relaxed, and now safe at last in the presence of her friends, she told them about Seamus Boggs' intrusion into her life, about the heartache of losing Harris just before discovering he would be a father, and finally about the dreadful shooting when Boggs broke into her home and threatened her. She trembled as she told it. Her emotions ran the gauntlet from fear to sorrow to anger through the telling. The others sat quietly, stunned by her account, their own emotions appearing to roll through the paces with hers.

Once or twice, Onaiwah had to finish a bit of the telling, but at last the whole story was out. Colette had revealed to them why she'd come, and why she felt so vulnerable.

"You did the right thing," Rob said.

Dark clouds hovered between Joseph's brows. "I wish Kashe and I had been there. I could've helped somehow."

"I doubt you could've done much, Joe. It happened like it did, when no one was around. I'm sure Boggs planned it that way."

Kashe nodded, but Joe only frowned.

"Well, you're here now," Jean said. "You and Onaiwah and Elaina are safe and will stay that way. As long as you need a home, we have one for you."

"I'm afraid we'll crowd you."

"Nonsense. We'll do just fine, won't we Rob?"

"Sure. You two girls and that little one won't take up much space at all."

"Onaiwah can stay with us," Kashe offered.

"Yeah, sure she can," Joe said. "If Lettie doesn't mind missing her a bit."

"It's up to her."

Onaiwah nodded. "Sure. I go to Joe and Kashe. That fine. I come back whenever you need me to help with Lainey."

Colette was glad Onaiwah was willing to stay with Joe and Kashe, and happy the two girls could get to know one another. Colette had Jean. Onaiwah would be good company for Kashe, who was nearly as new to the area as she was.

Finally, Colette gave them the money she'd brought for them, the money Seamus Boggs had demanded as payment for ruining them.

"You have to take it. I know you don't want to. I know you feel like I don't owe you anything. But you have to take it for Harris. You have to take it because he *did* owe you, and because I won't be able to stand it if you don't."

Joe and Rob and the women exchanged uncomfortable glances, but Jean understood, just as Colette had known she would.

"All right, Colette. We'll take it if it will give you peace about Harris." That was all she said, and Colette sighed with relief. The final bit of discomfort that had needled her since she'd first thought of coming here at last settled into peace.

After a few days, they fell into a relaxed routine that involved housework, gardening, and caring for their little ones. Rob came home late in the evenings, and out of courtesy Colette would often retire to her corner of the house behind a curtain to feed and cuddle Lainey while Rob and Jean had time alone. Rob would be off again early each morning.

Tom Durant dropped in to go over things with Rob a couple of times, and he was welcoming to her also. She could see why they all thought so highly of Tom. He was true to them. No wonder Nase liked him so well.

After a couple of weeks with Jean and Rob, Colette's thoughts naturally turned to Nase and the home he'd built and left behind. Now and then Jean said something about him, but Colette preferred not to ask questions -- until today. She couldn't help wondering about Manason's house. She knew from Jean's comments and earlier letters that it must not be far away. Jean had once said that it was *on the hill,* so Colette's eyes naturally drifted toward the rise behind Rob's property. The area was too wooded to tell if anything was up there, but she wondered...

"Jean," she finally asked as they stood outside scrubbing their clothes in a tub by the pump. "Where is the house Nase built?"

Jean wiped her hands on her apron and pointed to the northeast where the ground sloped upward. "Just up there, not even a mile. Can't see it from here, but he can see our chimney smoke through the trees when the leaves are gone."

Colette looked to the woods, imagining the house. She could feel Jean's eyes on her.

"Do you want to see it?"

A small but undeniable quiver of excitement stirred Colette. She grinned. "Could we? I mean, would it be all right? You don't think Manason would mind?"

"Course not." Jean laughed. "He's asked us to keep an eye on the place after Boggs... well, you know. Tom stays there sometimes, but he's gone to the new camp with the boys." Colette knew she meant Rob and Joe. Mrs. Gilbert always called them *the boys*, and lately Jean did, too. "Let's rinse these britches and get them on the line, then I'll take you up there. Kashe and Onaiwah will be here by then with the potatoes Rob ordered in town. We'll see if they can stay with the children."

Energized by a feeling of adventure she hadn't experienced in many months, Colette hurried alongside Jean to wring out the work clothes and pin them to the line that stretched across the side yard.

Jean had time to give Stephen his lunch, and Colette nursed Elaina before Onaiwah and Kashe arrived. They spent a few minutes unloading the potatoes into the root cellar at the base of the hill, and still not much of the afternoon had passed.

"Let's wash our hands at the pump," Jean said, "then we'll get out of these aprons and go."

Ten minutes later they walked up a grass covered path that wound serenely through the woods and up the gentle slope of the hill.

"I thought I would be tired of the woods after my long journey here," Colette remarked, "but I'm not. At times, I've needed to escape it. Sometimes I'd run to the river banks so I could see a bigger patch of sky. But I still love the trees."

Jean smiled, and as they hiked along at a comfortable pace, Colette kept talking, needing to release the feelings that had veiled her for so long.

"I remember my papa used to say the trees were the aristocrats of the forest. 'They're like old men, some of them, Colette,' he used to say. 'You have to respect them. Some are like strong young soldiers, straight and tall, waiting to do battle'. That's what he said. 'Some of them are like supple maids, bending and twirling in the light'." She laughed. "I told him that once. He said it was just like a girl to say such a thing."

Jean laughed, too. "Well, he taught you a lot of things my dad never taught me. He had the boys to tell things like that to, I guess. Maybe that's why you and Manason both think so alike when it comes to these things." Her voice faded away for a moment, leaving room for Colette to respond, but she decided not to say anything more. She didn't trust herself to keep from saying something Jean might misinterpret.

"There it is."

Colette looked up the path where it intersected a wagon trail that led into a clearing. The log house stood in the opening like a stately king, its stone chimney and veranda facing them like a solid, yet welcoming fortress. They strolled across the yard past the shed and small barn, past the pile of wood seasoning until it was needed to warm the house. They turned and took in the view down the hill to the treetops waving over the stretch of valley before them.

A stream glittered in the distance. Somewhere below the ocean of treetops waving at them, Jean's house hid shrouded, as did Joe's.

"Want to go inside?"

"Yes."

A shudder of some unknown emotion coursed up Colette's legs and into her core as she mounted the sturdy steps and crossed the veranda. Jean lifted the door latch and swung it open. A rush of cool air washed over her as they stepped inside. Dusky light filtered in through the wide windows. The empty quiet of the place filled her, and her anticipation rose.

To the right lay the kitchen. Even from where she stood just inside the door, Colette sensed the large openness of the other room. Her gaze swept quickly from floor to ceiling, taking in the huge fireplace that separated the main room from another room, probably the bedroom. She took in the tall ceilings, the loft, the stairs, the handsomely carved dining table and oak chairs. *Plenty of room here.* So like Nase to think of the future and the guests he would have, perhaps the family he would raise.

She turned and walked into the kitchen, Jean following.

"It's big," she said, hardly an adequate way to show Jean how impressed she was. The house had a big pantry, too, and another table in the kitchen, as well as a big black stove to cook on and warm the place.

"Cookee is jealous," Jean said with a smile. "He says he expects just such a kitchen in the wanigan at the new camp."

The well-built shelves were stocked with all manner of pots and pans and utensils. "Does Manason cook?"

"Well, he and Tom manage after a fashion."

"Mmm."

Sunlight dappled the room in tranquility, even as it spread its fingers into the main room to make the whole place feel serene, comforting.

"He keeps his office up there." Jean indicated the loft as they came back into the central part of the house. "Another bedroom is up there, too. But Nase still sleeps in the office."

"Then where does this go?" Colette asked. Before Jean could answer, Colette pushed opened the door to the room that was separated from the main room by the shared fireplace. She stopped, let her breath out slowly as she took in the master bedroom. The fireplace opened on this side, too, facing a heavy four-poster bed piled high with down ticking. It was the only room with curtains on the windows, and Colette noticed they were pretty -- not rough or rustic -- but pretty calico curtains. She fingered them thoughtfully.

"Kashe made them for him as a gift."

"She's a nice girl."

"Yes. I'm happy Joe found her."

Colette ran her hand across the beautiful pine dresser, picking up a light coating of dust.

"Why does he sleep in the office when he has this beautiful room?"

"Old habit, I suppose."

They went back into the main room, and Colette couldn't help sitting in the rocking chair angled in front of the fireplace.

"It's a beautiful house. It suits him. I hope he doesn't stay away from it for long."

"Oh, he'll come back sometime," Jean said, her voice laced with the same hopefulness.

Chapter Thirty-Nine

Manason's heart slapped like hammers on wood planks as he made his way through the trees in the waning afternoon. He wanted to run the horse up the hill, but didn't dare. He needed every moment available to think before he rushed in.

He just couldn't get over it, all the things Tom and the Gilbert brothers had such trouble telling him at the camp. *Colette is here.* His heart hammered to the beat of those three words, and he kept hearing them over and over again as he rode up the trail, pushing and ducking past branches that poked at him in the saddle.

He'd arrived at the new camp that morning, thinking only how good it felt to be back, and knowing it was where God wanted him to be.

The new camp looked great. Tom and Rob, and now Rob's brother Joe, could be thanked for that. He would make sure they were paid back in some way for all their work and sacrifice. That went for Jean, too. She'd put up with a lot, living like a widow during the hours Rob had spent away on Manason's behalf.

Look what had been accomplished, however. In the two years since the fire and his leaving, they'd gotten off to an incredible start, a start which would be sustained with the new equipment Manason had purchased, and the new claims Tom had sent for him to file at the land office in Washington. The future looked bright.

Then he had run into Tom, and Tom had greeted him with a funny look on his face, and the first thing he'd asked was not about the claims or the equipment, or even the trip, but whether or not he'd stopped by Jean's house before coming up to camp.

"No, I didn't think you guys would be there in the middle of the morning. Why, is something wrong with Jean?"

"Oh, no... no," Tom said.

"It's not Stephen, is it?"

"No. The boy's fine. I just wondered."

"You just wondered."

"Mmm-hmm." Tom pulled his hat down to shade his eyes, and suspicion gnawed at Manason's insides. Then Rob came over to slap him on the back and welcome him home. For a moment, Manason had relaxed and the world had tilted back into place. What was with Tom anyway, sounding so off like that?

"Been by the house?" Rob asked.

Manason glanced at Tom, who studiously avoided his gaze by examining the permanent layer of dirt imbedded under his fingernails.

"My house or yours?"

"Either one," Rob said, laughing a rather canned laugh, Nase thought.

"No. Came straight here. Figured to find you gents here."

They went over to the wanigan where cookee behaved the most normally of anyone, making a fuss over Manason in a most welcoming way, asking about the trip from Stu's mill, and setting him down to biscuits and gravy and boiled coffee, just like old times.

They all talked about the new projects then, but every now and again a strange glance slid between Rob and Tom.

"What's up?" Manason finally asked. "I got something growing out of my head or something? You keep looking at me and then at each other like something's wrong with me."

"Oh, nothing," Rob said.

"Naw," Tom added, "nothing. When you going home?"

Nase frowned. "I figured I'd ride out with you fellows tonight."

"Not tired, then?"

He shook his head.

Then Joe came in, covered in sweat and dirt. He'd been assisting a road crew laying corduroy across a swamp about two miles upriver.

"Manason Kade."

Manason didn't know Joe well, but he seemed to be cut from the same cloth as Rob. Nase was warmed to be greeted so openly and friendly-like by the man when they were only lightly acquainted.

"Good to have you back."

Manason shook his hand. "Thanks, Joe."

"You're welcome. Say..." Joe looked at the other two. "You tell him about our visitor, or has he already been home?"

"What visitor?"

A brief awkward silence fell over the men, then Joe scowled at his brother and Tom. "Well, you guys ought to be ashamed." He looked squarely at his boss.

"A friend has come up to stay for a while. I'm sure she'll want to know you're back."

"Meddling man," Tom murmured.

She? Manason blinked.

"Lettie Eastman's here. Ain't that so, Robbie? Staying with him and Jean right now."

Manason looked at Tom, who grinned sheepishly.

"Wasn't sure how to tell you," he said. "Guess we shoulda just come out with it."

"Yeah, why didn't you?" Nase looked back at Joe, who grinned. Joe knew. Tom knew. Certainly Rob must know. They all knew how he'd felt about Colette Eastman two years ago when he went away. They assumed he hadn't put all that behind him. Well, he had let her go until this minute. He had given her the chance to make her marriage work, and he didn't know if it had or not. He had gotten the news from Tom about Eastman's death, but nothing more. Colette had never contacted him, nor sent him a message through Jean. Maybe she didn't want anything to do with him. He was willing to live with that if God willed it.

But could that picture have suddenly changed?

"You think I couldn't handle it? Come on, fellas." He sipped his coffee as nonchalantly as possible. "So she's here. When did that happen?"

They told her all about Colette's sudden arrival and what had brought her to them. He had trouble, then, hiding the anger that swept into him.

"We all felt the same way," Joe said. "But at least she's safe now, her and Onaiwah, and that little gal of hers."

That was the first Manason heard of Colette having a baby. Too much information was coming at him, and it squirreled around in his head making him feel as if he were lost in a cedar swamp where everything was cedar trees and bogs, and he couldn't tell one direction from another on a cloudy day.

He moved through the rest of the morning and the afternoon only by force of will. His mind was already up the road meeting Colette. What would she think upon seeing him after all this time? More worrisome still, what would she *feel*?

It doesn't matter, he reproved himself. *She lost her husband not too long ago. Whatever kind of man he was, she must have loved him once, at least a little. I promised her I wouldn't interfere in her marriage, and I won't interfere now during her grief, either. She deserves that much from me.*

Finally the long afternoon ended, and they all decided to head home a little early. Clearly a concession to him, Manason figured. They must have known the anticipation was eating him, even though he tried to hide it. Tom said he'd just as soon stay at the camp tonight, and he went out the door whistling before Manason could argue.

On the road home, Joe veered off to his place, giving Manason a one-sided smile and a small wave when he said goodbye. Manason hitched his shoulders and touched the brim of his hat, reeling from the speculation in Joe's smile. At Rob's, they found Kashe and Onaiwah with the children. Manason couldn't help but stare for a moment at the little pink-skinned, dark-haired creature waving her fists and looking up at him from Stephen's crib.

"Where are Jean and Colette?" Rob asked.

"Up the hill," Kashe said, while both girls' eyes drifted to Manason. He ignored their stares.

"They went to Nase's house?"

"Yes," they both answered.

Manason stirred toward the door and then stopped. He wasn't sure what to do. Should he go up there, or wait here for them to return? He couldn't decide. Rob seemed to be doing his thinking for him.

"How about if you go on up without me, Nase? I'll stay with these little tikes so Kashe and Onaiwah can get on home."

"You sure?"

"Yeah, go ahead. Jean'll be mighty happy to see you."

"All right. I guess the house might need to be aired out some."

Rob nodded, and Nase let himself out the door as calmly as possible.

Mounting his horse, he turned up the short-cut path that led between their houses and urged it forward as hard as he dared.

*****

Reluctant to leave the house, Colette rose from the rocking chair. She wondered if Manason ever felt that way when he was here. She tried to imagine nightfall with the glow of the fire on the hearth. *Mmm.* What a pleasant thing it must be.

"We'd better get going, I suppose." Jean's voice sounded almost as reticent about their departure as Colette felt. "We haven't started supper, and I bet those two girls would like us to take Stephen and Lainey off their hands."

"I suppose you're right."

They went outside, Jean catching the latch on the door firmly behind them. Facing the valley, they admired the western sun, not quite setting, but already casting livid brush strokes of color across the sky.

Insects buzzed in the grass as they crossed the yard, but all sound faded as a rider came into the edge of the clearing. Both women stopped, startled, and then Jean cried out Manason's name, running to meet him while Colette hung back, stunned and thrilled all at once.

Manason swung his leg across the horse's neck and jumped to the ground. He met Jean's headlong rush with a laugh and picked her right up off her feet to swing her around.

"Miss me?" he asked as her feet touched the ground again.

"Course I missed you, you crazy man." Jean hugged him again.

With his smile hitched firmly in place and his right arm wrapped around Jean, his eyes slowly drifted to Colette. In the waning sunset, he and Jean came closer, and Colette forced her steps forward to meet them. Jean grinned up at her brother.

"You recognize her, don't you?"

He unhooked his sister and held out his hand. "Hello, Colette."

Colette reached for his hand, pulled in more by the way he said her name, the full, gentle timbre of his voice. Then his fingers clasped hers, and her heart kicked. Her lips lifted in pleasure. "Hello, Nase."

"Didn't expect to find you here in the Chippewa country."

"Me, either."

"Everything is all right?"

She nodded. "It's all right."

"Does Rob know you're back?" Jean interjected.

"Yeah... yeah." He seemed to find his present again, having gone away from it for just a moment. "I, uh, saw him down at the mill. We rode home together."

"Kashe told you we were up here?"

Nase nodded and found Colette's eyes again. He'd come up the hill to see her. She knew it now, knew he hadn't come home, but had come to her. The straight line of his brows, the way his gaze steadied on hers told her this even if he hadn't given it away with his answers to Jean.

She glanced at Jean who smiled with the same understanding. Once, Colette would have blushed, but not this time. This time she was too caught up in the undercurrent of Manason's arrival for Jean's awareness to matter. This time her spirit was already praying about what might come.

"Well, if Rob's home, then I should be there, too, getting his dinner. You'll come back down, won't you, Nase?" Jean held his arm. "I mean, I hate to rush away. But we can talk in a little while, can't we?"

"Sure." He kissed her forehead and hugged her again. "You'll make it back okay?"

Jean nodded. "I know the way. Colette can stay, though. There's no need for her to hurry. You can bring her down when you come."

Colette watched their interchange without comment. She wouldn't insist on going down with Jean. She would take this meeting with Manason for whatever God intended it to be.

Jean pressed her in a hug and said goodbye, then hurried off down the path, quickly disappearing out of sight.

Manason's gaze swiveled back to Colette, and he curved his lips in the lazy smile she remembered. "Mind if I bed the horse?"

"No, go ahead."

He walked back to the animal patiently cropping at the grass and picked up the reins. Colette followed him to the small barn and waited as he led the horse into her stall and poured grain into a feed bucket.

"I saw your little girl. She's a pretty little thing," he remarked.

"Thank you."

"Kind of took me by surprise, you having a baby. Though I suppose it shouldn't have." Manason loosened the saddle and pulled it off the sweaty horse.

Colette shrugged. The horse nickered, and his dusty, sweaty smell mingled with that of sweet hay, rising up around them, a calming smell.

"Well, it's been a long time." She sidled over to a rack on the wall and pulled off a brush, its bristles bent and splayed from wear. She edged closer to him and brushed the horse, finding comfort in having something to do with her hands.

"Real long."

Colette stole a glance at Manason as he hefted the saddle off to a far corner of the room, averting her eyes as he turned to come back.

"I've wondered about you." He rested his hand on the upper slats of the horse's stall. "Tom and Jean told me about Harris."

Colette nodded slowly, realizing again it didn't hurt to talk about Harris, not anymore. Only a small hollow gaped in the conscious part of her heart, as though she had woken abruptly from a surreal dream and couldn't quite recapture it. Harris had been who he was to her for such a short time, and then he was gone. "He never knew about Elaina," she said.

"I'm sorry."

She concentrated on the strokes of the brush. Manason tossed an arm load of loose hay into the manger.

"Did you ever -- I mean -- did things work out otherwise?"

She stilled and looked at him. Streams of events and memories ran through her mind. She remembered her last days with Harris, come too late.

"We had some better days before he died. Just not enough of them." She sighed. "They're over now, too."

Manason came around the horse and took the brush from her hand, tossing it aside. He touched her fingers, slowly coiling his own around them.

"Are you healed?"

Warmth rushed up her spine and washed down her limbs. She nodded, certain, as Manason raised her fingers to his lips and held them there.

Chapter Forty

Manason held Colette's hand and led her to the porch. They sat on the steps and talked long after the sun dropped over the horizon and darkness gathered the trees together. They sat in silence awhile, too.

Little by little stories about their lives during the past two years came out. She told him about the days after he went away, and how her marriage had found shaky footing, until death had parted her and Harris. She confessed new uncertainties over her abilities to raise Elaina, but also about how well she'd been provided for. She even told him of the fear that drove her to the Chippewa and what it was like to have shot a man.

Manason talked about that, too. He said he and Tom would make sure Seamus Boggs never bothered her again. He encouraged her to believe Boggs would be caught. He promised he would do whatever it took to see to that. Manason could tell his assurance convinced her, comforted her even, and just knowing she felt safe because of his words brought him no limit of pleasure.

He talked about his family, and the days after his father died. He told her all the things she'd probably heard before from Jean about Annie and Hank and Stu and their families. He told her how he'd missed the Wisconsin woods and the lakes and his place here on the hill in the Chippewa Valley.

Then they both grew quiet, until he stirred at last and offered to take her down to Jean's. But he knew... Lord, how Nase knew he loved her still, and that he wanted her to be his.

A week went by, and every day Manason made a way to see her. With each encounter, their relationship grew with a freedom it never had been able to before. Every time it was as though they had not only grown up together, but also as if they'd never been apart.

He was stricken with awe when he considered God's timing in finally bringing him back to Wisconsin. *For Colette, Lord?* he prayed, and was filled with expectation.

The same week, they discovered Seamus Boggs still lived. Tom delivered the good news that he'd been captured and sent up to the judge at the Brunet trading post to be tried. "I'm to testify at the trial. I'll be sure he gets what's coming to him," Tom told Nase with a wink.

So with confidence, Manason decided not to wait to ask Colette to marry him. She had told him she was healed, and he took her at her word. Once she had claimed she would never again be led by the fickle nature of her heart. She would be prayerful and certain about her decisions in the future. So now she would either accept or reject him, not because of impulse or emotion, but because it was the right thing to do. And Manason was ready to live with that -- he hoped.

He'd already asked Colette to come up to the house on Sunday so the two of them could spend the afternoon together after her morning worship with Rob and Jean. She'd promised she would come. But all Saturday long the hours dragged, and one thing or another troubled the job at camp. Finally, thinking more about the day to come than the one already at hand, Manason announced to Rob that he was going home. He gathered his things together and was just about to head out when Joseph stopped him.

Joe had a good-natured grin plastered on his face, but even though he was a congenial fellow and good company, agitation prickled Manason at being delayed yet again.

"Heading out?" Joe asked.

"Yeah, thought I'd take some paperwork home. Can't seem to get much done around here today." Manason walked toward his horse, hoping to shake Joe off.

"I know what you mean. Say, Kashe's wanting to have a picnic tomorrow. Can you come? Tom's coming, and Rob said he and Jean would make it. Kashe's inviting Lettie and Onaiwah, too."

Manason didn't know what to say at first. He hadn't been on a picnic in years, not since his other life in Michigan. Likely, Colette would be put on the spot and either have to turn Kashe down because of Nase's private invitation to spend the day with him, or else she'd accept, hoping to put off their own plans for another day. He didn't think he could wait until another day, and neither did he want to propose to her with the others so close by.

"If you don't feel like coming, that's okay," Joe offered, apparently sensing his reluctance. "We'll all miss you, but..." Joe shrugged. "You just want to stay home and take it easy?"

Manason grinned. "Well, something like that, I'm afraid."

"You aren't planning to spend all day working in your office, are you?"

"No, no work for me tomorrow."

Joe chuckled. "I'm glad to hear it. Well, just think about the picnic, okay?" He turned to walk away, but hesitated. A glimmer lit the corners of his eyes as he turned back to Manason. He chewed his lip. "I don't suppose Lettie is going to be able to come, either. Is she?"

"Well, she might -- if she'd rather," Nase answered sheepishly.

Joe licked his lips. "Uh-huh. Good luck with her." He laughed as he walked away shaking his dark, curly head.

What if Colette really did change her mind? Then Nase would feel compelled to tag along on the picnic just to be with her.

He fretted about the possibility until Colette knocked on his door late the next morning. Nase dried his hands on a towel and quickly ran them through his hair as he headed for the door. He shot a glance over the house to reassure himself that everything looked presentable by daylight, then he opened the door.

She wore a yellow bonnet and a flowered dress, her blue eyes sparkling so that her entire countenance reminded him of a spring bouquet. She jostled Lainey on her hip, and her breath came out in little jags from the hike.

"Hey," she said.

He must have a stupid smile pasted on his face, but he couldn't help it. His whole body buzzed with anticipation.

"Come inside. I'll get you something to drink." His words sounded breathy even to his own ears as the reality of his plans burst over him afresh. *I'm going to ask her today.*

"Water will do." She took off her bonnet and hung it on a peg next to the door, then settled into her favorite rocking chair and nestled Lainey in her lap. Colette called to Nase while he went to the kitchen, "I never realized how big Lainey's been getting until I carried her all the way up the hill from Jean's."

"I should have met you and given you a hand," he said, returning with the drink. "I wasn't thinking."

She sipped the water and set the glass on a split log side table. "It's all right. Lainey liked it." Manason sat down on the floor in front of Colette and played with the baby on her lap, eventually getting her to squeal.

"I didn't know if you'd change your mind about coming. I thought you might want to go on the picnic with Jean and the others."

"Oh, they gave me a hard time about coming up here instead, I'll tell you that."

"They did?" One glance past the baby girl revealed color creeping up Colette's neck.

"But I wanted to come." Her lashes lifted, and her clear blue gaze shot straight into his heart. He found himself staring at her as she added boldly, "I was afraid that if I went on the picnic, you wouldn't be there, and then I wouldn't get to spend this time with you."

She gave a little laugh and colored some more. She was probably embarrassed for speaking so candidly, but her honesty thrilled Manason and infused him with so much confidence he knew his question couldn't wait.

She looked away, but her eyes kept coming back to his. "Say something, Nase."

"We could spend all our time together if we married."

Slobbering on her fists, Elaina grew fussy. Colette bounced her on her lap. The baby squealed and pulled away from her, stretching her arms toward Manason. Her small, wet hand touched his cheek, reaching for him, and he drew Elaina off Colette's lap and tucked her into the crook of his arm. Lainey sat mesmerized in silence for a few moments, her eyes on the man holding her.

Glassy tears gathered beneath Colette's lashes, and with his free hand Manason reached up to catch them as they spilled onto her cheeks.

"Will you marry me, Princess?"

She tilted her head just enough to rest the curve of her cheek against his palm and nodded.

"Yes," she whispered. "I've prayed about it a long time. I will marry you, Nase."

Slowly he leaned up toward her, his hand still cupping her face. He stopped. He looked at her again, their faces so close, then moving closer still. Elaina wriggled against his arm. She cooed and grasped his hair and ears, cocooned between them as the softness of Colette's lips touched his, yielding and tender.

Home.

*****

"She is a beautiful bride, isn't she, Joe?" Kashe said as she wove a little circle of ribbons over the crown of Colette's hair.

Joe's brows lifted. "She is that."

Colette blushed as the two of them stared at her. The day had finally arrived. Joe would give Colette away.

"Are you sure about this? I mean, really sure, Lettie girl? You don't doubt that Manason is the man for you?"

Her chin came up, and she nodded. "This time I know, Joe. This time I'm hearing more than my own impulses telling me what to do."

His lips drew together, and he blinked with a slow nod. "All right, then."

"Joe? Will you pray with me before we go down?"

He nodded again, and she sighed in relief. He took her hand and Kashe's, and asked God's blessing on Colette's union with Nase. When Colette lifted her head at Joe's amen, she was ready.

"May I hug the bride?"

"You'd better."

Kasheawa was next, hugging Colette and offering her a warm, knowing smile. Then Joe reached for her arm, and Kashe opened the door to descend the log stairs to the room below where Colette's groom waited.

Somehow Colette knew everyone was smiling at her, but she didn't really notice any of them as she fixed her eyes on the one who was to her, the handsomest man in the room. He wore a black Sunday suit Colette never remembered seeing before. His waves of brown hair were smoothed back at the sides of his head, his brown eyes telling her how beautiful she was to him, and that he loved her. Waiting near the preacher, Manason stood poised as though he might fetch her from Joe before she reached the bottom of the stairs.

Finally, she and Joe stood before Manason and the preacher. Tom stood at Nase's side as best man, and Jean handed Stephen over to Rob and rose to stand beside Colette as her matron of honor.

"Who gives this woman to be married to this man?"

"I reckon that's me," Joe said. He squeezed Colette's arm gently before stepping back to sit beside Kasheawa.

Colette gave him a small smile, then returned her gaze to Nase. He took her hands in his and stroked them, and everyone else drifted away.

The preacher spoke, and she and Nase responded to his promptings with words of love and commitment, her heart crying out its promises to Nase more loudly than her lips.

The two of them flushed and smiled at one another as they exchanged rings .

Then the preacher quoted, "So if there is any encouragement in Christ, any comfort from love, any participation in the Spirit, any affection and sympathy, complete my joy by being of the same mind, having the same love, being in full accord and of one mind."

Colette had that dizzying sensation, like those she'd gotten when she was young, when the world fell away beneath her feet and she floated on air, buoyant with joy and all the unknowns of the future, which at this moment in time, ceased to matter.

Because at this moment in time, she was finally his.

Epilogue

1867

With a broom in hand, Colette stood on the front porch of the house on the hill and looked out over the treetops. Rusty leaves spun in a flurry across the lawn, and the mild autumn breeze brushed soft and warm against her face. She leaned the broom against the graying logs of the house and sat in the rocking chair on the porch. The old rocking chair creaked with wear, but it remained her favorite after seventeen years.

She'd been thinking about all those years, having recently found an old letter from Annie stuck in the pages of a book on her shelf. A letter she'd gotten shortly after she married Manason. She'd smiled when she found it, and stuck it in her apron pocket. Now, sitting in the rocking chair, she pulled out the creased, wrinkled sheet and read it again.

Dear Colette,

It's been several years, and I'm certain it comes as a surprise to you that I would write at all, knowing correspondence has never been one of my strong points. That has always been more Jean's forte than my own. I thought it fitting, however, that I send a word of welcome to our family, since we are not only friends -- however long lost, to be sure -- but sisters now also. At least, I suspect we will be sisters by the time this letter reaches you.

So, Colette, it appears you have caught the attention of my dear brother at last. I always thought you'd hoped to. I trust he is as good to you as I know you will be to him. I learned from him and Jean last year about some of your misfortune, and I do so want to tell you how sorry I am for it. I could only wish the best for you, Colette.

Perhaps we shall meet again one day, you and me and our broods of children. I'm certain there shall be broods. It just seems so like you.

She laughed out loud. Her childhood in Michigan lay far in the past. Life had brought change, but some things -- some people -- remained the same. Why, Annie had become no different after marrying and starting a family than when they were young, growing girls. Even now, Colette could hear Annie's chattering, illuminating Colette with her opinions and gossip. Whether or not Colette was interested or in agreement, mattered not at all to Annie.

She picked her gaze up from the letter at the sound of voices carrying up from the road; her men were coming home.

Tucking the letter back into her apron pocket, she kept her eyes on the trees until faces appeared with the voices, Manason and their sons. Sixteen year-old Grayson was the oldest, then Eldon at fourteen, and Kenton at eleven. Kent's laughter and Eldon's good-natured ribbing filled the clearing. Gray was in earnest conversation with his pa. Feeling the straining of his own youthful manhood about to burst upon him, he was daily beginning to challenge them with his own ideas and longings.

Colette stood as they came into the yard, scattering chickens in their path. She became aware of the quiet approach of someone gently pushing at the screen door behind her, and she glanced back as her beautiful Elaina stepped onto the porch.

"They're finally home," Elaina said. She shouted out to them, "Your supper's going to coagulate into a lump of muck if you don't skedaddle! I don't know why Ma puts up with any of you."

Colette laughed at Manason's chafed expression. He stopped in his tracks, placed his hands on his hips, and shook his head as Lainey marched down the steps and gave him a quick peck on the cheek.

"Hi, Pa. Did you get the paper?"

He pulled the rolled newspaper from his back pocket and handed it to her. She grabbed it and twirled off, heading back toward the house.

"Thank you?"

She blushed and spun around. "Thank you, Papa," she answered, then leapt up the steps and into the house, letting the screen door crack shut against its wood frame.

The three boys disappeared round the back of the house where they'd head straight to the pump, and Manason came up the steps. His back bothered him some days, and it looked as if today was one of them.

"What are we going to do with that girl?" He pu his arms around Colette, tugging her close

She sighed and folded herself into his embrace, inhaling his woodsy scent. "We'll think about it tomorrow."

He kissed her forehead where little strands of gray had cropped up among her dark, brown-gold waves. "That's not much of a plan."

"Well, I keep praying, but that's all I've come up with so far."

He chuckled and sighed. "Then that'll have to do." He put his arm around her and led her into the house where supper waited in the warming box on the stove.

That would have to be the plan, as it always was for everything -- not just for Lainey, but for their boys, and for all of the days ahead. Stilling their anxious hearts, they would pray, they would wait, and they would love.

The future would unwind from the palm of God's hand.

The End

About Naomi Dawn Musch

Naomi writes from the pristine north woods of Wisconsin where she and husband Jeff live as epically as God allows on a ramshackle farm near their five young adults and three grand-children. Amidst it, she writes about imperfect people who are finding hope and faith to overcome their struggles, whether the story venue is rich in American history, or along more contemporary lines.

Central to her stories is the belief that God blesses messes, and He delights in turning lives around. For that same reason, Naomi spent five years on the editorial board of the Midwestern Christian newspaper, *Living Stones News*, writing true accounts of changed lives. She also enjoys writing for magazines and other non-fiction venues that encourage homeschooling families and young writers.

She invites readers to say hello and find out more about her stories, passions, and other writing venues at **http://www.naomimusch.com** or to look her up on Facebook (Naomi Musch - Author) and Twitter (NMusch).